THE *Malibu* SECRET

BELLA CHRISTINA

Vinci Books

vinci-books.com

Published by Vinci Books Ltd in 2026

1

A CIP catalogue record for this book is available from the British Library.

Paperback ISBN: 9781036733933

The EU GPSR authorised representative is Logos Europe, 9 rue Nicolas Poussion, 17000 La Rochelle, France contact@logoseurope.eu

By Bella Christina

The Kensington Brothers

The Malibu Arrangement

The Malibu Destiny

The Malibu Secret

Bella Christina as Ainsley Keaton

Sconset Beach

The Beachfront Inn

The Beachfront Surprises

The Beachfront Reunion

The Beachfront Secrets

The Beachfront Girls

The Beachfront Sunsets

The Malibu Girls

The Beachfront Christmas

The Beachfront Retreat

The Beachfront Crush

The Beachfront Winery

Orchid Island

The Orchid Island B&B

The Orchid Island Restaurant

The Orchid Island Gallery

The Orchid Island Christmas

The Orchid Island Wedding

The Orchid Island Theater

Bella Christina as Annie Jocoby

Fearless

Fearless

Secrets & Lies

Trapped

Illusions

Beautiful Illusions

Deeper Illusions

End of Illusions

Ryan Gallagher

Exposure

Exposure

Focus

Close Up

Broken

Broken

Saving Scotty

Ever After

Always

Temptations

Dangerous Temptations

Twisted Temptations

Dark Temptations

Wicked Temptations

Bella Christina as Rachel Sinclair

Kansas City Legal Thrillers

Bad Faith

Justice Denied

Hidden Defendant

Injustice For All

L.A. Defense

The Associate

The Alibi

Reasonable Doubt

The Accused

The Hate Crime

Secrets and Lies

Until Proven Guilty

Southern California Legal Thrillers

Presumed Guilty

Justice Delayed

Insanity Defense

Wrongful Conviction

The Trial

Chapter One

TALLY

I slam my needle down on the tray. "For the love of—would you stop squirming?"

The redhead in my chair—who calls herself "Shallow" like that's a normal human name—flinches again as I try to finish the cursive "M" of "Mortimer" on her lower back. March isn't even over, and this is already boyfriend tattoo number five for the year.

"I thought redheads were supposed to have, like, superhuman pain tolerance," I mutter, dabbing away a tiny bead of blood.

"Sorry," she whispers, then immediately jerks again.

I shake my head, wondering what drives someone to permanently ink every temporary man onto their body. Part of me wants to lecture her about how these guys never stick around—trust me, I know—but another part of me almost respects her stubborn optimism. While I'm over here refusing to get even one romantic tattoo until I meet a unicorn who won't bail, she's collecting an entire gallery of failed relationships like they're souvenirs.

I cap my needle gun and step back. "Well, Mortimer has officially joined the skin parade," I tell the lovely Shallow, who's been my most loyal—and most idiotic—customer. "Right above the VIP entrance, as requested."

She's got a goddamn boyfriend museum all over her body. Slade occupies her left forearm (lasted three weeks), Nash rides her right shoulder blade (cheated with her cousin), Lincoln decorates her ankle (stole her cat), and Wilde (ironically the most boring) circles her belly button. The douchier the guy, the cooler the name. So, assuming that relationship between douchetude and cool names, that'll mean that good ol' Mortimer will be a wonderful guy who'll treat her like royalty. I mean, nobody names their kid Mortimer unless they're planning for him to grow up honest and dependable, right? Maybe the universe is finally cutting her a break. Or maybe she'll be back next month for a "Bartholomew" tramp stamp. Jesus.

She rubs her lower back—newly minted Mortimer territory—and wrinkles her nose. "I know, I know. Terrible name. But you ever see *Arsenic and Old Lace*?"

"The one where sweet little grannies poison lonely dudes with elderberry wine laced with arsenic, strychnine, and just a pinch of cyanide for a kick? Yep. Why?"

"Cary Grant's character was Mortimer," she says, jazz-handing like she just pulled a rabbit from a hat. And fair play—Cary Grant was basically the Ryan Gosling of his day, if Ryan Gosling had the voice of a British butler and eyebrows that could seduce you from across a football field. So maybe Mortimer has a fighting chance after all. Even if the name peaked sometime around 1943, when people thought Mortimer, Mildred and Hubert were names you'd actually inflict on a child.

Shallow slaps her card on the counter, wincing as she

rubs the fresh ink on her back. I ring her up, watching her go with a head shake. Ten bucks says she's back before Valentine's Day wanting "Poindexter" or "Eggbert" etched somewhere else. Girl better pray she doesn't fall for some dude with a name like Bartholomew Christopherson—she's running out of virgin skin at this rate.

Eight hours later, I'm finally clocking out. My fingers are cramping from the nonstop tattoo gun action today. Maya—my business partner and supposed "other half" of Manic Muse, my tattoo studio—texted at 6 AM with some bullshit about food poisoning. Yeah, right. More like she's nursing a hangover the size of Texas after that warehouse rave she "wasn't planning to attend" last night.

I need a drink the size of Jupiter right now. Thank god I'm hitting up our Malibu spot with Celeste and Liv tonight. Yeah, Malibu—land of the douche canoes—but what can I do? My bestie Celeste went and married Max Kensington, billionaire extraordinaire who practically has his name stamped on every grain of sand there. Their whole setup started like some medieval arranged-marriage bullshit that I thought died with corsets and the plague, and I thought she was batshit cray for doing it, but damn if those two didn't pull a romance novel twist. From "I can't stand his face" to "I can't keep my hands off his face" in record time. Love's weird like that.

I spot Celeste and Liv at our usual table on the Bluetide Grill deck, the ocean breeze tousling their hair. Despite marrying a billionaire, landing that screenwriting gig, and having little Violet at home, Celeste hasn't changed. There she sits in worn Levi's, a faded t-shirt, and those ridiculous rainbow Docs she loves so much. That knockoff Vuitton she haggled for in Cabo is perched beside her, red hair twisted into her signature messy bun. Max filled her closet with designer everything, but whenever she's with us, it's like the fancy shit stays home. Sometimes I wonder if she's just more comfortable this way, or if she's afraid we'll call her Princess Moneybags if she shows up in Prada. Maybe a little of both.

I slide into the booth, drumming my fingers on the table. "All right, ladies. Spill the tea. What's been happening?"

Celeste shrugs, tucking a strand of perfect hair behind her ear. "Nothing much, really. Just the usual."

"Right," I snort. "Just the usual mind-blowing sex with your movie-star-looking husband while you're raking in screenplay money. God, how do you survive the boredom?" I catch Liv's eye and she smirks. We both know the drill. In an hour, Celeste will check her watch and make her excuses —Max and little Violet waiting at home, the perfect little family in their perfect 20,000 square foot house. Meanwhile, Liv and I will order another round, maybe hit another bar after, stumble home whenever the hell we want. No texts to answer, no one to check in with. Just sweet, uncomplicated freedom. And honestly? I wouldn't trade it for all the Max-clones in the world. One-night stands don't come with custody arrangements.

Celeste sips her drink with that cat-who-got-the-cream smile. Must be nice getting laid on the regular—definitely one perk of the whole marriage package I hadn't considered.

"How's life treating you?" she asks.

"Jesus Christ." I blow my bangs off my forehead. "Today was a three-energy-drink nightmare." I dive into my highlight reel of the day's clients—the frat boy who fainted during his tribal armband and the middle-aged woman who wanted her ex-husband's name covered with a particularly anatomical mushroom. I roll my eyes. "So, yeah, when Maya decides to be 'sick,'" I say, making little bunny ears with my fingers, "my entire existence turns into a dumpster fire. Like, congratulations on your self-inflicted misery, now I get to suffer too."

Celeste's eyebrows shoot up. "So there's this guy at Max's studio who's been asking about you—"

"Hard pass," I cut her off. "I'm not about to make awkward small talk with some trust fund bro who keeps flashing his fancy-ass Philippe Patek watch at me like it's supposed to make my panties drop."

"It's Patek Philippe," Celeste says primly. "They're actually quite—"

"Jesus, who names their kid Patek?" I snort. "Though I guess it beats Mortimer. At least Patek sounds like he might know how to have fun without his mommy's permission."

Celeste laughs. "It's actually named after two guys who started it—Antoni Patek and Adrien Philippe. They created this super high-end watch company in Switzerland back in the 1800s. The Swiss don't mess around when it comes to timepieces."

"How do you know this random watch trivia?" I ask, shaking my head. "I thought Patek Philippe was some new luxury brand all the rappers started flexing in their Instagram posts like five years ago." Then I shake my head. Of course Little Miss Married-to-Money knows all about fancy-ass timepieces. I bet her husband could buy the whole damn factory with his pocket change. I take a deep breath, trying not to roll my eyes. Maybe she has changed after all.

"No, no," Celeste says, swirling her wine. "But it is weird how everyone suddenly cares about them. I always thought Rolex was the ultimate status symbol, but now it's all about Patek Philippe."

"Holy shit, is this what girls' night has devolved to? Drooling over fancy-ass watches worn by trust fund babies?" As soon as the words leave my mouth, I wince. *Nice one, Tally*. Celeste's husband Max probably has a whole damn collection of those Patek whatever-the-fucks stashed in some climate-controlled safe. And he's actually decent, despite the silver spoon. His brother Roman isn't half bad either—managed to fall for some crystal-waving tarot card reader, which still blows my mind. Maybe I've been too quick to write off the entire Kensington clan.

Celeste's eyes meet mine for a second before she loses it, cackling so hard her mascara starts to run. I'm right there with her, snorting like an idiot. Jesus, we're ridiculous—usually debating the merits of dick pics while normal people worry about climate change or whatever. But fuck it. Some people march with cardboard signs; we judge tattoo designs and talk shit. Not exactly solving world hunger over here, but at least we're honest about it—unlike that customer today who wanted "Deep" tattooed on her wrist while talking about her spiritual awakening at Coachella.

Later on, I'm driving home stone-cold sober. Five years ago, a cop pulled me over after girls' night. I got lucky—he let me go with a warning that still makes my hands shake on the wheel sometimes. Now I nurse one drink all night, tops.

The streetlights flash across my face as I grip the wheel, thinking about Celeste. It's not the hot-as-hell husband who looks photoshopped in real life. It's not his bank account that could fund a small country. It's that look in her eyes now.

A few years back, we were the same—not happy, but not unhappy. Both of us just existing, her with her screenplay rejections and her mom's cancer battle, me with my own shit. Now? That bitch radiates. She's crossed over from that gray zone of not-happy-but-not-unhappy into just plain happy. Meanwhile, I'm still stuck in that same twilight of not-happy-but-not-unhappy, watching the clock tick.

But I've made my choices. Damn right I have. The whole white-picket-fence-and-hubby routine? Hard pass. Same goes for popping out kids. While other little girls were playing house, I was mixing watercolors until they bled through the paper. Liv was the one obsessed with her Easy Bake Oven—no surprise she's slinging gourmet appetizers now. Me? Give me a Lite Brite or that impossible silver-screen Etch-A-Sketch any day. God, that thing was a nightmare at first, but once I cracked the code? Magic. One of my favorite foster families nearly lost their minds when I twisted those little knobs into the perfect Beatles Revolver album cover at age eight. Their faces when they recognized those four floating heads and that wild lettering? Priceless.

Love is garbage. It's not like my childhood prepared me for happily-ever-after. Mom chose prescription painkillers over stability, which meant I got the grand tour of the foster care system. Every few months, some government lackey in sensible shoes would interrupt my Etch-A-Sketch masterpiece to stuff my belongings into trash bags. And I never wanted to leave my mother. Never. I mean, sure, Mom was orbiting Saturn half the time, and I became a Hot Pocket connoisseur by third grade, but she was mine. Those substitute rando mothers with their fake smiles and forced hugs? Couldn't hold a candle.

And then—HOLY CHRIST—a deer materializes out of nowhere, eyes blazing like hellfire in my headlights. I wrench the wheel hard, tires screaming against asphalt as my Jeep launches sideways, the world spinning violently as metal crunches and glass explodes around me. Three, four rolls—each one hammering my body against the restraints until I'm hanging upside down, blood rushing to my skull. Those movie scenes where people walk away from wrecks? Complete horseshit. Every breath feels like knives between my ribs, and something warm trickles down my temple that I'm desperately hoping isn't brain matter.

It takes everything in me to dial 911, my trembling finger missing the buttons twice before finally connecting. The room spins like a carnival ride as I press the phone to my ear, darkness creeping in from the edges of my vision until I mercifully slip into unconsciousness.

Chapter Two

CAMERON

I'm working the ER when they wheel her in—dark hair with rainbow streaks spilling across the white gurney sheets, cheekbones that could cut glass even beneath the angry purple bruising spreading across her right side. My heart stutters when I realize it's Tally, Celeste's friend from both weddings. The fluorescent lights catch on the blood seeping through her torn blouse, revealing lacerations across her abdomen. Her eyelids flutter, consciousness slipping in and out like a tide, and her normally full lips are pale and cracked. My fingers tremble slightly against the cold metal rail as I guide the gurney toward Bay 3, remembering how she'd laughed at Max's reception, champagne glass dangling between slender fingers, completely unaware of my staring at her from across the room. Now those same fingers lie limp against sterile sheets, and I've still never spoken a single word to her.

The trauma team descends in a choreographed rush—one nurse cuts away her bloodied clothes while another starts an IV line, a third attaches cardiac monitors that immediately fill the room with urgent beeping. I call out orders as I check her pupils with my penlight: "Get a trauma panel, type and cross for four units, and push 1 of morphine." Her oxygen levels dip and I motion for intubation equipment. "Let's get her to CT stat—I need to rule out internal bleeding and head trauma before she crashes completely."

My fingers dig into her abdomen, probing for internal bleeding or swelling, the heat of her skin burning through my latex gloves. Her eyelids flutter—delicate as moth wings —revealing irises the precise blue of Mediterranean waters at noon. "Fucking perfect," she hisses through clenched teeth. "A Yalie doctor. Just my goddamn luck." Her gaze drops to my wrist, zeroing in on my watch gleaming under the merciless hospital lights - the antique Patek Philippe, given to me by my granddad on my 16th birthday. "Bet you've got a whole fucking vault of those at home, don't you, Scrooge McDuck?" A savage smile cuts across her bloodless face, that single dimple appearing like a battle scar before her eyes roll back, lashes slashing shadows across skin pale as death.

I shake my head. "Didn't go to Yale. Johns Hopkins." I tap the face of my watch—the only Patek Philippe I own, unlike my brothers who collect them like trading cards. Something in Tally's eyes tells me she knows me and thinks that I'm a trust fund baby playing at being doctor. Had she been watching me at those weddings too? My family is incredibly wealthy and she assumes I'm the same, which I admittedly am, thanks to a half-billion trust fund set up by granddad for all of us Kensington boys. Still, she probably doesn't know me as the black sheep of a dynasty, the one who chose a year in Kenya's dust with Doctors Without Borders over boardroom battles and trust funds. The one whose annual salary wouldn't cover what Roman makes in a day.

I can still see her at Max and Celeste's wedding—that burgundy halter dress that framed her shoulders like artwork, the slit that revealed legs strong enough to kick down doors. Her short dark hair shot through with defiant rainbow streaks. She stood there like someone who'd parked a Harley outside the church, and I couldn't look away if I'd wanted to.

Of course, being mesmerized by her meant I froze like a statue. My brothers would've strolled right up—Roman with that cocky grin, Silas with his smooth one-liners, Max already making her laugh. Ansel would've had her feeling like his oldest friend within minutes. Kalen would've channeled that rock star confidence, while Connor—despite those childhood years when he could barely order pizza without stammering—would've drawn on that Oscar-winner charisma. Even Asher, who treats romance like an abstract theorem, would've managed better than me. My palms went clammy just watching her from across the room. I've always been this way around beautiful women—admiring from a distance, tongue-tied and hesitant. The irony is I probably respect women more than any of my brothers, yet I'm the one who can never seem to approach them.

Which is why I'm still stunned—thunderstruck—that I convinced a woman like Alecia to marry me. My Alecia, with those freckles scattered like constellations across her nose, hair blazing like summer wheat under a merciless sun, and eyes that cut through me—green as absinthe and twice as intoxicating. Her laugh that first day slammed into my chest like a fist. How could a goddess like her even acknowledge my existence? But I knew—Christ, I KNEW—the instant I saw her that I would drown in her. And I did. And she did too. One weekend in her Arts District loft was all it took. I would have slit my own throat before letting her slip away.

Three years ago, her laugh was silenced forever when a drunk driver obliterated her car with my baby girl Stephanie inside. All because I couldn't handle a goddamn cold. We ran out of NyQuil, to my chagrin. I never run out of anything because I make sure to replace everything once it gets low. I never, ever just run out of toilet paper, paper towels, toothpaste, cold medicine, aspirin, anything that's necessary. Yet we did run out of NyQuil, a fact that haunts me to this day. Why, why, why didn't I get a bottle of NyQuil when I happened to be at the store instead of running out completely? But I didn't, so, that early morning when I was so sick, we needed to get some in the house ASAP.

The coughing fits had been ripping my lungs apart for hours when Alecia kissed my burning forehead at 1 AM and whispered she'd be right back. She took Stephanie because I was too pathetic to move. Three blocks away, that bastard plowed through a green light at 80 mph without touching his brakes. I heard the sirens screaming through our neighborhood and knew—KNEW—before my phone rang. My soul recognized the sound of my world ending.

I'd resigned myself to a life of solitude. Then I spotted Tally across the crowded room at Max and Celeste's wedding. My heart stuttered. The champagne flute nearly slipped from my fingers. I kept stealing glances at her while pretending to listen to some cousin's medical woes. Three times I started toward Celeste to ask about her friend, and three times I retreated. What would someone with galaxy-blue hair streaks and sleeve tattoos peaking beneath her cocktail dress want with a guy who spent his days in scrubs and his nights hunched over medical journals?

Now, here she is, and I'm attending her after her accident. The fluorescent lights cast a harsh glow on her bruised skin.

Her voice comes out like sandpaper. "Hit me with it, doc." She narrows her eyes at my badge, then recoils. "Dr. Kensington? Christ. You're Max's brother." She clutches the paper-thin sheet to her chest, fingers digging into the fabric. "Brilliant. Absolutely brilliant. Next dinner party at Max's, you'll have this little tableau burned into your memory, won't you? Me, splayed out like a science experiment." Her jaw tightens. "I'm guessing the hospital gown came after you got quite the anatomy lesson."

She didn't recognize me until she read my name tag. This realization hits like a sucker punch—while I'd been stealing glances at her all night at Max's two receptions, memorizing the curve of her smile, the way she cocked her head, and the way she threw her head back when she laughed, she hadn't even noticed me in the crowd. When she called me Scrooge McDuck, it wasn't because she knew who I was. She just took one look and decided. And hell, maybe she's right. I've held dying children in refugee camps and stitched wounds by flashlight, but at the end of the day, I'm still a Kensington. Maybe wealth clings to me no matter how far I run from it—like some designer aftershave I can't wash off.

I clear my throat. "Your CT scan and MRI results aren't back yet, but I need to ask you a few questions."

"Shoot," she says, wincing as she shifts position.

"Can you tell me how the accident happened?"

"Damn deer." She sighs. "Not that I should blame her—poor thing was just being a deer. But she darted across the road and next thing I knew, my Jeep was rolling."

I run through the standard checklist. Seatbelt? Yes. Airbag deployment? None to deploy—her '97 Jeep predates mandatory airbags. Windshield impact? No. Alcohol consumption? The lab work confirms what she tells me—BAC of .02, nowhere near the legal limit.

I glance at my watch. "What day is it today?"

She arches an eyebrow. "Depends. Has the clock struck midnight yet? Because if it has, we've crossed into Friday territory. If not, we're still clinging to Thursday by our fingertips."

Good enough. She seems to have a sharp memory, so I don't suspect a concussion. But I go through the rest of the protocol anyway. I check her pupils with my phone flashlight, ask her to follow my finger with her eyes, test her balance by having her stand on one foot, and quiz her about who the president is. She passes everything, rolling her eyes at my ministrations.

She finally grips the edge of the bed, her knuckles paling. "Listen, doc. I need to get out of here." Her jaw tightens slightly. "My tattoo studio on Mateo is in trouble if I don't show up. Maya—she's not the most reliable—called in sick yesterday, or maybe it was today? Is it past midnight or not?" She leans forward, concern in her eyes. "She might not come in again today, and if I'm not there, that's twelve appointments canceled. Twelve. That's rent money I can't afford to lose while I'm stuck here." She gestures toward the clipboard. "Please. Sign the papers."

I grip the side of her hospital bed. "Ms. Steele."

"Oh please." Her eyes flash, her voice dropping to a husky whisper. "You've seen me naked. Tally is just fine."

Yes, I've seen her naked and it is a sight to behold. Heat floods my face. "Tally," I say, my voice rougher than intended. I lean closer, close enough to catch the faint scent of her perfume beneath the antiseptic. "You cannot leave. Not right now, anyhow. Not when every minute counts after trauma like this. The protocols don't catch everything—I've seen patients walk and talk perfectly, then collapse hours later from a brain bleed no one detected. I won't risk that. Not with you. Celeste would kill me if you died on my watch."

She rolls her eyes and crosses her arms so tightly it's like she's physically holding herself together. "Goddamn it," she hisses through clenched teeth. "But yeah, I've heard of that talk and die thing. Liam Neeson's wife? Hit her head skiing, said she was fine, then—dead. And Jesus—Celeste's father." Her voice cracks. "Laughing with the EMTs one minute after that skier crashed into him. Next day we were picking out his casket because his brain just—" She makes an explosive gesture with her fingers near her temple. "Fuck. You win. Not risking that." Then she shakes her head. "But if Maya wants to call off again for another fucking hangover, I'm firing her ass and getting somebody I can rely on."

"You do that," I say with a smile. "Anyhow, need to do my rounds. I'll be back when I get the results back from your scans."

She salutes me like she's in the military and I leave her there, my pulse hammering so violently I can feel it in my fingertips. During ER rounds, her scent haunts me—Tom Ford Black Orchid invading my senses, making it impossible to focus. The black truffle, black orchid and black plum notes mixed with that intoxicating patchouli and chocolate—it's not just a perfume, it's her essence distilled. Dark. Dangerous. Utterly consuming. Like her. I want to drown in it.

A few hours later, I return with results that bring visible relief to her face. "The scans came back clean—no internal injuries," I tell her, watching her shoulders relax. "You'll probably need to stay tonight for observation, but you should be free to go home tomorrow morning."

And then I go about the rest of my rounds, the scent of Tom Ford's Black Orchid following me around like a ghost.

Chapter Three

TALLY

I swear, every time Cameron Kensington walks into a room, the temperature rises ten degrees. The man didn't just win the genetic lottery—his entire family bought out all the tickets. Put any Kensington brother in a suit and watch the photographers at *GQ* start a bidding war, but Cameron? At 38, he's aged like fine whiskey. When he runs his fingers through those dark waves or flashes those dimples—which he knows damn well what they do to women—I have to remind myself to breathe. Those sapphire eyes could make a nun question her vows.

But now I'm back at my apartment, and unless I wreck another vehicle, I've seen the last of Cameron. My poor Jeep—Jaspress, I called her, because I always loved the name Jasper but it felt too masculine for a car—is completely destroyed. Damn deer came out of nowhere. No work today either. The accident's still got me rattled, even though they discharged me from Cedars around 3 AM, plus, my left hand - the dominant hand, alas - is fucking stiff as hell. Cameron said it's strained. I can't grip a tattoo gun right now.

Cameron pushed for them to keep me overnight, but with no beds available except maybe a gurney in some hallway, they sent me home. If my brain had hemorrhaged while I slept, Mom would've hit the lawsuit jackpot—her opioid days finally paying off. But here I am at two in the afternoon, channel-surfing with a perfectly clear head. Guess I survived.

I am having a slight problem getting around, though, as my body is stiff from whiplash. Guess it's whiplash, because my scans showed nothing broken and whiplash is more of a muscle thing. Shit, I'll probably have to get some kind of neck brace. That'll be lovely at work. My regulars won't stop giving me shit about something like that.

A thunderous knock rattles my door. I lurch forward to answer it, but white-hot pain sears through my lower back, dropping me back onto the couch with a gasp. My muscles seize into concrete, each spasm a lightning strike up my spine. "COME IN!" I scream, desperation clawing at my throat. God, I don't even care who's there anymore—the devil himself could be on the other side of that door, but if he can drag me to the bathroom before my bladder explodes, I'll gladly follow him to hell.

Cameron steps through the door and my breath catches. Last night's green scrubs were one thing, but now—blue t-shirt stretched across shoulders that could carry the weight of the world, jeans hugging thighs that have clearly seen their share of training miles. His dark waves fall just past where they should, begging for fingers to brush them back. When he shoves his hands in his pockets, the motion pulls the fabric tighter across his chest and I have to bite my lip to keep from making a sound. That jawline could slice through diamond. Damn.

"Just checking on you," Cameron says gently.

I nod. "Hello there, Yalie boy," I say, my voice suddenly husky. "Sorry. Meant Johns Hopkins boy. Still playing doctor, I see. Anyhow, I really gotta use the little girls' room and—" My back spasms again and I cry out, the pain searing through me like a hot knife. He's at my side in an instant, his cologne hitting me before his hands do.

"I'd really like some help," I whisper, hating how vulnerable I sound.

When his fingers grip my waist, it's like being branded. Every nerve ending screams to life. Sure, I'd seen him at both of Max and Celeste's weddings—the first one that was as real as a Prada purse being sold from back of a Cabo van and the real tear-jerker one in England —but I'd dismissed him as just another perfect-faced Kensington with their obscene wealth and country club smiles. So he saves lives in Africa and has dimples that could make a nun question her vows. Big deal.

But holy hell, I wasn't prepared for this—this molten heat flooding my body as he practically carries me toward the bathroom. His breath fans against my neck, and I swear I can feel each individual exhale like a promise against my skin. My heart hammers so hard I'm certain he can hear it. God help me, I can barely remember my own name.

After finishing in the bathroom, I hobble into the living room where Cameron waits, armed with a warm towel and cold compress.

"Lie down," he says, gesturing to the couch. I stretch out on my stomach as he places the icy compress against my lower back. I flinch but bite my lip. The dragon tattoo that curls across that same spot took four hours and I barely winced—I can handle this.

"That's quite a bruise," he observes. "Black now, but it'll cycle through green, yellow, and finally a yellowish-brown before it's gone. Usually takes two weeks, though this one might need longer."

I manage a nod as he removes the compress. His fingertips begin working the tissue around the injury, sending little sparks racing up my spine. My breath catches. My muscles clench involuntarily beneath his touch. I close my eyes, suddenly aware of how long it's been since anyone has touched me like this—clinical as it may be. His hands are here to heal, not to explore, though my body doesn't seem to understand the difference. Wasn't there some study about endorphins from orgasms being natural painkillers? Maybe I'm just self-medicating in my mind.

His fingers work the skin around my bruise with practiced precision. "Increasing circulation," he explains. "Helps the blood flow, speeds healing. I promise I'm not being fresh."

My body begs to differ. I bite my lip to keep from saying so, amused by his quaint phrasing - "fresh." Cameron with his old-timey expressions, probably the kind of guy who says "swell" unironically. I never thought I'd be attracted to someone like him—this doctor who supposedly, according to Celeste, makes five-star meals on weekends and keeps a song-writing journal. Something about that combination makes my pulse quicken under his touch. Last boyfriend couldn't even microwave without setting off the smoke alarm because the dumb shit put a metal bowl into that microwave and set the damn thing on fire. I mean, who doesn't know by now that you can't put metal in a microwave? Kent Rogers, my idiot ex, that's who.

I've heard Cameron plays piano too, just like his brothers—especially Kalen and Ansel. A doctor with artist's hands. No wonder I can barely breathe when he's this close.

His voice drops to a rasp. "I need you to unzip your jeans. Just enough for me to see the bruising."

My fingers tremble at the zipper. The metal teeth part with a sound that echoes in my ears like thunder. I ease the denim down, revealing the thin strip of my thong and the curve of flesh beneath. The cool air kisses my exposed skin.

"It's spread lower," he murmurs, his breath warm against my back. Ice touches my skin—a shock that melts instantly into heat as his fingertips trace the edges of the bruises. His touch is clinical, but my body doesn't know the difference. Every nerve ending ignites.

Two decades of dawn runs and punishing squats have sculpted me here. I know what I am. And I know what his quickening breath means as his hands work over me.

He applies heated towels, but they're nothing compared to the inferno building between my legs. I bite my lip to keep from arching back against him, from begging his fingers to slip beneath the thin fabric, to feel his mouth replace the ice. I want to burn. I want to shatter.

Dammit. I'm burning alive. Every nerve ending screams, my skin electric under his touch, my core clenching with a need so fierce I can barely breathe. I have to do something before I combust.

I flip onto my back, the sudden movement making him jerk backward. His eyes—those impossible eyes that shift between oceanic blue and forest green depending on how the light catches them—lock with mine, pupils dilating instantly. He swallows hard, that perfect throat working as he tries to drag his gaze away from my exposed skin. I grab the hem of my shirt and yank it up, revealing the purple-blue stain across my abdomen. "This needs your attention too," I whisper, my voice husky, unrecognizable.

His hands hover, trembling slightly, before pressing the ice against my skin. I gasp at the shock of cold against heat. His fingers work the tender flesh, and I arch involuntarily into his touch. He's looking everywhere but at my face, while I'm desperate to capture those kaleidoscope eyes, to make him see exactly what he's doing to me.

"Doc," I begin.

"Don't call me doc, please. I'm not your doctor right now, god forbid. After you were discharged from the ER, I ceased being your doctor."

"You're so sensitive about that."

"I need to be. Because doctors can't do things like this with their patients."

"Things like what ?" I ask innocently. I slip open the first button of my blouse, then the next. The bruises from the Jeep accident map across my skin in purple-green constellations. Cameron's eyes widen as I reach behind to unhook my bra.

I slip open the first button of my blouse, then the next. The bruises from the Jeep accident map across my skin in purple-green constellations. Cameron's eyes widen as I reach behind to unhook my bra. This is reckless.

Celeste would never forgive me. Her golden rule: friends don't hook up with friends' relatives. Especially not her husband's brother. The Kensington family gatherings would become unbearable—and I've already missed their famous annual gala last year with the living art installation. Art is my weakness; I never miss the *Pageant of the Masters* in Laguna if I can help it, and from what I hear, Asher did something similar as that Laguna festival at last year's Kensington gala. I want to attend this year's gala where Asher's planning something spectacular again, and it'll be…uncomfortable…if Cameron and I hook up and I have to run into him there.

If Cameron and I crash and burn like all my relationships... but God, the heat spreading through me demands satisfaction in a way logic can't touch.

He's shy. I've watched him shrink into corners at both weddings, his eyes darting away whenever a woman approaches. Even with that jawline—the kind that could cut glass—and those broad shoulders straining against his tailored suit, he'd rather study the pattern in the carpet than meet a woman's gaze. I've seen them circle him like sharks, touching his arm, laughing too loudly at his mumbled jokes. Each time, he'd flush crimson and find an excuse to escape. If I want him, I'll need to be the predator here.

"Cameron," I say, arching my back until my breasts nearly graze his chest, "does this bruising look serious to you? Feel how tender it is." I'm pointing at the bruise across my now-bare breasts.

"I—Christ—I can't—" His pupils dilate until his eyes are almost black, fixed on my skin like he's drowning in it.

I shove him onto the other end of the couch. "You can and you will." I devour his mouth, and Christ, the taste of him—dark chocolate and sin. My body ignites. Bruises? What bruises? Back pain? Gone. There's only him, his hands gripping my hips hard enough to leave marks, his tongue claiming mine. He kisses me with a violence that matches my own, and I know with absolute certainty he'll obliterate every sensation except pleasure. I need him to burn through me like wildfire, scorching away everything but this moment. This isn't about connection—it's about consumption. He's a feast laid out before a starving woman, and I will take, take, take until there's nothing left of either of us. Right. Fucking. Now.

His voice breaks. "Oh, god. This is so wrong." He shakes his head even as his mouth travels from mine down to my neck, then finds my tender, sore breasts. My fingers work at his buttons, revealing a chest that could have been carved from Carrara marble perched right above an eight pack.

Damn, this man is fine.

My fingers trace the ridges of his abdomen. I've worked marble before—know the patience required, how the chisel must strike just so. For my final art class project, I'd copied Michelangelo's *David*, spending hours studying the perfect proportions, the tension in the muscles, the subtle asymmetry that makes it feel alive. That sculpture remains my favorite, though I create original pieces now. It captures human perfection in a way few things do.

Cameron's body rivals it.

"God, you're beautiful," I whisper as his lips trace my arms, my breasts, moving down to my stomach. "I need those endorphins flowing through me right now."

He looks up, eyes dark. "Orgasms are known to relieve pain."

"Yes, doctor," I breathe. "So get busy."

He rises suddenly, his hands gripping my shoulders as he pushes me back against the leather. His eyes darken, pupils dilating. "Your body is exquisite," he growls, voice dropping an octave.

"Right," I challenge, breath catching. "If you prefer Picasso's chaos to John Singer Sargent's *Madame X*."

"No." His voice is steel wrapped in velvet. "You're perfect." His mouth descends on the purple-black bruise marking my abdomen, tongue tracing its edges before pressing against the center. I gasp, arching involuntarily as his teeth graze my skin, his hands already tearing at the thin fabric barrier of my underwear. The sound of ripping lace barely registers as his burning mouth claims me completely.

Oh, yes. Yes. His tongue traces slow, deliberate circles, then flicks with perfect pressure against that sweet spot that makes my thighs tremble. I arch my back, fingers tangled in his hair as he slides one finger inside me, then another, curving upward in rhythm with each stroke of his tongue. My breath catches when he hums against me, the vibration sending electric currents straight to my core. God, this guy knows exactly what he's doing and I don't want him to ever stop. This is better than any painkiller I could ever think of. Good god, they should bottle this feeling - there would be no more Oxycontin addictions.

His fingers curl inside me, finding that perfect spot that makes my back arch off the couch. I gasp his name as he adds another finger, stretching me deliciously while his tongue traces hot, deliberate patterns that send electric currents through my entire body. The pain that had consumed me before Cameron arrived dissolves into nothing—replaced by a pleasure so intense it borders on unbearable. I claw his back, desperate for more, for him to fill me completely, but he refuses. Instead, he doubles down, his mouth relentless, his fingers moving with devastating precision until I'm trembling, begging, coming apart beneath him. He's determined to worship me this way, and God help me, I'm powerless to do anything but surrender.

I shatter into a thousand pieces, convulsing as wave after wave of pleasure crashes through me, but it's not enough—I need more of him. Cameron's mouth blazes a trail up my bruised skin, his tongue leaving fire in its wake until he collapses beside me, his breathing as ragged as mine. "This crosses every line," he says, his eyes still dark with hunger. "You're my patient."

"Then diagnose me, doctor," I gasp, my body still trembling. "I'm addicted to your touch—no prescription drug could ever compare to what your mouth just did to me. I'd swear under oath that this was purely medicinal, even as I beg you to do it again."

He shakes his head. "I didn't come over for this."

I cock my head. "What did you come over for?"

"I wanted to check on you. It's my day off, and I thought about you all last night while I was on shift." He plays with my hair, which is now long, but is still streaked with every color of the rainbow. "All I could think of is that you're Celeste's best friend and that made it personal that you were in my ER. I thought I should personally check on you, that's all."

I take a deep breath. "Well, I just took from you just now. What did you get out of that?"

He smiles. "Tally, if you only knew just what I got out of that. I made you feel better. And as much as you shattered by what I was doing, it's safe to say that you'll feel the painkilling effects for hours to come."

I smile, my voice dropping to a whisper. "Dr. Kensington."

His eyes darken as he grabs my wrist. "Don't call me Dr. Kensington. Not right now." His grip tightens. "Do you have any idea what I've risked for you? Ten years of medical training, my license, my reputation—all of it hanging by a thread because I couldn't keep my hands off you." His jaw clenches. "One minute I'm treating your injuries, and the next—"

"You're making me come so hard I see stars," I cut in, pressing against him. "God, when you touch me, it's like being struck by lightning. Better than any drug. You should see the way your pupils dilate when I moan your name." I drag my fingertips down his chest. "Forget opioids—the world needs what you do to me."

He lays on top of me, his breath hot against my neck. "It's biochemical warfare. Pure endorphin rush straight to the brain's pleasure centers." His hand slides under my shirt. "And I'm about to give you another dose."

And he does just that. For hours. He doesn't ever seem to tire, even as he never even considers taking even one climax for himself.

Chapter Four

CAMERON

Christ. What have I done?

I grip the steering wheel as I drive away from Tally's place, knuckles white. The medical board would have a field day with this—doctor sleeps with patient, loses license, film at eleven. But how could I resist? The way her Black Orchid perfume lingered in the air between us. Those Mediterranean-blue eyes watching me from beneath dark lashes. The curve of her waist under my hands, so delicate I could almost encircle it completely. Her beautiful full breasts consumed me—the weight of them, the heat, the way my tongue traced her nipples until she gasped my name like a prayer and a curse all at once.

Alecia's face flashes in my mind. Two years without dating anyone, and now this. The guilt sits heavy in my chest even as I remember Tally's sighs, the way she arched against me. I justified it as medical care—endorphins are nature's painkillers, after all. Those bruises from the accident looked agonizing, and when I arrived, she couldn't even make it to the bathroom without help.

For a few hours at least, I distracted her from her pain. At least that's what I tell myself.

I need to talk to someone about this whole situation, so I dial up Dr. Elias Stone. We've been tight since our Harvard Westlake days—the fancy prep school where the Kensington boys get polished. I'll have to admit I crossed a line with a patient, but Elias won't report me. We've got a brotherhood that runs deeper than DNA. Don't get me wrong—I love my actual brothers, all seven of them. But with Elias, it's different. He chose me, and I chose him. That kind of bond hits different than the one you're born into.

I call my friend as I'm driving home from Tally's.

"Eli," I say when he picks up. I check my watch—7:30 PM. He's been home for hours already. Lucky bastard with his pediatrician's schedule, nine-to-five with weekends off, while I'm pulling another double shift in the ER. That sports medicine fellowship can't come soon enough, but first —Sicily. One more month and I'll be on a plane, spending a year with Doctors Without Borders helping refugees. "I need to talk."

"Door's open, Cam," Elias says. "Sarah just put Molly to bed. Wine's breathing on the patio."

I hate barging into Elias' perfect little world. His life is exactly what mine was supposed to be when I married Alecia. We had Stephanie within a year after those "til death do us part" vows, never imagining death would claim her just two years later. Watching Elias with his clockwork routine, his beautiful wife, his four-year-old daughter, the age Stephanie would now be - it stings. We used to joke about the cosmic timing—both having baby girls who'd grow up as best friends. The four of us were inseparable: weekend cabins at Lake Mead, skiing trips to Mammoth, that amazing week in New York. Then suddenly, my world collapsed while his remained intact. I don't resent his happiness—I'm not built that way. But knowing he'll probably meet me alone on that terrace, without Sarah, because we're no longer two couples but a pair and a spare—that's the part that cuts deepest.

I get to Elias, and, sure enough, Sarah and Molly are nowhere to be seen. "Sarah is upstairs with Mol doing a puzzle with her," Elias says. "She's so bright that she helps her mom do 500-piece puzzles. Can you imagine?"

I nod and sigh. Yeah, it's difficult hearing about Molly's milestones just because Molly is the same age that Steph would be right now. And Steph was an extremely bright child, too - she was a little younger than one when she was killed, but she was ahead of schedule for her milestones - babbling in complete sentences, walking already, tracking objects with those intelligent eyes while she was still crawling, already knowing her colors. So she probably would've been able to help Alecia put together a puzzle, just like Molly is with Sarah. And it'll always be like this, I know - when Molly is going to kindergarten and learning her tables, I'll think that Steph should be doing the same. When Molly makes the swim or gymnastics team or whatever she's bound to do, I'll wonder what sports Steph might've liked. When Molly gets her driver's license, there'll be a pang that Steph isn't doing the same. When she graduates high school, goes to college, gets married…I'll always wonder about Steph. After all, they were the same age so all the milestones Molly hits, Steph would've hit them at roughly the same time.

But there's no way in hell I'm saying a word to Elias. What am I supposed to do—make him feel like shit because he's living my dream? The white picket fence, the whole package I'd sketched out in my head. Christ. One hint of how I really feel, and he'd get that kicked-puppy look, start dodging my calls. So I swallow it down, paste on a smile, and keep my jealousy locked behind my teeth where it belongs.

He hands me a glass of wine and settles back into his patio furniture. "So," he says. "What's going on?"

I stare at my palms like they might hold answers. "I don't really know." I exhale slowly. "I'm kind of..." My words trail off. "I might have..." I run a hand through my hair. "I met someone."

He lets out a low chuckle. "So…you ready to crawl back into the land of the living?"

I shrug, voice rough. "Land of the living's a stretch. But hell—if I'm even noticing a woman again, that's something. Ever since the crash, every woman I see just…nothing. Doesn't matter if she's kind, brilliant, drop-dead gorgeous—my heart's been a block of ice." I swallow hard. "But maybe—just maybe—the frost is cracking." I shake my head, bitter smile. "Still, I can't picture myself falling in love again. I couldn't survive another Alecia or Steph. So maybe I'll just play the field—flit from one beautiful face to the next, never anchor down. Beats rotting alone in a dark house, staring at the walls."

Elias leans forward. "How hot's this spark, really?"

My chest tightens. "Goddamn, it's a blast furnace. More intense than anything I've ever felt—even with Alecia. With her, love sneaked up on me over years of friendship. We were comfortable, predictable, hanging out, setting each other up with different people so we could hopefully double-date one day—until a drunken dare set our lips together one night and boom. So yeah, years of friendship until the night it wasn't just friendship. That relationship was the epitome of slow burn. But this thing with Tally? It's thermonuclear." I press my palms to my temples, as if my skull might split open.

He raises an eyebrow. "You've seen her before she crashed into the ER?"

I nod, eyes distant, replaying the moment. "First at Max's fake wedding to Celeste—she stormed in like a riot. Hair cropped short, streaked in neon, tattoos spilling down her arm, that dress hugging every curve. She looked like she'd drag me through asphalt and laugh the whole way. Totally the opposite of Alecia's cashmere-and-pearls sweetness. Alecia was a kindergarten teacher. Tally is a tattoo artist. Those two couldn't be more different if they tried. And yet—Tally's raw power, her fierce beauty—it obliterated me the second I glanced her way. No type? Forget that. I've got one now."

Elias and I talk for several more hours before I head out of his place.

After leaving Elias, my car seems to drive itself to Tally's place. With three days off from my ER rotation—a rare luxury in my four-day, 12-hour shift schedule—I find myself calculating how many hours I could spend making her forget about her injuries. My mind lingers on the thought of her smile breaking through the pain. She'd need help getting around, someone to cook meals, maybe assistance slipping into a bath.

My hands tighten on the steering wheel. Two days of playing caretaker, of being needed in her space, before she'd be mobile enough to manage without me. Though I wasn't sure I wanted her to.

I smile at the irony—after spending hours making her writhe and moan beneath me, I never once thought to ask for her number. Calling Celeste isn't an option; Tally made it clear she wanted this kept between us. Fine by me. I'm not looking to announce whatever this is to the world. A fling? No, that sounds dismissive. Hooking up? Christ, I'm 38, not some college kid. I've saved lives in African villages and navigated emergency rooms during the worst nights imaginable. There has to be a better word for what I want—which is to show up at her apartment, strip her bare, and lose ourselves in each other until we can't move. Not dating, certainly. Just pure, electric connection. A liaison? An arrangement? A tryst?

I head over to her apartment. Just like before, she hollers for me to come in instead of getting the door herself. That can't be good. Has she been stuck on that couch this whole time? Sure enough, when I step inside, there she is, sprawled out with an ice pack wedged under her lower back. Her face brightens when I take a seat beside her.

"Thank Christ you showed up. I tried being a hero after you left—thought I'd fix myself something to eat. Big mistake. My back seized up again and I fumbled my damn phone. Now it's somewhere in kitchen Narnia while I'm marooned here with this ice pack. Was seriously wondering how I'd survive without Uber Eats for the foreseeable future. And, well, with the phone on the floor somewhere and me stuck here, how the hell would I summon Uber Eats? I was faced with starving to death." She sighs dramatically. "Had to call in reinforcements at the shop too. Some agency's sending over a temp artist named Blade. I mean, seriously? Blade? Might as well name yourself 'Needle' or 'Ink.' Anyway, looks like I'm on extended vacation whether I like it or not."

I shake my head. "No way. Forget Uber Eats. Let me get you real groceries. Just tell me what you want." My hands are already itching to help, to fix, to provide. It's my default setting—caretaking. "Actually, I'll order from Instacart. That way I don't have to leave you here alone again."

"My notebook," she says, wincing as she shifts position. "Get it from the spare bedroom. It's next to my sketchbook."

I duck into the first bedroom, finding only rumpled sheets on an unmade bed.

"Not that one!" Tally calls out. "The other spare!"

In the second bedroom, I spot her notebook on a small table, but freeze mid-reach. The space around me is transformed by color and form—watercolor landscapes capturing impossible light, their sunset hues bleeding into cerulean skies above jagged mountain silhouettes. A collection of small marble figures crowds the windowsill, each no larger than my palm: a dancer with one leg extended in an arabesque so delicate the stone seems flexible; a falcon with individually carved feathers poised for flight; a child's face with eyelashes so fine they cast hairline shadows. The walls themselves are a riot of framed sketches—hands in various poses, eyes with different expressions, the curve of a shoulder rendered in charcoal. I've stumbled into her secret gallery, a hidden chamber of her soul.

And all around are watercolors of a woman who looks much like Tally, but older and sadder. In one, she sits at a weathered kitchen table, her fingers curled around a chipped blue mug, steam rising in ghostly wisps. In another, she stands at a window, her silhouette backlit by a pale winter sun, one hand pressed against the frosted glass. The third shows her asleep in an armchair, a book fallen open on her lap, reading glasses dangling from fingertips. I gasp at how Tally has captured this woman—the same green-blue eyes, the same straight raven hair now threaded with silver, but with crow's feet etched deep at the corners and a downward tilt to her mouth that speaks of years of disappointment. Something shifts inside me. This isn't just a hookup anymore. I'm standing in the presence of someone whose soul bleeds onto canvas, and I'm desperate to understand the woman behind the brush.

I bring the notebook out and Tally narrows her eyes at me. "Took you long enough. What, were you checking out Marisa in there?"

"Marisa?"

"That's my mother. Well, sometimes she's 'Mom,' sometimes she's 'Marisa,' and sometimes she's 'hey bitch.'" A half-smile flickers across her face. "Depends on where we stand. 'Mom' is when I'm worried about her, 'Marisa' is when I'm pissed, and 'hey bitch' is for when we're actually tight." Her arms fold tight across her chest. "Today? Definitely Marisa."

"What happened?"

She looks away with a shrug. "Called her after you left. Needed help getting around. She had 'plans.'" Tally makes air quotes with her fingers, then swipes quickly at her eye. "Translation: she's in some new dude's bed, and I'm SOL. Classic Marisa—always ditching me for whatever rando she thinks might be her Prince Charming this week. Never mind that they all ghost her faster than a heart attack. But hey—" her voice catches, "—at least someone's getting a happy ending."

I can't help but smile. Looks like we both got dealt a bad hand in the parent department. Dad chose Jack Daniels over his family for two decades straight. I wonder if her father was in the picture at all.

"Dad caught a bullet in Iraq," Tally says, like she's plucking the question straight from my head. "Died when I was 4, but I never really knew him because he was deployed for years." Her eyes narrow, jaw tightening. "You know what kills me? Those suits in Washington throwing around words like 'casualties' and 'collateral damage.' That was my father. A real person." She traces a finger along the rim of her glass. "Mom was apparently fine before. After he died... opioids were the only thing that could make her forget."

The parallels hit me like a punch. My mother died, dad drowned himself in whiskey. Her dad died, mom disappeared into Oxy. Difference is, my brothers and I landed with loaded grandparents who could handle raising eight rowdy boys. Tally clearly wasn't so lucky.

"Your mom was using?" I ask carefully.

"Yeah." She shrugs like we're discussing the weather. "I got real good at the foster care shuffle. Mom would clean up just long enough to convince a judge she was mother-of-the-year material. Two weeks later, she'd be tweaking in the cereal aisle at Ralph's." Her smile doesn't reach her eyes. "Eventually I kept a go-bag under my bed. You learn to see the signs." Then she shakes her head. "Look at me, oversharing. I blame the good shit painkillers."

I inhale deeply. "We're not that different, you and me. We both lost a parent to grief. My dad drowned his sorrows in whiskey and vanished for two decades. Your mom..."

"Yeah," she cuts me off. "Except you got a silver spoon to suck on while daddy dearest was checking out. In the game of who got the shittiest end of the stick, trust fund boy doesn't win. Nice try, though."

I give a slow nod. "Pain doesn't check your bank account before it moves in."

She tilts her head, conceding. "Touché. Now hand over that notebook so I can list what I eat. Word is you're some kind of kitchen wizard."

That makes me laugh. I'm no Gordon Ramsay, but I can handle myself in the kitchen. Sunday mornings are sacred—just me, a mug of dark roast, and whatever chef is demonstrating knife skills on TV. My cookbooks are all dog-eared and annotated. There's something meditative about the steady rhythm of a knife against a cutting board—it quiets my mind the same way playing Chopin does, or filling journal pages with verses no one will ever see. Roman teases me about being the "sensitive Kensington," but I stopped being offended years ago my brothers' ribbing. My masculinity doesn't need defending just because my Spotify lacks Slayer.

Tally scrawls her food preferences on the notepad I hand her. Pizza tops her list, followed by various proteins—chicken, seafood, tofu. No beef or pork. Raw onions are apparently her nemesis. I nod, mentally cataloging ingredients while tapping out an Instacart order. Once that's done, I join her on the sofa and lift one of her feet onto my lap. "Delivery's on the way," I say, pressing my thumbs into her arch. "I'm guessing you wouldn't mind a massage?"

Her eyes roll back as her lids fall shut. "Jesus Christ, yes," she hisses through clenched teeth. "Even better than what you did to me earlier." The corner of her mouth curls into something dangerous. "Other men attack that like they're defusing a bomb with oven mitts, but you..." She arches her back, a small moan escaping her throat. "Your hands should be registered as lethal weapons."

I feel my pulse hammering in my throat. Tonight, there'll be no stopping at my just pleasuring her. The heat in her eyes when she looks at me is unmistakable—scorching, demanding. And I'm already burning to give her exactly what she needs. For medical purposes, of course.

For thirty minutes, I work Tally's feet with practiced hands, drawing out those little groans that tell me I'm hitting the right spots. Her head falls back against the cushions. I know exactly where to press to ease tension—a skill that beats most painkillers, though not quite as effective as an orgasm. That'll come later. Right now, I'm focused on the delicate arch of her foot, the curve of her heel, each toe getting individual attention as I knead and press with just the right pressure. Back when Alecia carried Steph, I'd studied foot reflexology to help with her pregnancy discomfort. Turns out the human foot is like a control panel for the whole body—press here for back pain, there for headaches.

There's a knock at the door—the Instacart delivery I ordered. I haul in bag after bag of groceries and head straight for the kitchen. When I open Tally's freezer, I'm greeted by a sad army of frozen dinners standing at attention—Lean Cuisines, Amy's, Bellisio's, Stouffer's, Marie Callender's. The fridge isn't much better: a lonely six-pack of Heineken and some bottled water. That's it.

I shake my head, feeling something tighten in my chest. Something about seeing her empty fridge hits me harder than it should. I've always been the guy who rushes in to fix things, especially for women like Tally—the ones with the tough exteriors and vulnerable cores. It scares me how much I want to be the one she leans on, even though I know she'd hate the very thought of needing anyone. Still, looking at this barren refrigerator, I can't shake the feeling that she really does need someone in her life to care about her. Can that someone be me?

While Tally shifts between ice packs and heated compresses on the couch, I set to work on my signature dish. The kitchen comes alive as I flatten chicken breasts with quick, practiced strikes, then prepare a filling of tangy goat cheese, wilted spinach, and sweet-tart cranberries kissed with honey. I roll each breast around the mixture, coat them in fragrant herbs, and sear them in shimmering olive oil before they hit the oven. Water bubbles in two pots —one for potatoes, another for fresh green beans. I notice a pristine food processor on her counter, looking suspiciously unused amid evidence of a frozen-dinner lifestyle. When everything finishes cooking—timing perfectly orchestrated —I transform the potatoes into a cloud of garlicky, herb-flecked comfort. Minutes later, I'm carrying two steaming plates to the living room, hoping good food might ease her pain better than any compress.

Tally takes a bite of the chicken and closes her eyes. "Holy shit," she says, licking her lips. "This is—" She takes another bite, this time with a forkful of the garlic mashed potatoes. "How the hell are you a doctor? Did you, like, go to culinary school too?" She stabs at a green bean, dragging it through the mashed potatoes and gravy on her plate before popping it in her mouth. "The cranberries with the goat cheese? Genius. And these beans—" She points her fork at me. "You're wasted in medicine, I swear to god."

I can't help but smile. "After peeking in your fridge and freezer, I'm thinking you only consider me a great cook because—"

"Because my culinary hero is a cartoon character on a can? Fair." She flashes a grin. "Fun fact though—Chef Boyardee was actually real. Ettore Boiardi, Italian immigrant. Had this fancy restaurant in Cleveland before he started canning spaghetti."

"Impressive trivia," I say, amused. "Though having a Michelin-star background doesn't exactly elevate those little meat-filled UFOs to gourmet status."

Tally quirks an eyebrow. "What are you now, the food police?"

"Hardly." I shake my head. "Just your average Western medicine guy. We don't do the whole lifestyle counseling thing. Our approach is more 'here's a prescription, good luck.'"

Tally cocks her head. "Shouldn't doctors be all over what their patients eat?"

"We try," I say with a half-smile. "But telling someone to eat broccoli and dust off their exercise equipment usually gets me a 'whatever, Doc, just write the prescription.' So we adapt. Hence all the medications for conditions that proper diet and exercise could prevent." I shrug. "Besides, I'm only an ER doc. It might not be up to the primary care docs to lecture about diet and exercise, and it's really not up to ER docs to do that."

Her fingers brush my forearm, and I swear my skin tingles where she touches. "But you practice what you preach, right?" She settles back against the pillow, those eyes still challenging me.

"Looks like you do too," I say, though I'm puzzled how she maintains that toned physique with what I saw in her kitchen.

"Don't judge my empty fridge," she says. "I do Sweetgreen salads three times a week and Tender Greens on Santa Monica. When I'm working, it's Zinc Cafe on Mateo. Plus my daily shake—kale, berries, protein stuff. Those sad frozen dinners? Just for when tattoo bookings are slow and I'm watching my pennies."

"Well, good to know that you don't live on Lean Cuisine," I teased. "That shit's full of sodium, you know."

She finishes her meal, looks at me and says "so what's for dessert?" Then she raises an eyebrow, and I know what she's getting at. I lift her into my arms, feeling her weight settle against my chest as I carry her to the bedroom. Her fingers trace the line of my jaw as I lay her on the bed, her dark hair fanning across the pillow. When our lips meet, she tastes like the red wine we shared. I trace the tattoo spiraling down her shoulder, following its path with my mouth until she arches beneath me. Our clothes find their way to the floor, and I take my time exploring every inch of her, memorizing the sounds she makes when I find a sensitive spot. We move together, skin against skin, her nails digging into my shoulders as our bodies find their rhythm. Time dissolves into an exquisite haze of two bodies coming together, again and again, until dawn breaks through the blinds, painting golden stripes across her flushed skin and the sheets beneath us.

Chapter Five

TALLY

Holy shit, last night was volcanic. The pain in my body vanished the moment Cameron's hands gripped my hips, replaced by a hunger that clawed at my insides. That man doesn't just fuck—he devours. His body is sculpted perfection, all hard planes and raw power like some Kensington family birthright, and Christ, when he finally thrust inside me—let's just say "generously endowed" doesn't begin to cover it. I lost count of how many times I shattered, each orgasm more violent than the last until I was practically sobbing, begging him not to stop. Therapeutic? It was fucking transcendent. Now I'm waking up to cold sheets and his scent lingering on my skin.

The clatter of pans and soft footsteps from my kitchen wake me up. Minutes later, Cameron appears in the doorway with something I've only seen in movies—an honest-to-god breakfast tray complete with a tiny vase holding a single red rose. Where the hell did he find a tray in my apartment? And the vase, not to mention the rose?

And this fancy China plate? Did he conjure all of it from thin air?

He slides onto the bed beside me, balancing his creation. My stomach growls as I take in what he's made: Eggs Benedict with smoked salmon instead of Canadian bacon, a puffy Dutch Baby pancake drowning in lemon curd and fresh berries, and a bowl of plump strawberries. After last night's... workout, I could eat the entire tray, silverware included.

I take one bite of the Eggs Benedict and nearly moan. "Holy shit, did you actually make this Hollandaise from scratch?"

The sauce is silky perfection—lemony, buttery, with just the right amount of tang. I've watched enough cooking shows to know this isn't some packet mix or blender shortcut. This is the real deal—the kind of sauce that requires whisking your arm off while praying to the culinary gods that your egg yolks don't scramble. The kind of sauce that gets chefs Michelin stars and makes home cooks cry.

He kisses my forehead. "Of course."

I shoot him a side-eye. What the hell does he think this is? I didn't sign up for some fairy-tale bullshit with him. We're not Celeste and Max playing house. This is about scratching an itch—a really good, toe-curling, back-arching itch that he happens to be phenomenal at scratching. Multiple times. But forehead kisses? That's crossing a line.

I stare at the Dutch Baby pancake, its golden crust puffed up like a cloud around the edges and sinking into a buttery crater in the middle, dusted with powdered sugar that's melting into the heat. "What are you eating?" I ask, cutting into the eggy goodness with my fork. "And where did you get all this fancy shit? The silver tray with these little scrolly handles, that blue glass vase with the single rose, and especially the heavy-ass cast iron skillet you needed to make this phenomenal—and I mean fucking phenomenal—pancake?"

I know the groceries came from the Instacart dude—I saw the paper bags. But the rest? My cabinets are as empty as my bank account at the end of the month. My fridge typically contains nothing but half-empty takeout containers and a six-pack.

Cooking is against my religion. No mom in my rearview to teach me, and I never gave a damn about learning. I was too busy with charcoal-smudged fingers, hunched over whatever scrap of paper I could find, or molding creatures from Play-Doh until my knuckles ached. Some foster homes got it—they'd see me drawing on napkins and spring for those cheap watercolor sets, the kind with the neon-bright colors that kindergarteners use. I once had a friend who'd eat the paint, just took it out of the tray and bit right into it. That's the kind of watercolors I'd get, the kind that kindergarteners eat, but I'd make beautiful portraits out of that shit. I'd make clay from flour stolen from the pantry, water from the tap, and whatever else I could swipe. Art from nothing—that was my superpower.

Cameron shakes his head. "Already had breakfast. I'm one of those ungodly early risers—4 AM. Been that way forever, which is perfect for my hospital schedule. Start at five, done by two." He gestures to the table setup. "Swung by my place for supplies. Cast iron's non-negotiable for a proper Dutch Baby. But good on you for knowing how to make a Dutch Baby pancake and for knowing it requires a cast iron skillet."

He nudges my arm, and I can't help but nudge back. "So, you ate?" I ask. "When did you do that?"

"At four this morning. Just had my usual protein shake. Berries, spinach, avocado."

Figures he's a health nut. Though I'm hardly one to talk —my breakfast routine is basically the same. Frozen blueberries, chocolate collagen powder, peanut butter, and kale when I remember to buy it. Right now, though, out of all those things - meant to go to the store, but got into an accident instead, so no store. But blending is the extent of my "cooking" skills.

I feign offense about his comment about my knowing that a Dutch Baby pancake requires a cast iron skillet. "I'm not completely clueless about cooking. Dutch Babies are just oven pancakes, so of course you need a cast iron skillet." I try to look indignant, but my eyes keep drifting back to his face. Damn, he's beautiful.

"So," he says as he gently clears my bangs off my face. Again with the intimacy bullshit. How do I put this to him? I'm not here for romance. Just pure analgesic, therapeutic, mind-blowing sex that makes me forget my own name let alone my painful back. Cameron's right - orgasms are nature's painkillers. I don't feel a single twinge in my back right now, mainly because I came so many times last night that I lost count. Cameron is amazing in bed, as I knew he would be, because he's so damn good at oral. He knows how to please a woman, and, right now, I'm extremely pleased. "Let me run you a bath. Epsom salts and Peppermint oil will help loosen up your sore back."

I bite my lower lip so hard I taste blood. "Cam," I say, my voice sharper than I intended. "This is all fucking amazing. This food, last night—Jesus Christ—I mean, my thighs are still trembling. I have no goddamn idea how you got up at 4 AM when we were fucking till 2. But I need you to hear me." I lean forward, gripping the edge of the table. "I'm not just allergic to romance, I'm fatally allergic. Like anaphylactic shock, dead-in-minutes allergic. You do not want to get tangled up with me. I'm not a cute little storm—I'm a fucking Cat Five that levels everything in my path." I jab my finger on the table. "Just so we're crystal fucking clear."

A look crosses his face, there and then gone. He's hurt. But he needs to know the score. I don't do relationships. Not after watching my mom's love life play out like a horror movie on repeat. She collected men like trading cards while collecting her daily dose of prescription pills. Every new guy was "The One"—until he wasn't. They'd stick around a week, maybe a month. Pepper—seriously, who names their kid Pepper?—lasted a whole year, setting the record.

In college, when I nearly got expelled for my drinking and landed in mandatory therapy, my shrink connected the dots. Mom wasn't just hooked on opioids; she was hooked on men. Couldn't breathe without one. When they inevitably split, she'd turn into this desperate creature—driving past their houses at 3 AM, blowing up their phones, creating fake profiles to stalk their Facebook pages. Then came the depression, the threats. "I'll swallow these pills." "I'll slit my wrists." "I'll drive off the bridge by the interstate." She never followed through, but I lived in constant fear she would.

"Co-dependent," my therapist called it. Whatever fancy label you slap on it, the lesson stuck: relationships equal destruction. And that's one family tradition I'm breaking.

He finally says, "I guess we're just having fun, then." He looks at me with those kaleidoscope eyes—a swirling collision of cerulean blue, jade green, and honey-gold flecks, all framed by lashes so thick and dark they look like they've been painted on with India ink—and I feel a twinge of something that might be pity. He's hunting for a woman to love, to cherish, to wrap in cashmere blankets and protect from the world's sharp edges. Somebody like his dead wife —Celeste mentioned she taught kindergarten, probably in some brick schoolhouse with a white picket fence where the children wore uniforms.

I can see them together in my mind—not plastic-perfect Ken and Barbie, but Cameron and Alecia, names that sound like they were embroidered onto matching monogrammed hand towels hanging in a powder room. Him, in cable-knit sweaters the color of aged bourbon, crisp seersucker pants with knife-edge pleats, probably captained the rowing team at Harvard- where I know he got his undergrad because Celeste told me so -where he aced every class and graduated Magna Cum Laude. Definitely belonged to one of those secret societies where they drink from silver cups and swear blood oaths by candlelight. Her—honey-blonde hair falling in perfect waves, willowy limbs wrapped in buttery-soft cashmere twin sets in pastels, that effortless beauty that comes from generations of good breeding and expensive face creams. Sorority girl from Yale—because Harvard doesn't have sororities, and I'd bet my left arm his precious Alecia needed that sisterhood connection—who drove a sleek silver Audi with leather seats that never saw a coffee stain. I picture them at their lake house, sipping French-pressed coffee from hand-thrown pottery mugs on their private dock, listening to whippoorwills and bullfrogs while planning which artisanal bakery in Bridgehampton they'll visit for fresh scones before their couples' tennis lesson.

At any rate, whatever white-picket-fence, Sunday-dinner-with-the-in-laws life he's imagining, he won't find it with me. I'm a hot mess—the kind who eats cold pizza for breakfast, has more tattoo ink than clean laundry, and considers tequila a food group. I'm the kind of woman who has her electricity cut off because she forgot to pay the bill three months running, who eats cereal straight from the box at midnight, and who has seven unfinished tattoo designs scattered across her coffee table right now. My Jeep was held together with bumper stickers and prayer. I'm as far from that Yalie Alecia with her willowy blonde goodness, trust-fund smile, and cashmere-soft life as anybody can get —with my ink-stained fingers, colorful vocabulary, and body that's basically a walking art gallery—so Cam just has to be set straight before he gets any more stupid ideas.

"Yeah," I say. "And last night as hella fun."

He smiles, his eyes crinkling at the corners. "I'm off today and tomorrow too. So, there's lots more fun to be had." His lips brush mine, soft at first, then hungrier. I sink into the sheets, my body already humming with anticipation. Yes, this is exactly what I need. Nothing but mind-blowing sex that makes my toes curl and my spine arch, that drowns out the constant throbbing ache I now carry everywhere. His fingers trace my collarbone, then drifts lower, leaving goosebumps in their wake. Every touch ignites something primal in me, like he's flipping switches I didn't know existed.

And then he makes love to me. Not the frantic, sweat-soaked tangle from last night that left marks on the wall, but something deliberate and devastating in its tenderness. His eyes never leave mine. And as much as I want to hate it—because each careful, measured thrust feels like he's staking a claim rather than scratching an itch—goddamn, I don't hate it.

Which fucking terrifies me to my core.

Chapter Six

CAMERON

I'm Tally's for the next 36 hours—completely hers—and my skin still burns where she touched me this afternoon. I made her breakfast, then made love to her until neither of us could breathe right, until we were slick with sweat and gasping each other's names. Now evening's falling, and I'm already aching to take her out, to see her in candlelight, to watch other men's eyes follow her and know she's coming home with me.

After Alecia, I went two years without a woman's touch. Two years of cold showers and emptiness. Now with Tally, it's like a dam breaking. The way she arches beneath me, the way she claws at my back, the way she whispers filthy demands against my neck—Christ, I've never wanted anyone like this.

We're in her bed right now, our bodies still trembling from the aftershocks. She's already created distance—sitting up, reading a book, the sheet barely covering her ink-adorned skin. God, the sight of her makes my blood surge all over again. I reach to brush a strand of hair from her face and catch that look—sharp, warning, electric. My hand freezes mid-air.

Every touch outside of sex feels like crossing a minefield with her. Stroke her cheek? Glare. Brush her hair back? Flinch. Touch her calf when we're not making love? She tenses like I've burned her. The only exception is the foot rubs—"purely medicinal," she insists, though I've memorized the exact pressure that makes her eyes flutter closed.

Her unspoken commandments are crystal clear: Don't hold my hand during movies. Don't kiss my forehead. Don't touch my back in the bath unless you're inside me. Don't kiss me unless it leads to more. Every rule is another wall in her fortress.

Tonight I'm taking her to my jazz club. I'll be at the piano, pouring out songs I've written. I need her to see this part of me, raw and exposed. I need to crack through her armor.

But I'm already anticipating the battle: "It's not a date." She'll recoil if I pull out her chair. She'll bristle if I open her door. She'll shut down if I try to slow dance with her. And still, I'll follow every damn rule because the truth is hammering in my chest—she's resurrecting parts of me I thought died with Alecia and Steph. One wrong move and she'll bolt. And I can't lose her. I won't.

I say "So," but what I really want to say is nothing at all—just reach across the space between us and run my fingertips down the soft skin of her forearm, feel the goosebumps rise beneath my touch. My hands physically ache with the need to touch her. Not sexually—though God knows I want that too—but the simple, primal connection of skin on skin. That's just me, though. I touch. I hug. I'm the one crushing my brothers in bear hugs, the one who still kisses my father's cheek like I'm eight years old, the one who wraps my new stepmother Patricia in a hug so tight she laughs. But with Tally? I'm paralyzed, hands clenched at my sides, terrified of that icy glare she'd give me. "What do you say about going to Indigo tonight in Hollywood?"

"What's there?"

I shrug. "I hit up open mic night once a month. Piano, vocals, the usual. I write my own stuff, so—"

She cuts me off with a laugh that makes me wonder what I said wrong. She's shaking her head. "Jesus Christ. You're like someone ordered a romance novel boyfriend from a catalog. Top of your class at Hopkins, saving refugees with Doctors Without Borders, cooking better than a five-star chef, those ridiculous foot massages, and let's not even get into what you can do in bed. Now you're telling me you're some kind of singer-songwriter too?" Another head shake. "Look, you need to understand—I'm damaged goods with trust issues a mile wide. Go find yourself some preppy Elizabeth in a cashmere sweater set, driving a Volvo, and who'll smile politely at your perfection because she's too proper to scream about anything, even in bed."

What can I possibly say? Yes, before Tally, I exclusively dated women who wore pearl earrings with their tennis whites. Alecia would sooner die than mar her porcelain skin with ink—partly on principle, partly because the woman used numbing cream for bikini waxes. She was just the latest in my parade of Sarahs and Blairs and Ashleys, all with their monogrammed weekend bags and family summer homes in the Hamptons. Trust fund babies or corporate climbers, they all drove German cars and ordered white wine spritzers.

None of them set me on fire like Tally does. With the others, sex was scheduled, quiet, efficient—like filing paperwork. With Tally? Christ. We've broken in every surface in her apartment, and thirty minutes ago I had her against the wall, my first time ever doing that. Now I'm already plotting how to get her alone in the bathroom at the jazz club tonight.

But it's not just the physical stuff. There's something about her wildness that feels like oxygen after years of breathing filtered air. When she said I should find someone "too proper to scream," something clicked into place. I don't want proper. I want real. I want Tally.

I lean against the doorframe. "Injury or not, you need to get out of the house. Sitting around isn't good for your back. You need movement—like dancing."

"Seriously?" Tally snorts, her Mediterranean-at-noon eyes glinting with mischief. "After what we've been doing all afternoon, I've had more than enough 'movement' for one day." Her lips curl into a smile despite herself. "But fine, I'll check out this jazz club with you. You any good?" She catches herself and rolls her eyes. "Never mind. Of course you are. Mr. Perfect-At-Everything probably dances like Fred Astaire and sings like John Legend."

"Hardly," I say. "And I can't create like you do. Can't bring a blank canvas to life or shape clay into something meaningful. Your talent is... extraordinary."

"Oh, I know I'm good," she says, tracing a finger along one of her tattoos. "I'm a badass artist. I just don't have your ridiculous range of skills."

I reach for her hand, my thumb brushing over her fingers, earning me the death glare, so I take my hand away again. "You sell yourself short. Your art speaks to people in ways I never could." The memory of her body against mine flashes through my mind—her generosity, her passion. She might claim she can't cook or play an instrument, but her talents run deeper than she knows.

"Okay," I say. "So, we're on for tonight then."

Tally's eyes narrow as she lays in the bed. "Yeah, as long as I don't bump into anyone who knows both me and Celeste." She winces. "She'd have my head on a platter if she found out about this." She gestures between the two of us. "Not that there's a 'this' to find out about. Which is exactly the issue."

"I don't follow. Why would Celeste mind?"

"God, you have no idea." Tally leans forward. "She practically worships you. All her in-laws get the royal treatment, but you're her golden boy. Every time we grab drinks, I get the Cameron highlight reel—how your heart's too big for your own good, especially after everything with your wife and baby. How you're the only Kensington who didn't sell his soul for fame, fortune or both." She stretches, showing her flat stomach and my mouth waters. "She's made it her mission to find you some perfect woman who'll love you like you deserve." A humorless laugh escapes her. "If she knew about us, she'd murder me on sight. She knows my relationship track record looks like a five-car pileup, that I'm an absolute train wreck and the last thing she wants is for you to be my next casualty." Tally meets his eyes. "Which you will be. Remember, this is just fun."

"Oh, I see what's happening here. Saint Cameron meets Rebel Tally." I shake my head, scrambling to prove I've got an edge too, but come up empty. No recreational drug use in my history. Never stumbled home drunk behind the wheel. Never thrown a punch in a bar—or anywhere else. That's Roman's domain. Sure, I surf some Saturdays and tackle black diamond slopes with my brothers, but while they live for the adrenaline rush, I'm just along for the ride.

The responsible Kensington—that's been my role since Dad walked out when I was 14, leaving me holding everything together. I became the stand-in father figure overnight, despite some of my brothers being just a year or two younger than me. Strangely, I never resented it. Something about being their rock when they'd come to me with tear-stained faces asking when Dad was coming home—it filled a need in me. That same instinct led me to medicine in underserved countries, and if I'm honest with myself, it's part of what pulls me toward Tally. Each time she calls herself a "hot mess," a "Cat 5 Disaster" or a "train wreck," something in me lights up. I want to be her safe harbor. Not that I'd ever admit that to her face—she'd probably launch me through her apartment window for even suggesting she needs someone to catch her when she falls.

Nonetheless, that's what I'm dying to do.

Catch her when she falls.

Chapter Seven

TALLY

I'm sprucing myself up for tonight's date with Cameron. He's crashing here through tomorrow, so I sent him out to grab clothes and an overnight bag—and now that he's actually gone, I can't help missing him. Missing him! His flawless physique, those piercing eyes, a jaw sharp as glass, the grin that reveals perfect dimples, and his dark, tousled hair that's begging for a trim. I'd love to be the one to cut it—because I'm pretty good with scissors—but that feels way too boyfriend-and-girlfriend-y for me. Not now, not ever. I even find myself craving the warm notes of his sandalwood-and-bergamot cologne, some high-end scent that only Ivy Leaguers like himself knows about.

But I've drawn a hard line: nothing beyond sex. No hand-holding at the jazz club, no gentle strokes on my forearm—or god forbid he brushes my bangs out of my eyes with that look he gives me. If he does, I'll lose it. I'm a wreck, he'll get tired of my rules and my mess, and eventually he'll settle down with his Elizabeth or Sarah or Claire, hand in hand in a Volvo, driving just under the speed limit.

For now, though, I'm here for the mind-shattering sex and the multiple orgasms—pardon, "pain-killing sessions." He's right: we "worked out" for hours today, slamming against walls, lathering each other in the shower while he worshipped me with his mouth and I returned the favor, christening every piece of furniture in my place—twice. And dammit, he's also right that since he first relieved my back pain yesterday—his lips, fingers, and tongue going deeper than I ever imagined—I haven't had a single spasm.

But I can't grow attached. He's here only until tomorrow, then back to his ER shifts—and next month he's off to Sicily for a year with Doctors Without Borders. So I can't get used to him or count on him. If my back remains a chronic issue, I'll just have to find another kind of relief.

Cameron shows up at my door looking like he stepped out of a men's magazine. The distressed jeans hug his thighs just right, and those leather captain lace-ups add an inch to his already impressive height. His dark t-shirt stretches across his chest under a perfectly tailored blazer. I can tell he wanted to bring flowers—his hands keep fidgeting like they're missing something—but thought better of it. Points for reading the room.

"You look beautiful," he says, his eyes traveling from my face down to my legs in the black dress I chose specifically because it shows off everything I've earned at the gym. The fabric clings to curves I've sculpted through countless squats and planks.

"Hmmm..." I say, checking my watch. "Where are we eating?"

"At the jazz club. No reservation needed."

One raised eyebrow is all it takes.

Two hours later, we're hunting for our scattered clothes,

and my stomach is growling loud enough to drown out any jazz band.

Then we get into his car, which surprises me. I expected he'd be driving an Aston Martin or some other gleaming beast with an engine that purrs like a pampered tiger, the kind his brother Max drives. But he doesn't. It's a base Porsche Cayenne in white, all clean lines and understated luxury. The leather seats cradle me like butter-soft gloves, and the dashboard glows with subtle blue lighting. A beautiful car, expensive even, but it's less than $100,000. Max would consider this car slummy, like something you'd donate to a charity auction.

We get to the club, a place that practically begs for a haze of cigarette smoke hanging in the air—even though indoor public smoking's been banned for years. The exposed brick walls are stained with decades of nicotine ghosts, and between them hang these vibrant, electric-blue and hot-pink Warhol knockoffs of Coltrane and Holiday with their eyes half-closed in musical ecstasy. The only illumination comes from amber-tinted glass lamps on each table, casting everyone's faces in that perfect golden-hour glow that hides flaws and deepens shadows. On the center stage is a gleaming black baby grand, its lid propped open like a shark's mouth, waiting for Cameron to run those long fingers across the keys and croon into the vintage microphone that dangles above it. God, I hope he doesn't suck—nothing worse than watching someone you know bomb. But something tells me he'll be brilliant—men like him always are, infuriatingly perfect at whatever they decide to try.

I pick the burger, Cam goes for the fried chicken, and he orders wine for the table. Christ, my stomach's in knots watching the first few performers, knowing he'll be up there soon. Fifth in line, and the bastard looks cool as ice. Relaxed. Like he's done this a thousand times. Meanwhile, my heart's doing the cha-cha in my throat. I'm sweating through my shirt for him, and he's just sitting there sipping his Pinot Noir like he's not about to bare his soul at that piano. Maybe I should take his calmness as a good sign? Hell if I know.

It's finally his turn. He mounts the stage in three deliberate steps, his gaze locking onto mine through the amber light that makes everything feel like a fever dream. "This is an original," he announces, voice low and rough against the chrome microphone, fingers already commanding the keys like they're extensions of his nervous system. The crowd doesn't just applaud—they erupt, a volcanic recognition that sends vibrations through the floorboards beneath my feet. While others tonight offered the comfort of familiar classics—the flirtatious tease of "Ain't Misbehaving," the raw wound of "God Bless the Child," the soaring escape of "Fly Me to the Moon"—Cam is about to cut them open with something they've never felt before.

The first chord slams into the room like a fist, a minor seventh that doesn't just hang but suspends time itself. His fingers attack the keys with violent precision, each note a confession torn from somewhere primal. The melody doesn't just unfurl—it claws its way through the room, a wounded animal both dangerous and beautiful. I see him not just practicing but exorcising demons in his house, transmuting the death of the two people he loved most in the world into this brutal, gorgeous catharsis.

When he finally sings, the room doesn't just fall silent—it stops breathing. His voice isn't just bourbon but lightning in a bottle, electric and devastating, burning everything it touches. This voice couldn't exist anywhere but here, in this moment, between us. Each syllable feels ripped from his chest, secrets he's kept locked away now bleeding into the open air, and somehow—God help me—directly into my veins.

Yes. He has the fucking goods. Every note he sings rips straight through my chest. The melody crawls under my skin, the words punch me in the gut, and that voice—God, that voice—rough like whiskey and broken glass, shattering at the edges when he can't hold back the pain anymore. I feel the devastation pouring out of him, the raw wound of losing his wife and baby girl bleeding into every syllable. This isn't just a song—it's his soul being torn out through his throat, and I can barely breathe watching him survive it.

Holy shit. I'm getting chills watching Cam pour his soul into that piano. His fingers dance across the keys, building this intense crescendo that reminds me of all these classical composers I used to listen to with my mom when she was sober—Mahler, Moszkowski, Chopin, Rachmaninoff, Liszt, Schubert, Ravel, even a piano version of that haunting Max Richter piece I've always loved, "On the Nature of Daylight." But he's not just copying them; he's channeling something raw and personal through those notes. The jazz bassist behind him catches my eye, nodding along as he adds these perfect off-beat punches that make the whole thing come alive. Before I know it, I'm wiping my cheek and standing up, hands stinging from clapping so hard—and I'm not the only one on my feet.

When Cam weaves his way back to our table, I get my answer about whether he's a regular. "Doc Cam!" someone calls out. At least five different people high-five him or grip his shoulder as he passes. This is definitely his territory.

He eventually sits back down while more people swarm the table to congratulate him. Cam's all smiles, chatting everyone up like it's nothing. I gotta hand it to him—I'd be crawling out of my skin with all this attention. Put me in a crowd and I turn into a human panic button. Like that time my paintings somehow ended up in this underground gallery that got invaded by punks. They circled me like leather-jacketed vultures, five or six deep, telling me I was "revolutionary" or whatever. First off, compliments make me want to dive under the nearest table. Second, back the fuck up and give a girl some breathing room, especially when I'm trapped in a basement that suddenly feels like someone sent up the punk bat signal. The whole thing was bizarre anyway—my stuff is basically fancy portraits with blurry edges, total John Singer Sargent knockoffs. No idea why the safety-pin crowd lost their collective shit over it.

He turns to me, all grins—that crooked, dimpled smile that makes his eyes crinkle at the corners—and I play it cool even though inside I'm dancing the Air Walk like a teenager at her first concert. "Yeah, you got some chops there." I turn away and sip my wine, the tart Pinot washing over my tongue as I try not to show my hand too much. Then I shake my head, my silver hoop earrings jingling against my neck. "Aw, who am I kidding? You were fucking amazing out there. The lyrics, the melody..." My voice trails off as a lump forms in my throat, because his haunting baritone over those minor chords brought tears to my eyes, reminding me of Mom.

Yes, right now, she's Mom, even though I'm not technically worried about her. I told Cam that I only called my mother "Mom" when I'm worried about her, but that's not necessarily true. I actually call her Mom when I'm feeling nostalgic, too, and there's something about this entire evening—the amber glow of the stage lights, the smell of beer and perfume mingling in the air—that's making me nostalgic for her.

And that's when it hits me. Before the pills, before her skin went from porcelain to pockmarked, Mom was someone else entirely. Dad's death changed everything—suddenly those graceful hands that once flew across piano keys started shaking, reaching for Oxy bottles instead. Her face hollowed out until her cheekbones looked sharp enough to cut glass.

Before Dad died, Mom was a concert pianist, a professional who used to fill concert halls. As I was only 4 when he died, I didn't really know that version of her. But Daniel—probably the only halfway decent boyfriend she ever had before she spiraled and chased him off—uploaded her performances to YouTube. Millions of views and thousands of comments from strangers who have no idea that the woman with the "transcendent talent" and "extraordinary sensitivity" has problems staying sober, to put it mildly. I watch those videos religiously, like prayers to a god I'm not sure exists anymore.

Even during my childhood, between the highs and the disappearances, she'd have these moments of clarity. She'd sit at our secondhand upright, and suddenly our shitty apartment would transform into Carnegie Hall. Those rare performances—her fingers dancing across ivory, her face serene—they're the memories I cling to when everything else about her tries to fade away.

God, I used to listen to her play and get goosebumps racing up my arms like little electric currents. She wrote her own compositions, too, even if she couldn't sing a note without sounding like a strangled cat. And I guess Cam playing like that kinda brought me back to where I was 7 years old, sitting on the worn velvet of the piano bench next to my mother playing a Mahler piece on her baby grand, the notes rising and falling like waves in a storm that still haunts me to this day.

The day that baby grand disappeared also still haunts me. Mom got that death benefit check—nearly half a million for war widows back then—but two years later? Gone. Turns out street level Oxy costs a hell of a lot more than the dealers advertise, especially when you factor in bail money and lawyers' fees every time she got busted. Plus paying for endless rehabs that never stuck. Not to mention all those foster homes I bounced through - had to hire lawyers for that, too. So when the money dried up, she started selling everything that wasn't nailed down. That piano though... when it left our house, it felt like someone cut out a piece of my soul.

And now here's Cam, playing just like she used to—all instinct and heart, letting the music breathe instead of strangling it with precision. Mom could take something everyone knows— “Claire de Lune,” “Moonlight Sonata,” “Rhapsody in Blue” —and transform it with these little improvisations that made you hear it fresh. She'd bend those classics until they became something new but familiar, like she was revealing what the composer meant all along but couldn't quite say.

He smiles and reaches for me, but pulls back when I flinch. "Glad you loved it."

"I did." I take a swig of whiskey and grab my purse. "Ladies room."

Bullshit. I'm calling my mother. We haven't spoken in weeks except for that one call after the accident—which she blew off—but after those memories hit me, I need to hear her voice. So, I go outside the club and into the alley way and call her.

"Tally!" Mom answers immediately. "How are you?"

"Fine, fine," I say, swallowing the urge to ask why she couldn't be bothered to play nurse after my accident. But honestly? I'm glad she didn't show. If she had swooped in with her Florence Nightingale act—or more likely her Nurse Ratched routine—Cam wouldn't have stepped up. And Cam's version of TLC beats Mom's any day. Not that Mom's all bad. Our Phase 10 marathons are legendary, and she destroys me at chess every damn time. But "playing games" with Cam? Whole different ballgame. Trust me on that.

"How's the recovery going?"

"Pretty solid," I say, wincing as I rub my lower back. The spot where Cam worked his magic is throbbing again. Maybe I could lure him into the bathroom for another round of his hands-on therapy?

"So what's up? I can hear piano music—you're at a bar. You never call from bars unless something's on your mind."

She's right. I don't do social calls from noisy venues. But how do I explain that this gorgeous guy at the piano is reminding me of her playing the baby grand while I grew up? That those are the few good memories of my childhood, because when she was playing, she was sober, and when she was sober, I always prayed she'd stay that way so I wouldn't be taken away again? That watching Cam play makes my chest ache with memories of her? That some nights I fall asleep counting imaginary dollars, wondering how many tattoos it would take to buy her a Steinway—something she might love more than the pills or the men who leave bruises on her arms and empty spaces in her cabinets.

The words tumble out before I can stop them. "Want to crash at my place for a few days?"

There's dead air on the line while I mentally kick myself. Cameron's back at work soon, but he's off by mid-afternoon, so he'll probably stop in after his shifts to check on me. I'm in no rush to get back to Manic Muse—Blade's handling the shop just fine and my left hand isn't healed, so I can barely hold a needle let alone create - so I'll let Cam take care of me if he wants to. Am I seriously asking my mother to come and stay when I could have more of Cam's brand of pain relief? Too late now.

Her silence screams the answer. Mom's got better things to do—probably some new deadbeat keeping her bed warm. Or maybe it's the fact she can't pop pills under my roof. I made that boundary crystal clear years ago.

"Tal," she finally says, "I'd love to, but—"

"Forget it," I cut her off, hating the sting behind my eyes. "Gotta run. My friends probably think I've fallen in."

God, I can still hear her voice from my childhood: "Tally? You fall in or what?" And the way she'd warn I'd "float away" when I chugged too much water. Why do those stupid sayings still gut me?

"Tally, call me tomorrow, okay?"

"Yeah." Part of me actually believed she'd say, "Of course I'll come, you need me." Stupid. She's my mother, not a Hallmark channel character.

I slide back to the table and lock eyes with Cam.

"My back's killing me again," I say with a meaningful look. "Unisex bathroom. Sixty seconds."

I shoulder through the packed dance floor toward the bathroom, only to find a line snaking down the hallway. Figures. Saturday night, club's rammed, everyone's bladder is full of overpriced drinks. I chew my lip. We'd be assholes to monopolize the bathroom while people are crossing their legs outside.

When Cam appears behind me, I grab his wrist. "Change of plans. Your car."

His mouth curls into that slow smile and we weave toward the exit. Careful not to touch more than necessary, obviously.

Chapter Eight

TALLY

We get to Cam's car, and he slams the seat back as I lunge for him, my body crashing onto his. I dig my fingers into his shoulders, pinning him against the leather while his mouth devours mine. His kiss ignites something primal—all teeth and tongue and desperation—the kind that leaves my lips raw and throbbing for days.

He grips my hips with bruising force, his fingers pressing into my flesh, making it clear this isn't some rushed car hookup. His hands slide to my lower back, finding that spot that's been white-hot with pain since the accident. The same spot that turns molten when he makes me come so hard I see stars, whether it's with his wicked mouth or that long, thick, perfect cock that ruins me for anyone else.

I tear at his zipper, fingers trembling with need, and he surges up against my palm, hot and hard beneath denim. His breath comes in ragged bursts against my neck, both of us panting like we're drowning in each other. Still half-dressed, my skirt hiked up around my waist, I put the love glove on him and then take him inside me with one violent thrust that sends electricity crackling up my spine. The sound that tears from his throat mingles with my own desperate cry as my body stretches to accommodate him.

I ride him savagely in the front seat of his Porsche, my hips slamming down with enough force to make the suspension groan, the windows fogging with our ragged breath as headlights occasionally slice through the darkness, illuminating our reckless, desperate claiming of each other.

He eases into a slower rhythm, his fingers working the knots in my back, each movement dissolving the pain bit by bit. I let out a breath and rest my head against his shoulder, feeling the heat of his skin against mine. There's a pressure building in my chest, words I don't dare release. How do I tell him that watching his fingers dance across those piano keys broke something open inside me? That yeah, the sex has been mind-blowing, but seeing that other side of him was what truly wrecked me? No way. Some things, once said, can't be unsaid. So I swallow hard and stay silent.

Afterwards, I'm laying there with my head on his rock-hard chest, counting each thump of his heart against my ear like a metronome. His fingers weave through my tangled hair, gentle as a summer breeze, and I'm letting him—fucking letting him—which tears at my insides like barbed wire.

I never let a dude do this intimate shit after sex. Not the hair-stroking, not the cuddling, not the goddamn vulnerability hanging in the air between us. What the hell is happening to me? It's only been a couple of days, for fuck's sake. I barely know which side of town this guy lives on. Never let a dude past the steel-plated door I installed around my heart years ago. So how is Dr. Perfect managing to slip through the microscopic cracks I never even knew existed, like water finding its way through concrete?

I glance back toward the club. "We should probably head inside. Don't you get, like, a trophy or something for playing that well?"

Cameron's laugh is soft, almost shy. "It's just open mic night. No prizes, just people sharing what they love."

"So where'd you learn to play like that?" I ask, tilting my head.

His fingers are still tangled in my hair, and I can tell he's waiting for me to swat him away any second. His touch is hesitant, like he's petting a cat that might scratch. "Got a toy piano for Christmas when I was three. One of those little ones—like Schroeder in the *Peanuts* cartoons. Instead of just smashing the keys, I tried to make actual music. Mom noticed right away." His voice softens. "She was good at seeing things like that." He pauses, looking past me. "Started lessons before my hands could even reach an octave. After she died—I was seven—playing became everything. Helped me process what I couldn't say."

I swallow hard, thinking about Cameron's mom. According to Celeste, Catherine was diagnosed with breast cancer while pregnant with Max. The doctors told her that terminating would probably save her life, but she chose her baby instead. She died just months after Max was born. Cameron was seven when she passed—unlike his brothers, he was old enough to have real memories of her. I can picture her walking him to his first day of kindergarten, cheering as he stood on a surfboard at four years old (a crazy Kensington family tradition), and bundling him up for ski lessons at five (another Kensington thing—their dad believed kids should learn scary stuff before they're old enough to overthink it). Now Cameron's talking about how she noticed his musicality and nurtured it. I can't help wondering if his younger brothers like Max and Ansel resent him for having those extra years with her—for knowing the woman they never really got to meet.

I put my head back on his chest. "Your playing reminds me of my mother," I say, and then immediately regret it. I don't want to open that can of worms, not with him. Don't want to tell him about how Mom's hot mess makes mine look like normalcy.

Too late.

"Your mother played?"

I nod. "Yeah." My throat tightens. "Juilliard. IMG Artists was her agent. The whole package." I want to stop talking but can't. "She'd play these haunting Chopin nocturnes that would make you cry, then laugh at me for crying. Called it weakness." I trace a pattern on his skin. "When my dad was deployed, she'd book these fancy L.A. gigs, drag me 3-year-old me along, make me sit perfectly still for hours." I swallow hard. "After Dad died, she... God, I still miss her music sometimes. Even knowing what came after." My voice breaks. "Beautiful things don't last in our family."

I can't believe how much I'm spilling on him. Shit I've locked away for years, never told a soul—not even Celeste and Liv. Sure, they know the headlines—Mom's Oxy addiction, the parade of foster homes, the revolving door of rehab centers. But they don't know how I ache for her beauty. Not her face, though God knows that was stunning before the drugs hollowed her out. I'm talking about when her fingers hit those keys. That piano wasn't just an instrument—it was her goddamn religion. She worshipped at those ivory keys, loved them more fiercely than she ever loved me or my father. I've never told anyone how it gutted me when she lost it. Because when those repo men dragged that baby grand across our living room floor, leaving gouges in the hardwood like open wounds—this was long after IMG dumped her —they weren't just taking furniture. They were ripping out her voice box. And mine too.

Cameron's silent, just running his fingers through my hair. What the hell could he say? One wrong word that sounds like pity, and I'd bite his head off. But now I've dumped my mom's story on him—this beautiful, brilliant, talented woman who could've been anything, now just another addict with nowhere to go. She bounces between the streets and whatever loser's couch she can crash on. Keeps her phone, though. Always the damn phone. I've called her a dozen times in the past few months, offering her my spare room. She always refused. Maybe she thinks I'd cage her somehow. Lock her in and throw away the key. Christ. What am I supposed to do with that?

His voice drops to a whisper. "Tally, I—"

"Let's go back into the club," I cut him off, my heart hammering against my ribs. Whatever's coming next—some bullshit sympathy or worse, something real—I'm not ready. My throat tightens. I just handed him a piece of me I can barely hold myself, and now his eyes have that look. That fucking look. My fingers twitch toward the door handle. Classic Tally escape plan: shatter the moment before it shatters me.

Back at the club, something's different. The vibe's shifted between us. Cameron's eyes follow me across the room, holding something heavy I've never seen there before. I pretend not to notice, but fuck—he's catching feelings. I can see it plain as the ink on my arms.

And damn it all to hell, I'm not mad about it.

Chapter Nine

CAMERON

Back at work after staying with Tally for two days straight, and I have to put my head down and deal. The ER doors whoosh open every few minutes, bringing the metallic scent of blood from gunshot wounds, the acrid stench of burnt rubber clinging to car accident victims, elderly women clutching their lower backs from bladder infections, and wide-eyed ladies in labor whose knuckles turn white as they grip their partners' hands. An appendicitis or two comes through the door, faces flushed with fever and twisted in pain. I do what I do—assess vital signs with steady fingers, order CTs with a few quick taps on the keyboard, and deliver news with the practiced calm that comes from years of practice. "You'll be the proud recipient of an emergency appendectomy," I tell a college kid, trying to ease his fear with a touch of humor, before sending another patient upstairs to bring new life into the world.

After my shift ends, I exhale deeply and head to Tally's place. It feels strange having something genuine to anticipate after leaving the chaos of the ER. Getting off at 3 PM has always felt odd—my brothers are still grinding away at their desks, Elias is still buried in paperwork at that time. I discovered Tally's shop, Manic Muse on Mateo, is open from 7 to midnight. It's conveniently close to her apartment in the Arts District. Once she returns to work, I plan to suggest aligning our schedules. Not because I'm clingy—I'm practical. Sicily looms just weeks away, and I'm desperate to bank every possible moment with her.

She's awakened something in me that's been dormant for years. Call it selfish, but I need to stockpile memories of her to sustain me through twelve months with Doctors Without Borders. And selfishly, I want to leave such an impression that when I return a year later, she'll still be waiting.

When I arrive at her place, Tally yanks open the door, her head tilting to one side. "'Bout time," she says. "I'm fucking starving."

Progress—she's actually standing at the door instead of hollering for me to let myself in. Her left hand, the one she needs for her tattoo work, flexes repeatedly at her side. I catch the deliberate demonstration, the silent argument that she's healing.

"Don't even start," I tell her, watching her fingers curl and straighten. "Another week minimum. Rush back to those needles now and you'll regret it for months."

She shakes her head. "Shit. Maya's calendar is packed solid. Blade could take more clients, but my regulars are loyal as hell. They'll wait for me or nobody."

I nod. "Because you're that good. Hey, what about your painting? Give it a couple days, then try that. Doesn't demand the same precision grip as tattooing. Might actually help rehabilitate that left hand. Baby steps back to your art, you know?"

"Yeah. I guess that's something."

I go into the kitchen and whip up a quick dinner - grilled salmon and asparagus with a big green salad - and open a bottle of wine. As we sit and eat at her dining room table - distressed wood because Tally has excellent taste in furnishings - Tally shakes her head. "You know, I could get used to this, but I don't want to. You're leaving soon, so I have to figure out how to eat once you're gone. Been thinking about taking a cooking class in my spare time."

I laugh and take a sip of the wine. "Glad I could inspire you."

"It's not that you inspired me so much as I realize how pathetic I've been, not knowing how to cook. And if there's one thing I don't like to feel like is pathetic. So, yeah. Have to be self-sufficient, so…"

"I could teach you to cook," I say. "Just the basics, and then you can get some good cookbooks to continue on."

She shrugs, but I can see that she'd like me to teach her a few things.

So, for the next two weeks, I arrive after my ER shifts with grocery bags and patience. I guide her hands as she butterflies chicken breasts, show her how to test salmon with a fork's edge, and demonstrate the perfect poached egg wobble. I teach her how to make risotto the right way—standing at the stove for what feels like forever, adding broth one ladle at a time, stirring until her arm aches. When she tastes that first creamy, perfect bite, the look on her face makes every minute worth it.

We create a rainbow of sauces—velvety béchamel transformed with cheese, onions, or tomatoes; pungent pesto;

rich ragout; creamy Alfredo; bright Romesco, made from almonds, sun-dried tomatoes and red peppers. She curses when her hollandaise breaks but beams with pride when the second attempt turns silky. I teach her the subtle variations of the basic Hollandaise sauce—mornay with its nutty cheese, soubise's sweet onion undertones, nantua's delicate seafood essence, aurora's vibrant tomato hue, and English sauce's herbaceous brightness. Tally absorbs it all, her questions as sharp as her chef's knife, her practice sessions becoming increasingly confident.

"See?" I say, watching her drizzle golden hollandaise over perfectly grilled salmon. "Master the foundations, and everything else is just creative combinations. That sauce works magic on practically anything."

She sighs, licking a drop of sauce from her thumb. "Holy shit. I actually made hollandaise that didn't break. And mayonnaise from scratch. You're like a culinary Gandalf or something."

"Just passing on the basics," I say, watching her taste the sauce again. My chest tightens as I imagine her making these recipes after I've left for Sicily. I picture her standing here alone, nourishing herself with something I taught her, and it soothes an ache I didn't know was there. But I swallow those thoughts before they reach my lips—Tally would roll her eyes if she knew I was worried about her eating properly without me.

I catch myself thinking she'll fall apart without me and roll my eyes at my own arrogance. This is Tally we're talking about—the woman who told me that she stitched up her own forearm after a motorcycle accident. She survived twenty-nine years before I stumbled into her ER bay.

Still, I can't shake this urge to be the one who brings her coffee in the morning, who makes sure she eats something besides takeout. A year in Sicily stretches before me like an ocean I have to cross alone.

Focus, Cameron. There will be refugees who need your hands steady, your mind clear. Not daydreaming about the curve of her shoulder blade under your fingers.

Though as distractions go, she's exquisite.

Chapter Ten

TALLY

These past few weeks have flown by, and I've shocked myself by not wanting to kick Cameron out of my apartment. And it's not just because he's good in bed. It's the way he is—how he actually listens when I talk. Most nights after he comes over, after the takeout containers are empty and the sheets are rumpled, we end up dangling our legs off my fire escape, city lights blinking below us.

Last night, the words just kept flowing between us until 3 AM. I found myself telling him about the first tattoo I ever designed—the one that made me realize I could turn pain into something beautiful. He told me about holding a newborn baby during his first rotation and knowing right then that medicine was his calling.

Tonight, we're again on my fire escape, sharing a bottle of wine, passing it back and forth, not even bothering with glasses. We're talking about me right now, and I'm explaining how I came to become an artist. "Art saved me. Every time they moved me to a new foster home, I'd find something to draw with. Didn't matter if it was crayons or a ballpoint pen stolen from some social worker's desk. I'd make these little Play-Doh figures and hide them under my bed so they wouldn't get thrown out." I met his eyes briefly before looking away. "Couldn't exactly tell Mrs. Whatever-her-name-was how terrified I was that my mom would never get clean, you know? But somehow I'd paint this storm, or this broken bird, and later I'd look at it and think, 'Oh. That's how I feel.'"

And then he puts his arm around me, and I let him. "You're worried about your mother, now, aren't you?"

Cameron gets it. Gets that I should probably hate the woman who turned my childhood into a three-ring circus, but I don't. I fucking love her. Not some TV fantasy mom, but mine—messy, real, mine. I've spent my whole life trying to see past her chaos to the love I know is there. Even now, when she can't be bothered to visit her daughter in the hospital after a goddamn car wreck, I'm not mad. Just see a broken woman doing her broken best.

"Yes," I say, nodding as I take another pull on the wine bottle. "Every day I wonder if she's dead in an alley somewhere. Homeless people get treated like garbage—beaten, burned, worse. Or maybe this time she'll finally OD. Or some random hookup will put her in the ground." I swallow hard. "And I keep thinking I should protect her somehow, you know? But how the hell do you protect someone who's basically a ghost?"

I swallow hard. Cameron's arm stays wrapped around me, warm and steady. "You know what's funny? I actually tried the whole prayer thing once. My first foster family—I was seven—they were super religious. Dragged me to this huge church with stained glass windows that made the light look like it was bleeding. Every Sunday for a year, I'd kneel there in my stupid frilly dress and beg God to fix my mom.

Like, please make her stop taking pills, please make her stop bringing home these creeps, please just make her...my mom again." I let out a short laugh. "Spoiler alert: God ghosted me."

A few more sips of wine and I dangle my legs over the sides of the fire escape. "So, tell me what drew you into medicine."

He smiles. "I've always been the black sheep. While my grandfather built his empire and most of my brothers climbed the corporate ladder after him, I wanted something different." He counts off on his fingers. "Kalen's got platinum records, Connor's got movie premieres, and the rest—Max, Roman, Silas, Asher, Ansel—they've all got corner offices and stock portfolios." His smile softens. "After Dad left, I spent years patching up my brothers' emotional wounds. Made me realize I wanted to heal people for real." He shrugs. "Thought about psychiatry until I learned it was more about prescriptions than conversations. So I packed my bags for Somalia, then Syria with Doctors Without Borders. Now I'm at Cedars, putting people back together after their worst days—gunshots, car wrecks, whatever comes through those ER doors."

I swirl my wine glass. "So what's next after Sicily?"

"Sports medicine fellowship." He leans back. "I'm done with the ER after this."

"Sports medicine?" My eyebrows shoot up. "Seriously?"

He shrugs, those broad shoulders moving under his shirt. "The ER's killing me, honestly. And Caspian—he's Roman's best friend—wants a doctor for his chain of MMA gyms. Professional fighters need someone who understands their bodies." He takes a long sip of wine, his throat working. "Plus," he adds, voice softening, "I'd get to see my brothers more. Roman and Max both train there."

And we talked like that until the sun slashed through the blinds, bleeding gold across his face.

It's moments like this—his fingers tracing my tattoos, his voice wrapping around me—that will fucking haunt me when he's gone.

Because when he leaves for Sicily, he won't come back to me. That truth burns in my gut, carved deeper than any ink under my skin.

Chapter Eleven

TALLY

Tonight's our last real night together before Cameron ships out for a year—if he ever comes back at all. We've had a good run though. Mind-blowing sex. Food that makes me moan. He didn't just cook for me; he dragged my ass into the kitchen and showed me how. "Give a girl a fish, feed her for a day; teach a girl to fish, feed her for life," he'd say with that stupid grin.

And Jesus, the way he makes my coffee. Better than any barista. He gets these beans from some hipster roaster I can't even pronounce, grinds them in that fancy machine he bought me (which I'm definitely keeping), and adds cream and sugar like he's got my taste buds mapped. That first sip every morning? That's another thing I'll miss when he's gone.

At least when Cam's gone I can finally see my girls again. I've been dodging them because the minute I walk in with this stupid grin plastered on my face, Celeste will know. And I can't lie to her—I'd have to spill that I've been screwing Cameron Kensington, Dr. Perfect himself, and she'd lose her shit. First, she'd say I'm corrupting him (trust me, that ship has sailed), and second, she'd remind me I'm just going to break his heart and the last thing Cam needs is another fucking tragedy. She'd be right about that part. I'm still not relationship material, and Cam deserves someone who doesn't have my particular talent for disaster.

Celeste's been blowing up my phone about Happy Hour, but I keep making excuses. I don't lie, but damn, I'm Olympic-level at leaving shit out. If I can see them without bringing up where I've been, maybe I can dodge the whole truth bomb. So yeah, the only upside to Cam leaving is getting my friends back.

Tonight, I'm going to bring him into my world. There's an exhibit in a warehouse downtown—one of those industrial spaces with exposed brick and steel beams where the hipsters hang out. It's a pop-up tattoo art thing that's only running this weekend. They've got these massive blown-up photographs of intricate back pieces hanging from the ceiling, flash sheets from the 1950s under glass, and this badass chick from Seattle doing live sessions right in the middle of the floor. You can literally watch skin transform while sipping overpriced craft beer from the makeshift bar.

I'm pumped for tonight with Cameron. Last time, he dragged me to this hole-in-the-wall jazz club where he absolutely killed it on stage—his voice and that piano? Pure magic. But of course, my phone has to ring right now.

"Tal," Mom's voice wavers on the line. When her number pops up, I always answer. Could be anything—she's passed out somewhere, or some dickhead boyfriend put her in the ER, or maybe—just maybe—she's finally ready to get clean. And if it's that last one? I'd drop everything. In a heartbeat. Yeah, she turned my childhood into a shit show of foster homes and chaos, but she's still my mom. She's still the woman whose fingers could make a piano weep, who almost played with the fucking LA Philharmonic before Oxy stole her away. The same woman who somehow traps my king every damn time we play chess, even though I'm ranked 1700 and she just plays for fun. My brilliant, broken mother. So when she calls, I answer. "I need help."

I ask where she is.

"Cedars," she says. "ER. I'll explain later. But could you come and get me?"

Cedars-Sinai. Where Cam is still on shift. What if he's the one who treated her? Would he even know who she is? He's only ever seen her in my paintings, never in person or photos. Doesn't matter. I'll have to cancel with him tonight—it's his last night before leaving, but my mother comes first. Besides, maybe I need the distance. He's flying out tomorrow anyway. No point prioritizing him over my mother who actually "needs me" for once. She's never needed me before—always had some loser boyfriend to lean on, one right after another. Never alone long enough to ask me for anything. But now she's calling for help. Cam will understand. Of course he will. He'll board that plane to Sicily tomorrow and forget I exist before they even retract the landing gear.

I sigh into the phone. "I'll be right there." At least I'm not at the shop today. Mom's never been one for patience. If I'd told her I couldn't come until after my shift, she'd be hitchhiking before I hung up, thumb out on the highway, looking for her next temporary savior with a couch and a bottle of pills.

I get to Cedars and see my mother waiting for me in the waiting room, her coat draped over her arm even though it's fucking July. I don't see Cam anywhere, of course - I'm sure he's busy on his shift.

“Mom,” I say. “Let’s go.”

She nods. "Thanks for coming to get me, Tally."

I bite my tongue so hard I taste blood. The question burns in my throat: Why not call one of your deadbeat boyfriends? But the image of her empty bedroom flashes through my mind—drawers yanked open, closet bare, not even a goddamn note. Been there before. So I swallow the words, knowing they'd send her running faster than anything. From now on, I'll tiptoe around her moods like I'm crossing a minefield. That's my life now. Every day I'll come home wondering if her shit's still there or if she's ghosted me again. If she even agrees to crash at my place for any period of time. Fuck. No way out of this one.

“Sure, Mom,” I say. “Listen, maybe you could crash with me for awhile?”

To my astonishment, she nods. “Thank you, I’d like that.”

I slide behind the wheel of my new Jeep, Sophie—RIP Jaspress—and steal glances at Mom as we drive to my place. Her face is blank, unreadable.

At my apartment, she does a slow spin in the living room. "Fancy digs, Tal. Arts District must cost an arm and a leg, huh?"

"It's not cheap," I admit. "You can have the spare bedroom. And I actually cook now, so we can save some cash eating in."

Mom's eyes light up. "I know every food bank in the area. Good stuff too—fresh strawberries, potatoes. You cook, I'll forage."

I try not to roll my eyes. Like she'll stick around long enough to make a single food bank run. I need to accept the truth: she could vanish in the middle of the night or while I'm inking someone's bicep. No warning, no goodbye note.

Can't exactly handcuff her to the radiator. She's like one of those stray cats that lets you pet it but keeps one eye on the exit. Physically present, mentally halfway gone already.

Mom sits down at the dining room table, running her hand over the distressed grain like she's caressing a lover. "Beautiful table," she says, her eyes gleaming with something I can't quite place. "You always had the eye for beauty, Tally. Guess I'm not surprised that you're an artist."

"Tattoo artist," I snap, my jaw clenching. Maybe she didn't know what I did. After all, growing up, I was just an artist, period. On those rare fucking occasions when Mom got her shit together and somehow convinced a judge to give her custody, she'd marvel at what I created—right before disappearing on another bender. I busted my ass at UCLA, got my BA in Art while working two jobs. I can make canvas bleed with acrylics and watercolors, and I've always been a badass sculptor, but tattooing? That's where I found my goddamn salvation.

"Tattoo artist," she echoes, her voice hollow. "Why did you decide to become a tattoo artist?"

I shrug, my shoulders tight as piano wire. "Not much money being a regular artist, so I took my talent where I could make enough money to eat and pay for utilities. I own the studio down the street." I lock eyes with her. "Used the money the government gave me when Dad was blown to pieces in Iraq to open the shop." I raise an eyebrow, daring her to comment. My blood boils thinking about how she pissed away not just $100,000, which is what I got, but a half-million dollars of death money. Plus the monthly survivor's benefits. All of it gone down her throat while I, the fucking daughter, was smart enough to build something lasting. Then I shake my head, my fingernails digging crescents into my palms. I have to stop this toxic comparison shit. She's Mom and I'm me. Two different women, two different choices, one giant fucking gulf between us.

She nods. "I always knew you'd become somebody," she says, her head dropping. "Unlike me. I'm just a hot mess." Then come the tears, and fuck if that doesn't wreck me every time. Only sociopaths and liars claim they can watch a parent cry without feeling like they've been gutted.

"Mom," I say, wrapping an arm around her bony shoulders. "We're both hot messes, so there's that." I exhale, memories flooding back—age 8, 9 and a half, 11, 13, 15—each time CPS yanked me from home because Mom was spiraling again. But they never took me out of the house because I reported her. She was always a disaster, but I'd rather die than report her. I knew what foster care felt like. It was always some busybody neighbor spotting her tweaking in Ralph's, or cops catching her driving wasted. That bitch teacher Ellen Davos called CPS just because Mom missed Parent-Teacher night. Once, her own dealer reported to CPS because she owed him money and he was pissed. But the CPS reporting never came from me. I never betrayed her.

Every single time they took me away, I'd think: This is it. This will be her wake-up call. She'll get clean now. But she never did. Yet here I am, watching her sob in my living room, and some stupid part of me wonders if this time might be different. If maybe she's finally ready to get clean, to return to the piano, where her fingers used to make magic before the drugs stole everything. I'm thinking this time is it, that the last pill she took is the last pill, period, but how goddamn naive is that?

I lean toward her. "Mom? You ready to quit?"

She shakes her head, tears spilling down her cheeks. "Oh, Tally. I've been clean six months now. But something's wrong." Her shoulders heave with each breath. "I'm seeing things—people. They talk to me. I don't recognize them, but they're always there."

"Wait—six months clean?" I blink, trying to process this. "When did this happen? Why didn't you tell me you were getting help?"

Her face hardens. "That's your response? Not concern about the strange voices and phantom people?"

"Well, that's probably just withdrawal after all those years using."

"Fuck you, Tally." Her eyes flash.

And we're off. "What? What did I say now?"

"You clearly know jack shit about addiction. I only ever took pills—Oxy, that's it." She wipes angrily at her face. "You never even bothered to learn the first thing about what I was going through, did you? Or you'd know hallucinations aren't part of it."

"I don't understand—"

"I'm telling you I've been clean half a year," she cuts me off. "So explain why I'm suddenly seeing things that aren't there."

"I'm pretty sure long-term use can cause—" I stop myself. Who am I kidding? I don't know the first thing about this. She's right—I never looked into it. Too much baggage there.

"No, it can't," she says quietly. "My counselor at the halfway house explained all this. Some addicts get psychosis from quitting cold turkey, but not these specific hallucinations." She looks up at me, suddenly small. "Tally, I'm terrified."

"Well, what's your theory?"

She rubs her temples. "Grandpa Jim had bi-polar disorder. Ended up in a psychiatric facility, completely detached from reality." She winces. "God, I shouldn't talk about him like that. Mom always said he was 'off his rocker,' but now that I'm facing similar symptoms, I see how cruel those descriptions were."

I lower myself onto the chair. "Grandpa Jim? Was I ever around him?"

"Never," she says, her eyes fixed on the floor. "He became this family ghost after they committed him to a mental health facility. Not a 'loony bin' or 'funny farm' or whatever awful nickname people use. I didn't learn the truth until Mom finally opened up after his passing." Her gaze meets mine, vulnerable and frightened. "bi-polar disorder can jump generations, Tally. Like a stone skipping water." Her fingers flutter between us. "My grandfather suffered, his children escaped it, and now... me? I'm terrified I'll slide further away until I'm trapped in some hallucination where you can't reach me in." She clutches my hands. "Promise you'll get me help if I disconnect completely. I've survived homelessness before, but wandering the streets lost in delusions?" She swallows hard. "That possibility terrifies me more than anything."

Just then, Cameron shows up. My phone's been buzzing all night, but I've been too wrapped up with...Mom? I shake my head. Who am I kidding? I'm already building walls. Better to fortify them now than watch them crumble when he meets some gorgeous Italian doctor in Sicily. She won't have a maybe-bi-polar mother with a rap sheet of addiction. No, this woman—Gia, let's call her—will have glossy dark curls, espresso eyes, and a laugh that makes everyone turn. While I'm here trying to figure Mom out, they'll be saving lives together. Bonding over crashed patients and diseases that Americans pretend don't exist anymore - tuberculosis, typhoid fever, cholera, malaria. They'll stumble out after grueling shifts, collapse at camp with wine and war stories, and the rest writes itself. Ridiculous? Maybe. Inevitable? Feels that way.

So I need to cut the cord now. Focus on Mom instead. If she's really clean, that's huge. The bi-polar disorder thing needs professional eyes—I'll book something tomorrow. Maybe if I can get my mother back, it'll soften the blow when Cam's "Sorry, I met someone" text finally comes through from halfway across the world.

Mom gazes at Cameron, her eyes practically sparkling. “You’re the doctor at Cedars,” she purrs, batting her lashes. “Excuse me.” Then she leans in and whispers, “Tally, can I borrow your foundation, concealer, mascara, and eyeliner?”

I can’t help smiling. For someone who struggled with addiction for so many years, she looks astonishing. She’s a bit thinner—thankfully I learned to cook just in time, so I can put some weight back on her with some healthy food—but her blue-green eyes still shine, her smile is as radiant as ever, and her thick chestnut hair hasn’t thinned a bit. Still, I know her: she’s trying to doll herself up for Cameron as if he’s one of her conquests, which, of course, he isn’t. I go along with it.

“Sure, Mom.”

Cameron watches her head into my bathroom. I hear drawers clicking open and closed until she locates my makeup stash. While she rummages, I stare at him, trying to memorize every detail of his face. I might never see him again—and I have this urge to paint him later, because apparently I’m a glutton for punishment.

“Is that—”

“Yep. It’s her,” I say, shaking my head. “That’s why I said ‘sure, Mom.’ And…tonight’s off. I can’t trust her not to bolt the minute I step out, and an underground art exhibit isn't really her scene."

"That's fine," Cameron replies. "Do you mind if I stay here with you two? I'm leaving early tomorrow, so..."

Dammit. He's stunning, kind, brilliant—and unforgettable in bed—but I know this is goodbye waiting to happen.

Mom emerges from the bathroom, her face perfectly made up, and Cameron's eyes go wide. "Your mom looks just like you," he whispers. "She could pass for your sister."

I nod. My mother has always been beautiful, so it's a compliment he thinks we resemble each other. "Thanks, Cam."

I still haven't answered his offer. He could stay, but Mom will flirt nonstop and make him uneasy, and I'm not sure what the three of us would even do—watch a movie? Or maybe he'd play chess with her, and knowing him, he'd crush her just like everything else. Whatever happens, there's no chance of anything happening between us tonight. Our bedrooms are too close, and the thought of Mom overhearing...makes me shudder.

I plaster on a fake smile. "Actually, Cam, Mom's reappearance has drained me mentally and emotionally." Not entirely a lie. "And you probably need your sleep. Your flight leaves at 6, after all."

He nods slightly, his eyes dimming like someone just turned down his internal brightness. The words bubble up in my throat—how I know I'm just keeping his bed warm until he finds some perfect doctor in Sicily with olive skin and a tragic backstory, or return to the states and find a country club princess who his family would approve of. Someone who makes sense on paper. Someone who isn't covered in ink with a mouth like a sailor and mommy issues deeper than the Mariana Trench. I swallow hard. Better to rip the Band-Aid off now than watch him slowly realize I was never enough.

"Okay," he says, hanging his head. "I get it."

I punch his arm, my knuckles grazing the crisp white cotton of his sleeve. "Knew you would." My throat tightens like someone's wringing it out. "So. Yeah." I swallow so hard it echoes in my ears, blinking back the hot sting behind my eyes. "Um, have fun in Sicily." The words hang between us, pathetic as a deflated balloon. Have fun in Sicily? *Jesus Christ, Tally.* I can practically see him wading through refugee camps, stethoscope around his neck, sweat darkening that perfect hairline while he diagnoses Ebola, Typhus, Malaria—all those diseases Americans think disappeared with polio. Yeah. Real fun.

He lets out a long breath. "Don't worry about me. I've got sixteen hours to Rome to catch up on sleep," he says, running a hand through his hair. "Was actually planning to pull an all-nighter with you at the exhibit so I'd pass out the minute I buckle in. Beats staring at the seat-back screen for half a day."

I toss my hair back, flash a smile that doesn't reach my eyes. "Well, Cam, if you're pulling an all-nighter, you're doing it solo. Sorry." My voice doesn't crack, thank god. My fingers grip the doorframe so hard my knuckles go white, but he can't see that. Who am I kidding, though? Whether he stays tonight, wrapping those arms around me in a way I never thought I'd allow, or leaves right now—the end result's the same. He'll find someone else eventually, and I'll be gutted either way. But maybe—just maybe—shoving him out now will dull the edge of what's coming. A little.

My mother's jaw drops, her eyes wide as dinner plates. I just shrug.

"Oh! Cameron, right? Please, don't mind my daughter

—she doesn't know what she's saying. I insist you stay. I'll grab my things and find a nice hotel nearby—"

The word bursts from me like a thunderclap. "NO!" I catch myself, but too late. Cameron's just an excuse for her —a convenient escape hatch. If she walks out that door tonight, that's it. Game over. She won't be back. And after all this time maneuvering to get her here, under my roof... Christ, I'm not letting her slip away again. I eye Cameron, mentally calculating the fastest way to get him out of my house.

"So, Cam," I say. "I guess this is goodbye."

His brows draw together in a tight line, and his eyes—those damn blue eyes that got me into this mess—cloud over with hurt. I watch confusion ripple across his face, then settle into a quiet sadness. No flash of anger, though. God, I wish he'd just yell at me, call me names, storm out. A shouting match would be so much cleaner than this silent collapse of everything we might have been.

"Okay," he says quietly. Then he produces something out of his pocket. A jewelry box. "Here. I was going to give this to you so you can remember me. You might as well take it."

I nod and take the box, keeping my eyes fixed on a spot over his shoulder. Looking inside the box would crack me open, and I can't afford that—not when he needs to walk out that door. "Thanks," I manage, my voice flat as week-old soda. Better he remembers me this way: the tattooed ice queen shoving him toward Sicily with both hands. Let him hate me a little. It's a gift, really. The last one I can give him.

The door clicks shut behind him and I'm left alone with the jewelry box, a lump rising in my throat. Holy shit. He remembered. That day he was over and I'd circled this exact necklace in the magazine, drooling over something I couldn't justify dropping that kind of cash on.

I lift it from the velvet, watching light dance across the different colored stones. Ruby bleeds into topaz, sapphire is nestled against emerald. There's also deep purple amethyst, and that perfect beryl that's not quite blue, not quite green. In the bathroom mirror, I fasten it around my neck with trembling fingers. It settles against my collarbone like it was made for me, and fuck, I'm actually tearing up over jewelry. Mom always said I could spot beauty a mile away, and this thing is practically screaming it.

My phone's right there, and my thumb hovers over Cam's name. But Mom's sudden appearance—and her bombshell about possibly being bi-polar—has thrown my world sideways. Tomorrow's a marathon: I need to make doctor appointments for Mom, and help her shop for her now-skeletal frame, basic necessities, go on a Sephora run. I need to lock this place down so she can't vanish on me again.

So tonight, it's just Mom, me and my new necklace. Mom needs me focused on her, not on Cam—especially when I'm pretty damn sure he's already forgotten about me.

Chapter Twelve

CAMERON

A month later, and I still can't get Tally out of my mind. Her scent - Tom Ford Black Orchid with its heady notes of truffle and ylang-ylang - haunts me like a phantom, lingering in the collar of my white coat even after three washes. I bought a bottle at Nieman Marcus before leaving, keeping it on my nightstand in Sicily where I spray a single mist each morning, just so I can feel like she's around. Her eyes haunt me the most - Caribbean-clear blue-green that darkens when she laughed, with flecks of gold near the pupils that caught the light when she tilted her head just so. The photo from the jazz club captures her mid-laugh, head thrown back, exposing the constellation of freckles across her collarbone. I had it printed on archival paper, framed in burnished silver, and it's the first thing I see each morning on my nightstand next to my bed.

While I'm working, my mind narrows to the task at hand. Twelve-hour shifts blur together in the makeshift clinics we've established in conjunction with the University Hospital of Palermo. I clean wounds inflicted by smugglers, set bones broken during desperate escapes, and listen to traumatized Libyan refugees describe horrors in halting English or through our overworked translators. Their eyes haunt me—hollow with suffering yet somehow still hopeful. When a young man with cigarette burns across his back thanks me, or a mother squeezes my hand after I treat her fevered child, Tally's face recedes from my thoughts—though never completely.

When I get to my tent and stare at the picture of us—her raven-black hair with rainbow streaks falling across her shoulder, revealing her beautiful swan-like neck—I feel it. I feel her warmth radiating through the glossy paper. We were "together" for only thirty-eight days, but I know now that I felt drawn to her strongly from the moment I saw her across the crowded ballroom at Max and Celeste's first wedding, her light sapphire-emerald eyes catching the light as she laughed. And then again at Max and Celeste's second wedding in England when, once again, I couldn't take my eyes off her.

That magnetic pull I felt wasn't some temporary infatuation. It was visceral and real, like a current running between us. But Tally apparently didn't feel the same—I've sent twenty-seven unanswered texts and called her eleven times, desperate for a video call just to see those beautiful eyes again, to watch how they crinkle at the corners when she smiles—but my phone remains stubbornly silent. So, the message is crystal clear. She wants nothing to do with me.

I've felt worse pain—when Alecia and Stephanie died, I thought I'd never breathe normally again. But this ache where Tally used to be isn't trivial either. Here in Sicily, I'm treating refugees who watched their families murdered before enduring torture themselves. Their suffering dwarfs mine, I know. But pain doesn't work like that, does it? It can't be neatly ranked and filed. This particular hurt has its own signature, sharp and precise as a scalpel.

I really believed Tally might be my second chance.

Now there's just this hollow space where that hope used to live.

Chapter Thirteen

TALLY

"Tally," my mom calls from outside the bathroom. She insisted I take a pee test once I started vomiting every morning and couldn't keep anything down. So I went to CVS and bought ten different pregnancy strips, praying at least one would say I wasn't pregnant. But every single one lit up instantaneously—plus signs, "pregnant," double pink lines—whatever they use to make it painfully clear you're expecting. "What do the tests say?" she asks.

I slump on the toilet, head in my hands, and exhale. Everything had been going so well. After batteries of tests with a shrink over at Cedars, Mom got a latent bi-polar disorder diagnosis. The doctor explained to both of us that she'd likely shown bi-polar disorder symptoms forever, but they stayed hidden under the stress plus her Oxy habit. Once she quit the pills, the bi-polar disorder surfaced, and he prescribed a cocktail of lithium plus Abilify. It's working wonders—she's stable and happy.

Since then I've been cooking for her so she'd gain weight, and I even dropped my F45 weight-lifting classes so

I could take her to Pilates five afternoons a week after my 7 AM–4 PM shift. She's loving it, getting stronger every session. She's talking about getting a job to "pay her keep," not that I care much when she does. I bought her a whole new wardrobe on my credit card. She's started a little herb garden on our terrace—chervil, rosemary, basil and upside-down tomato planters dangling from the ceiling. Mom has a real green thumb, and I've been enjoying her fresh herbs in every meal.

For the first time since Dad died, life seems peaceful for her. I was even planning to squeeze a baby grand piano into our cramped two-bedroom apartment—as soon as I 86 an old bookshelf and unused desk—and watch her play again. Helping Mom, plus my tattoo gigs and catch-ups with Celeste and Liv once or twice a month, nearly erased the pain of losing Cam. He's called, texted, tried FaceTime countless times, but I never pick up. I want him to move on, find someone who fits him better, because I'm not that person for him and never was.

And now this. A baby. Damn. What am I going to do? We're stuck in this tiny apartment—two little bedrooms, one for me, one for her—and there's no asking Mom to move out. She's too fragile. I'm not sure she'd remember to take her meds, eat properly, keep up with exercise, make doctor's appointments or get to bed early enough to avoid triggering her symptoms—she's such a night owl. In other words, I don't trust my mother to take care of herself without me. I'm keeping her together. I still hold my breath every fucking time I go to work for fear that when I get home, she'll be gone. Still hold my breath every time I go to sleep that I might wake up and she'll be gone. Same thing for when I go out with the girls.

Fuck! The girls! No way I'm telling Celeste who knocked

me up. She'd go ballistic. She's still clueless about me and Cam, and I'm keeping it that way. Christ. I'll have to feed her some line about a random hookup, which she'll never buy since I don't do casual. Never have.

And protection? Dammit, we used protection, all kinds of fucking protection. The pill since I was sixteen, plus Cam's condoms every damn time. How the hell did this happen? Roman's wife Lilith would probably flip her tarot cards and say some mystical bullshit about the universe having plans. And maybe she'd be right – because what else explains a pregnancy that bulldozed through two forms of birth control? The universe clearly wants this kid to exist, and I had absolutely no say in the matter.

I emerge from the bathroom, tugging at my jeans that already feel snug across my middle. "Guess I'll be hitting up the stretchy pants section soon." I scan our cramped apartment, mentally rearranging furniture to figure out how the hell I'll fit a baby in this place. "Where the hell am I supposed to put a crib?" Mom's stuff is barely unpacked—she only moved in weeks ago. No way I'm asking her to sleep on that lumpy couch when this whole knocked-up situation is not her circus, not her clowns. Hell, it's barely even my fault considering we were so careful. But I know Mom—give her one uncomfortable night and she'll be halfway to Timbuktu by morning. Not happening.

Mom's not sure how to take this news. She looks like she wants to be all happy about her first grandkid, but, then again, if she says one fucking word of congratulations, I'll cut a bitch. She knows that. Poor Mom.

"Well," she finally says. "At least the father is wealthy, or comes from a wealthy family at any rate."

"He *is* wealthy," I say. "Makes six figures, around 300 large a year at the ER and plus he has a trust fund. They all do. Celeste tells me that each of the brothers have at least a half a billion in trust, because the Granddad made it that way." I shake my head. "But that's neither here nor there, Mom. I'm not telling him about this baby." I cross my arms in front of me. "I mean, I'll tell him there's a baby. I'll have to, because word will get around to him. Celeste will know, and she'll tell Max, and..." And what? Why would Max announce the baby to Cameron? Nobody knows about us. But he might let it slip - "did you hear that Tally's having a baby?" Somehow, someway, the jig will be up with Cameron, if not Max slipping then maybe I'll run into Cameron at some Kensington function in the future. At any rate, there's about a zero percent chance of him never finding out I had a kid so...better tell him something.

Dammit. He's exactly the kind of guy who'll demand we "do the right thing"—and that "right thing" is the last thing I would ever want. Other girls fantasize about their big day—what dress, what flowers, how many bridesmaids, where the reception is, who takes the photos, yada yada blech. Not me. I refuse to trade my independence for some guy. No one gets veto power over my life choices. Especially not Cam, dropping to one knee and sliding a diamond on my left ring finger. He doesn't know this baby is his. So I've got to beat him to it: call him, and drop the hammer of the fake story I'll create—I got plastered right after he left (and yeah, he'll do the math), slept with a rando and now I'm pregnant. End of story. No fuss, no compromise. Cam will hate me? Fine. Let him.

Better he hates me than learn the truth and smother me. He'd fly home early from Sicily and start bossing me around: "Tally, have you taken your vitamins?" "Don't eat sushi." "Working till midnight again?" "Your mom shouldn't be around little Liam—or Vanessa." "Don't meet the girls; you'll drink." He'd turn into my dad—who I barely knew—and hell no, I'm not letting that happen.

And anyway, women drank and smoked constantly in the '50s and '60s, and guess what—there weren't more birth defects from booze than there are now. The spike back then in birth defects was from missing vaccines and taking toxic shit like Thalidomide, not wine. So if I need a glass after a crappy day, nobody's grabbing it from my hand.

But goddamn it, having a kid means giving someone veto power over everything I do. A baby will own my life just as surely as any diamond ring ever could.

I hold up my hand. "Mom," I say, my voice already cracking. "Don't. Fucking. Move."

She freezes.

The scream rips out of me like something feral, tearing my throat raw. I slam my fists against the wall, kick over the coffee table, sending magazines flying. My lungs burn but I can't stop—won't stop—until every cell in my body is vibrating with it. "ARE YOU FUCKING KIDDING ME?" I shriek at the ceiling. "CONDOMS! THE GODDAMN PILL! WHAT MORE DO YOU WANT?" My knees hit the floor as I pound my fists against the carpet. "We weren't some drunk teenagers fumbling in daddy's car! WE DID EVERYTHING RIGHT!" Tears stream hot down my face, mascara probably turning me into some horror-show clown. "This is punishment, isn't it? For screwing Cam? Well FUCK YOU!" I'm not even sure who I'm screaming at anymore—God, the universe, my own stupid body betraying me.

Mom sighs. "Tally," she says. "I just want you to know that I support you in whatever you do." She nods meaningfully, and I catch her drift.

This is the Mom I remember from the good days—the

sober stretches between pill bottles and strange men in our house. The one who squeezed my sweaty little hand on the first day of kindergarten when I was too scared to let go. Who didn't bat an eye when I watched Simba's dad die for the fortieth time in one weekend. Who'd crack open *The Giving Tree* night after night until the spine was worn through. Who never, ever questioned my desire to get an art degree from UCLA. When other parents would've pushed me toward something "practical," Mom helped me research art careers on our ancient desktop. That's how the tattoo studio dream was born.

And oh, *The Giving Tree!* That damn book still wrecks me. A tree giving everything—apples, branches, trunk—until she's nothing but a stump for some ungrateful old man to sit on. Some see that story as beautiful sacrifice; others see a toxic relationship. All I know is I still cry every time, just like when I was four and somehow already understood that love sometimes means giving everything to someone who might never say "thank you."

My hand drifts to my stomach. Soon I'll be giving pieces of myself away too. I wonder if I'm setting myself up for the same raw deal as that tree, making sacrifices for someone who might never appreciate them. But then I remember my mother reading to me, her voice steady even on the hundredth time through, and I think maybe there's something beautiful in the giving after all.

"No, Mom," I say, feeling calmer now after I threw my fit. "Not an option." I sigh. "I'll march in the streets for the rights of others to choose, but for me…no. I'll have this kid and somehow, someway, I'll make it work." I sigh. "Even though I'll obviously have to find a bigger place."

Chapter Fourteen

CAMERON

One day, I stumble back to my tent after eighteen straight hours at the clinic. My scrubs are stained with blood that isn't mine, and the Sicilian sun beats down mercilessly. Outside the medical tent, Amir waits for me, his weathered face breaking into a smile that reveals three missing teeth. He presses a small loaf of bread into my hands—still warm, though I can't imagine where he found an oven in this camp. Yesterday, Fatima brought me homemade wine in a plastic water bottle. Last week, Youssef insisted I take a tiny wooden Christ figure, assuming I pray to the same God he does, just in a different way. The Libyan man in the corner tent—I can never remember his name—gave me a Farmla, the traditional tunic now hanging in my quarters.

I don't ask where these gifts come from. I suspect family heirlooms, the last possessions they managed to save while fleeing. I accept them all with the reverence they deserve. These people who have lost everything—homes bombed, children murdered before their eyes—still laugh around campfires at night. Meanwhile, my brothers sit in Los

Angeles penthouses and mansions worth much more than this entire camp, with Roman and Max together worth more than the entire Libyan GDP of $47 billion. All of us, even me, with half-billion-dollar trust funds, courtesy of Granddad. The contrast leaves me dizzy sometimes.

And my living arrangements are typical of Doctors Without Borders, too. A canvas tent that sags when it rains, where seven of us doctors sleep on metal-framed cots with thin mattresses that leave my back aching. The bathroom's a plywood stall with a hole in the ground that reeks by midday. We eat whatever the cook manages with limited supplies—often beans and rice for days straight. I've learned to shower with half a bucket of water and perform surgery by headlamp when the generators fail. So, yeah, this life is as far away from the glamorous life of my brothers as could possibly be imagined, but the work has been so exhilarating that I never mind the spartan conditions. Wouldn't trade this experience for all the money in the world.

I'm greeted by an unexpected sight when I walk into my shared space—Tally's name flashing on my phone screen. My heart skips as I accept the video call. Her face fills my screen, but her usual confident smirk is missing.

"Tally!" I can't help the grin spreading across my face, even as I notice the way she's fidgeting with her rings—something she only does when she's nervous.

"Cam," she says, her voice softer than usual. She chews her bottom lip, her eyes darting away from the camera. "There's something I need to tell you."

"What is it?"

Tally's eyes dart away before meeting mine again. "Well, here's the thing." She inhales deeply, her chest rising beneath her faded Wheezer concert t-shirt. "I got really stupid one night. Right after you left. Got sloppy drunk and...ended up with a new guy. A one-nighter. And, well, I'm knocked up." Her fingers twist nervously at the frayed hem of her shirt. "Thought you should hear it from me."

My heart seizes like it's caught in a vise. The bustle and noise of the other doctors in this tent fades to white noise. Tally is pregnant? By some random stranger? "It was a one-nighter?" My voice sounds hollow in my ears. "Did you ever hear from the guy again?"

She shrugs one shoulder, the movement making her raven hair slide across her collarbone. "Nope. I actually don't remember the whole thing. That happens with me with tequila - I feel fine after four shots or whatever, and then by the fifth shot..." Her lips curve into a smile that doesn't reach her eyes. "One tequila, two tequila, three tequila, floor. That's me."

White-hot rage floods through me, my fingers curling into fists so tight my knuckles crack. I imagine finding this faceless bastard and unleashing violence until he's unrecognizable. Because what she's describing isn't consensual—it's predatory, calculated, criminal. This bastard took advantage of a passed out woman. That's rape.

I close my eyes, feeling my pulse hammer in my temples.

And then it crashes over me like an icy wave. Tally is pregnant. Her hand rests protectively over her still-flat stomach. She's going to have a baby. Not mine—that thought twists in my gut like a serrated blade—but she'll need someone when I return. She'll need me.

But she hasn't asked for my help. Does she want it? I have no idea. This is Tally, after all—the woman who once told a biker twice her size that his skull tattoo looked like a constipated hamster. Yet...she's single, living in that cramped third-floor walkup with peeling paint and a bathroom sink that never stops dripping. She has a newly-sober mother who's probably still trembling through each day. She owns a tattoo studio with rent due on the first, payroll due on the fifteenth, and equipment that breaks down when she can least afford it. She really has a lot on her plate—a plate that's cracking under the weight. I could really help out, could steady that plate before it shatters completely. If only she'd let me.

"Tally," I say, watching her fingers nervously twist the silver rings on her hands. "Is this why you've been avoiding my calls and texts all along? You've been afraid of telling me about the baby?"

She shakes her head. "No. That's not why at all."

Something cold slides through my chest. There's more to this—something keeping her at a distance while I'm stuck in Sicily and she's back in Los Angeles. I've been picturing us together, building something real. Hell, I'm now even imagining myself helping raise her baby, regardless of who the father is. But the wall in her voice tells me everything.

"Then why have you been avoiding me?"

She sighs. "Cameron. It's been fun—"

The words hit like a slap. Fun? That's what she calls what happened between us? I haven't felt this alive since before the accident took Alecia and Stephanie from me. After losing my wife and daughter, I disappeared into myself, existing but not living. My songs became my only voice—just scratching notes in journals between hospital shifts. But with Tally, I started breathing again. She's like oxygen after years of drowning.

"Tally," I say, my voice catching in my throat as I lean forward, elbows on my knees. "I haven't just been having fun. I feel that there's something here for us. I thought you might feel the same."

"Cam," she says, twisting one of her silver rings around

her finger, her crimson lips pursing slightly. "Here's the thing. You're all into me because I'm a bit wild, a bit different, I'm not your Malibu Barbie doll that you usually date." Then she shakes her head, her jet-black hair swinging across her shoulders, the purple tips catching the light. "No. Not Malibu Barbie doll, sorry. That's an insult. I think that was your brother Roman's type until he met Lilith. And Max, too, until he was forced together with Celeste and, well, the rest is history there, isn't it?"

She looks up at the ceiling, her long lashes casting shadows on her cheekbones, before turning to her sleek silver laptop. Her fingers, adorned with blood red nail polish, fly across the keyboard. She nods triumphantly as she brings up a picture of a Barbie doll wearing a cashmere sweater dress in a soft heather gray, with glossy chestnut hair cascading down her back, chocolate brown thigh-high boots hugging her plastic legs, and a buttery leather satchel hanging from her tiny arm.

I get the reference immediately - she doesn't see me with the Los Angeles plastic-surgery enhanced women with their platinum blonde hair and suspiciously perky assets, the super model types that some of my brothers admittedly pursued - Roman and Max mainly, although Ansel has certainly had his moments. No, she sees me with the kind of woman who exudes Ivy-League elegance - more natural beauty with a hint of old money, dressed in crisp Ralph Lauren separates, pearl earrings glinting in her ears, weekends spent at a weathered cedar-shingled summer home on Nantucket. I admit, with a pang in my chest, Alecia fit that mold perfectly, from her honey-blonde bob to her boat shoes to her house in the Hamptons, a house she inherited from her father.

She sighs. "Look, let's be real. We had amazing sex, but

that high won't last. And when it fades..." She makes a face. "You'll see me—really see me—and wonder what the hell you were thinking." She examines her fingers. "Face it, we're from different planets. The only place we click is between the sheets." She shrugs one shoulder. "Eventually some socialite with a beach house who gets excited about organic kale will catch your eye, and I'll get the 'it's not you, it's me' speech. I'm just saving us both the trouble."

I narrow my eyes. "Tally, stop deciding for me. I'm a grown man who can choose who I want to be with." I shake my head. "Have I dated pearl-clutching socialites who think tattoos are for criminals? Women who drive overpriced eco-cars and treat organic kale like it's a religion? Sure. But that's not what matters here." I lean closer, my voice softening. "I see you, Tally. Really see you. And whatever's happening between us feels real. Different doesn't mean wrong. Hell, I'm probably not what you pictured for yourself either."

Tally's voice drops to a whisper, barely audible over the static of the video call. "Cam. Don't make this harder than it is." Her fingers dance while she stares at them instead of looking at me through the screen.

Words tumble out of my mouth before I can stop them, my voice rising with each sentence. "Let me help, Tally. The baby's coming, and with your mom's condition—I mean, the meds are working now, but bi-polar disorder is unpredictable. Your apartment's tiny, that fire escape is a death trap, and there's so much to prepare for. Baby-proofing, midnight feedings, diaper changes. I know how to—"

Her eyes flash, emerald turning to jade. I'm still talking when the screen goes black, the abrupt silence deafening. She's hung up.

I call back immediately, my thumb jabbing the screen

hard enough to hurt. Straight to voicemail. I fire off three texts in quick succession. No response, not even the dancing ellipsis of a reply being typed.

I rub my temples, feeling the throb of a headache forming beneath my fingertips.

Nice work, genius. Way to sound like a condescending ass.

Chapter Fifteen

TALLY

I glare at Mom when she cracks open my bedroom door. "Don't even."

She steps in anyway, her eyes knowing. Of course she heard me hang up on Cam. His whole "let me rescue you" bullshit had me seeing red. That's exactly why I'm keeping this baby situation to myself—I don't need him swooping in like some knight in shining armor.

My gaze drifts around my cramped bedroom. Baby gear will never fit in here. And with Mom staying until her meds stabilize, we're practically sardines. But whatever. My mess, my problem.

"Tallulah," Mom plants herself at the foot of my bed. "He deserves to know about his child."

"Nunya," I mutter, picking at my chipped nail polish.

"Excuse me?"

"None. Of. Your. Business."

Mom's arms fold across her chest. "Like hell it isn't. This affects me too." She ticks off on her fingers. "First, it's wrong and karma's a bitch. Second, that man seems decent

—unlike the parade of losers you usually drag home. Third, have you looked around this shoebox lately? You need help." She gestures at the mess surrounding us. "I know you want me here, and honestly, I need to be here. Someone has to make sure I stay on my meds until I'm back on solid ground." Her voice softens. "I can't go back to that dark place, Tally. I just can't. So I need you—and I'm woman enough to admit it."

I know what she's getting at. At the very least, I need to figure out a way to get a bigger place. Because this shoebox with its cracked plaster ceiling and temperamental radiator won't work. And her calculating mind is thinking that Cameron will just buy me a bigger place. Maybe in the suburbs where I don't have to hear ambulances and police cars 24/7. I mean, this neighborhood, the Arts District of Los Angeles, is generally safe and I love it - it's walkable, full of galleries with their stark white walls and exposed beams, craft breweries serving hazy IPAs in Edison-bulb-lit spaces, vibrant murals splashed across brick buildings like a rainbow explosion. It's just my vibe.

But any time you get thousands of people crammed into these converted warehouses and lofts, sirens are gonna happen at all hours, their wailing echoing between buildings like trapped ghosts. It just is. So, I'll have to think of a sleeping infant who won't be asleep for long once he or she hears those ear-splitting sirens blaring through our paper-thin windows. But live in the suburbs? The baby will sleep, well, like a baby.

Which is another thing I'll be giving up for this kid - my apartment where the sirens and street noise blend with Jamal from upstair's Ziggy Marley blasting through my ceiling at 2 AM. Last Tuesday he banged on my door with a paper bag that left grease stains on my fingers, and I ate still-warm scones while he showed me his latest canvas - all violent reds and cosmic purples that matched the yarn wrapped around his dreads. Yesterday, Bettina from downstairs buzzed me down to borrow tequila for margaritas, her septum ring catching the light as she talked about some French body horror flick, gesturing wildly with hands heavy with her own metal creations. And tonight the bass from the punks' apartment down the hall is making my coffee mug inch across the counter, their party spilling into the hallway where some guy with a green mohawk just offered me a joint through my cracked door.

These are my people, and I'll be trading all of that in for a cookie-cutter house on a tree-lined street where sirens are never heard, where there will be awkward block parties and men in pressed khaki shorts and pastel golf shirts with baseball caps covering their sunburned balding heads and wives with highlighted bobs who will be selling tacky costume jewelry through some multi-level marketing company or maybe be selling Pampered Chef stuff at wine-soaked home parties.

But I'll have to do it for her. Or him. Because this cramped third-floor walkup with its peeling paint and the constant wail of sirens outside isn't a place to raise a kid. And my mother, with her knowing looks and barely concealed I-told-you-so's, knows the only way I can afford some cookie-cutter split-level in Oakridge Estates or some other boring suburban neighborhood is if Cam gets involved. It'll have to be a house, too, not some beige-carpeted apartment with paper-thin walls. I want this kid to have a backyard with actual grass, maybe a maple tree they can climb, not just concrete and cigarette butts. I want them to hear birds in the morning, not the thudding bass from 2B or the screaming matches from 4A.

Moving to the suburbs seems cringe to me, but it won't to the kid. And the kid, and my mother to a certain extent, will have to come before me.

I sigh. "Mom, I'll just have to figure it out. On my own. I know I need a bigger place and I know that this neighborhood isn't a place to raise a kid. Not if I want a kid who doesn't want to wake up at 2 AM when the sirens rush through because somebody got their face smashed in with a beer bottle or some junkie is foaming at the mouth on the sidewalk. I know this kid will be better off in the suburbs." And, at that, I bolt to the bathroom, barely making it before violently heaving into the toilet. Christ, I've been puking my guts out for weeks now, can't even keep down fucking saltines, but somehow, just the thought of moving to the suburbs makes me want to rip my own stomach out through my throat. But maybe I could psyche myself up for it.

Maybe I'll watch one of those shows on HGTV where some perky couple with daddy's credit card looks at three different cookie-cutter houses that are all on streets named after trees but with "character" and just enough edge to convince themselves they're not becoming their parents.

Oh, who am I kidding? How would I ever afford that? My tattoo place does pretty decent business, but this is Los Angeles - houses *start* at a mil. I'll have to come up with two-hundred grand just for the fucking down payment, two hundred grand I don't really have right now.

But I'm still not telling Cam the truth about the baby. I'll see a financial advisor who can help me figure this thing out. Maybe take out a loan - my tattoo studio has been in business for seven years, since I was 22, and it's been pretty solid the whole time. I'm a decent credit risk.

Mom gives me that look—the one that sees right through my bullshit. "Tally, you need to tell me what's really going on. What's the real reason you won't tell Cameron about the baby?"

"What do you mean? I told you. I don't want him to interfere with my life. With the baby's life. I don't want him to become like a ball and chain to me and you know he will."

Do I really know that though? Celeste has a kid with Max—Violet. They both work long hours, though Celeste works from home now. After Violet was born, she left Dreamscape Studios to focus on screenwriting and has crushed it career-wise. She's never once complained about Max trying to control their parenting. When issues come up with Violet, they figure shit out together. As it should be.

But aren't they unicorns? In my mind, I see two parents, faces twisted with rage, squaring off across a gleaming granite kitchen island like boxers in a ring. The mother wants the kid to go to art school because that's what the kid wants, the father wants the kid to go to some soul-crushing prep school where rich kids learn to become even bigger assholes. Then the kid grows up and still wants to be an artist, so the Mom wants the kid in art school, but the asshole father wants the kid to become a lawyer, and won't pay for schooling unless the kid agrees to his vision of the kid's future.

Then I see the mother dragging herself out of bed at 2 AM, panic clawing at her throat, pressing trembling fingers against a burning forehead, while the father buries his useless head under a pillow, snarling about how he survived childhood without being "coddled." Then the kid, white as death, convulsing on the ice-cold tile, appendix already ruptured and spewing poison, and the mother's scream ripping through the house like a chainsaw, pure hatred blazing in her eyes as she lunges at the father. "FUCK YOU,

THOMAS, YOU GODDAMN WORTHLESS PIECE OF SHIT!" Yeah. That's the reality - it wasn't my reality because Dad wasn't around, but it's the reality in most of my friends' homes growing up.

I can't help thinking about my friend Sonya from fifth grade. Her stomach was killing her, but her dad wouldn't let her mom drive her to the hospital. "It's just a stomachache," he kept saying, even yanking the car keys away while Sonya's mom was sobbing, begging to take her in. By the time they finally got her to the ER, her appendix had ruptured. Three weeks in the hospital instead of a simple overnight stay. I know Cameron would never pull that shit—he's a doctor, for Christ's sake—but it's just one more example of how things go sideways when parents can't get on the same page about their kid.

Hard fucking pass on that nightmare.

Mom narrows her eyes at me. "Tallulah. I wasn't exactly Mother of the Year, and I'll own that. But I know when you're holding back. What's really going on?"

I exhale so hard my bangs flutter. Fuck. There is more to it. Another reason I'm keeping Cam at arm's length. And it circles right back to the woman sitting across from me.

What if this baby inherits Mom's wiring? Her bi-polar disorder jumped from her grandfather straight to her, skipping a generation like a goddamn genetic time bomb. I've dodged that bullet - knock wood - but my kid? The math isn't just "not in our favor"—it's a fucking sentence waiting to happen. And when—not if—those symptoms start showing up, I need to handle it my way. Christ, normal parents lose their shit over bedtimes and screen time—imagine the absolute nightmare when your kid's screaming about monsters that only exist in their fractured brain.

And Cameron? The guy's already survived a battlefield

of emotional carnage. He deserves something pure, something untainted. Not some ink-stained disaster with mother issues and a kid who might need psychiatric holds instead of timeout. I clawed my way through hurricane-force chaos—it's burned into my DNA. Survived Cat 5 chaos once, can do it again if the kid loses the genetic lottery and inherits Mom's mental illness. But Cameron's the superhero who held his shattered family together when their dad bailed, who stitches up broken refugees and literally saves lives at Cedars while I'm drawing pretty pictures on skin. He deserves better than being dragged into the hellfire of my family's demons. I won't fucking do that to him.

I roll my eyes. "No, Mom, it's not that deep. I don't need someone dictating my life choices, and I sure as hell don't want that for my kid either. I mean, yeah, I'll guide them, but on their terms. If they're running around with a toy stethoscope, maybe they've got Cam's medical gene, and I'll support that path. But if they're smearing paint everywhere and dropping Basquiat references before kindergarten, I'm not letting some guy squash their creative spirit because 'artists starve.'"

"Tally," Mom sighs, "what makes you think Cameron would be controlling? He seems level-headed to me."

"Because—" I throw my hands up, then let them fall. "Okay, fine. Maybe he is chill. But what if he's not? What if he turns into this helicopter parent who micromanages everything and screws the kid up?"

Mom gives me that look—the one that sees right through me. "And what if the baby inherits my issues? And you don't want him dealing with that burden."

I slam my palms against the kitchen counter. "That's not it!" The words explode out of me, and Mom's eyebrow arches in that knowing way. Damn it. She's always said my volume rises with my bullshit. I might as well have tattooed "LIAR" across my forehead. Her lips purse, and I know she's pieced it together. Fine. Whatever. If this baby comes out wired like her, I'll handle it myself.

"Oh," she says. "But it is it." She shakes her head. "Don't even try to lie."

I sigh. "That is it. But not all of it. Most of it is because I…" I trail off, twisting my rings around my fingers. Mom waits, that patient look on her face that always makes me crack.

"Fine. I'm terrified he'll wake up one day and realize I'm this massive mistake. That someday I'll overhear him telling his fancy doctor friends about his 'tattooed phase' before he got serious about life. That if he gets roped into being with me just because we have a kid together, he'll one day look at me across the breakfast table with this kid between us and think about the bullet he didn't quite dodge."

Now, Mom's crying. "Oh, Tally." She says my name three times like it's a spell that might fix everything. "I did this to you, didn't I? Made you build these walls? I dragged you through a childhood where nothing ever stayed the same. I should've been your rock—told you every single day how amazing you are. Then maybe you'd believe you deserve Cameron. Because you do deserve him, baby. You do."

I blink. She means well, but she's got it twisted. I know damn well I deserve Cameron. That's not what keeps me up at night. What scares me is how different our worlds are, and how eventually the shine will wear off. When it's 3 AM diaper duty and screaming matches about private versus public school, he'll look at the tattooed mess across from him and wonder what the fuck he was thinking.

But fine, she's right about the trust issues. Probably

comes with the territory when your childhood address changed more often than people change their goddamned underwear. Not that I'll say that out loud. She's already carrying enough guilt about the bi-polar disorder genes I might be passing down.

I roll my eyes. "I know I deserve Cameron, Mom," I say, my voice tight. "But I'm not exactly what he's looking for. He's probably dreaming of some trust fund princess who summers in the Hamptons and wouldn't be caught dead with ink on her perfect skin. The kind of woman who'd rather die than wear the same outfit twice and thinks a Birkin bag is a basic necessity."

"And how exactly do you know that?"

"Celeste filled me in. His precious Alecia taught kindergarten while living off daddy's money and jetting off to her Hamptons mansion every summer. Trust me, Mom, guys like him don't trade in their perfect porcelain dolls for tattooed girls like me. That's not how the world works."

Mom's voice softens. "Tally, honey. This goes both ways, you know. When's the last time you dated a guy who wore pressed khakis instead of leather? Who probably has NPR programmed in his car instead of KROQ? Who probably has never created an urban mural?" She tilts her head. "Remember how you and Jake followed the Drop Kick Murphys around the country that one summer and that was the guy you saw yourself with? I'm guessing Cam's idea of a wild night involves wine that doesn't come in a box. But here you are, falling for him anyway."

I sigh. Mom's words hit like a sledgehammer. This clear-eyed, rational woman—this stranger in my mother's skin—makes me wonder what kind of person I'd be if I hadn't spent my childhood hiding in closets while she screamed at invisible demons. But fuck that. My art work became my lifeline in that house of horrors. Every canvas I painted and sketched was a scream I couldn't let out, every color a feeling I couldn't name. Pain carved me into who I am.

"Jesus Christ, fine! I'm fucking crazy about him, okay?" The truth rips out of me. The sex? It demolished me. But it's HIM. I close my eyes and his scent floods back—Dior's Sauvage Elixir, so goddamn dark and spicy it makes my knees weak. So opposite to his golden-boy vibe that it gives me whiplash. I drown myself in Black Orchid for the same reason—to warn people there's danger beneath my skin. He's got hands that stitch up war refugees by day and coax jazz from piano keys at night with such raw emotion I had to hide my tears in the dark club. He sees straight through my bullshit. Nothing about him screams future asshole—he's not the type who'd crush our kid's dreams.

And that terrifies me more than anything. I'm drowning in feelings for a man who deserves someone who didn't grow up feral. Someone whose damage doesn't run soul-deep. On paper, we're from different planets. And sometimes "on paper" is all that matters to people like him.

Mom leans in, eyes laser-focused. "So the truth is out. You're absolutely fucking obsessed with Cameron, this gorgeous doctor who would walk through fire for you. You're carrying his child. What the hell is your problem?"

"Me." My voice cracks. "Like Taylor Swift says, I'm the problem, it's me." My chest feels like it's being crushed. I'm self-sabotage personified, the hurricane that destroys everything it touches. I dig my nails into my palm until it hurts. Everyone else figures their shit out eventually, right? Maybe I could stop being such a disaster long enough to not obliterate the one perfect thing that's ever happened to me.

Or maybe not. Either way, I'm taking this secret about the baby to my grave.

Chapter Sixteen

TALLY

Mom clears her throat one afternoon while I'm standing in her kitchen, my baby bump now unmistakable beneath my tank top. "So..."

I glare at the sushi menu I'd been eyeing on my phone. Deleted. I'd ranted for weeks about how women had babies for centuries without all these fucking restrictions, but here I am—no raw fish, no alcohol, no coffee. My copy of *What to Expect When You're Expecting* sits dog-eared on my nightstand, and my fridge is packed with enough spinach, avocados, and almonds to choke a horse. All for the folate. My tattoo clients have started bringing me decaf as a joke after I nearly bit someone's head off during a consultation.

"Brinley," I whisper, touching my stomach. The ultrasound tech had shown me last week—definitely a girl. Brinley Steele. Sounds like someone who could kick ass.

Mom tries again. "So... I've been researching. There are tests now—DNA markers that might indicate if Brinley could inherit my bi-polar disorder. Not guaranteed, but it might help you decide about telling Cameron he's the father."

I shrug. "Yeah, been there, done that research. But what's the point? So I can freak myself out every time she sneezes? The doc said even with the markers, she might never get it. And I'm still not telling Cameron. End of story."

I've made up my mind about him. Mom's little heart-to-heart last month almost cracked me, but I've cemented that wall back up. Poor guy. Not like it's his fault. Since I dropped the baby bomb on him, we haven't spoken. His name lights up my phone at least twice a week, but my finger hovers over "decline" every time. One conversation leads to another, leads to me spilling everything, and then what? Some bells you can't unring.

Mom shakes her head and I point at her. "Spill it to him and you're back on the streets." Total bullshit, obviously. She knows damn well I'd never kick her out.

It's wild seeing her so stable on these meds. Like someone flipped a switch. I've got plans, too—clearing out that old desk and bookshelf in the living room. Who needs paperbacks when everything's on my Kindle? That space is begging for a baby grand. She's got the chops to play again, maybe even make some real money at it. There's gigs all over—events, session work with local bands, clubs. She could actually support herself doing what she loves instead of suffocating me with attention. Funny how she's morphed into this hovering mama bear now, when she was practically a ghost during my childhood. Like she's cramming 29 years of parenting into six months.

She just laughs and shakes her head. "You're going out with the girls tonight?"

I sigh. Yeah, I'm meeting up with Celeste and Liv tonight. Haven't told them about Brinley yet. Been telling myself I'm just waiting for that second trimester safety zone, but who am I kidding? The second I open my mouth, I'll blurt out who knocked me up, and Celeste will lose her damn mind. Can't even blame her. She'll see it like I seduced some innocent lamb and now I'm going to wreck him like I wreck everything. She knows my relationship track record is a dumpster fire, and she's protective of Cameron. But I've gotta come clean eventually. The real question is whether she can keep her mouth shut around Max. If Max finds out, he'll tell Cameron in a heartbeat, and then I'm completely screwed.

"Then have fun."

I nod, no longer terrified she'll vanish into thin air while I'm out. Those first weeks after she showed up, I'd rush home from the shop, heart in my throat until I spotted her on the couch. Now I know better. She's sticking around—acting like an actual mother for once. And damn if I don't need that right now. Never in a million years did I picture myself pregnant, let alone grateful for my mom's presence. She's hardly winning parenting awards—the woman who taught me to forge her signature in third grade isn't exactly Dr. Spock—but having her here, watching her fold my laundry, somehow makes this whole baby thing feel possible.

I step into the bar and spot the girls already nestled in a booth. For months I've been dodging drinks with flimsy excuses—"I don't feel well," "I'm just tired"—which aren't outright lies, since I am usually wiped out and sicker than fucking hell. Still, it's hardly the whole truth, and they've started to notice. After all, our ritual is a glass of wine, a plate of appetizers, and at least a couple hours of catch-up, every few weeks if not more often. Even Celeste, juggling Max and their new baby Violet, rarely misses our nights out. I've loved having them in my back pocket, but tonight it's time to come clean.

They're mid-conversation when I arrive. Celeste is careful not to ramble on about Max and Violet—she knows how boring that can gets, even if her husband really is the gorgeous billionaire goddess-worshipper of her dreams.

"Hey, bitches," I greet them, sliding into the booth. Hugs all around. My heart pounds: it's go-time.

"Tally," Celeste says, leaning forward. "We've already ordered a bottle of wine in your honor. No more lame excuses about why you can't join us."

"About that..." I clear my throat. "There's something I've been hiding."

Liv perks up. "What is it? You knocked up or something?" She laughs—until my silence makes her realize she hit the nail on the head. She shoots a look at Celeste. "We were actually teasing about that before you showed up. We've been scratching our heads over your no-drinking streak. I mean, none of us go crazy except when we're all together, so... spill. What gives?"

"I'm pregnant." I close my eyes for a second, then open them again. I'd rehearsed a whole different story—that the father was an avant-garde artist I hooked up with after a gallery opening, that he tragically overdosed, so there'd be no awkward co-parenting questions. I killed him off in my head to dodge the "What about the dad?" interrogation. But suddenly, the truth feels right.

Celeste holds her hand out to Liv, her crimson nails gleaming under the fluorescent lights as Liv reluctantly slaps a crumpled five dollar bill into her palm. "Told you," she says with a smug smile that crinkles the corners of her cat-like eyes. "Bow down to the queen. If I say something, it's usually the gospel truth."

Oh great, they've been making bets about the state of my uterus. Not that I can blame them. I would do the same thing if I were in their position, probably wagering a twenty instead of a measly five. I would treat the whole thing like a joke too, while secretly dying to know every juicy detail.

Olivia leans forward, her honey-blonde hair falling across her shoulder as concern floods her deep blue eyes. "Don't be offended," she says, her voice dropping to a gentle murmur. "We're not trying to make a joke out of this. But we did make a bet. I lost that bet, by the way, because I can't imagine you with a kid—you who once said you'd rather swallow razor blades than change a diaper. But what I don't know is whether congratulations are in order or something else. How do you feel about this?"

I glare at them both. "How do you think I feel? I'm freaking the hell out."

Celeste's smile turns apologetic. "The bet was a dick move. I'm sorry. But I've suspected for weeks. And remember Roman's wife, Lilith? She did that tarot reading and said you had a baby in your cards. That's why we ordered wine—to see your reaction. Not exactly BFF behavior, I know. But seriously, what can we do to help you, anything at all?"

I appreciate their concern, I really do, but Mom's already on this. She's been googling morning sickness remedies non-stop. Spoiler alert: nothing actually works except ginger, peppermint, and choking down bland food. She even found some research on acupuncture and dragged me to appointments. It helps... barely. Mom's been to every doctor visit too. The girls couldn't go to doctor's appointments anyway with their crazy work schedules, which is partly why I haven't leaned on them. No point making them feel guilty about something they can't change.

“I’ll let you ladies know if there’s anything I need.” But they both know I won’t actually tell them about anything I need because I don’t do that.

Celeste puts her hand on mine. “I’m serious, Tally. Anything at all.”

I just nod.

"Who's the father?" Liv blurts out, because of course that's what they're really dying to know.

Shit. Here we go. If I lie, that lie's gonna boomerang back and smack me right in the face someday. Not maybe—definitely. What if the baby pops out with Cameron's dimples or that weird cowlick he's got? What if Mom loses her cool and spills to one of his buddies or brothers? She's been giving me the silent treatment for days over this whole "don't tell Cameron" thing. And if this all blows up? I'll have Cameron breathing fire down my neck plus Celeste and Liv looking at me like I just keyed their cars. Can't afford to lose my girls. Not now.

They're both staring at me, waiting. My brain's spinning like a slot machine, no jackpot in sight.

I chew my lip raw before finally asking, "Vault worthy?" They know what that means. Our sacred pact: anything in the vault stays buried. Period. Break that trust, and the betrayed gets to air one of your dirty secrets as payback. Works like a charm since we've all got skeletons we'd rather keep closeted. Mutually assured destruction—the cornerstone of any solid friendship.

Celeste leans forward, eyes gleaming. "Yeah?" The way she stretches that single syllable tells me everything—she's caught the scent of drama. Her fingertips drum once against the table as she waits for whatever bomb I'm about to drop. And honey, this one's nuclear-grade juicy.

"Liv?" I say.

"Absolutely. That's a given. Remember how you kept my Vegas hookup under wraps when I was with Jed?" Liv says, and I bite my tongue. Jed was her "forever guy" back then, despite the glaring red flag of her needing a secret Vegas fling while they were together. But some lessons you just have to learn the hard way. I honored the vault anyway.

Celeste hasn't cashed in her vault privileges yet, but we both know it's inevitable.

My pulse throbs in my ears as I force the name past my lips. "It's...Cameron."

Liv's palm shoots out immediately, and Celeste smacks a five-dollar bill into it with a defeated sigh. I let my head fall back. "Seriously? Was I that obvious?"

Celeste rolls her eyes. "Come on. You wreck your Jeep, tell me Cameron was your doctor, then start ghosting us? I knew you had a guy, and Liv said you were probably hooking up with Cameron. The man couldn't tear his eyes off you at both my weddings."

"What the fuck? He was not staring at me."

"Everyone saw it but you," Celeste says. "I didn't mention it because—"

"Because I'm toxic waste to guys like him. I get it."

"God, no," Celeste says. "I just thought Cameron wasn't ready to date anyone. And why point out something the whole reception could see?" Her face lights up. "Holy shit. You and Cameron making a baby together!"

Liv shoots Celeste a warning look that screams *shut up*. She understands why I put this in the vault—I'm not planning to tell Cameron anything. Celeste is too starry-eyed to connect the dots. I expected her to rip me a new one for dragging Cameron into my bed, but she's practically glowing. I can read her mind: if I married Cameron, we'd basically be sisters—or at least both have the last name of Kensington. Close enough for her.

Celeste's eyes go wide. "Hold up. Please tell me you've already told Cameron? That you two have been steaming up the international phone lines and figuring out your baby game plan?" She leans forward, her voice dropping. "You're not seriously thinking about keeping him in the dark about his own kid, are you?"

I say nothing, and Celeste shakes her head.

"Oh hell no. You can't pull this on us, Tally. Sorry, but I'm calling a vault exception."

Crap. She's invoking the loophole we all agreed on: if the secret's so explosive that no one could possibly keep it locked up, we break the vault. But Olivia has to sign off, too.

I glare at Olivia with the fiercest stink-eye I can muster—hoping she'll veto the vault exception. If she does, Celeste stays silent. If she doesn't…well, damn it, I just fucking played myself. I'll have to break this to Cameron. What kind of mess have I gotten into? I thought I could trust these two. Apparently not.

"Tally," Olivia says gently, "you know we love you. But this won't stay under wraps. And when it comes out—not if, when—we're all screwed. You're asking Celeste to betray Max, because you don't think he'll feel betrayed when it comes out that you kept his brother's kid secret from him? And we can't say you didn't tell us—everyone knows you share every detail, and Celeste is a shitty liar so Max will automatically know the truth. He'll know Celeste knew about the kid and that is a straight-up betrayal. Think it through."

I exhale in frustration. This is why I'm terrible at chess

—why Mom wipes the board with me. She's a natural; with training she could go pro. I only have my ranking from junior tournaments, and I was merely decent. Yet here I am, failing to think three moves ahead: I've set Celeste up to betray Max. Why didn't I see that coming?

Because I've been only thinking about myself. That's the ugly truth. I've been utterly selfish. Yes, I'm scared: scared Cameron will feel trapped and resent me down the road; scared he'll try to control my life and the baby's; scared that I'll love someone who ultimately might not want to stay. But showing that kind of vulnerability? That's something I've never been good at.

I blow out a long breath. "Fine. I'll tell him." Dammit. But Olivia's right—a secret this nuclear has a half-life of about five minutes. Better to detonate it myself than wait for fallout.

Celeste's face softens. "Tal," she says, leaning forward. "Why wouldn't you tell him? What's really going on?"

I fidget with my tattoo sleeve, tracing the outline of the phoenix on my forearm. "Pick your poison. But mostly? I'm terrified of disappearing into his life. I've always done whatever the hell I want, whenever I want. No compromises, no explanations, no apologies. My life, my rules." I swallow hard. "I know the kid's already gonna change that. But him too? That's...a lot of people having opinions about my choices." I inhale deeply, my chest tight.

Celeste leans back in her chair. "Welcome to adulthood, Tally. When you let someone into your life, you have to consider their needs too. It's actually not the worst thing."

I stare at my glass of sparkling water, wishing it was tequila. "Growing up, I learned to count on exactly one person—me. Nobody else ever showed up when it mattered." I pause, looking at my scarlet nail polish.

"Changing that mindset won't happen overnight, but I'm trying." I take a deep breath. "And now there's my mother to deal with."

"Right," Celeste says. "You've told us about her staying with you. How is she? I mean, we know you've always worried about-"

She doesn't need to finish that sentence. Every time my phone rang after midnight, my stomach would drop like I'm on a roller coaster—wondering if this is finally it, if some cop found her body dumped somewhere or if she OD'd in some stranger's apartment. Having her under my roof means I can at least sleep through the night without being terrified about getting *that* phone call.

I nod. "Remember all those years of pills and loser boyfriends? Turns out there was something underneath it all—bi-polar disorder. When she finally got clean and was still seeing things that weren't there, they ran tests. The genetic markers confirmed what her symptoms were showing. It's not a hundred percent certain, but the doctors are pretty convinced." I shrug. "They prescribed medicine for treatment of bi-polar disorder, and she has responded so well."

Olivia's eyes go wide. "Oh my God, tell me everything! This is huge, Tally!"

I nod. "Yeah, well, she's no June Cleaver, but she's still my mom. Back before the pills, before Dad got killed in Iraq, she was actually pretty amazing." I swallow hard. "The doctor explained that losing Dad probably triggered her bi-polar disorder, and she started self-medicating to silence the voices. That's their theory, anyway."

"What about this treatment?" Celeste asks, leaning forward.

"Lithium and Abilify." My voice catches. "It's like someone flipped a switch and gave me back my mom. She knows she put me through hell, and she's trying to make up for it. Comes to all my prenatal appointments, brings me ginger tea when I'm puking my guts out. She's actually acting like a grandmother-to-be. And there's talk about her playing piano again."

Celeste squeezes my hand. "That would be incredible. I know what those memories mean to you."

"Fuck yeah, it would be." I blink back tears. "Sitting next to her on that bench, watching her hands fly across the keys—those were the only good parts of my childhood before everything went to shit. But I'm not counting on it. Hope is just disappointment waiting to happen."

Celeste's eyes light up. "I've got an idea, Tally! Hear me out—Cameron's got, what, nine more months in Sicily? You need to tell him in person."

I roll my eyes. "Sure—let me just win the lottery tomorrow so I can fly to Sicily on a whim. I've got a tattoo studio to run, and I'm not made of money like your husband."

Celeste lays her hand over mine. "Exactly why you should take Max's plane. Surprise Cameron. You can't just drop 'we're having a baby' over FaceTime."

"That's just it—I already told him I'm pregnant. I panicked and blurted out that I'd had a one-night stand, got wasted, and woke up pregnant. I know—it's not my finest hour, telling some bullshit like that. But I couldn't keep the pregnancy from him. The grapevine runs too deep with you, Max, and the whole Kensington clan."

Celeste giggles.

"What's so damn funny?"

"You, thinking you'd get away with lying about the baby's father."

"Why wouldn't it work?"

"Have you seen the Kensingtons? They all look like clones. Even the dad. My husband's got green eyes, Roman's are dark, the others shades of green, blue, hazel—but line them up and it's obvious they're kin. Genetics in that family are bullet-proof. Your baby will look like a Kensington, guaranteed. She'll be beautiful, with you as her mom and Cameron as her dad—but she'll have that family face. You'd never fool anyone."

Touché. She's got a point. Some families have wildly different kids. Definitely not the Kensingtons. Jesus. You'd need sunglasses just to look at the whole pack of them together—like someone cloned a Calvin Klein billboard eight times over. Same thick hair you want to run your fingers through, same jaw you could open a beer bottle on, same cheekbones that could slice bread. Tall as redwoods, every last one. The kind of men who make you forget your own name when they look at you. Even their old man's still got it. So, yeah, it's true that they all look alike, so the genetics are strong and my kid will probably come out as a clone, too. Same as Celeste's kid, Violet - she's definitely a Kensington. Unmistakably a Kensington. Brinley will probably be the same.

"I fucking panicked," I snap, voice raw. "I didn't know what else to say."

"Alright," Celeste says, tone clipped. "So Cameron knows you're pregnant. You still need to look him in the eye and tell him he's the father."

I grit my teeth. "Looks like Blade's stuck at Manic Muse a bit longer."

"Blade? Who's Blade?"

"The agency's temp tattoo guy. Ever since the accident, I've been drowning in clients and Maya's been a no-show half the time. I don't know what drama she's spinning, but she's called in sick more than she's shown up. I'd fire her ass yesterday if she wasn't so goddamned talented and she knows that her talent is the only thing keeping her around." I run a hand through my hair. "But yeah—you're right. Cameron deserves the face-to-face."

Celeste's eyebrows flick up. "So you'll let Max lend you his private plane?"

I stare. "You don't know me at all, do you? Hell no. You think I'll torch thousands of gallons of jet fuel just for my ass to fly solo? And you offered it without even asking him! He might need it himself—now get this through your head. I'll fly Delta coach to Rome, then I'll catch a puddle jumper to Sicily." I shift uncomfortably in my seat. "Thirteen hours trapped in coach with a baby doing gymnastics on my bladder? Just strap me to a medieval torture rack and be done with it. Might be more fun."

Her deflated sigh is almost tangible. "Okay. But—" She shakes her head. "You're right. You'd never squander that much gas just for yourself."

I lean back. "And neither would you. We're both tree-hugging, planet-saving maniacs, remember?"

My chest tightens. Mom… she's been killing it holding down the fort, but can I really trust her for days while I'm staring down Cameron in Sicily? What if I come back and she's vanished?

Celeste scans me, cool and sharp. "Don't fret about your mother. If she's stable, she can bunk with us. Rosa's got that gorgeous ADU by the pool—the one with hardwood floors, a fireplace, a Jacuzzi tub—she'll keep an eye on her."

ADU my ass. That "tiny house" behind Max's pool is a full-blown mansion: at least a thousand square feet of luxury. Hell, once the kid's here, I wouldn't mind moving in there myself.

I glance between Celeste and Olivia. "Thanks, you guys."

"What for?" Celeste tilts her head.

I hitch one shoulder up. "Thought you'd want to murder me when I dropped the Cameron bomb."

Celeste's brow furrows. "Why on earth would that upset me?"

"Come on. We both know I'm relationship kryptonite, and Cam's...well, Cam. I half expected you to shove me through the nearest window for corrupting your precious brother-in-law."

She lets out a little laugh. "Oh, Tally. Please. You two are literally two of my favorite humans. Seeing you together is just—" She presses her fingers to her lips and makes a kissing sound. "Perfection. And besides, you both deserve so much happiness. I mean, Cameron, what he's gone through these past few years? I kind of love that you'll be the one healing his heart. And I know you can."

Liv leans forward, eyes sparkling. "Okay, but spill. What's he like?" She fans herself dramatically. "That man is grade-A gorgeous. Always thought he was the best-looking Kensington. Something about that whole saving-the-world vibe that makes the pretty package even better."

"Oh my god," I say, rolling my eyes so hard they practically hit the back of my skull. Just thinking of Cam in that way sends a flush of heat across my cheeks. "He's amazing in bed. I won't go into details, but the man knows exactly where to touch, when to be gentle and when... not to be. He really likes women. And not in a sleazy womanizer way, but in that rare 'actually listens and pays attention' feminist way. And you know how generous he is with his time? All those late nights at the refugee center?"

"Yeah, and he feeds the homeless, too, once a month at

St. Mary's," Celeste says, twirling a strand of her rust-colored hair. "Rain or shine, even during that torrential rainstorm last winter."

Of course he does. I'd expect nothing less from Cameron with his perfect jawline and those sapphire eyes that crinkle at the corners when he smiles.

"Well," I say, leaning forward until our foreheads are nearly touching. "Let's just say that he's generous like that across the board." I raise my eyebrows until they practically disappear into my hairline. "Yes, it's exactly what you're thinking—the man gives and gives until your toes curl. But also, he taught me to cook that lemon risotto everyone raved about at dinner. He helped me recover from my accident, massaging my back and applying cold and warm compresses, and helping me get around the apartment when I couldn't really move. And we talk for hours about anything and everything, just like best friends, and goddamn, he listens when I speak. I know this is true because he gives me advice and knows when I don't really need advice but just need to laugh. And we have the same sense of humor - dark. He's..." I sigh, my breath catching slightly. "Damn perfect, is what he is. Too good to be true."

Olivia sighs, her diamond tennis bracelet catching the light as she lifts her champagne flute. "Oh. You're so lucky to snag Cameron." Her lips, glossed to perfection, curve into a wistful smile as she drapes her toned arm across Celeste's bare shoulder. "And you're so lucky to have Max. Not as lucky as Tally is to have Cameron," she adds, twirling a strand of her honey-blonde hair, "just because I have a thing for those broad-shouldered doctor types who spend their entire lives saving others, but you're damn lucky, too, Celeste."

We stay, laughing and eating until 10 and then I drive home.

The streetlights blur as I drive, my fingers drumming the wheel in rhythm with the radio. What was I so worked up about? Celeste's face when I finally spilled—that knowing smile, the way she rolled her eyes like, "About damn time." Of course she'd be in our corner. That woman has seen me through three catastrophic breakups, two career changes, and that time I tried to cut my own bangs after too many tequila shots. If anyone was going to champion this relationship, it would be her.

I get home and Mom is waiting for me, sitting on the couch, watching a show while knitting. Just a normal mother in a cramped two-bedroom with her daughter. Crazy. After growing up in one foster family after another, it seems surreal to see her there.

Mom glances up from her knitting. "How are the girls doing?"

"Great. Celeste thinks I should fly to Sicily and tell Cameron about the baby in person." I roll my eyes. "Like I want to haul my pregnant ass on a plane while this kid practices kickboxing on my bladder. But maybe she's right."

Mom's needles stop clicking. "Tally, honey, you can't just drop in on a refugee camp. There are protocols. He probably couldn't even step away from his duties to see you."

"Since when are you the refugee camp expert?"

She shrugs, resuming her steady rhythm. "YouTube. I've been watching documentaries. Those doctors have it rough—working non-stop in overcrowded camps, swatting mosquitoes all night, barely sleeping. It's chaos. And you'd need a pharmacy's worth of vaccines just to visit."

I sigh. Trust Mom to be the voice of reason when Celeste and I are being ridiculous. Besides, the thought of squeezing into an airplane seat for sixteen hours straight makes my back hurt just thinking about it.

So. Not like I can FedEx a pregnancy test to some refugee camp in Sicily with "Surprise, Cameron!" scrawled on it. Guess I'm stuck waiting for him to get back. Shit. Why did I lie about the baby? What the hell was I thinking? Not exactly my finest hour.

I collapse onto my bed, staring at the water stain on my ceiling that sorta looks like Australia. What am I doing? In a few months, there'll be an actual human being that I'm responsible for. Looking around my disaster zone of a bedroom—yeah, I'm so not ready. My chest constricts like someone's tightening a vice around my ribs. Fuck. A panic attack. Been years since the last one. Heart hammering, room spinning, can't catch my breath.

I've been keeping Cam at arm's length, but maybe... maybe I need him. And that terrifies me more than labor. I don't do "needing people." Foster care taught me that lesson real quick. As a kid, I'd grab onto anything—a stuffed animal, a favorite book, a kind word—when everything went sideways. But those foster families, even the good ones, they were just temporary characters in the Tally Show. Nothing permanent. No one stays. That's the rule I've lived by.

Mom's been amazing, coming to every doctor's appointment with me, but none of this feels real.

She knocks. "Can I come in?"

"Sure," I call out.

She sits on the bed beside me. "Tal, I need to apologize for what I put you through growing up."

I wave at the ceiling. "Mom, don't worry about it."

"I do worry," she says softly. "I don't understand why you don't hate me."

I shrug. "No idea. But I don't."

She shakes her head. "Tally, you need to know I never stopped loving you—even when I lost custody all those times. You probably thought I chose pills over you. But I was terrified—of the hallucinations and the voices that started after your dad was killed. The pills silenced them, made the hallucinations stop. I wish I'd seen a doctor when it began, but I can't exactly hop in a time machine to fix it."

I narrow my eyes. "Wait—so you'd been having these hallucinations and voices back then?"

She nods. "Yeah. I didn't want to scare you. Once I was on the Oxy, everything went away, so I didn't think you needed to know."

I sit up. "Then why were you so confused when they came back?"

"Denial," she admits. "I couldn't accept that I was mentally ill, so I convinced myself nothing was wrong and blocked out that it had happened before. The idea of completely losing touch with reality terrified me. But with your help, I faced it."

I sigh. "Mom, it's okay. Water under the bridge. And right now, with the disaster that has become my life, I have zero motivation to try to dredge up the past. The present time is consuming me right now. Because I just don't know how I'm going to make all this work."

"You'll make it work, Tally. With my help. And hopefully Cam's."

Cam's help. He probably hates me. Why would he trust me with anything important after what I did? The weight of my secret presses against my chest like a stone.

God, I need to talk to him. My stomach knots at the thought of facing him, watching his expression shift as the words tumble out of my mouth.

I exhale slowly, counting to five. Nothing to do but wait for his return. By then, Brinley will be here. And I'll still be trapped in this shoebox apartment because rent's rent and beggars can't be choosers.

The ceiling seems lower today. I swear the kitchen and living room are getting closer to each other, like the trash compactor scene in Star Wars, only slower. Much slower.

Chapter Seventeen

TALLY

Time flies when you're knocked up and broke. But finally—a fucking miracle—the bank approved my loan for a house down payment. Should I be shitting myself over juggling both a mortgage and a $200,000 personal loan? Probably. If I default, they'll strip Manic Muse of every needle and ink bottle. Whatever.

Now I just need to find something under seven figures that isn't in actual Skid Row. Though even that hellhole has perks—it's near the Arts District, which means close to my studio. And I need a place close to my studio because no way am I commuting across this city. The 101 turns into a goddamn parking lot, and I refuse to waste hours of my life sitting in traffic, especially with a baby at home. Mom's already agreed to babysit while I work, which is... questionable at best. But beggars can't be choosers, right? Especially with this loan hanging over my head like a guillotine. One missed payment and those repo vultures will swoop in before I can even flip them off.

My days blur into a hamster wheel—fifty-plus hours at

the studio, then dragging Mom through open houses until my feet throb. By the sixth showing yesterday, the realtor's voice had become white noise. Every property fails some critical test: this one's in my price range but sits in a neighborhood where my car would be stripped overnight; that one's safe but would triple my commute; another has the perfect location but only two bedrooms. Mom keeps saying "compromise," but at my price limit of $800,000, I shouldn't have to settle for a place where I can touch both kitchen walls at once. Might as well be hunting fucking unicorns.

Finally, after thirty straight nights of real estate hell, I find the fucking unicorn. If I had to walk through one more overpriced shoebox with an agent chirping about "potential," I might tattoo their listing on their forehead—backward, so they can read it in the mirror.

It's a foreclosure and is a perfect little three-bedroom 1920s cottage in Echo Park, just five miles from the studio. Honey-colored hardwood floors that creak in all the right places. Morning light pouring through windows framed by ancient oak trees and a giant pepper tree in the backyard. The neighborhood hits that sweet spot—hip enough for decent coffee and late-night tacos, but not so packed that I'll fall asleep to a symphony of sirens like I do in my Arts District apartment.

I sign the house papers just in time—this baby's ready to make her grand entrance in a few months.

Saturday morning, Celeste and Olivia show up armed with tape guns, cardboard boxes, and a U-Haul the size of Texas. They both swear they're here because I've saved their asses enough times, but the truth? We'd walk through fire for each other. I've also hired some eye candy with muscles to haul the heavy stuff down from my third-floor apartment

—mama's not about to risk going into labor on the stairs. Celeste even dragged Roman along, her brother-in-law whose biceps have biceps. He and Max have become workout buddies lately, crushing triathlons together like it's their religion. Roman's basically what would happen if Superman and Thor had a baby, so he'll definitely come in handy with the move. Max? He's out of the country finalizing a movie deal, so bullet dodged there for him.

Roman gives me a look when he walks in, but doesn't mention the whole Cameron-baby situation. Either the Kensington family text chain hasn't blown up yet, or he's just being his usual mind-your-own-business self. Which is weird, considering he and Cameron used to be practically attached at the hip. Though lately he's been spending more time with Max—all those crack-of-dawn training sessions for stupid triathlons have them bonding like frat brothers.

"Lilith's on her way too," he says. "Wouldn't take no for an answer."

Fan-fucking-tastic. Cue the crystal collection, goddess prayers for Brinley's protection, and sage smudging around my belly button. She'll probably whip out her tarot deck and try to predict whether I'll end up with a ring on my finger. Look, I actually like Lilith—she might be the kindest soul I've ever met. It's bizarre she ended up with Hurricane Roman, though watching her somehow tame that storm has been impressive. But I just can't pretend those shiny rocks of hers do a damn thing except look pretty on her shelf.

Lilith appears a half hour later, her dark hair bouncing with each step, wearing a pastel yellow sundress that practically glows against her tanned skin. That megawatt smile of hers could power my entire tattoo shop. Does the woman ever have a bad day? I somehow doubt it. I'm envious of her Disney princess vibe—the way people just naturally gravitate toward her, offering help or smiling back like she's sprinkled them with fairy dust. Not that I'd trade my tats and resting bitch face for her sunshine and rainbows routine.

She gives me a big hug that smells like patchouli oil and that herbal shampoo they sell at the co-op for seventeen bucks a bottle. "Tally, I've been dying to see you since I heard about the baby." Then she digs through her fringed macramé bag and pulls out—you guessed it—a crystal. It's opaque and white, like a chunk of frozen toothpaste. "This is Selenite. If you put it in your nursery, it'll cleanse the space." She rummages again and produces another rock, er, crystal, this one jet-black and lumpy as a lump of coal. "Black tourmaline. It'll shield your baby from negative energy."

Oh, fucking fantastic. She gives me two of the most boring crystals in the world—one that looks like someone's forgotten ice cube and another like something Santa would give to a kid on his bad list. Couldn't she have given me one of those really beautiful, funky ones, with purples and dark reds swirling together like a galaxy, something mysterious and beautiful that I could at least display without visitors thinking I'd picked up random gravel from a parking lot?

I force a smile, pocketing the crystals. It's sweet, really—she genuinely thinks these magic rocks will keep my kid safe or whatever.

But she's not here to give me woo-woo crystals. She's here to help and before I can say anything else, she's already grabbing the heaviest boxes and muscling them down the stairs to the U-Haul. Hard to be annoyed when she's doing the heavy lifting I shouldn't be doing anyway. Seven months pregnant means I'll take whatever help shows up, even if it comes with a side of crystal bullshit.

Twelve hours later, we're all sprawled across my new living room floor with pizza boxes and beer bottles scattered around us. Everyone except me, that is—I'm nursing apple juice like it's liquid gold. Seven months pregnant and I still can't bring myself to have even one sip of beer, though the doctor said it probably wouldn't hurt anything at this point. But hell, I've made it this far sober.

"So," Roman says, cutting through my thoughts, "when exactly are you planning to tell my brother he's about to become a father?" He cocks an eyebrow at me over his beer bottle, his other arm wrapped protectively around Lilith. She's nestled against him, her head tucked perfectly into the crook of his shoulder while he absently kisses her forehead every few minutes.

My chest tightens watching them. Not since those two pink lines appeared on that damn pregnancy test have I felt such a sharp ache of longing. Roman and Lilith have everything—that bone-deep certainty someone's always got your back. And here I am, running from it. Because what was my reason again? Oh right—I don't want to be fucking smothered.

“When he gets back,” I say. “In five months.”

Roman rolls his eyes. “You know it’s bullshit keeping him in the dark, don’t you?”

The words "none of your goddamned business" burn on my tongue, but I swallow them. I'm the one lying to his brother about the baby, after all. Cameron's got his loyalty, not me. I've seen the photos of Cameron with little Stephanie—the way he'd toss her into the air, catching her squealing with those surgeon's hands. I know he'd be the same with Brinley. Cameron's itching to rebuild, to find Wife 2.0 and Baby 2.0. Not replacing what he lost—he'd never—but filling that crater in his life with something tangible. As if rescuing refugees or saving lives at Cedars Sinai forty hours a week isn't tangible enough. Celeste says he wants his "forever girl." That phrase alone makes my skin crawl. Forever girl? I'm barely managing to be a today girl.

"I know, but I can't drop this kind of bomb on him from across the world. He needs to focus on saving lives over there. You think he can do that with thoughts of my carrying his kid keeping him up at night?" The justification tastes sour even as I say it.

Roman's knuckles go white around his beer bottle as he takes a long swig. His jaw clenches like he's biting back words. Lilith whispers something in his ear, and the tension drains from his shoulders like she's flipped some hidden switch. It's wild how she transforms him. Celeste says he used to be the kind of guy who'd cut in front of you in line and then blame you for being in his way. Now? He holds doors open and remembers birthdays. Though right now he's glaring at me like I keyed his car, which is fair. After all, I'm keeping his brother in the dark about the tiny human growing inside me that shares their DNA.

He finally sighs. "Fine. But when Cameron finds out you kept this from him, he won't just be pissed at you. He'll be pissed at all of us for being accomplices."

He's probably right—if he was talking about any other Kensington brother. But Cameron? Cam listens first, judges later. He sees the why behind the what. He'll get it once I explain.

Right?

Chapter Eighteen

TALLY

Once the last box is unpacked, I wheel in Mom's surprise—a baby grand piano for my new sun porch. God, I fucking love that porch. Floor-to-ceiling windows frame the backyard where this massive pepper tree towers like it's been there since dinosaurs roamed. I can already picture myself scaling its branches, not just when Brinley's old enough to join me, but next week if I feel like it. I'll build a "treehouse" for her that'll double as my sketching sanctuary. The yard's already decked out with birdhouses, feeders, and this fancy raised garden bed. Mom can handle the planting—I kill cacti by looking at them—but she's itching to grow everything from cucumbers to kale. Lately I've been craving veggies like crazy. Brinley's turning me into some kind of health freak from the inside out.

When the movers position the piano, Mom descends the stairs and freezes. "Oh, Tally! You didn't!"

I just nod. "Sit. Play something."

She cracks her knuckles one by one, takes a deep breath that fills her lungs completely, and launches into Ravel's

Gaspard de la Nuit. Her fingers dance across the ivory keys, coaxing out the delicate, crystalline notes that patter like midnight rain against a windowpane. The haunting melody hangs in the air, deceptively simple at first, before her hands begin to blur with the gathering complexity of the piece, her body swaying slightly as the tempo quickens and the music darkens.

Her fingers fly across the keys like she never stopped playing. Eyes closed, body swaying, she navigates this insanely difficult piece like it's nothing. Watching her, I'm seven years old again, cross-legged on the floor, wondering how those hands that make my sandwiches can create something so magical.

Just like when I was seven, I sit cross-legged on the floor while she plays, her fingers dancing over the keys. Bach, then Chopin, then Debussy's "Reverie" - a piece that I love even more than Debussy's more familiar "Claire de Lune" - then something I don't recognize but sounds like raindrops. Five grand for that baby grand—worth every penny I shouldn't have spent. The shop's killing it lately, though. Blade turned out to be tattoo gold, drawing crowds that spill over to my chair. Even Maya finally got her act together, her line work tight as hell now. Between the three of us, we're booked solid for months. Then there's the celebrity factor—I still get goosebumps remembering how I nearly fumbled my machine when Chris freaking Hemsworth walked in. One A-lister and suddenly everyone wants ink from the same shop.

I'm grinding harder these days, banking hours and cash. Baby girl's coming, and babies aren't cheap. College funds, art classes if she's got my creative streak, maybe private school with those fancy enrichment programs. My mind runs the numbers, making plans that oddly don't include

Cam's wallet. Stupid, really. He could pay for four years of Juilliard without blinking. But something in my gut says he'll do the bare minimum—cut the required checks but nothing more. Wouldn't stretch far if he pushes for that joint custody he'll probably demand.

I look at my mom and smile. "You've still got it. Why don't you ring up that agent at IAG? He'd book you in a heartbeat."

"You really think I can handle that kind of pressure again?" She twists her hands together.

"Absolutely. You're—"

The pain slices through me mid-sentence, hot and sharp. My first contraction. I double over, gasping for air. Shit. Should've dragged my ass to those Lamaze classes after all. Couldn't stomach it though—all those beaming couples with their matching outfits and synchronized breathing. Would've twisted the knife, especially with these damn pregnancy hormones making me fantasize about Cam moving in, the three of us becoming this perfect little family. Pure fucking delusion. Because right behind that cozy picture comes the panic—walls closing in, choking the life out of me. Gotta remember that feeling when I see him. Can't let some biological chemical trick convince me it's love.

Mom's face goes serious. "Come on," she says, grabbing the pre-packed hospital bag from beside the door. "Time to go to LA General." It's the closest hospital, just off the freeway. I never bothered with a proper birth plan—what was the point?—and now I'm picturing myself screaming on some cold metal table, legs splayed like in those ridiculous movies where women give birth in five minutes flat. Giving birth doesn't seem like—

Another contraction rips through me like barbed wire

being dragged through my insides. And then—a warm gush between my legs soaks my sweatpants and puddles on the hardwood floor. What the actual fuck? It's my first birth. I'm supposed to have hours of contractions, time to get settled at the hospital before this happens, yet here I am, standing in my living room in a puddle of amniotic fluid. My mother watches me with those knowing eyes and nods.

"Happened exactly like this when I had you," she says, already guiding me toward the door with one hand while grabbing towels with the other. "Water broke right away. Steele women don't mess around. Let's get you to the hospital before you drop that baby on your new floor."

She drives me to LA General in her ancient Camry that smells like vanilla air freshener, weaving through mid-morning traffic like she's qualifying for NASCAR.

Twelve excruciating hours later, after cursing every deity and male human who ever existed, Brinley enters the world.

Chapter Nineteen

CAMERON

After a year in Sicily's sun-scorched refugee camp—where I'd bandaged blistered feet, delivered babies in makeshift tents, and held the hands of dying children—I still woke each morning with purpose burning in my chest. My hands would tremble with fatigue as I stitched wounds by lamp-light, listening to the soft whimpers of children separated from parents during desperate sea crossings. Yet each small victory— a fever broken, a smile returned—reminded me why I chose medicine. Even on the worst days, when the Mediterranean washed another body ashore or when medical supplies ran dangerously low, I felt alive knowing each suture I placed mattered.

And if sometimes, during those rare quiet moments beneath star-filled skies, my mind wandered to Tally's emerald eyes or the possibility of a child with her dark hair and smile and somebody else's stubborn chin... well, I buried those thoughts beneath tomorrow's patient charts.

But it's time to go home, and my stomach knots with a tension I can't explain. I want to see Tally—her wild dark hair, those green-blue eyes that flash when she's angry, the curve of her tattooed shoulders. Even after all these months in Sicily, her image hasn't faded. When I close my eyes, I can still trace the outline of the phoenix rising up her forearm, still hear that throaty laugh. That's how I know what I feel is real, at least for me. The ache in my chest when I think of her hasn't diminished with distance or time. It might not be real for her—she might have forgotten me entirely—but it burns in me like a fever.

So, after a grueling 16-hour flight where my knees cramped against the seat in front of me and the recycled air left my throat parched, I'm home again. My sprawling Brentwood house with its gleaming marble countertops and cathedral ceilings suddenly seems as cold and empty as a mausoleum. It's because I've spent the last year in dust-covered canvas tents that flapped in the Mediterranean wind, sharing cramped quarters with 7 other doctors whose snores and whispers became as familiar as my own heartbeat. We worked 12-hour days under buzzing fluorescent lights, our scrubs stained with sweat, blood, and spilled coffee, then unwound by eating lukewarm MREs, drinking whatever booze we could find, and playing cards on upturned supply crates until our eyes burned. After that kind of raw, visceral chaos—that kind of purpose—winding down to a gigantic empty house with nothing but the hum of the central air and the ticking of an antique grandfather clock just seems soul-crushingly depressing and lonely.

Plus, I've got nothing but time on my hands. I quit the ER before my deployment to Sicily, and my Sports Medicine fellowship doesn't kick off until early next year. Six months of freedom—or six months of staring at my ceiling. Depends how you look at it.

I slip on my leather jacket and head out that night to

Indigo, the dimly lit jazz club where I can lose myself in music for the open mic night. I need the press of bodies tonight, the clink of glasses and murmur of conversation drowning out the hollow echo in my chest. This emptiness has shadowed me since Alecia and Stephanie were killed in that accident, but now it's a gaping wound, raw and throbbing, because Tally—with her vibrant laugh and constellation of tattoos—carved herself into my life only to vanish.

My phone sits heavy in my pocket, screen blank where her name should be, my dozen messages floating unanswered in digital limbo. And somewhere across town, she's cradling another man's child, tiny fingers wrapped around her slender wrist.

In Sicily, the endless parade of desperate faces and makeshift medical tents kept the pain at bay—twelve-hour days of sweat-soaked scrubs and the metallic tang of blood on my tongue left no room for heartache. But now, beneath these familiar city lights, I can finally name the ache behind my ribs. My heart isn't just broken—it's shattered.

I nurse a whiskey neat, then another, as regulars drift over to my corner booth—Sal with his perpetual five o'clock shadow, Marlene whose bracelets jangle with every gesture, and old Pete who still wears the same faded Coltrane t-shirt. The amber lights of Indigo cast everyone in a honey glow while saxophone notes curl through the pristine air of the club.

This place feels like my version of the Cheers Bar from TV—most faces light up when I walk in. The bartender slides my usual across without asking, and the manager keeps glancing at the baby grand in the corner, his eyebrows raised in silent question. After a year away, they're hungry to hear me play again, and my fingers are already twitching with muscle memory.

But I don' t feel like playing tonight. I slouch against the bar, nursing a whiskey neat, letting the amber liquid burn my throat while I scan the dimly lit room. The open mic stretches for an hour, the stage bathed in blue light that makes everyone look like they're drowning. I watch a girl with dreadlocks coax haunting melodies from her cello, a middle-aged man in a rumpled suit who makes his saxophone cry, and then the house band takes over— piano, sax, upright bass, and drums, all gleaming under the spotlight.

And then Marisa steps onto the stage, which almost makes my glass of whiskey slip through my fingers in shock. Her silver bangles catch the spotlight as her fingers dance across the keys, first in gentle ripples, then in cascading torrents. When the saxophonist launches into an improvised solo, she shadows him, note for note, then spins his melody into something entirely new. The bassist grins, accepting her challenge, and soon they're trading phrases like boxers trading jabs – quick, precise, relentless. Tally had mentioned her mother played, but this isn't playing – it's breathing music. It's alchemy.

My chest tightens watching her hands – hands so like her daughter's. Each chord progression twists the knife deeper, a reminder of the woman whose skin I've memorized but whose heart remains frustratingly out of reach.

She catches my eye across the room, smiles, and nods. I return the gesture.

After an hour, the band takes a break, and Marisa makes her way over to me. "Cameron," she says. "You're back."

"I am," I nod. "Your piano playing is incredible. When did you start performing here?"

"Just a month ago," she says. "Tally surprised me with a

baby grand, and it's like my fingers remembered what to do."

A baby grand in that tiny apartment? Where would it fit?

Marisa soon answers that question. "We found this adorable 1920s bungalow in Echo Park." She sweeps her hand through the air. "You should see it—front porch, sloped attic ceilings, original hardwoods everywhere. I swear you can almost hear the ghosts of flappers laughing with their cigarette holders, dancing until dawn. There's this magnificent pepper tree in the backyard that must've been just a sapling when the house was new. Now it towers over everything. Perfect compromise for Tally—she was dreading suburban life, but this way she gets a real house without leaving the city. No more neighbors stomping overhead or complaining when the baby cries. And it's close to her studio. Best of all worlds for Tally."

Tally moved into a house after her baby was born. It made sense—her old apartment would have felt like a shoebox with both her and her mother tripping over each other while trying to care for a newborn.

I nod. "Well. Tell Tally I say hi."

She hesitates, her gaze locked with mine. Something flickers behind her eyes—a question, maybe, or a confession—as she studies my face. Her lips part, then press together, once, twice. I arch an eyebrow, silently urging her forward, but whatever courage she'd gathered dissolves with a small shake of her head.

"I'll tell Tally I saw you," she murmurs.

Then she's gone, swallowed by the sea of bodies around us.

Chapter Twenty

TALLY

The bedroom light blazes on at 3 AM. Mom's silhouette hovers in the doorway.

"Get the fuck out of here!" I snarl, blinking against the assault. Like I need this shit. Brinley's already got me on some twisted newborn schedule where five minutes of sleep feels like a luxury. I just got her latched, fed, and back down after what felt like the hundredth time tonight. For once, I'd actually drifted into real sleep—the kind where your brain fires up those weird-ass dreams. Nothing cool, though. No wild sex or superhero flying. Just the classics: wandering naked through Target while everyone pretends not to notice, or showing up to a final exam for a class I'd forgotten existed. Seriously, brain? With all the tattoo designs I've created, you can't cook up something better than me failing calculus again?

"I won't get out of here!" Mom screams right back.

Oh, fuck. Is she drunk? If she's fallen off the wagon, I'm calling the psych ward to come get her. I used to cut Mom all kinds of slack, but that was before Brinley. Now I'm lucky to get three hours of sleep, which means I show up at Manic Muse ready to throat-punch anyone who breathes wrong. My hands shake so bad I can barely hold the tattoo gun steady. One slip-up and I'm screwed. No sleep means no steady hands. No steady hands means no job. No job means no house. And the thought of my baby girl homeless keeps me up at night—when I'm not already up with her. So if Mom's popping pills again—or drinking, which she knows damn well she can't do even if booze wasn't her poison of choice—I'm gonna completely lose my shit.

I bolt upright at the sound of Brinley's wail. Shit! I glare at Mom before dragging myself to the nursery. When was the last time I slept more than forty consecutive minutes? I scoop up my screaming bundle, collapse into the rocking chair, and guide her to my breast. As she latches on, I rock and wonder how our species survived this long. Between the endless feeding, the diaper changes that require hazmat suits, the random crying jags, and getting puked on more times than I can count—who signs up for this willingly? And some women do this multiple times? Christ. At least I dodged the Kensington twin curse. Cameron's brothers came in matching sets—twice. If I had two of these tiny sleep-terrorists instead of one? Just hand me the straitjacket now.

I narrow my eyes at Mom. "Any particular reason you decided to barge in my room and blind me at three in the morning? Some of us have to drag our asses to work by seven." I blow out a breath, glancing down at the squirming bundle in my arms. "Though I guess the little gremlin here was about to wake the whole neighborhood anyway, so consider yourself pardoned."

She rubs the back of her neck. "Look, I ran into Cam

tonight. The way you're hiding this baby from him—it's not right. He should know he has a child."

Cam's back. I nod. Should be doing cartwheels or some shit, but my brain's running on fumes from zero sleep.

Then it hits me like a freight train—Cam's fucking back. No more hiding Brinley. No taking back the truth once it's out there. I'm gonna have to swallow whatever comes next. If he goes all helicopter boyfriend, that's on me. If he whips out some gaudy-ass diamond and drops to one knee, I'll have to crush his dreams right there. He'll probably at least want to play house, and I'm about as girlfriend material as a cactus on a good day. Now? With my hormones making me either homicidal or a human sprinkler system? Forget it. Yesterday I lost it and started sobbing over a goddamn Pampers commercial. A commercial! Some corporate asshole in a suit designed that shit specifically to manipulate people, and I fell for it. And it wasn't even one of those sad-puppy ASPCA spots that normally turn me into a blubbery mess.

"Well, thanks for telling me. And you didn't tell him, did you?"

Mom shakes my head. "No way. You'd have kicked me to the curb if I told him. That's the only reason I kept quiet. But damn, Tally, he looked wrecked when I saw him at Indigo last night."

"Wrecked? Please." I snort, bouncing the fussy baby against my shoulder. "What's he got to be miserable about? I'm the one doing life without parole with this little demon. Meanwhile, he's out there living his best bachelor life, playing his piano and singing for an appreciative crowd. Cry me a fucking river."

Jesus, I'm being a total witch today—worse than my

usual charming self. Blame it on the toxic cocktail of my natural cynicism mixed with these hormone tsunamis.

I shake my head. "Didn't mean that. I'm just so exhausted I can't see straight and…" The tears ambush me right there in the rocking chair while Brinley nurses, oblivious. "What the fuck did I do here? I've gotta stand at the shop today for eight hours when all I want is to hibernate for a week. Every shirt I own is decorated with baby puke. These hormones are making me crazy and…."

How do I even say this next part? That sometimes when I look at this tiny human, I fantasize about handing her to some random stranger on the street, then crawling into bed and pretending none of this ever happened. God. She didn't ask to exist. And here I am, thinking about pawning her off—exactly what Mom did to me more times than I can count...

"Tally," Mom leans forward. "Tell me how you really feel about Brinley. Complete honesty. It matters."

I shake my head. The truth is too monstrous to voice. I'm supposed to be a mother now. Aren't mothers programmed to fall hopelessly in love at first sight? Isn't that maternal instinct supposed to make everything worth it—the sleepless nights, the cracked nipples, the body that feels like a stranger's, the hormonal rollercoaster, the complete demolition of the life I knew?

But when I look at her, I feel... nothing. She might as well be some creature from another planet. When I stare into those eyes, I don't see my daughter. I see a stranger who hijacked my body and my life.

I drag my hands down my face. "Oh, Mom, I'm drowning here. Some days I think about adoption—just handing her over to someone who knows what the hell they're doing. Yesterday I almost tattooed a butterfly on this guy who asked for a dragon. A fucking butterfly! When the dude asked for a dragon! My hands shake so bad from being up all night that I can barely hold the gun steady. And clients have to repeat themselves because my brain's just... mush. One of these days I'm gonna nod off mid-session and burn someone, and there goes my business, 'cause I'll be sued." I swallow hard. "But I can't stop working with that $200,000 loan hanging over my head. I'm trapped, Mom. All because of this...this tiny person I didn't ask for."

Mom gives a slow nod. "We need to find someone who can help with the baby."

"Who? I'm broke, Mom. This house is eating me alive. Should've stayed in my crappy apartment. Yeah, there wasn't room for us all, but it was one helluva lot cheaper than this house and I didn't have to take out a massive personal loan to live there." I shake my head as I burp the little monster. "We could've made it work. I could've crammed Brinley into my room. Yeah, it couldn't have worked long-term, because at some point, she needs her own room, but I guess I could've crossed that bridge when I came to it. But now..." I shake my head. "It's so close to everything going to shit. I lose my business and that's it. We're all out on the fucking street."

"Tally." Mom's voice cuts through my spiral. "Take a breath. This isn't the end of the world. Every new mother has stood where you're standing, running on fumes and wondering how they'll make it through another day."

I might not be the first woman to go through this.

But it sure feels like I am.

Chapter Twenty-One

CAMERON

My phone buzzes with a text from Tally's mom, just a day after our chance encounter at The Indigo. Last night when she'd asked for my number, I'd handed it over despite finding the request a bit strange. Now, staring at her message, I understand exactly why she'd been so eager to get my contact information.

I hope you can come over tonight. I'll cook. But you need to talk to Tally and she's not in a good place, so she might not contact you. 7?

Sure. Am free tonight, don't have a job to go to as I am transitioning into sports medicine and my fellowship doesn't start for six months.

Oh my goodness, that would be perfect! Tally could use your help, even if she won't come out and ask for it. See you at 7?

See you at 7.

I shake my head, staring at the message. Not from Tally. From her mother. Of course. Tally would sooner walk barefoot across hot coals than ask anyone for help.

Something clicks into place inside me, like a dislocated shoulder being reset. For the next six months, before my sports medicine fellowship starts, I've got nowhere to be. I could be there for her—help her figure out this whole baby thing. Even if the kid isn't mine, it's a part of her.

And God help me, I'd still walk through fire for that woman.

Chapter Twenty-Two

TALLY

I snap my gloves on at the tattoo studio, the latex cracking like a warning shot. "Twitch one more time and your phoenix gets a dick for a head," I tell the guy in my chair, who's been jerking every time the needle hits his shoulder blade. He laughs, all nervous teeth. The businessman waiting his turn scrolls through his phone, pretending not to hear me tell him he's "dancing on my last functioning nerve cell" when he asks—for the third time—how much longer.

But the needle in my hand moves like it's possessed by something holy today. Each line flows black and perfect into skin. No tremor, no hesitation. Like those stories nurses tell—how some dying patient will suddenly sit up, eat a full plate of hospital meatloaf, laugh at old jokes. Family members start calling relatives: "Come quick, she's better!" Then the monitors go silent. Seems like I'm getting a similar second wind from god knows where.

I wipe ink from a perfect wing tip, wondering if this is the last dance.

After eight hours on my feet, I drag myself through

the front door to find Mom's lasagna waiting on the table. Brinley's cooing in her bassinet, not a care in the world, and somehow my closet's stocked with clean clothes I definitely didn't wash or fold and Brinley's is as well. I'd be screwed without Mom, which makes her schedule even more miraculous—she races to pound out jazz standards at Indigo three nights a week, and fills in the other evenings at The Ember Room on Sunset with whatever band needs a pianist. Between all that, she still manages to keep my kid alive and fed while making sure I don't drown in baby spit-up and dirty onesies. I don't deserve her.

But her smile is a little off. She's up to something. Dammit. What is her game?

"What?" I ask her.

She shrugs. I just look at her, trying to figure out what she's hiding. Because she's hiding something. That much is plain.

And then I hear the doorbell ring and my heart stops. I look at Mom. "What did you do?"

She shrugs again and walks towards the door and there stands Cameron on my front porch, on the other side of the screen door. Holy. Fucking. Hell. Cameron stands there like sex incarnate in that dark t-shirt stretched tight across his chest, those stone-washed jeans hugging every goddamn inch of him, and those boots that make me want to be stepped on. His wavy hair falls just below his ears, begging for my fingers to grip it. My skin burns like I've been branded, every nerve ending screaming his name. My heart slams against my ribs so hard I swear he must hear it. Before the baby, just looking at Cameron made me wet. Now? These postpartum hormones have turned me feral. I want to tear his clothes off with my teeth, pin him to the mattress, and fuck him until neither of us remembers our own names.

Just then, Brinley starts her high-pitched, ear-splitting wailing, and the spell between us shatters like dropped crystal. Cameron's head snaps toward the sound, and something shifts in his face—a flicker of pain followed by a softening around his eyes. His fingers twitch at his sides, as if reaching for a bottle or a burp cloth that isn't there. I can see the muscle memory etched into his body.

After all, he lost his baby daughter, and I'd bet my favorite tattoo gun he was the type who not only changed diapers at 3 a.m. but probably sang lullabies while doing it, the kind of father who warmed bottles of mama's breast milk to the perfect temperature while she caught precious hours of sleep. He has that gentle-but-capable energy of a man who wouldn't dream of doing the bare minimum, but insisted on carrying his full half of the parenting load—maybe even more.

I force a smile. "Cam. Come on in." I shoot daggers at Mom, who's standing there with this shit-eating grin plastered across her face. I'll get her back for this ambush later. Still, seeing Cameron doesn't completely suck—partly because the chemistry between us could power a small city, but mostly because he might be my ticket out of this mess with Brinley. Maybe he'll take her. Permanently. Because I can't do this.

Brinley deserves someone who actually wants her around. I know what it's like growing up wondering if you're wanted—though with Mom, it was different. Even bouncing between foster homes, I knew somewhere deep down she loved me. She just couldn't beat what was eating her alive from the inside. With Brinley, there's no addiction clouding things up. No complicated excuse. The truth is simpler and uglier: every time I look at her, something in me just... recoils.

Cam walks in as Brinley continues her hungry cry. I drag myself to her room, scoop her up, and collapse into the rocking chair. Christ, this kid's stomach is a black hole. Makes that stray cat I had—the one that howled for food like it was being murdered every two hours—seem reasonable. I get her latched and fed, change her diaper, and then find myself just staring.

Fuck me, she's gorgeous. Total Kensington through and through. Celeste nailed it when she said those genes bulldoze everything else. That dark hair. Those killer blue eyes with lashes that could start a damn fan club. Cameron's eyes, exactly. No way in hell anyone's buying she's not a Kensington. Kid hit the genetic jackpot.

I carry her to the living room and collapse onto the couch. My eyes burn, and I blink back tears I don't even understand. Exhaustion, maybe? For six weeks straight, it's been nothing but ink-slinging at Manic Muse all day, then tag-teaming with Mom at night. The second I drag my ass through the door, she's grabbing her purse to play piano at Indigo or Ember. No breaks. No sleep. Just me, Manic Muse and Brinley, around the fucking clock.

Or maybe I'm crying over what I did to Cam. Christ. Hiding his own kid from him while he was saving lives in Sicily? Ghosting him like some coward? Looking at him now, standing there in my living room with his perfect jawline and those concerned doctor eyes, I feel something crack inside me. When I look at Brinley, there's this weird emptiness. But when I look at him—her father—it's like someone turned the volume back up. And yeah, okay, maybe knowing he didn't run off with some sexy Italian doctor in a white coat makes it easier to admit my feelings for him. Either way, I'm drowning in guilt over the whole damn mess.

He's staring at Brinley, and I can see it in his eyes—the moment it clicks. Shit. The Kensington genes aren't exactly subtle. Those eyes, that chin—it's like someone photocopied his family features onto my little girl's face. My stomach knots as I watch him connect the dots. No more hiding behind lies. Time to rip off the Band-Aid and tell him what he's already figuring out just by looking at her—that little nose is pure Kensington, just like her father's.

I take a deep breath. "Cameron, meet Brinley. Your daughter."

His face freezes. "My—? But you told me—"

"I know what I told you." My voice cracks despite my attempt at nonchalance. I stare at a knot in the hardwood floor, counting the rings. My heart hammers against my ribs while my stomach twists itself into sailor's knots. The sight of him standing there—God, he looks good—makes me want to run to him and run away at the same time. What if he never forgives me for this?

Cameron's eyes lock with mine. "Why lie about her father?"

I exhale slowly as Mom bustles in with a steaming lasagna. She sets it down, beaming at Cameron and me. "Off to work," she announces, her fingers brushing my cheek. "Behave yourselves. Or don't—I'm hardly one to judge." With a theatrical wink, she's gone.

My stomach growls loudly. These days I'm perpetually famished—thank god breastfeeding torches calories like nobody's business. Between the baby and the drama, I haven't eaten a thing since yesterday.

"Sit down, and eat. I'm starving."

I settle Brinley into her bassinet beside me, her tiny coos

like background music while I pour Cameron's wine. The rich burgundy splashes into the glass, and I swear it winks at me as I reach for my sparkling apple juice. My mouth waters for just one sip of that Cabernet. Just one. But my milk-heavy breasts remind me why that's not happening tonight—or any night soon. I eye the bottle of wine and sigh. Add it to the list: wine, sleep, hot showers, spontaneous anything... all sacrificed at the altar of motherhood. The list grows daily.

Cameron obeys like a good boy and sits his ass down at the table. God, this is weird as fuck. A year of radio silence, when before Sicily we could jabber all night long. And yeah, we could do other things all night too, but it was the talking I missed most. That feeling when someone just gets you, you know? When you don't have to explain your jokes or apologize for your opinions. When someone sees all your rough edges and thinks they're perfect just as they are.

But now? Crickets. I've already demolished one plate of Mom's lasagna and I'm working on seconds, plus some salad with veggies from her garden that she's been babying all summer. Cameron just sits there across from me, not saying a damn word, which is freaking me out. His eyes keep darting to Brinley, but his face gives nothing away.

I can't take it anymore. The elephant in the room is about to suffocate me. "Say something about your daughter, please." My pulse is going like a jackhammer. I've really screwed myself this time, haven't I?

He nods. "Processing it." He shakes his head. "Why would you lie?" And then he narrows his eyes, and my heart sinks. Yeah. I probably really did screw up here. What if I screwed it up for good? What if he feels like he can't trust me? I guess I should think about that as a distinct possibility. Why would he trust me after this?

I take a sip of apple juice from a wine glass, my fingers trembling against the delicate stem. "Not my finest hour," I say, swirling the amber liquid like it's a fine Chardonnay. I always drink apple juice out of a wine glass because I like to pretend it's wine. As if this pathetic ritual could fool my brain into thinking I haven't surrendered every last pleasure to the tiny dictator laying beside me. But the glass doesn't change the taste, and it doesn't change the facts. This kid has hijacked my body, my identity, my whole damn life—and there's no escape clause in this contract.

His jaw tightens as he stares at me. "Not your finest hour?" The words come out clipped, controlled. "While I was in Sicily, I kept thinking about coming back here to find the man who—" He stops, swallows hard. "The man you claimed took advantage of you when you couldn't remember. I wanted to make him pay." His voice drops lower, trembling with barely contained emotion. "Do you have any idea what that was like? I've treated actual assault victims, women who've been through hell, and here you are..." He looks away, his knuckles white. "Using something that devastating as a convenient story to explain away our child."

Shit. I'd basically told him I was date-raped and knocked up. Who does that? But the thought of him picturing me willingly climbing into bed with some random dude felt worse somehow—like I'd cheated on him, even though we weren't together. My fingers trace the outline of the tattoo on my wrist, the one I'd gotten after my last epic screwup. Should've learned my lesson then. This lie was even worse than the truth, and now I was stuck with it, watching his face fall as he tries to be the good guy. Again.

I swallow hard. "Cam, I'm sorry. God, I'm so sorry. I just..." My voice catches. "I freaked out."

"Freaked out." He doesn't look at me, just stares at his

empty glass before reaching for the bottle. "And why exactly would telling me the truth be so terrifying? Is sharing a child with me really that unbearable?"

"Yes," I blurt. The word hangs between us like a slap. His shoulders stiffen, jaw clenching as he absorbs the blow. I watch his eyes go flat, distant. Shit. No taking that back. Idiot, idiot, idiot. "Wait, I didn't—"

"Save it," he cuts me off. "Message received. Apparently the idea of me in your life is your personal nightmare. Well, tough luck—we have a kid now. A kid whose name I never got to choose, by the way. So I guess you're stuck with me, no matter how badly you wish I'd disappear."

How do I tell him that the last thing I want is for him to disappear? I don't just see a lifeline when I look at him—someone to help with Brinley or take her off my hands like some kind of horseback-riding cavalry coming to save my ass. I want him because...he's Cam. Beautiful, sweet Cam who brews me coffee with the best beans, knowing exactly how I take it. Cam with his magic hands giving foot and back rubs that would make a massage therapist jealous. He actually listens when I rant about clients, then offers advice that works. Before Sicily, he taught me to cook so I wouldn't starve, but he'd rather be in the kitchen himself, putting Gordon Ramsay to shame. That whiskey-tinged voice when he sings breaks my heart, and he plays piano better than my professional pianist mother. When I forget my coat, his own is around my shoulders before I can shiver. He runs bubble baths with water at the perfect temperature. His heart is enormous—the man lived in a tent for a year helping the poorest of the poor. Cameron will be an amazing dad, and goddamn it, I should just let down these walls and let him be that amazing dad.

And Jesus, he's incredible in bed.

But I just can't get past the fact that I love my own style, I'm set in my ways like concrete, and I'd rather eat glass than share my space with some dude's recliner and sports memorabilia. My house is MY sanctuary—blood-red walls screaming with personality, a chandelier that explodes with bubbles of light, and a mural of jazz musicians so vibrant it practically bleeds sound. Marilyn Monroe stares down with sleeve tattoos that would make a biker jealous. My throw rug in the living room, right in front of my multi-colored couch, is a riot of swirly colors - pink, purple, blue, yellow. My shower curtain? A psychedelic elephant that hits you like an acid trip every morning. Every inch is me, raw and unfiltered. No compromise. No apologies.

And, of course, along with his no-doubt beige-on-beige bachelor furniture comes the death of everything that makes me ME. I can already feel my tattoo ink fading at the thought. I wasn't fucking built for this sharing-a-bathroom, compromise-on-dinner bullshit. No way in hell. And now with Brinley? Christ. I'll be trapped, cornered like some wild animal forced into domestication, watching my spirit shrivel up and die while I become some hollow-eyed version of myself serving goddamn pot roast on Sundays. I'd rather set myself on fire.

My brain's spinning with all this crap about how I don't need someone barging into my life, trying to sand down my edges and stuff me into some cookie-cutter mold. Then my mouth just opens, and I swear on every tattoo I've ever inked that it's the sleep deprivation talking. The hormones. The fact that my life's gone completely sideways.

"Don't leave," I hear myself say. "Just... take her. Take her away so I don't have to look at her anymore." The words hang there like cigarette smoke. Christ. That's exactly how I feel, but did I really just say that out loud?

I've just blown it completely. No guy—not even Cameron—would stick around after hearing that. "Take my daughter away so I never have to see her face again"? Who even says something that cruel? In other words, I not only want to be rid of her but be rid of him too. After everything else I've put him through, this is definitely his breaking point. Those words can't be unsaid. They're hanging between us now like a goddamn neon sign of my deepest, darkest thoughts. Freudian slip or whatever—that shit came from somewhere inside me.

But Cameron's reaction catches me off guard. His granite jaw unclenches. Those ice-chip blue eyes of his thaw right in front of me.

"Tally," he says, voice gentler than I deserve. "Are you saying you want me to take Brinley? That you never want to see her again?"

Shit. Cat's out of the bag now. This is Cam. My Cam. If I can't tell him the ugly truth, who can I tell? These feelings are eating me alive anyway.

"I feel nothing when I look at her," I say, my voice barely above a whisper. "Nothing good, anyway." My throat tightens. "Fuck, Cameron. Where's that magical mom-glow everyone promised? That rush of love that's supposed to make everything worth it? I keep waiting and waiting and—nothing. Just this... resentment. Like I'm staring at this tiny wrecking ball that demolished my entire life. Some days I fantasize about leaving her on someone's doorstep with a note pinned to her blanket, like I'm living in some Dickens novel."

He nods. "Do you have thoughts about hurting yourself or Brinley?"

I nod back. "Yeah. Not hurt her, but myself." I stare at a coffee stain on the floor. "Last night I counted ceiling cracks at 3 AM while she screamed in the next room. My tattoo gun slipped yesterday—client jerked away just in time. One bad Yelp review about burns, and my shop's done." I take a breath that catches in my throat. "Sometimes I'm driving along the coast, and I think about just... walking into the ocean until there's nothing but blue." I look up at him. "I won't though. Mom's finally sober, finally got a diagnosis. If I disappeared, she'd be back on the Oxy before my body washed up. She needs me to count her pills, drive her to therapy, be her goddamn lifeline." My voice shrinks. "So Brinley isn't why I don't go through with drowning myself. Just Mom. Sometimes when Brinley cries, all I see is this tiny thief who took everything from me. And I fucking hate myself for it."

I suck in air like I'm drowning while Cam's eyes bore into mine. His fingers brush the hair from my face—so gentle it hurts. That same gesture I used to flinch away from now feels like the only thing keeping me from shattering. It screams that he sees me—really sees me—and hasn't run for the hills.

"Tally," his voice cuts through the roaring in my ears. "This isn't you. It's postpartum depression ripping you apart." His jaw tightens. "The statistics don't lie. Women who've been through hell like you have—bounced between foster homes, abandoned, neglected—they're prime targets. Add your mother's bi-polar disorder into the mix, and you're fighting a war on multiple fronts, because the family history of mental illness might make you vulnerable. We need to get you help before this thing devours you whole."

"Worse than this?" My voice cracks.

"Remember Andrea Yates?" His words hit like ice water. "Five children. One bathtub. Five tiny bodies, one drowned after another. That's postpartum psychosis—when the depression mutates into something monstrous. I'm not saying you'd ever—" His voice breaks. "But I refuse to watch this disorder consume the woman I love. Not when we can kill it first."

The woman he…loves? My heart slams against my ribs like it's trying to escape. His words hang in the air between us, casual as a grenade with its pin pulled.

"How do you know so much about this?"

"Psych rotation," he says, his eyes darkening. "Had mothers grip my wrists until their nails drew blood, begging me to take their babies away before they did something unforgivable. Women who couldn't sleep because every time they closed their eyes, they saw themselves dropping their newborns from tenth-story windows. Mothers who'd wake up with their hands hovering over their child's throat, terrified of what they might do if they blacked out for even a second. These weren't monsters, Tally. They were just women whose own minds had turned against them. Like yours is doing now."

The tears come without warning, hot and fast down my cheeks. Something inside me cracks open at Cam's words. Not broken. Not a terrible mother. Just a woman with a chemical imbalance—something fixable, something with a name.

His arms encircle me, solid and warm as I dampen his shirt with my crying. "Shhh," he murmurs against my hair. "We're getting you help. Tonight."

I pull back just enough to see his face. "Tonight? Without appointments or waiting lists?"

"I can write the prescription myself." His voice is steady, certain. "There's a new medication specifically for post-partum depression—Zuranolone. Two weeks of daily pills that work differently than standard antidepressants. The success rate is remarkable."

When he brushes my bangs aside, his fingertips linger against my skin. Then his lips press against my forehead—gentle, reverent. Every instinct screams to push him away, to maintain my walls, but I find myself leaning into his touch instead, releasing a breath I didn't know I was holding.

"Aren't all pharmacies closed right now?" I ask, looking at the clock.

"I'll get it from the hospital," he says. "Matter of fact, going right now. I'll be back in a couple of hours."

He leaves, and I stare at the door before my eyes drift to Brinley, who's actually giving me a break for once. Her face looks almost angelic when she's not screaming—right fist curled over her belly, head tilted like she's listening to something far away. The Green Day *American Idiot* onesie I special-ordered rises and falls with each tiny breath. That stubborn tuft of dark hair sticks straight up from her crown, a cowlick identical to Cameron's. Something tightens in my chest, not quite love, but maybe its distant cousin. When she sighs in her sleep, I catch myself wondering what she's dreaming about. I have my own dream too—that someday I'll scoop her up and finally feel that thunderbolt everyone promised. That she'll transform from this life-hijacking tiny tyrant into something else entirely: my daughter. For real this time.

Cameron returns after what feels like forever, prescription bag in hand. "Got it," he says, shaking out a small pill. "The pharmacist said this stuff is pretty potent—you might notice a difference by morning. Give it a couple weeks, and the postpartum fog should lift and you'll be back to yourself."

I attempt a smile. "Not sure the world's ready for the return of regular Tally."

His expression softens. "The world might not be, but we are. That little girl in that bassinet needs the real you—tattoos, attitude, and all. The meds just help clear the path back."

I sigh. I hope he's right. Because if he's not, I'll feel more hopeless than ever.

Chapter Twenty-Three

CAMERON

I'm a father again. The realization hits me like a tidal wave—exhilarating and terrifying all at once. My fingers tremble as I think of holding another tiny hand in mine. Brinley. Even her name feels different on my tongue than Stephanie's did. It should. They're different souls, different hearts. Steph will always occupy that sacred corner of my memory, just as Alecia does. But now there's this new space opening up, unexpected and precious.

I run my hand through my hair, exhaling slowly. Tally lied to me, yes. But that's pure Tally—all sharp edges and steel walls. She'd rather cut herself than be caged. To her, having me thrust permanently into her life must feel like wearing handcuffs. Tally chooses her people carefully, deliberately. Being stuck with me because we had a kid together? That's her worst nightmare. If circumstances were different, and she wasn't forced into it, maybe she'd have chosen me. But now? With a baby between us? I'm just another thing she didn't ask for.

Tally clears the table without a word. I watch her movements, the slight tremor in her hands, the dark circles beneath her eyes that even her careful makeup can't hide. I have a proposition that might save her. She's drowning—anyone can see it. The prescription I wrote should help with the postpartum symptoms, but medication alone won't fix the impossible schedule she's keeping. Ten hours standing at her tattoo station, then home to Brinley's cries while her mother plays piano in smoky clubs until dawn. No wonder she's running on fumes. But her business would collapse without her there every day, so she needs to keep a marathon schedule there at the studio. Her mother told me that Tally's business secured a loan that was used as a down payment for this house, so if she takes a break from her business, she might lose her business and her house of cards would cave in.

Tally's situation is impossible. The tattoo studio demands long hours if she wants to keep the lights on, and her mother only helps with the baby until 7 PM before heading off to her piano gigs. The second Tally walks through her front door, she's on full-time mom duty without a break. Between running a business and raising a newborn single-handedly through the night, when is she supposed to sleep?

I could step in. With my six-month sabbatical, I could take Brinley, give Tally room to breathe. But there's the logistics. Fifteen miles between Brentwood and Echo Park might as well be fifty in L.A. traffic. Shuttling back and forth daily would exhaust us both. And Tally needs the overnight relief most—those 3 a.m. feedings that leave her hollow-eyed and stumbling through her days. I want her to bond with her daughter, not resent her. There has to be a better solution.

I reach for her hand. "Tally, let me help you."

She nods, her mascara tracking down her cheeks. This from a woman who once tattooed through a bar fight without flinching.

"I can't do this anymore, Cam," she whispers. "Take her. Please. I feel nothing when I look at her, and I'm drowning here. My clients are repeating themselves because I can't focus. Yesterday I nearly passed out with the needle still buzzing. My whole business—everything I built—it's slipping away."

I squeeze her fingers. "I'll take her home with me if that's what you really want. But this medication will help, Tally. And when it does, you might see her differently. You might want to be her mom."

She nods, her hands trembling visibly. "What exactly are you offering here?"

I take a deep breath. She's going to run for the hills when she hears this, but here goes. "Let me move in temporarily—just six months. I've got time. Left the ER before Sicily, and my sports medicine fellowship doesn't start until next year." I lean forward. "You need sleep, Tally. I can handle Brinley's midnight screams, diaper blowouts, all of it. I can tell from a cry whether she's hungry or needs changing or just wants to be held. You pump, I'll handle night feedings." I meet her eyes directly. "And I'll be there for you too. Cooking, cleaning, whatever you need while you're working at the shop. No strings attached."

All I want is to support her and the baby, to make sure they have everything they need. Knowing Tally, she'll probably flip me off and insist she doesn't need anyone's help. Then what? I'd hate to involve lawyers, but I won't be shut out of my child's life. Not an option.

She inhales slowly, her shoulders rising, then falling as she exhales.

"I need some time to process this," she says finally.

I nod, relief washing over me. She didn't slam the door in my face.

It's something.

Not sure what, but it's something.

Chapter Twenty-Four

TALLY

When Cameron suggests moving in, I nearly throw my arms around him. God, I've been praying for this—someone to actually help. Mom tries, but with her bi-polar disorder, she needs solid sleep. She staggers home from the clubs at 3 a.m., crashes until noon, and by the time I drag myself back from the tattoo studio, she's already applying her makeup to head out again. Our schedules barely touch. Meanwhile, I'm running on fumes, working all day and up with Brinley's feedings all night. The thought of someone taking even one of those 2 a.m. bottles makes me want to weep with relief.

But shit—it's Cam. Cameron fucking Kensington. The man I've been trying not to fall for. Him moving in? My stomach knots. We'd be like some married couple, sharing a bathroom, seeing each other's morning breath, living in each other's space day after day. The walls of my house suddenly feel like they're closing in. If he moves in here, I'm trapped.

Only one way this can work.

I take a deep breath. "All right. You can move in here to

help with Brinley." The words come out in a rush. "Look, I need help most at 3 AM when she's screaming her head off, and I can't exactly have you driving back and forth at all hours while I'm trying to get enough sleep to function at work. That's just... ridiculous." I glance around my cramped apartment. "But you've got that gorgeous place of yours. Are you sure you want to squeeze in here? There's barely room to breathe."

He starts to say something, but I interrupt.

I clear my throat. "Look, I need to set some ground rules. If you're moving in, we're strictly roommates. No benefits. No...entanglements. It'll mess with my head." I force myself to meet his eyes. "Just friends raising our kid together. And we both need to be free to date other people."

His expression shifts from confusion to something harder to read. "I understand," he says quietly. "Platonic co-parents only."

"Exactly. It's not like we had anything serious before anyway. Just great sex and..." My voice trails off. I'm such a liar. I remember how he'd snort-laugh at the most ridiculous parts of *What We Do In the Shadows,* how he'd quote *It's Always Sunny in Philadelphia* at random moments, matching my twisted sense of humor beat for beat.

It was those nights on my rusty fire escape, stars above us, city below, talking until our voices went hoarse. Him actually listening when I rambled about my childhood. Me hanging on every word about his travels. How sometimes our hands would find each other's in the dark without either of us acknowledging it. How I'd catch myself wondering what it might be like to wake up to that face every morning, not just after hookups.

He nods. "I get it. If there's sex, there's…"

"Strings," I say. "At least in my head. And we've already

got enough strings between us to make a damn symphony orchestra." I fidget with the sleeve of my tattoo, tracing the outline of a swallow. "Before, when we hooked up, I knew you had a plane ticket with your name on it. An exit strategy. I could enjoy the ride knowing it had a final stop." I look up at him. "Great sex. Great laughs. But temporary. The way I like it."

"Because when people leave," Cameron finishes for me, "you can finally exhale."

Damn him for knowing me so well.

I fidget with my sleeve, tugging at the ink-stained cuff. "Look, I need the help—like, desperately need it. But fair warning: you'd be bunking in the attic. Total *Jane Eyre* vibes, minus the whole setting-things-on-fire part." I wave my hand upward. "It's actually pretty sweet up there. High ceilings, decent floors, windows that actually open. Was saving it for Brinley's playroom someday, but..." I catch myself rambling and smile. "Celeste told me about your Brentwood house. How you're basically neighbors with Spielberg and Reese Witherspoon. Trading celebrity neighbors and a mansion for my Echo Park shoebox is a serious downgrade. But I can't move in with you in Brentwood—it's an hour in traffic and I'd lose my mind sitting in traffic for hours every day."

He inhales slowly. "Okay."

"Okay?"

"Yeah. I'll move in. Roommates who raise a kid together."

"Oh, thank God." My arms twitch with the urge to throw them around his neck, but I plant my feet firmly on the floor. One brush of skin and these pregnancy hormones would short-circuit my common sense. The air between us practically crackles, same as always. One touch and we'd be tearing each other's clothes off before the ink even dried on our little roommate agreement.

Holy shit, I have actual help now! My shoulders drop three inches as I exhale. Cameron's going to be amazing with Brinley, and maybe I'll finally get more than four consecutive hours of sleep.

But him living here? Recipe for disaster. Every time he walks by smelling like sandalwood and clean laundry, my hormones will do the cha-cha. And I basically told him to date whoever he wants because we're "just roommates." If he brings home some perky nurse, I'll smile and nod while mentally setting fire to her scrubs.

This arrangement has "terrible idea" written all over it. Whatever.

Brinley has someone else to rock her at 3 AM, and right now, that's all I give a damn about.

Chapter Twenty-Five

CAMERON

After spending that first night at Tally's, I swung by Elliot's place. I'd already grabbed my clothes from home and wanted to drop by and see my friend before heading back to her. We'd worked out an arrangement—I'd move in, but I had to be home by ten every night. That's her bedtime, non-negotiable. The woman needs her eight hours or she turns into a sleep-deprived demon at the tattoo studio. Her words, not mine. Something about "wanting to stab the next person who asks for a butterfly tramp stamp."

I swirl the wine in my glass, watching the ripples across Elliot's pool mirror the amber liquid. The evening sun casts long shadows as I finally break the silence.

"So, what's your take on this whole Tally situation?" I ask, though I can practically hear his response already. Elliot's going to think I've lost my mind—moving in with a woman who's keeping me at arm's length, all to be near a child she tried to claim isn't mine. He'll see right through me, know that I'm hoping proximity will spark something more than co-parenting. That beneath all my doctor's logic,

I'm betting everything on the foolish notion that sharing a roof might somehow build us into the family I can't stop imagining.

Elliot snorts. "You' re delusional if you think that setup will last between you two. Not with all those unresolved feelings hanging in the air."

"My feelings, anyway. I doubt she feels the same."

"Oh, come off it." Elliot rolls his eyes. "Every woman I've ever met wants to put a ring on your finger yesterday—Sarah included." His mouth quirks up at the corner, and I shake my head. His wife definitely does not have designs on me. "You're like catnip to the female population. The GQ looks, the humanitarian hero complex, that bleeding heart of yours. Throw in the trust fund and the MD after your name, and you're basically irresistible. So yeah, I'm betting Tally's plotting to rope you in as we speak."

I can't help but smile. If anyone's the one being pursued here, it's her. She's like some wild, beautiful creature that won't be tamed, while I'm just the guy standing at the fence with an apple, hoping she might come closer. Sad, but true.

I grip my coffee mug tighter. "Look, I want to be in my daughter's life. Tally's calling the shots right now. A custody battle would be hell for everyone, especially Brinley. Besides, I'm between jobs—sabbatical until my sports medicine fellowship starts. Perfect timing to step up."

"And when the fellowship begins?"

I shrug, trying to look more confident than I feel. "We'll cross that bridge later. By then, hopefully we'll be together. Maybe a bigger place in Echo Park, hire a nanny."

"Your Brentwood house isn't an option?"

"She'd have to commute to her studio. It's a non-starter."

“And your fellowship is at UCLA, right?”

"Right."

"And UCLA's what—five miles from Brentwood? Fifteen from Echo Park?" He tilts his head, eyebrows raised. "You're bending over backwards while she gives nothing."

"Then maybe I can go ahead and talk her into moving into my Brentwood home," I say. "Again, I'll cross that bridge when I come to it."

I don't mention the commute she'd hate, or how ridiculous it would be suggesting she relocate her Arts District tattoo studio to Beverly Hills, which is the closest retail area to my house. Those pristine, spa-like tattoo places in Beverly Hills? Tally would sooner set herself on fire than work somewhere with cucumber water and ambient music.

Eliot leans forward. "So what's your plan to convince her this isn't just some temporary thing?"

I shrug.

"Right. You'll figure it out as you go." He rubs his temples. "Christ, Cameron. You're putting an awful lot of faith in future-you to solve this mess."

I just nod. "What's wild is how Tally keeps pushing me to see other people. Like she's giving me permission to date around while we co-parent. I'm all in for raising our child together, but bringing another relationship into this situation? That feels like asking for trouble."

Elliot shoots me a knowing look. "But I can tell you're considering it—thinking maybe dating someone else would make her jealous enough to finally claim you. Tale as old as time. Fair warning though—even if that works to get her attention, it won't address why she's keeping you at arm's length in the first place. Have you figured out what's behind all those walls she's built? Why she runs from anything resembling commitment?"

I let out a sigh. "Tally was bounced around foster homes

like a pinball. Every time she thought she'd go back to her mom for good, something fell apart. Turns out her mother was battling bi-polar disorder without even knowing it until recently. She's on meds now, doing okay." I rub my neck. "But the damage is done. Tally doesn't believe anything lasts. She's learned to count on exactly one person—herself. Makes her stubborn as hell and allergic to letting anyone in. I'm basically trying to scale a fortress with nothing but my bare hands."

Elliot leans forward, his eyes narrowing. "So, if there weren't a kid involved, would you keep pursuing Tally? Just curious if your interest in this woman who keeps you at arm's length is because there's a kid between you two or whether there's something real there for you."

My answer erupts before he finishes the question.

"Hell yes," I say, slamming my palm against the table. "I'd crawl through broken glass to be with her. And don't ask me why because I can't—I just—" I drag my hands through my hair, my chest burning. "She shattered me awake. After Alecia and Stephanie, I was a ghost. But those 38 days with Tally? I felt blood pumping through my veins again. Every morning I woke up starving for her. So yes. I'd still fight for her even if Brinley had never taken a single breath on this earth."

I meant every syllable, but hearing those words come out of my mouth shocked even me. Christ, this is the second time I've let my guard down. Just yesterday, I called her "the woman I love" right to her face. Did she notice? The flash in her eyes tells me she did. And now she's going to bolt like a startled deer.

Way to go, genius.

Chapter Twenty-Six

TALLY

Cameron stayed the night after finding out about Brinley, and holy shit—I finally SLEPT. Like, actually fucking slept. He got up with her three different times, handling those midnight feedings with my pumped breast milk like some kind of baby whisperer. I was so goddamn unconscious I didn't even dream. Dinner at 7, hammering out our new arrangement settled by 7:30, and then I face-planted into oblivion. It was my day off from Manic Muse—Mondays we lock that shit down tight—and I didn't resurface until 7 the next evening. So, yeah, slept like the dead for 24 hours straight. When I zombie-walked into the living room, Mom had vanished to her gig, and there was Cam, cradling Brinley in the rocking chair. My uterus practically exploded. Marriage proposal from me was right on the tip of my tongue.

But I swallowed it back. Even when he announced he'd made chicken parm—MY WEAKNESS—from absolute scratch. Even when he poured me sparkling apple juice in an actual wine glass like I was some kind of queen. I inhaled that food like a death row inmate getting her last meal. Jesus Christ, his sauce should be illegal—fresh tomatoes he boils and peels himself, simmering all day like he's channeling some ancient Sicilian grandmother. Which technically he is—his mom was Sicilian, though somehow blonde while the rest of her family looked straight out of a Roman fresco.

It took superhuman restraint not to climb him like a fucking tree right there at the dinner table. To not rip his clothes off and ride him until neither of us could walk straight. But I CAN'T. We're "platonic roommates" now. The second we cross that line, my brain will short-circuit, convince me this is real, and I'll bolt so fast I'll leave a me-shaped hole in the wall. The ONLY way this works is if I mentally file him under "Geoffrey from college"—strictly roommate territory. Nothing more.

Tonight, I finally get to see my girls. First night out since Brinley popped into the world and strapped me to the house like some kind of adorable ball and chain. Celeste and Olivia have visited, sure, but there's a difference between them coming over while I'm trapped in mom-mode versus me strutting into our Venice Beach hangout as just Tally again.

And holy shit, do I feel amazing. Cameron's been on night duty for five days straight. After hibernating for a full twenty-four hours that first night, I've been sleeping like the dead every night since. Eight nightly uninterrupted hours will make you feel superhuman after months of zombie-mode.

That prescription for the baby blues must be working too, because I've finally had that moment everyone talks about—that lightning bolt of pure, overwhelming love for my daughter. I'm not just seeing a tiny screaming machine anymore; I'm seeing this perfect little person. She's actually a good baby when she's not demanding food or diaper changes (which, yeah, still happens two or three times a night, poor Cameron). The rest of the time she just lies there, making those little baby noises, waving her tiny fists and kicking her feet. And that smile—fuck me—when her whole face lights up, it's like staring into the sun.

I pull up to The Sea Glass, our beach-side watering hole, and spot the girls at one of the outdoor tables. After a round of hugs, they all just stare at me.

"What?" I ask, patting my face. "Do I have spit-up on me somewhere?"

Celeste tilts her head. "No, it's just... you're glowing. Like, actual new-mom glowing."

I snort. "Trust me, a week ago I was the poster child for sleep deprivation. My skin was this special shade of greige—you know, when you're so tired you're both grey and beige? But Cam moving in has been a game-changer. Five days of actual sleep has done more for me than all the fancy serums in the world. I've slept more this week than I did during Brinley's entire first two months combined."

Celeste's hands fly up in a T-shape. "Hold up. Cam moved in? With you?"

I nod. "Yeah, but we've got rules."

"Rules?"

"Boundaries. We're not a couple. No hooking up, no cuddling, nothing like that."

Celeste gapes at me like I just announced I'm giving up oxygen. "You're kidding me. Why on earth—"

"Girl," Olivia cuts in, waving her hand like she's overheating, "I cannot fathom how you resist climbing that man like a tree every damn day. Especially when he's doing all those sexy domestic things—cooking dinner, folding laundry, handling diaper duty. Sweet Jesus." She fans herself harder. "The first time I saw a man that fine changing my baby's diaper, I'd be dragging him to the bedroom before he could wash his hands."

I exhale slowly. "Look, I know it sounds crazy. But my head's a complete mess right now. If we keep the physical things off the table, I can convince myself he's just some guy sharing rent." I let them process that ridiculous notion—Cameron Kensington, walking magazine cover, relegated to 'roommate.' "Plus, I told him we're both free to date other people. Not that I'm looking." I shake my head. "It's this weird primal thing—I'm only interested in him. Like my body chemistry is locked onto the father of my baby. His scent drives me wild while random guys do nothing. Pure biology. Can't fight nature."

I absorb the reality of our situation. Cameron could be with anyone. So could I—at least in theory. But who am I kidding? My eyes slide right past every other man on the street like they're invisible. Meanwhile, there's Cameron, rocking Brinley to sleep while I get a full night's rest. There he is, drawing me a bath with just the right amount of bubbles, brewing coffee exactly how I like it, or cooking dinner without being asked.

There he is, bonding with my mother - a few days ago, I walked in to find him and Mom hunched over the chess board, his forehead creased in concentration as she studied him with grudging respect. A day later, they were at the baby grand together, his fingers following hers across a haunting melody she'd written years ago. Every damn time he does these things—these perfectly Cameron things—I have to physically restrain myself from dragging him to bed and keeping him there for days. Instead, I swallow hard and look away.

Celeste shakes her head. "You're playing with fire. You're telling Cameron that he can date anybody he wants? And what if he takes you up on it?"

My stomach knots at the image of Cameron with someone else—his hand on another woman's back, that smile directed at her instead of me. I dig my fingernails into my palm.

"It's fair," I manage. "I can't give him what he needs. The whole wife-and-mother package? That's not me. I'd suffocate. With Cameron being nothing but a roommate, I can breathe because there's no pressure. But he deserves someone who wants the whole deal, and I care enough to step aside if that happens."

"Really?" Olivia asks. "Tal, would you really be okay if Cameron meets somebody else?"

I force a casual shrug, though my throat tightens. "If Cameron meets his dream woman, I won't stand in his way. Sure, I'll miss having him around—he's been amazing with everything. But he wouldn't abandon us completely. He'd probably even help find a nanny to pick up the slack if he remarries somebody else."

Celeste and Olivia just sit there, giving me those looks. The ones that say they can see right through my bullshit. And they're right. The thought of Cameron with another woman makes me want to punch something. Or someone. But what choice do I have? He deserves to be happy, and I'm a walking disaster area.

I suck in air through my teeth, blinking back the hot sting behind my eyes. Cameron kissing someone new. Cameron's hands on someone else's body. Some faceless woman wearing his ring, carrying his baby. Jesus. If that happens—when that happens—it'll gut me like a fish. That's the kind of pain you don't come back from.

I raise my glass. "Listen, this meeting tonight was not supposed to be 'the poor Tally' show. Now come on, ladies, fill me in on all the gossip I've been missing since Brinley was born."

Olivia nearly spits out her wine. "Oh my God, you won't believe this bride I had last week. Demanded we serve sushi —at an outdoor wedding. In August."

I scrunch my nose. I love sushi, but it needs to be fresh. Sushi at an outdoor wedding in August. No. Just no.

"What about you, Celeste?" I ask.

Celeste scrolls through her phone, then holds it up to show me a photo. "Max took this of Violet at the beach house. And I just sold a series treatment to Netflix. I'll be the showrunner!"

We all clink our glasses at that one. Celeste is so amazing. Just a few years ago, she was struggling to sell any of her screenplays. Now she'll be developing a whole series!

"And Patricia?" I ask, my voice dropping.

Celeste's eyes light up. "Mom's scans came back clean again. Remember how gray she looked a few years ago? Now she's planning a cruise with Cameron and Max's dad."

I nod, thinking about the experimental treatment Max paid for—the one her insurance wouldn't cover. The one that costs more than my yearly mortgage payments.

"So, give me the Hollywood dirt," I say. This is our ritual - Celeste is a screenwriter and her hubby is a major movie studio CEO, so she knows it all.

Then Celeste lunges forward so abruptly her necklace clatters against the table, her voice dropping to a hiss. "So Bryce Harrington? Complete nightmare on set. Threw an actual tantrum—like, screaming, stomping, the works—because they gave him green M&Ms instead of blue ones. Fired two PAs on the spot." She stabs her finger against her wineglass with each syllable. "And Madeline Frost? God. She trapped my husband against a wall at the Vanity Fair party, practically frothing at the mouth about her 'revolutionary' skin care line until security had to intervene." Olivia and I lock eyes, electric with gossip-lust, then practically dive across the table, knocking over a saltshaker in our scramble to get closer.

Yes. This is the good shit. Just normal, everyday stuff. Coming home to my kid, but also knowing Cameron's got my back when I need a minute to breathe. Win-win-win situation right here.

Unless Cameron hooks up with someone. Then we're in uncharted territory.

But I'll dynamite that particular problem when it explodes in my face.

Chapter Twenty-Seven

TALLY

I walk in after visiting the girls and find Cameron in the living room, Brinley nestled against his chest in one of those baby slings I used to mock—yet seeing him like that makes me melt. He's folding laundry, and the instant our eyes meet, both his face and Brinley's light up. She kicks and reaches for me, as though she already knows me. At barely three months old, she's already showing personality, and, thanks to whatever is in my meds, I can't help but feel overwhelmed with love every time I look at her.

"How were the girls?" Cameron asks, unfastening Brinley from the sling and passing her to me. She cups my cheeks and coos; I choke back tears.

"They were… the girls," I shrug. "They both think I'm nuts for our arrangement." I want to admit I feel insane too—only a madwoman would risk losing a man like Cameron. "Who's my beautiful girl?" I ask Brinley while she gurgles, coos, smiles and grabs my nose. I shake my head at her. "Who's my beautiful girl?"

God, I'm doing the one thing I swore I wouldn't -

cooing at a baby in a sing-song baby-talk voice. But I can't help it. She really is my beautiful girl and I need to tell her that.

Cameron watches us for a second, a huge grin on his face. And then he motions to the piano. "Sit at the piano. I've written something for Brinley—a song I want to play at Indigo this Friday. Tell me what you think. Oh, and don't worry: I've asked Patricia to watch Brinley so we can have a night out."

I slide onto the piano bench beside him, confident this melody will be stunning; Cameron never does anything halfway.

He taps the keys and smiles. "Your mom actually helped me craft the melody. She's an incredible composer with this offbeat perspective—something she shares with many creative minds who live with bipolar. Even under treatment, her creativity is as vivid as ever."

As he plays, he talks about historical figures linked to bipolar: Beethoven, Van Gogh, Virginia Woolf, Tolstoy, Churchill, Hemingway, even Isaac Newton. "I really admire your mom," he says softly. "Her courage to face her challenges and ask for help—that's something extraordinary."

I love the song, from its haunting minor-key melody to the raw, honest lyrics that catches in his throat. The song isn't dripping with saccharine sentiment like some tracks famous musicians have written for their offspring. Take "Isn't She Lovely" – those sparkling piano riffs had me hooked until I discovered Stevie Wonder penned it for his newborn daughter. Suddenly all I could hear was the musical equivalent of a diaper commercial. Don't even get me started on Creed's "With Arms Wide Open" with its overwrought vocals practically drowning in father-son tears. But not all parent-to-child musical offerings make me want to gag. Radiohead's Thom Yorke crafted that eerie, dissonant lullaby that feels more like a beautiful nightmare than a nursery rhyme, and Alanis Morissette's song for her kids, "Ablaze" has razor-sharp lyrics that cut through the typical baby-talk bullshit. Cameron's song belongs in that rare category – it's got teeth and truth, with syncopated rhythms that make your hips move and lyrics that make your heart ache.

I clap when he's finished with it and Brinley, who's sitting next to us in a special high chair with little cartoon giraffes on the tray, starts pumping her tiny fists and chubby legs like she's auditioning for a baby mosh pit. She doesn't laugh—apparently babies don't do that until they're around six months old—but she smiles so wide I can see her pink gums gleaming. She gurgles and makes those wet, bubbly baby sounds that somehow sound like pure joy.

I scoop her up, feeling her warm weight against my chest, her baby powder scent filling my nose. And it's such a revelation to look into those big blue eyes and actually feel that rush of warmth spreading through my chest that everyone talks about. When she grabs my nose with sticky fingers and makes that hiccuping gurgle sound, I don't fantasize about flagging down the first person walking by and begging them to take her—I just want to hold her closer.

I stare at Cam, genuinely impressed. "That song... wow. When did you come up with it?"

"Just scribbled it down during the 4 AM feeding," he says with a modest shrug. "So you really think it's good enough for tomorrow at Indigo?"

Tomorrow. At Indigo. My stomach flips before I remind myself: not a date. Definitely not a date. We're nothing like that.

"Absolutely," I manage, my smile feeling stiff. "But listen, Cam—"

He holds up a hand. "I get it. Just friends hanging out. No expectations."

"Right. And if some gorgeous woman catches your eye..." The words taste like vinegar, but I force them out anyway. "You should totally go for it."

Did those words actually leave my mouth? Christ, they did.

He just shrugs and says nothing.

Cameron changes the subject, thank God. "Tal, my family's doing our every ten years mountain thing next weekend. Up at Mammoth. Granddad's place is ridiculous—calls it a cabin, but it's basically a mansion on a lake. We do all the rich-people water sports." He hesitates. "I want them to meet Brinley. You should both come."

My throat tightens. Shit. The whole Kensington clan? I could bullshit some excuse about the shop, but the truth is, I'm interviewing two new artists next week. If I hire them both, we'd finally have enough coverage that I could actually take a weekend off. God knows the three of us have been running ourselves ragged.

Plus, Celeste mentioned she's going. Having her there would make it less... intense.

But still. A weekend with his family? That's crossing into territory that feels dangerously... couple-y. I shake my head at myself. This is exactly the kind of overthinking that makes me want to run. Another fucking landmine in this arrangement I suggested and now regret—but still need. I just can't dive headfirst into whatever this is without completely losing my shit.

I take a deep breath. "Okay, I'll go to your family's gathering." My stomach knots as I picture walking in with

Brinley on my hip. Seven brothers, all staring daggers at the woman who lied about their niece being fathered by some rando instead of their beloved doctor brother. God, I'm going to need at least three shots of tequila to survive this. Too bad I'm breast-feeding, otherwise I'd have that tequila. But Brinley deserves to know her father's side of the family, no matter how uncomfortable it makes me.

Time to face the firing squad.

Chapter Twenty-Eight

TALLY

Welp, Cameron was not kidding when he said that his family's mountain retreat is a chalet, not a cabin. The massive structure looms against the snow-capped Sierra Nevada mountains, all gleaming cedar and floor-to-ceiling windows that catch the alpenglow at sunset. Mammoth's powdery slopes rise in the distance—a skier's paradise built on the sleeping giant of a volcano that last spewed lava seven centuries ago. The Kensington retreat sprawls across three levels, with ten bedrooms decked out in plush fur throws and rustic-luxe furniture that probably costs more than my Jeep and tattoo equipment combined.

Since it's August, there's no actual skiing or snowboarding—just a lakeside house and a weekend full of boating, waterskiing, kayaking, and whatever other fresh hell awaits. My only goal is to make it through without wanting to punch one of the Kensington brothers, though I'm sure each of them will give me ample reason.

First up is Roman, the most likely culprit. He's toned

down since marrying Lilith—maybe her psychic powers really did soften him—but a leopard never changes its spots entirely. I have a hunch we'll be at each other's throats before the weekend's over. He's fiercely loyal to Cameron, so at least his asshole behavior will feel justified.

Next is Max. I never warmed to him after how he treated Celeste when she first moved in—she was practically hired to marry him and desperately needed the money, yet he behaved as if she didn't belong in their own home. I haven't forgotten, and now I've given him solid reason to be pissed at me, so he's another prime candidate for conflict.

Then there's Silas, CEO of a major jewelry empire who regularly deals with royalty. Full of sarcasm, cold superiority, and convinced he's better than everyone else, he'll relish calling me every name in the book.

The rest should be manageable. Connor, despite being an Oscar-winning A-List actor, is apparently shy and insecure—a real sweetheart, according to Celeste. Kalen, the pop star, is always daydreaming, so he won't cause trouble. Ansel is more like a loyal puppy: all energy and little bite, so he'll back off but will probably rib me. And Asher? He'd sooner psychoanalyze me than shout insults—and since we both love art, we might actually have something worthwhile to talk about.

I check my phone for the fifth time in an hour. No missed calls from Mom. This weekend marks her first time alone in the house since moving in with me, and my stomach's in knots. She's been religious about her meds—that little chiming alarm on her phone going off like clockwork. The pills have worked miracles. Gone is the woman who'd ditch me for whatever loser bought her drinks, who'd pop pills like candy, who'd forget I existed when a new man came around. But what if she walks out that door while I'm gone? What if that alarm doesn't go off? Or worse—what if she hears it and ignores it? Two missed doses and she could spiral, and just like that, I'd lose her all over again. My hands won't stop shaking at the thought.

So, yeah, this should be a relaxing weekend on the lake, but it seems full of landmines for me.

When I step inside, I spot the biggest landmine of all. Silas—ever the sneaky bastard—either missed the memo that Cameron's now living with his baby's mother, or he noticed and just didn't care. Or maybe he simply enjoys stirring shit. Whatever the case, he's invited some woman named Dr. Willow Rosewood to spend the weekend with us. And the way he zeroes in on Cameron for an introduction tells me he's plotting a classic setup.

"Cameron!" Silas calls as Brinley squirms in the sling on my chest and Cameron hauls our mountain of gear through the doorway—not just suitcases but all the baby essentials: diaper bag, high chair, travel crib, toys. He's pulling it all on a red wagon. Silas meets my eyes and gives me that look—like he's already penciling in how to piss me off before brunch. Forget Roman. Silas is now the prime candidate for the guy who'll make me want to cut a bitch by Sunday. "So good to see you. You remember Dr. Rosewood, right?"

Of course Cameron remembers her. And of course Dr. Willow Rosewood is the human embodiment of every nightmare I've ever had about pretty, perfect women. She's at least 5'10", with huge blue eyes, thick chestnut hair so glossy it makes me want to shriek, and a face so symmetrical it hurts. Legs for days, flawless smile—she could be the poster child for Natural Beauty skincare.

I glance at her, then down at myself, and ugh. My breasts are still swollen from nursing and my stomach a soft

Buddha pouch, thanks to zero workouts since the baby arrived. I haven't had the energy for Pilates or P90X in months. Next to Willow, I feel like a soggy sandwich. I can't help resenting her perfect flat stomach and perky ass and perkier breasts.

She's a doctor too—probably a Yalie or Hopkins grad like Cameron. Sure enough, Cameron wraps her in a hug, pecks her cheek, and they launch into memories of med school at Hopkins.

I need Celeste. Now. I have to learn everything I can about this Willow Rosewood.

And Celeste apparently brought her nanny along, Esmé, so I can have some alone time with my friend this weekend. As long as she doesn't mind that Brinley will be ever-present in her little sling on my chest this weekend.

Boy, I envied Celeste having a nanny when it was just Mom and me tag-teaming Brinley. Now that Cameron's in the mix, though, he's better than any nanny, mainly because he's so easy on the eyes and, yes, I still fantasize about him all the time.

I spot Celeste by the sliding glass window that opens onto the deck and yank her outside by the arm. It should be peaceful out here—I can hear bullfrogs croaking, whippoorwills calling, and beyond the trees a deer and a flock of wild turkeys meander through the underbrush. The lake is glass-smooth at dusk, with only a handful of boats still out, though tomorrow morning it'll be crowded again, I'm sure. Despite the calm, my heart is pounding.

Because I'm the idiot who convinced Cameron we weren't a couple. I'm the one who pushed him to date other people. And now, looking back into the living room at Cameron and Dr. Willow deep in conversation—probably medical talk, or more Hopkins hijinks, though what kind of hijinks happens in med school, I have no idea—I realize he looks perfect next to her. If anyone could be Daddy's money all grown up, with a mansion in the Hamptons and another in Ojai or Big Sur, it's Willow.

Celeste squeezes me in a hug. "I'm so glad you made it. Max didn't think you would."

"Yeah, yeah," I mutter. "What's the deal with Dr. Willow?"

Her eyes go wide. "Oh—Silas decided Cameron's been in mourning long enough and, well, invited Willow." She makes a face. "Silas knew Willow back when he was an undergrad at Harvard—they lived down the hall from each other. When Cameron came to visit Silas in those days, Willow had this massive crush, but Cam was with Alecia, so nothing happened. Later, Silas ran into Willow at an art opening, and that gave him the bright idea to set her up with Cameron for the weekend."

"And they already knew each other from Johns Hopkins?"

"Right. She was a couple years behind him, and he became her mentor during her first year."

I roll my eyes. Of course: this beautiful, wealthy doctor has liked Cameron forever, and that sneaky Silas thought it'd be great to throw them together in front of his baby mama.

"Tal," Celeste says softly. "This is what you wanted, right? For Cameron to be happy with someone? You told me—"

"I know what I said." I hunch my shoulders and stare back through the window at Cameron and Willow, still talking, still laughing. "I meant it. I'm not right for him. He deserves happiness. But damn, it hurts to watch him with the woman who might finally give him that."

Celeste slips an arm around me as I lean over the railing, my hands gripping the smooth wood. Brinley is asleep on my chest—any second she'll wake up crying, and I'll have to feed her, rock her. But for now, I'll take this time. I'll dig up every scrap I can about Willow Rosewood. After all, if I truly love Cameron—and I do, more than anything—then Willow might be the one to bring him the joy he deserves. Even if, in my darker moments, I'll probably imagine plunging a knife into those perfect eyes.

I twist a strand of my jet-black hair around my finger until the tip turns purple. "So Silas knows Brinley is Cam's?"

Celeste's emerald eyes narrow to slits. "Oh, he knows. That's why he ambushed you with Willow this weekend. He saw you and Cam were attending together and thought, perfect setup for revenge." She leans forward, her coffee breath mingling with the cloying scent of her vanilla perfume. "Silas is the one with the grudge. He thinks what you did—passing off Cam's baby as some random hookup's kid—was unforgivable. In his book, you're officially Bad News with a capital B."

"So he's playing matchmaker." My fingernails—hot pink nail polish and all—dig crescents into my palm. People always think they know the whole goddamn story. Sure, hiding Brinley's paternity looks terrible on paper, like I'm some calculating bitch.

Was I wrong? Absolutely. But nobody saw me at 3 AM, staring at my ceiling fan's hypnotic circles, replaying that moment I almost called him in Sicily, phone clutched so tight my knuckles went white. Nobody understands what it's like growing up watching your mom trapped in relationships she never chose, her spirit dimming with each passing year. I wanted Cameron in my bed, not making decisions about my life. And what if my pregnancy had pulled his focus when those refugees—desperate faces pressed against chain-link fences—needed him more?

I bang my head softly against the textured wall, feeling each tiny bump against my skull. Other women would've seen Cameron for the jackpot he is—those surgeon's hands with perfectly trimmed nails that save lives by day and work magic by night, that deep laugh that rumbles through his chest and makes you feel like the only person in the crowded room, the way he actually listens, head tilted slightly to the right. And Jesus Christ, he can make me see stars in bed, constellations I didn't even know existed.

I get why Silas wants to "rescue" his brother from me. Doesn't mean I have to like it.

Celeste leans forward, her eyes serious. "Tally. Listen. If things changed with Cameron, you need to tell him. Before it's too late and you regret the whole arrangement. Do it now."

I shake my head so hard my earrings jangle. "Commit to Cam? I can't even commit to a fucking tattoo design for longer than five minutes. What right do I have getting territorial about him dating Willow? That's just me being a selfish bitch." I shake my head again just as Brinley is waking up. "No. He deserves someone who can give him what he needs, and that's not me." My voice cracks on the last word.

Celeste's arm slides around my shoulders. "Tally," she says softly. "You love him, don't you?"

"Fuck." I swipe at my eyes with the back of my hand. "Yeah. I do. Love him so much it fucking hurts. Physically hurts. That's the whole goddamn problem. I love him enough to know when to walk away."

That old saying about setting someone free if you love them? It's bullshit. I don't want him coming back to me. I want him finding someone who isn't broken, who doesn't have my baggage. Someone who can make him happy.

And knowing that's not me? It feels like someone reached into my chest with a tattoo gun and inked "FAILURE" across my heart.

Chapter Twenty-Nine

CAMERON

My brother Silas has always been a meddler, but this time he's crossed a line. Word around the family is he's harboring the biggest grudge about Tally lying about the baby. Somehow he's appointed himself the judge of my love life and decided Tally isn't suitable. My opinion? Irrelevant, apparently.

This weekend at the family retreat, I walked in to find Willow Rosewood—my med school classmate who's now running pediatric oncology at UCLA—sitting in the chalet's living room. Silas then proceeded to fling us at each other's heads. After an awkward catch-up where I learned her husband passed from cancer three years ago, I cornered my brother.

"You're seriously matchmaking while Tally's in the next room?"

Silas didn't even have the decency to look embarrassed. "Absolutely. Bumped into Willow at some gallery thing, got talking about you. Your wife's been gone about as long as her husband. She admitted she always had a crush on you. Seemed perfect."

"Silas, I have Tally—"

"But you don't," he interrupts. "You're just her roommate, nothing more, remember?"

Of course I never told any of my brothers about my arrangement with Tally. Instead, Tally confided in Celeste, Celeste blabbed to Max, and before I knew it, the whole Kensington clan was in on our business. Damn it—why can't anything in our lives stay private?

I exhale and glance toward the deck where Tally and Celeste are chatting. That's where my heart is—nowhere else.

Except hers clearly isn't with me. If it were, she wouldn't keep pushing me away. She lied about Brinley being my child because she'd decided to raise the baby alone. She insisted our living situation was purely platonic and that we were both free to date whoever we wanted. I never agreed to any of that. If it were up to me, Tally and I would be married by now, living in a spacious Echo Park house—with room for me, her, Brinley, and Marisa. In fact, ideally we'd have that main house plus an ADU for Marisa so she'd have her own space yet stay close enough for Tally to check on her—make sure she's eating right, sleeping enough, taking her meds.

But it's not up to me. Tally's calling the shots, so here I am—sleeping in the attic of her modest three-bedroom home, encouraged to date other people, and fully aware that we aren't "together." Silas sees it too—he knows how much Tally's taking advantage of me. Not that I mind. I love Brinley. I gladly handle the 3 AM feedings and diaper changes, read bedtime stories with Tally curled up next to me, and cover childcare while Tally works. My presence not only helps her but also frees Marisa to accept more piano gigs—she just started tutoring wealthy kids in Malibu.

Soon I'll begin my sports-medicine fellowship, and we'll all have to adjust again. But by then, Brinley should be sleeping straight through the night—no more 3 AM wake-ups for anyone.

I roll my eyes. "Just let me live my own life how I want, okay?"

"Okay. But Willow knows nobody here but you and me, and Tally has Celeste here, so..."

Damn him. He's really pulling this guilt trip about Willow not knowing anybody here when he's the one who dropped her in my lap without warning? And where does that leave Brinley? I can't just dump my kid on Tally all weekend. This whole situation is turning into a complete disaster.

"Cameron," Silas says, draping his arm across my shoulders. "Unanswered prayers, remember?"

That Garth Brooks song hits me like a punch to the gut. Sometimes what you think you want most in the world would actually destroy you if you got it. Like when you're the only one who can't see how toxic a relationship is, how it's eating you alive while you keep begging for more.

Silas's gaze hardens into a warning. I can read it as clearly as if he'd spoken: Let Tally go. Some doors are meant to stay closed, no matter how badly you want what's behind them.

"Silas—"

"Doing it out of love, bro. Nothing but love. Remember that."

I sigh and walk over to Willow, who's chatting with Connor. My movie star brother smiles that million-dollar smile at her, ever the gentleman despite the daggers his fiancée Alys is shooting from across the room. Alys Sanders - the new face of Dior. A-list actress. Yet she's a soul-sucking harpy who somehow convinced my kindest brother to propose. The wedding's in two years, and none of us can figure out how to save Connor from this union that will destroy him in the end.

Something clicks as I watch Connor and Alys. We all see Alys for what she is—everyone except Connor. What if my brothers see something in Tally that I'm blind to? What if those red flags they keep pointing out aren't just overprotectiveness?

Our father walking out when we were kids made us a unit. We protect each other. We tell hard truths.

Silas isn't trying to sabotage me by bringing Willow here. He's trying to save me.

I need to at least consider what my brothers see that I don't. I need to give Willow a chance.

God, that's going to hurt.

But I'll do it.

I'm sure it's in my best interest.

Tally is an unanswered prayer. Perhaps she needs to stay that way.

Chapter Thirty

TALLY

This weekend is turning into my personal hell. Every time I look over, Cameron's laughing at something Willow said, or Willow's touching Cameron's arm, or they're sharing some private joke. And all the brothers are eating it up—not just Silas with his knowing smirks, but even Max, the traitor.

Case in point - the activity for that first morning, kayaking.

"Tally, you're with Celeste," Max announces when we reach the dock, pointing to the blue kayak while practically shoving Cameron and Willow toward the red one. I try to bail—I hate kayaking, always end up soaked, and someone needs to watch Brinley anyway. But Rosa's already bouncing my daughter on her hip, waving us off like we're teenagers at prom. Celeste grabs my arm, whining about needing a partner since Max and Roman has already claimed the green kayak for themselves. Apparently Lilith's off at some crystal-waving convention in Big Sur, teaching baby psychics how to separate fools from their money. Those two—Max and Roman—are the oddest bromance I've ever seen, but whatever. At least someone's having fun.

Kayaking done, we move on to mixed doubles tennis. And once again, the master of ceremonies for the day, Max, unsubtly pairs Cameron and Willow with each other.

Meanwhile, I'm stuck with Asher. Just my luck. I can barely hit the ball over the net, and Asher, while in as great of shape as his brothers, apparently has the coordination of a newborn giraffe. We're gonna get destroyed

Cameron—that golden boy—plays like he's auditioning for Wimbledon. Willow's no slouch either. They absolutely destroy Connor and Alys in the first match—not exactly a shocker. Connor holds his own, but Alys acts like she doesn't want to break a nail so she doesn't even try.

Next up, the dynamic duo of Cameron and Willow take down Max and Celeste, who actually put up a decent fight. Then it's our turn. Poor Asher—brilliant mind, killer abs, terrible backhand and forehand, for that matter. Between my wild swings and his awkward lunges, we didn't stand a chance. Game, set, and total humiliation.

So yeah. Between the kayak thing, the doubles tennis thing and just the way that Silas keeps shooting me the stink eye while looking at Cameron and Willow approvingly, I couldn't miss what was happening between Willow and Cameron if I tried.

The after-dinner show is what clinches it. Two fucking baby grands sitting side by side in the old man's palace—who lives like that? Cameron and Willow slide onto the benches like they'd been itching for this moment all night. She hits every note he does, both of them criminally wasting their musical gifts on regular paychecks. They volley lyrics back and forth—from Elton's heartbreakers to Billy's ballads, then Tori Amos' raw confessions and Radiohead's beautiful misery. Her voice pours out sweet and smooth against his perfect whiskey-rough edges. I watch them lean into each other between verses, their hands flying across ivory, and thought: shit, that's what belonging to someone looks like.

Watching them together hurts like someone's taking a cheese grater to my insides. Cameron and this Willow chick —they just fit. Their voices blend on "Goodbye Yellow Brick Road" like they were born to harmonize, their fingers dancing across the piano keys in perfect sync. Fuck. I can already see how this plays out: them building their little love nest while I'm home alone with Brinley, Cam and I passing her back and forth like some kind of human baton. I never thought I'd be another statistic, another mom with a custody agreement. But here we are. Game over.

I tell myself this was what I wanted.

But that's bullshit. What I really want is to wake up one day as someone who doesn't break out in a cold sweat when Cameron talks about picking out china patterns. Someone who sees his kind eyes and steady hands and thinks "forever" instead of "trapped." Someone better than me.

The ink on my skin tells my story, but I can't tattoo myself a new personality. Cameron deserves his white picket fence dream.

So I'll smile and nod when he mentions Willow's name, even while my stomach twists into knots that would make a sailor proud.

Chapter Thirty-One

CAMERON

I hate to admit it, but Willow's growing on me. Smart, successful, single—she ticks every box my family thinks I need. And this weekend? My brothers might as well have worn T-shirts saying "Operation: Hook Cameron Up With Willow."

The kayaking setup was their first move. I'd naturally assumed Tally and I would share one, until Silas oh-so-helpfully pointed out that "poor Willow" was all alone and needed a partner. Then Max—that traitor—jumped in with some bullshit about wanting to paddle with Roman because of their "triathlon training schedule." Right. As if I couldn't see through that excuse to pair Tally with Celeste, leaving me no choice but to climb into a kayak with Willow. The whole time, Max avoided my death glare while Silas smirked. Subtle as a heart attack, these idiots. And Max? Never thought he'd join the matchmaking schemes. Asshole.

I caught myself enjoying Willow's company out on the water, then immediately felt a stab of guilt. When she tossed her head back and that musical laugh spilled out, something in my chest lightened. She gets my jokes—the stupid ones, the dry ones, all of them—in a way most women don't. Tally appreciates my humor too, but with Willow it feels... different. We ended up abandoning the kayaking for swimming, circling the overturned boat like sharks. Every failed attempt to climb back aboard sent us into fresh fits of laughter, the kayak flipping and dunking us back into the water again and again.

Tennis doubles were next on the agenda. Perfect, I thought. I can partner with Tally and make up for the kayak situation. But Max had other plans.

"Cameron with Willow, Tally with Asher," he announced, clipboard in hand. My stomach knotted. This felt different than before—at least in the kayaks, Tally had been with her best friend. Now she was paired with Asher, who she barely knows.

"Actually, I think—" I began.

Silas caught my eye and mouthed, "Unanswered prayer," our code for hopeless causes.

Right. Tally doesn't want me. Willow does.

I resigned myself to my tennis partner, who turned out to be incredible. We demolished the competition, our high-fives and victory dance looking like we'd been a team forever.

Now I'm in the kitchen making dinner for everyone while Tally feeds Brinley. Willow gets sent in to help me, and she's chopping vegetables as I stir the sauce for chicken parm—Tally's favorite. I glance through the doorway at her bent over the high chair, that familiar ache spreading through my chest. Loving someone who doesn't love you back is its own special kind of torture, especially with Willow hovering nearby, clearly being pushed in my direction. And, yes, I do love Tally. Desperately. But what is it they say? If you can't be with the one you love, love the one you're with? Yeah, right.

Dinner gives way to the evening's entertainment, and I discover Willow at the piano. Her fingers dance across the keys with practiced ease as she launches into "Piano Man." I can't help joining in, our voices blending in perfect harmony. We flow from Billy Joel to Elton John, then Lady Gaga to Tori Amos, finishing with Radiohead's "Creep" and "Karma Police." Something clicks between us—a musical shorthand that feels eerily familiar, as if we've been performing together for years.

Later, I find Tally alone on the deck, her face tilted toward the stars. When she turns and smiles at me, my stomach twists. I'd been half-hoping for jealousy, for some sign that seeing me with Willow all day had bothered her. That smile—so genuine, so uncomplicated—leaves me more confused than ever.

Tally's lips quirk into something not quite a smile. "So, Willow, huh? You two planning a big weekend?" She punches my arm with just enough force to sting.

"Yeah," I manage, searching her face. "I was going to—"

"Listen, Cam." Her voice catches. She blinks rapidly, those beautiful eyes suddenly glassy. "I want you happy. That's all." She turns away, but not before I catch the tremor in her jaw.

The lake stretches before us, black and still. Tally leans further over the railing.

"You deserve everything good," she finally says, voice steadier now. "And I can't be that for you. When I see you with Willow, I see possibilities. Real ones."

"Tally, I don't want-"

She tilts her head back. "Stars are something else out here."

"They are. Tally—"

"Don't." Her tattoos seem darker against her suddenly pale skin. "Take Willow out. Give it a real shot. Brinley and I will manage. She's sleeping through most nights now anyway." Her fingers trace invisible patterns on her jeans. "The sooner you accept we're not happening, the sooner you find someone who can give you what you deserve. And Cameron?" Her eyes meet mine. "You deserve everything."

The baby monitor in Tally's hand crackles with Brinley's wails. She catches my eye, then glances pointedly between me and Willow, who's just stepped onto the patio. Her eyebrow lifts—a silent blessing I never asked for. I sigh and tilt my head back. The night sky unfolds above us, exactly as Tally described: stars scattered like diamond dust across black velvet. August perfection. Beside me stands Willow—all thick chestnut waves and compassionate eyes. The pediatric oncologist. The woman Silas cornered me about earlier: "She's into you, man. Like, really into you." On paper, we're perfect: two medical professionals dedicated to healing the most vulnerable. Anyone who can hold the hands of cancer-stricken children day after day must possess a rare kindness. My body responds to her—that's undeniable. But my heart feels nothing of the electric current that shot through me the moment I first saw Tally across Max's wedding reception. This feels like homework. That felt like destiny.

My pulse races as I clear my throat. "I was thinking, when we're back in LA, we could grab dinner, maybe catch a show? They're doing *Death of a Salesman* again—always been a favorite, despite the whole crushing-weight-of-failed-dreams thing."

There. Ball's in her court. *Satisfied, Tally?*

"I'd be into that," she replies with a quick smile. "Silas mentioned you're taking time off from medicine. My schedule's pretty fixed—four days on, three off, twelve-hour shifts—but we can make it work." Her fingers graze my forearm, sending electricity through my skin that my brain refuses to acknowledge. I catch myself scanning the room for Tally instead. She's probably in Brinley's bedroom right now, nursing the baby. The living room holds only my brothers with their dates. Dad and his new wife Patricia arrive tomorrow.

I spot the Trivial Pursuit box coming out through the patio doors. "We should head back in," I tell Willow, nodding toward the house. "Game night's starting." My pulse quickens slightly—random facts are my superpower, though Asher's encyclopedic brain makes victory nearly impossible.

Inside, Willow becomes my teammate alongside Max and Celeste, but something feels off as I take my seat. The empty chair across from me seems to mock my situation. I catch myself imagining Tally there instead of Willow—Tally high-fiving me over correct answers, Tally kayaking with me earlier, Tally waiting in my bed tonight. The ache of missing her body against mine hits suddenly. I understand her hesitation though; sex plus cohabitation equals commitment in her mind, and I've learned how quickly she bolts when feeling trapped.

When Asher says he wants to join, I can't help but groan. The guy's our resident genius—he absorbs information like those movie and TV characters who flip through books and instantly memorize every page. Think Reid from *Criminal Minds* or Will Hunting from *Good Will Hunting.* Yet this is the same man who regularly loses his phone even though it's in his back pocket, who asks us if we've seen his sunglasses when they're atop his head. Brilliant and hopeless simultaneously.

We divide into four teams: our foursome, Silas's group, Kalen's crew (including Ansel's insufferable girlfriend), and Asher flying solo—the only fair arrangement given his abilities.

Somehow, miraculously, our team clinches victory an hour later. As everyone celebrates, I realize Tally never returned after going to feed Brinley. I slip away upstairs and find them both asleep—Tally sprawled across the bed, Brinley peaceful in her crib.

I can't fight it anymore. Willow's been driving a wedge between us, and it's killing me. My body aches for Tally's touch like a man starved for oxygen.

I take Brinley out of the room and place her in the adjoining room. We can hear her through the baby monitor, so there's no danger. But I need my daughter out of the room because I'm determined to ravage her mother and I don't want to scar her for life.

"Hey," I growl against Tally's ear as I get into bed next to her, the heat of my breath stirring her from sleep.

She jolts awake and I immediately claim her mouth, my tongue seeking hers with urgent need. Her lips part beneath mine as she arches against me, the thin cotton of her nightshirt doing nothing to hide the heat of her skin. She responds with a soft moan, her fingers digging into my neck, pulling me closer until there's nothing between us but sweat and desire. Then suddenly she tears away, chest heaving, eyes wild with want.

"Cameron, we're breaking the rules," she gasps.

"Those rules don't exist here," I murmur, my voice

rough as my hands slide beneath silk, finding her slick and ready. "The cabin has its own laws."

Her back arches sharply, a ragged moan escaping her lips as Willow's very existence evaporates from our world.

We crash onto the bed with such force the headboard slams against the wall. My fingers dig into her tattoos, memorizing every line as I bury myself inside her. She's burning against me, her spine a perfect arch as her nails tear into my shoulders, drawing blood. The sharp sting of her teeth on my neck sends electricity down my spine as I drive deeper, harder. Her wetness floods around me, her inner muscles gripping me like she's afraid I'll disappear. When she comes, it's violent—her entire body convulsing, eyes rolling back, a primal sound ripping from her throat. I don't slow down. I pound into her relentlessly, the wet collision of our bodies echoing through the room as she locks her legs around me in a vise grip. Even as we devour each other, I feel tomorrow's ghost between us. Each desperate kiss is contraband I'm smuggling across the border of her defenses. In LA, she'll become a fortress again. Tonight, there's only this savage connection—her body branded against mine, her taste seared into my mouth, our thundering hearts trying to break through our ribs as I explode inside her, claiming what I know I'll lose.

Christ, I've been starving for her. Three hundred and eighty-eight days since I last tasted her skin. No wonder I'm shaking, no wonder I can't stop. Or maybe it's simpler than that. Maybe it's just that somewhere between Sicily and here, I fell so hard for this woman that I can't find my way back up.

Doesn't matter. We make love until dawn breaks, scorching her bedroom gold, her ink-black hair spilled across the pillow like a confession. My heart hammers against my ribs when I finally surrender to what's consuming me.

"Tally, I'm in love with you," I rasp, my voice breaking. "I'm so fucking gone I can't breathe when I'm not touching you. I'd marry you right now, this second, if you'd just say yes."

Her answer? She crushes her mouth to mine, nails digging half-moons into my shoulders, pulling me inside her again with a desperation that burns. Not a single word. The silence between my confession and her body's response screams everything I was afraid to hear.

At dawn, after we've marked each other in ways that will linger for days, making love no less than 7 times, although I eventually lost count, Tally's voice slices through the sweat-soaked sheets.

“This was our last night,” she whispers. "And please... keep trying with Willow."

I knew it was coming. Doesn't make it hurt any less.

It is what it is.

In twenty minutes I'll be downstairs, smiling across pancakes at the woman I'm supposed to want, while the one I actually do pours coffee like nothing happened.

Wrong doesn't begin to cover it.

Chapter Thirty-Two

TALLY

Jesus Christ. Last night was...like drowning and finding air at the same time. The way our bodies crashed together—lightning strikes across bare skin—his hands everywhere at once, my nails leaving crescent moons down his back that I hope hurt this morning.

Perfect addiction, lethal dose. I practically threw his clothes at him at dawn when Brinley's hellish screaming erupted next door. Couldn't let anyone—especially Willow with her perfect smile—discover he'd spent the entire night fucking me. Because I know I need to cut him loose. Someone has to be the goddamn adult here, carve that line in concrete. And that line screams: Cameron deserves someone who isn't the train wreck that is Tally Steele.

Yet I begged him to ruin me again. And again. And again. And several more times before we finally broke apart. A weakness I can't afford, but what defense did I have when he slid between my sheets, his mouth hot on my neck, his cock hard against my thigh? For all I know, spending the day with flawless Willow left him desperate, and I was just...his favorite sin. I need to bury last night in the "Never Again" graveyard and walk away. But God, the way he made me come undone...

After nursing and changing Brinley, I strap her into the papoose against my chest. Her tiny fists punch the air while her feet kick rhythmically, happy gurgles bubbling up as we head downstairs to face everyone. At least one of us is looking forward to this morning.

Cameron's already in the kitchen with the others, his black t-shirt stretched across shoulders that have no business looking that good. He hands me coffee—cream and real sugar, exactly how I need it—his fingers lingering against mine, eyes saying everything about last night without a word. My stomach flips, but I force myself to step back. Whatever happened between us has to stay there. Willow deserves her shot with him, and I won't be the reason she doesn't get it, even if I have to physically drag my gaze away from him every time he looks at me like that.

Cameron's eyes meet mine, glinting with mischief. "How did you sleep, Tally?" I bite back an eye roll. He knows exactly how I slept—I didn't. Not with his body pressed against mine all night, his hands exploring every inch of me until sunrise, my voice growing hoarse from calling his name. My thighs still ache from being wrapped around him all night, and the marks on my neck needed extra concealer today.

My body aches in all the right places as I stretch. "Like a baby," I say, though every cell in me is still vibrating with electricity. My muscles burn with the sweet soreness of marathon sex, my skin still hot where his hands gripped me. Christ, I haven't pulled an all-nighter like that since—I can't even remember. Worth every second, but I'm going to crash hard later. Cameron's eyes are bloodshot, pupils still dilated when they meet mine. If we both disappear for naps today, everyone will know that we're both exhausted for the same reason.

Shit. How am I supposed to act normal around him today? Every time I look at him, I'll see last night—our first time since before Sicily, before the baby, before everything went sideways. For over a year, I've been dodging him while my trusty bedside vibrator got one hell of a workout. Then last night happened. One look, one touch, and boom—we went up in flames. Like striking a match in a room full of gasoline.

The whole family's gathered around the massive dining table, Willow included. They've laid out a buffet-style breakfast that could feed a small army, which is exactly what I need after the marathon session Cameron and I had last night. And several times more at dawn. And twice more before we finally crawled out of bed. I catch myself grinning and quickly school my expression. Let's just say there's a damn good reason I'm about to demolish this breakfast spread.

The food line forms, and I spot Cameron behind me, deep in conversation with Willow. Her voice floats over—husky and articulate with this musical quality that makes me want to punch something. She's rocking jeans and one of those casual tanks that somehow makes her biceps look sculpted and her chest look like it defies gravity. I bite back a sneer—isn't this exactly the scenario I've been angling for? After what happened last night, I know Cameron's a sure thing. One word from me and boom: engagement ring, massive house—not in Brentwood (too damn far from my tattoo studio), but maybe right in Echo Park. But the very thought of Cameron waiting at an altar somewhere, ready to lock this down, makes my chest tighten until I'm eyeing that lake out back like it's my only escape route.

And how, exactly, do I know that Cameron is mine if I want him? It wasn't just the way he fucked me last night like a man who'd been starving in the desert for forty days. It was because he said those words to me, his voice raw and desperate against my skin. Maybe he doesn't even remember it in the frenzy of our bodies crashing together like we were trying to break each other, but he grabbed my face between his hands and swore he loved me, swore he'd marry me tomorrow if I'd let him. Heat of passion? Maybe. He said it so casually I thought I'd hallucinated it. But I remember it now, burned into my memory like one of my own tattoos. And, Christ, there's a part of me—a part that's growing by the second, consuming me from the inside out—that wants to scream YES and claim him forever. Not just because Brinley deserves the childhood I never had—stable, wanted, protected, with two parents who can’t keep their hands off each other—but because I'm so fucking in love with Cam it terrifies me, like standing at the edge of a cliff and feeling that urge to jump.

So when Cameron catches my eye while chatting with Willow, I give him a nod and flick my gaze toward her—my silent permission. Despite last night, despite everything. This ache in my chest will fade eventually. What wouldn't fade? The suffocation of a shotgun wedding, the trap of vows spoken for all the wrong reasons, the prison of a life built on obligation rather than choice. Some cages have no keys.

I shake my head. Last night belongs in the file marked "Mistakes I'll Never Make Again," even if my body screams otherwise for the next forty-eight hours. Too bad. I've made up my mind.

My sanity can't afford another night like last night.

Chapter Thirty-Three

TALLY

That afternoon, I vanish. I can't bear another minute with Cameron's eyes following me everywhere. Breakfast had been torture—every time I glanced up, those blue eyes were watching me, stripping me bare across the dining table. I latch onto Celeste like a lifeline. Besides Cam, she's my only familiar face here, and I shadow her movements with desperate determination.

After the dishes are cleared, I practically drag her outside. "Let's explore the woods," I suggest, needing pine-scented air to clear my head. What was the point of a mountain retreat if you stayed cooped up indoors? I hand Brinley to Cam with a clipped "We'll be back later" and escape before he can protest. The last thing I need is what his hungry gaze promises—sneaking away until dinner to finish what we started last night and this morning. I could read the invitation in every look he gave me. But I wouldn't give in. Last night was already one mistake too many.

Celeste and I walk into the woods, the cool mountain air

filling my lungs. I try to focus on getting away—the pine smell that makes me forget the city, birds calling out, maybe even animals watching us from the trees. I press my nails into my hand. This weekend was never about Cameron and me breaking our no-sex rule just because we're not at home. And Cameron has no right—none at all—to push me into thinking this trip changes things between us. I hate that my body still wants him when he looks at me. That's bad enough. What's worse is that my heart still wants him. My soul. So, yeah, I need to get away from all of those feelings pronto.

Celeste stops and does a slow three-sixty. "Please tell me you memorized our route," she says, squinting at the towering pines surrounding us. "Because my phone's got zero bars out here."

I freeze mid-step. Half a mile from the house, surrounded by trees that smell oddly like vanilla extract, and not a single trail marker in sight. All because I couldn't stand another minute under Cameron's gaze, those eyes tracking my every move. No compass. No water. Nothing. Watch us end up as some nature documentary footnote—two idiots who wandered off and got scavenged by black bears after we collapsed from exposure. Bears don't even hunt humans, they just clean up what's left.

And speaking of bears…I freeze mid-sentence when I spot a black bear clinging to a nearby tree trunk, his dark eyes fixed on us. My lips curve into a smile. Unlike their grizzly cousins, black bears rarely pose a threat—they're the introverts of the bear world. And, really, grizzlies don't pose much a threat, either, despite that infamous case of two grizzlies killing campers in one night in the 1970s, an incident so rare that it inspired a book and a TV special. In general, all bears leave people alone.

"What's with the grin?" Celeste asks, following my gaze.

"Bear," I whisper, nodding toward the tree.

Celeste's eyes widen. "Jesus! Don't. Move."

"Relax," I say, keeping my voice low. "He's just curious. Even if it's a mama with cubs nearby, she'd just huff a warning. They're not the monsters people think they are."

Something about this unexpected encounter pulls me away from thoughts of Cameron. Out here, with distance between us, I can finally admit the truth to myself: I want him as fiercely as he wants me. Last night when he whispered about love and marriage between kisses, my heart raced—and not from fear.

Marriage terrifies me? Absolutely. But standing here in the woods, I'm grateful for the space to realize how much I already miss him.

Celeste grabs my arm, her nails digging into my skin. "Tal. Tell me you know how to get back."

I shake her off. "I don't. But we find a stream, we follow it downstream, we find civilization. Simple." I lock eyes with her. "This isn't some horror movie where one of us ends up as wolf food while the other crawls out of the wilderness half-dead, drinking their own piss to survive."

"Wolves?" Celeste's voice jumps an octave, her face draining of color. "There are actual wolves out here?"

"Christ, Celeste!" I snap, whirling around. "Yes! Wolves with razor teeth and glowing eyes that hunt screenwriters specifically!" I push aside a branch that whips back, nearly hitting her. "Lucky for you, all those damn movies you mainline for 'work' have prepared you perfectly for this exact scenario."

"Tally-"

I shake my head. "Those predator attack movies like *The Grey* and *Frozen* - the stuck ski lift movie, not the Elsa and

Anna movie - get it all wrong. Wolves avoid humans whenever possible, just like bears do. Wolf conservation groups despise that kind of fearmongering—it just leads to more hunting." I can't help but roll my eyes. "Even Great Whites, despite what *Jaws* would have you believe, typically steer clear of people."

Celeste lifts her chin. "I'm well aware of shark behavior, thank you very much. When Max and I started surfing together, he prepared me for Great White sightings. My first encounter? Total panic attack. Max couldn't stop laughing. These days?" She shrugs with casual confidence. "I barely notice them anymore."

I nod. "Bears and wolves tend to avoid humans. Mountain lions, though..." I pause dramatically, watching Celeste's eyes widen before I crack a smile. "They usually keep their distance too."

Celeste scans the trees nervously. "Where did you learn all this wildlife stuff?"

"Just something I've always loved." A flock of wild turkeys crosses our path, their iridescent feathers catching the light. "One of my foster families had this remote cabin. I'd disappear for hours with my sketchbook. After a few close encounters, I figured I'd better understand what makes animals tick—or attack. Turns out, most just want you to respect their space."

I shoot Celeste a look, and she gets it. I've hiked plenty of trails before. I never got lost then, and I won't now. Even when I'm not paying attention, my brain catalogs every fallen log and distinctive tree.

"You're sure you can get us back?" Celeste's voice pitches higher, doubt written all over her face.

"Trust me, Celeste."

We reach a stream, and I peel off my boots and socks, sighing as the cool water rushes over my feet. Perfect. This hike is exactly the reset I needed before heading back to face Cameron. I need to set boundaries—last night was a mistake, not a standing invitation. He needs to focus on Willow and stop fantasizing about something that's never happening again.

Celeste glances at her watch, but kicks off her shoes and peels away her socks anyway. We settle side by side on the stream bank, letting the current wash over our bare feet.

I spot movement in the shallows and point, grinning. Tadpoles. "See those? When I was a kid, I'd scoop up tadpoles in jars and watch them at home. I was obsessed with catching that moment—you know, when the tail shrinks away and those tiny legs push through."

Celeste's laugh rings out, the tension visibly melting from her shoulders. She's finally forgetting about being lost. "I tried that too! Mine always ended up belly-up before anything interesting happened."

"Tap water," I say with a knowing nod. "It's like poison to them compared to this." I swirl my toes through the clear stream. "I only had one survivor that went the distance. Watching those legs sprout and that tail disappear—like witnessing magic. After that, I retired from my tadpole-snatching career. Mission accomplished."

We sit, side by side, watching the tadpoles dart around like tiny black bullets. I'm transfixed, heart hammering against my ribs.

"You know," I say, my voice barely audible over the roaring in my ears, "I wonder if I could rip myself apart and rebuild completely. Like these tadpoles—they dissolve their own bodies from the inside out to become something else entirely." Thunder growls in the distance. The air crackles with electricity, raising the hair on my arms. Two PM. Storm coming. We need to go, but I can't move.

"What do you mean?" Celeste's eyes burn into me.

"Just—" My throat constricts. "Some creatures destroy themselves to evolve. What if I could tear down everything I am?" My fingers dig into my thighs. "Become someone who doesn't hyperventilate at the thought of forever with Cameron."

Celeste grips my shoulder, her nails leaving half-moons. "That's what you really want, isn't it?"

"God, yes." The words rip from me. "I'm desperate to be the woman who deserves him on his knee. Who can wake up to that face for fifty years without running. Who can love him back with the same fucking intensity that he loves me. Who can say the words 'I love you' back to him when he says it to me."

"Cameron says he loves you?"

My skin flushes hot, then cold. Last night floods back—his words branded against my neck, my back arched, both of us slick with sweat, trembling. "Yeah," I whisper. "But..." Christ. I almost told her how he'd confessed his love between our fourth and fifth time, his voice breaking as he pushed inside me again. "Never mind." I sniff the air and it smells like rain.

"But?" She elbows me. "Go on, Tally."

I shake my head. "Nothing. Forget I said anything." Then I shoot her a look that she knows means to back off, which sucks for her, because I HATE it when somebody starts to say something and then doesn't finish. But I'm not telling her about last night.

"Tally-"

"Let's get back before it rains."

So, Celeste and I head back to the chalet. We crunch through the ground and, before I know it, we're back where we need to be. I hear Celeste breathe a sigh of relief, which tells me that there was at least a little part of her that was afraid that I really didn't know the way back, which means that she gives me little credit for not being an idiot.

We get in there and the chalet door swings open as Michael Kensington arrives with Patricia—Celeste's mother and his new bride. Patricia's cheeks glow with a vitality I barely recognize compared to the hollow-faced woman of a few years ago, when cancer had whittled her down to bones and will. Now her fitted sweater shows off arms toned from those five-weekly Pilates sessions she mentions in every conversation, and her legs look strong enough to power through those Peloton rides she documents religiously on Instagram. The way she gazes at Michael—like he personally hung the moon—makes perfect sense. He's cut from the same cloth as Cameron: gentle eyes, ready smile, the kind of man who'd give you his last dollar without hesitation.

Roman practically bounds across the room to his father. I nearly do a double-take watching them embrace, Roman's arm slung around Michael's shoulders as they walk in together. The sight is as jarring as seeing Roman and Max sharing inside jokes these days. For months, Roman wouldn't even stay at family gatherings if Michael showed up—now here he is, beaming like a lighthouse.

"Dad," Roman says, lifting Brinley from Cameron's arms. "Meet your granddaughter."

Michael cradles her with practiced hands, his face softening. "She's Cameron through and through," he says, then catches my eye. "Beautiful work, Tally. Absolutely beautiful."

I glance toward Cameron, who's sipping wine beside Willow. "She is," I agree.

Michael bounces Brinley in his arms, her chubby legs kicking with delight. "So, Rome," he says with a grin, "when are you and Lilith planning to make one of these adorable creatures?"

Rome's face breaks into a smile he can't contain. "Well, I wasn't supposed to say anything without Lilith here, but..." He runs a hand through his hair. "Hell, I can't keep it in. We're expecting. Four months along already."

The room erupts. Everyone crowds Rome, clapping his back and offering congratulations while someone pops champagne. Glasses appear in everyone's hands except mine and Michael's, of course. Me because I'm still nursing, Michael because he's a recovering alcoholic.

I hang back, grateful for Roman's news stealing the spotlight. While Michael entertains Brinley and the others swarm Rome with questions, I slip away to my bedroom, collapsing onto my bed to stare at the ceiling in blessed quiet.

A knock sounds at my door about thirty minutes later. I brace myself to face Cameron—ready to shut him out even though part of me wants to pull him in and keep him here all weekend. Saturday to Monday morning would make for quite the sex marathon.

But when I open the door, it's Michael standing there with Brinley in his arms, his expression gentle and hopeful enough to draw a smile from me.

"Am I interrupting?" he asks.

"Not at all," I say. "I just needed some space from the celebration downstairs. Congratulating Roman seemed like something for family, and—"

"You are family," he interrupts, carefully transferring

Brinley into my waiting arms. "You gave me my first grandchild. That makes you family in my book."

My eyes well up unexpectedly. I bite back mentioning Stephanie, the grandchild he never knew because of his long absence. No need to reopen old wounds.

I gesture toward the French doors. "Want to sit outside?"

Every bedroom in this mansion has its own private balcony—all ten of them. The price tag for this chalet must be astronomical. Granddad Kensington could probably purchase a small island if he ever sold this place.

Michael follows me out, and we settle into the chairs. "So quiet up here," I remark. "Going back to the city will be an adjustment, even though I'm in the quieter outskirts now."

He clears his throat. "Yeah. So." His mouth opens, then closes, a fish gasping on land. His eyes flicker to Brinley, then back to me. I can practically see the questions forming behind his furrowed brow. Will his granddaughter be shuttled between homes like luggage? Or will Cameron and I create some semblance of a normal family? And I know exactly what he's hoping for—the gold band, the ceremony, the whole traditional package that would let him sleep at night. The worry in his eyes says it all: he doesn't want Brinley bouncing through life like a pinball, he wants roots for her.

"You want to know the score on Cameron and me, right?" I ask him.

"Yeah." He furrows his brow. "I don't get what's going on down there. Cameron's hanging out with that beautiful woman down there, you're up here. When I asked Roman what's going on, he said to talk to Silas. Silas then told me that he brought Willow with him because he wanted to set her up with Cameron." He shakes his head. "Make it make sense."

I stare at him, my chest tightening until something inside me snaps. The laughter bursts out of me like glass breaking—sharp and dangerous. God, it's all so fucking ridiculous! Me burning for Cameron. Cameron supposedly burning for me. Silas playing puppet master, except I've already cut my own strings. And poor Willow—thrown into our emotional dumpster fire while Cameron happily lets himself get distracted. My laughter turns manic, tears pricking my eyes. This weekend isn't just a mess—it's a Dalí nightmare, melting clocks and all, with the four of us - me, Cam, Brinley and Willow - trapped in a landscape that's twisting more by the minute.

I exhale, looking at Michael. "I wish I had words for this feeling." If anyone would understand the instinct to flee, it's him. The man vanished from his family's life for over two decades. Talk about running away.

"Tally." His voice softens. "I think I see what's happening here."

"Do you?" I meet his eyes.

"You're terrified of letting someone in." He leans forward. "And that's the only thing I can think of, because I know Cameron and he wants to be with you." He shakes his head. "The way my son watched you when you walked away downstairs—it's like you were taking all the oxygen with you. Cameron loves completely. Always has. I wasn't there for most of his life, but these past few years have shown me he's still that same determined little boy at heart."

I force a smile, desperate to redirect. "What was he like back then? As a child?" Part of me wants to escape Michael's uncomfortable insight about my fear, but another part genuinely craves these glimpses of Cameron's past.

“Well, I left when he was 14.” He nods. “22 years I was gone, and when I came back, Cameron opened his arms to me, no questions asked. And that didn’t surprise me, because he was always so kind. So gentle.”

I smile and bounce Brinley on my lap, eager to hear more.

"In middle school, Cameron was something else," Michael says, his eyes distant with memory. "Popular kid, varsity everything—football, hockey, the rowing team. But he used that status differently than most. One time, this bigger kid was shoving a freshman into lockers. Next day, that bully showed up with a black eye, wouldn't look anyone in the face for weeks."

That's the Cam I know.

"At lunch, he'd scan the cafeteria for the kid eating alone, drag his chair over uninvited. Ask questions and actually listen to the answers. Same thing with the homeless folks downtown—he'd roll up with a bag of McDonald's, sit on the curb, and share a meal like old friends catching up."

Michael's voice softens. "Found a cardinal once, stunned from hitting our picture window. Cameron scooped it up, cradled it in his palm. Tapped its tiny chest with his fingertip until it started fluttering. Even breathed into its beak." He shakes his head. "Always figured he'd be a veterinarian. The number of half-dead creatures that boy nursed back to health in our garage—squirrels, field mice, even a baby raccoon once. Had a real gift."

I lean forward, my voice dropping. “How did you find out what happened at Harvard Westlake with Cam?” The name of that ultra-exclusive prep school always makes my stomach tighten.

"Silas told me everything." His eyes lock with mine. "He and Asher were just seventh-grade nobodies when Cam was already ruling ninth grade. But Silas—God—he worshipped the ground Cam walked on. Said his brother was untouchable, had everyone eating from his palm, yet never once lorded it over anyone. Even threw these legendary parties where he'd personally make sure every single outcast got an invitation. Every. Single. One."

My heart pounds as it clicks into place. Silas. Of course. The same fierce loyalty that made him idolize Cameron is why he dragged Willow here—not to sabotage but to save his brother. The realization hits me like a physical blow. What I've been calling Silas's dick move was actually something far more primal—a desperate act of protection, of love so intense it borders on devotion.

"Which is why Silas brought Willow here," I say.

"Yeah. Silas always looks out for Cameron. But I think Cam hates the meddling. Maybe Silas should've just let things unfold between you two. Am I right?"

I stare at the horizon, searching for words. The sun dips behind the mountains, bringing that Sierra Nevada chill that sneaks up on you even in August.

"I'm getting cold," I say. "Want a blanket?"

He nods. I slip inside and return with two soft cashmere throws, tucking one around his shoulders before wrapping myself in the other. His question still hangs in the air. Should Willow be here, or should Cameron and I have space to work through our mess alone?

The answer seems clear—Cameron and I need time alone to figure this out. But that only works if I can stop sabotaging myself. Meanwhile, the sun sets and the house below fills with people who probably whisper about us the moment we leave a room, making up stories about a relationship they know nothing about.

I clear my throat. “Michael, I don’t know how to answer

that question. So I'll table that for now. At any rate, whether or not Willow should be here this weekend, the fact is that she is here, so the damage is done. But I appreciate your concern. I really do." I reach over and cover my hand with his and smile at him, even though I'm not feeling that smile.

We probably should have space to work things out. But we're not getting it and it is what it is.

I just hope everything doesn't spiral out of control.

Chapter Thirty-Four

CAMERON

The weekend vanished in a blur. The day after my night of passion with Tally, I caught myself checking the time, calculating how long until I could slip back to her room. But I didn't. Instead, I pulled her aside after breakfast, needing clarity. Her answer couldn't have been clearer—she wanted me to give Willow a real chance. So the following evening found me on one of Granddad's many private decks with Willow, the mountain air just cool enough to notice but not enough to mind. We talked until the small hours, our voices eventually dropping to whispers as the house slept around us. By the time I glanced at my watch—2 a.m.—I had to marvel at myself: from all night having sex with Tally to all night talking with Willow. Whatever else was happening in this mess, at least my endurance wasn't the problem.

And I found myself really liking Willow. She's intelligent and funny, with an uncanny ability to mimic different voices and mannerisms - Robert De Niro, Bill Clinton, Meryl Streep, Taylor Swift were some of the celebs she mimicked and she's amazing at it. She performs these spot-on impersonations at a nightclub as part of an amateur standup routine—something we have in common since I also perform at a club, though I sing and play piano.

We're both Johns Hopkins-educated doctors too, which gave us plenty to reminisce about. We traded stories about our instructors and rotation experiences, especially Dr. Harwood with his signature move: saying something profound, crossing his arms, then popping his eyes dramatically. I nearly fell out of my chair when Willow nailed his impression. We also laughed about Dr. Yang, the most straight-laced instructor you'd ever meet by day, who transformed into an Eddie Van Halen-level electric guitarist by night with his own band.

Naturally, after the time with Willow, the drive back to LA with Tally stretched into six hours of carefully chosen words. We chatted about movies, traffic, anything but what hung between us. My fingers tightened around the steering wheel whenever silence threatened. Once, at a red light, I caught Tally studying my profile, her expression unreadable. I wanted her—not Willow with her perfect résumé and infectious laugh. Yet as I merged onto the highway, part of me wondered if I was being stupid. How many men would kill to have a brilliant doctor with kind eyes looking at them the way Willow had looked at me?

Crossing our threshold felt like shedding a lead coat. Six hours from Mammoth to LA with Willow's name hanging unspoken between us had been torture.

The moment we arrived, Tally beelined for her mother. "Did you take your medication? All of them? On schedule?" She grabbed Marisa's wrist, tapping the Apple Watch she'd bought specifically to track her mother's rest patterns. That's Tally—scrutinizing sleep stats before even setting down her bags. Some might call it hovering, but I've always seen it differently: her vigilance is her love and devotion for Marisa made visible. The same intensity radiates when she gazes at Brinley, or when she turns those eyes on me. The difference is that loving me seems to suffocate her, while loving them gives her air. I'm learning to live with that contradiction.

"Tally," her mother complained. "You have to stop hovering. I'm doing well. I promise you I don't miss a dose of my Lithium or Abilify. Now go away." Marisa smiled, though, and hugged her daughter. "Missed you."

"Missed you too."

Tonight Marisa and I will inevitably drift to the piano for our usual duet. Her concert-trained fingers dance across the keys, challenging me to keep pace. It's like our chess matches—I hold my own, but her mind works in brilliant, unexpected patterns. Her bipolar disorder, which causes her so much pain in daily life, transforms into pure creative genius when she plays music or plots her next chess move.

God, if I somehow end up with Willow—which I don't want, despite her impressive résumé—I'd ache for what I'd lose. Not just Tally, but these evenings: Brinley's gurgling at dinner, Marisa's impromptu concerts before she rushes off to her nightclub gig, this makeshift family we've patched together.

It could happen, though. It really could.

But one word from Tally and I'd drop everything. She's still the only one I truly want. She's still endgame for me.

Even knowing she might never feel the same.

Chapter Thirty-Five

TALLY

Cameron's going out with Willow tonight. Their first date. I've been staring at the bottle of Tito's in my cabinet for twenty minutes, wondering if vodka might dull the ache of watching him get ready to see her. And goddamn it, if I weren't nursing Brinley, I'd be into that bottle of vodka so fast…

Willow is like some cosmic joke the universe played on me—beautiful, brilliant, and worst of all, genuinely likable. She even called me earlier, apologizing profusely for the way she got my phone number - Celeste gave it to Max, who gave it to Silas, and then to her. The brothers seem suspiciously enthusiastic about pushing Cameron and Willow together—and me firmly out of the picture.

When my phone rang and I heard, "Tally, this is Willow," I managed a casual "Oh, hey, what's going on?" while my pulse thundered in my ears and I blinked back tears. And it's not hormones making me emotional—it's pure self-loathing. Here's Cameron, this incredible man who wants commitment, and what am I doing? Practically gift-wrapping him for another woman. If there were an award for self-sabotage, I'd be accepting that trophy with both hands.

Willow's voice is melodious on the phone. "I just wanted to check if you're comfortable with Cameron and me dating. Given your... arrangement with him and little Brinley, I'd hate to cause problems. I've always believed in women supporting women, you know? So if you have any reservations..."

I catch myself mid-eye-roll. One word from me and she'd retreat. But to what end? The mere thought of committing to Cameron makes my chest tighten, like being trapped in a shrinking box. What right do I have to say, "Don't date him, Willow—even though I won't either"? That would be beyond selfish. Cameron deserves better. I need to put his happiness first, even as I feel the first crack spreading across my heart.

I force a smile that feels like it might crack my face. "You and Cam have fun with whatever you're doing. Take pictures. Text them to me. Don't do anything I wouldn't do."

"Oh, thank you!" Her voice jumps an octave, practically vibrating with relief. "The last thing I wanted was to get between—I mean—and you're absolutely sure?"

"I'm sure." My fingernails dig crescents into my palm. Not sure. Not even close. Every cell in my body screams for Cameron to wait for me, to pause his entire goddamn life while I figure out mine. But if I never get my shit together, he might as well be chasing a mirage across the desert until he drops dead of thirst.

So, yeah. Cameron is taking Willow to fucking Somni. Five hundred dollars per person just to eat. PER PERSON. And that's before the wine pairings that cost more than my weekly grocery budget. My stomach actually clenches when I hear this, like someone's twisting my insides with pliers. Not because I'm dying to eat gold-flecked whatever-the-hell they serve there. God, I'd probably use the wrong fork and get escorted out by security. That place is for people who own islands, not people like me. But Cameron? CAMERON? Mr. I-Don't-Care-About-Material-Things is blowing the equivalent of one of my mortgage payments on dinner? He must be gone for her. I want to vomit. I want to scream. I want to throw myself into traffic.

Cameron appears in the doorway, ready to leave for his date. My eyes narrow at his outfit—distressed jeans paired with that gray blazer and t-shirt he always wears. Not exactly fine dining attire.

"Enjoy Somni," I call out, shifting Brinley against my breast as she nurses. My smile feels plastered on while my chest constricts watching him leave to wine and dine someone else.

He stops, turns. "Somni? Who said anything about Somni?"

"Celeste mentioned it. I think that Max told her that's where you were going."

He laughs, shaking his head. "My brothers are trying way too hard with this Willow thing. Now they're wish-casting my date. But I'm not spending fifteen hundred on dinner with someone I barely know."

I exhale slowly. "So where are you taking her?"

"Girl and the Goat."

Still nice. Not break-the-bank expensive, but he'll probably drop a couple hundred once cocktails and dessert are factored in.

"After dinner?" The question catches in my throat.

"Tally—do you really want these details?"

"I need to know. Otherwise, I'll just picture you back at her place."

"Just an art gallery opening Asher told me about."

An art gallery. My stomach drops. He knows how much I love those—the hushed conversations, the wine in plastic cups, the electric feeling of discovery. That should be me tonight.

Cameron glances at his watch, but his eyes linger on me. He gestures toward the couch, and I sink into the cushions with Brinley nestled against my chest. I tuck the blanket around her tiny form, and she drifts off, oblivious to the ache spreading through my chest.

"Tally," he says, voice low. "Just say it, and I'll cancel with Willow."

My throat tightens. "God, I've been wrestling with this all day. If I'm honest? The thought of you with her—with anyone—kills me."

His phone appears in his hand. "She'll understand." His thumb hovers over the screen until I reach out.

"Don't. You deserve someone who can make you happy. And she's perfect, isn't she? Beautiful, young widow just like you, another doctor. The whole package."

"Tally—"

"Please go."

He rises slowly, reluctance in every movement. "I'll... see you later, then?"

I force my lips into what must be a brittle smile. "Have fun." I wave him away, watching as he hesitates at the door. "Don't worry about me. I won't wait up."

He leaves and my mother glides into the living room, dressed up for her gig that night at Indigo, all sequins and red lipstick like she's twenty-five instead of fifty-five. "Tally," she says, voice razor-sharp. "I need to talk to you."

I nod, my jaw already clenching. "Let me put Brinley down," I say. "Be right back."

I put Brinley in her latest onesie, bright yellow with a duck face, and press my lips to her forehead, breathing in her baby-powder smell, trying to steady myself.

"Okay, Mom, what's up?" I drop onto the couch, bracing for impact.

She slams her hand over mine. "Aren't you carrying this whole thing with Cameron a bit too far?"

"What are you talking about?" My voice comes out like broken glass.

"He just went out on a date with somebody else, that's what I'm talking about." She shakes her head, earrings swinging violently. "What the hell are you doing?"

"Mom," I say, squeezing my eyes shut so hard I see stars. "I'm sending him off to be happy with somebody because he sure as hell won't be happy with me."

"Tally," she hisses, "You need therapy. You need to talk to somebody before you blow the best thing that ever happened to you."

"Mom, I've had therapy, remember?" My laugh is bitter acid. "It was court mandated therapy when I was a kid and being shuffled around from one home to the next." I slam my fist against my thigh. "The last thing I want to do is talk to somebody who'll bring up all this shit."

"Tally, that's what therapy is for."

"Well, I'm not ready for that," I snap, my voice cracking. And then I shake my head, rage boiling up from somewhere deep and dark. Goddamn it. This is her fault. If she didn't make my childhood such a fucking nightmare, I wouldn't have the baggage I have now and I'd be able to give Cameron what he wants from me, which is to be his wife.

But life doesn' t work that way, does it? It's not a choose-your-own-adventure book where you can flip back to page 47 and pick door number two instead. My whole life is a tangled web of consequences, and when I think about it, I never would've met Cam, period, if I had had a normal childhood. After all, I met Celeste because I took that Soul Cycle class in West Hollywood when I was 23. I only lived in West Hollywood because I'd stayed with a foster family there when I was 16—six months of actual stability that felt like heaven. After college, I wanted to recapture that feeling, so I got an apartment three blocks from their old place.

Without that foster family, without that particular neighborhood, I never meet Celeste at that class. Without Celeste, I'm not at that specific Happy Hour on that specific night, which means no car accident. And even if by some cosmic joke I still somehow crossed paths with Cameron, he never would have given me a second glance if I wasn't Celeste's friend who'd just been hospitalized.

Guess there's a silver lining to every dark cloud. If I hadn't such a shit show of a childhood, I might never have crossed paths with Cameron. Or found Celeste, the sister life never gave me but somehow delivered anyway. Maybe I should be sending Mom a thank-you note instead of getting mad at her.

"Mom," I say, keeping my voice steady. "I hear you. I do. But I've got this handled."

Her eyebrows lift. "And if they click over dinner? If they laugh and talk for hours and then—"

"End up at her place..." The words stick in my throat. My mind floods with images I can't bear: Cameron's lips on someone else's, his hands tracing unfamiliar curves, his eyes —those eyes that make me feel like the center of the universe—focused on another woman.

Christ. Maybe I do need that therapist after all.

Chapter Thirty-Six

CAMERON

The seasons change, and with them, my feelings for Willow deepen—an unexpected complication. At home, Tally still occupies the same space, our lives intertwined through Brinley's care.

Willow's schedule as a pediatric oncologist dictates our relationship: three nights of dinners and conversations with her are all I can get, because four days a week she's at the hospital, doing the most physically and emotionally draining work possible. The remaining four nights find me at home, where Tally, her mother and I fall into domestic rhythms—sharing meals, Marisa and I playing piano together, board game competitions, and movie nights with commentary. Brinley transforms daily, her laugh now filling rooms, her sleep finally uninterrupted through the night. Tally has grown into motherhood, needing me less for midnight feedings.

My life splits neatly: four nights of family dinners with the woman I dream of marrying, three nights of possibility with someone new, all while guilt gnaws at me for leaving the woman I love alone with our child. This impossible equation balances only because Tally herself insists on it as a solution.

The text from Willow arrives like a grenade with its pin pulled. She wants to meet Brinley—properly this time, not like that brief introduction at the chalet months ago.

"Tally," I say, matching her fold-for-fold as we tackle the mountain of baby clothes on the couch. Across the room, Brinley's walker bumps against the coffee table, her five-month-old giggles punctuating the silence between us. The gray tabby—Tally's compromise between wanting Brinley to have a pet and her own limited bandwidth, as Tally doesn't have the time or patience for a higher maintenance pet like a dog—weaves between the walker's wheels. "Willow's been asking about spending time with Brinley."

Tally's hands freeze mid-fold over a yellow onesie. She nods mechanically, but her eyes tell a different story. "Right. Of course." Her voice thins as she smooths invisible wrinkles from the fabric. "If you two are getting serious, she should probably know..." The sentence hangs incomplete as she turns away. "Excuse me. I just remembered something."

"Tally—"

"It's fine, Cameron." Her back is to me now. "Introduce them."

I watch her retreat, conflicted. Willow could be my future, which means she and my daughter need a relationship. That's just reality. Isn't it?

Still, it feels like a knife twisting deeper.

Another wound in this maze where every turn leads to pain.

Chapter Thirty-Seven

TALLY

The leather of Dr. Wynn's couch creaks as I shift my weight. Three months of therapy sessions, and I still feel like an imposter here. Mom finally wore me down about getting help, but I've kept it from Cameron. No need to add "sending his ex to therapy" to his conscience. Dr. Wynn thinks my secrecy is ridiculous—she never says it outright, but her raised eyebrow when I mention keeping Cameron in the dark speaks volumes.

"Tally." Her voice breaks through my ceiling-staring trance. "How are things?"

"Shitty," I mutter, my head rolling side to side against the cushion. "Cameron wants Willow to meet our kid." The words taste bitter. "They must be getting serious."

Dr. Wynn's silence is deafening. No reassurance that I'm jumping to conclusions. No mention of "catastrophizing"—that beautiful term she taught me that perfectly describes my talent for imagining worst-case scenarios. Lately, I've been more skilled at catastrophizing than at my actual art.

Instead, she gives me that blank-faced therapist stare and says, "What if it turns into something real?"

I exhale. "I'll shatter into a million pieces. Won't ever be whole again."

She shifts closer. "Would you stop them if you could, Tally?"

I squint at her. Ridiculous. Obviously I would. I could, but I won't.

"Sure," I say. "But Cameron deserves happiness."

"And you don't?"

There it is. Strange this hasn't surfaced before now, after twelve Tuesdays at $150 an hour—money I barely have.

Is that my issue? That I've decided I don't rate joy? And if so, when did I decide that? All this time I figured I kept Cameron at arm's length because of the revolving door of foster homes, the lesson beaten into me that attachment is pointless since everyone vanishes eventually. People are temporary. Or like my mother, they stay just long enough to break you.

I sit up. "I deserve happiness. Of course I do."

"But do you really believe that?"

I shake my head. "I'll have to think about that."

That night, I find myself alone with my thoughts. Mom's out performing, Cam's out with Willow and Brinley's busy terrorizing the cat from her walker, her giggles punctuating the quiet house as she gnaws on her tiny fist. I dust off my easel and pull out a fresh canvas—something I haven't done in months.

Painting has always been my emotional outlet, the place where truths emerge that I can't quite speak aloud. Dr. Wynn's question haunts me as I mix colors: "Do you truly believe you deserve happiness?" The brush moves almost without my conscious direction. Why am I so fixated on

Cameron finding joy with Willow when it leaves me with nothing?

Two hours disappear. I step back and see her staring back at me—Sibley Flynn, my old CPS caseworker. Those unmistakable eyes, blue pools of melancholy that followed me through every foster placement. She was my only constant in those chaotic years.

I find myself searching for her contact information online. She's still with LA County DCFS. Before I can reconsider, I've scheduled an appointment. Perhaps she holds some key to why I've always felt unworthy of love.

I'm not deluding myself that excavating old wounds will magically fix things with Cameron. That ship has sailed. But understanding this piece of myself—that feels like a step I need to take.

Chapter Thirty-Eight

TALLY

With Willow coming over to meet Brinley today, I've got the perfect excuse to make myself scarce. I head to Van Nuys to see Sibley Flynn at the regional office, my stomach knotting with each mile closer. I need answers about those missing years—the ones my brain apparently decided were too much for me to process. Funny how minds work, building walls around the worst parts to keep us functioning.

Sibley's face lights up when I walk in. Her arms wrap around me in a hug that smells like vanilla and printer paper.

"Tally," she says, stepping back to look at me properly. "What a wonderful surprise when I saw your name in my calendar. I love watching my kids grow up and succeed. And here you are with your own tattoo studio—you've really made something of yourself."

I nod. "The business is thriving, but I'm still..." My fingers twist together in my lap. "I started seeing a therapist. Yesterday she asked me something I couldn't answer, not until I went home and picked up my brushes." I meet Sibley's eyes. "I painted you. Your face just appeared on the canvas, like my hands knew something my brain didn't."

She leans forward, elbows on her knees. "I'm listening, Tally. You know, in all my years of fostering, few adjusted to life's curveballs like you did."

"Maybe that's exactly it." The words catch in my throat. "I was offered something real—this man who's..." I press my palm to my chest. "He's everything, Sibley. And I pushed him away. Worse—I practically gift-wrapped another woman for him." My laugh sounds hollow even to my ears. "I told myself it was for his happiness, but the truth is, I'm terrified I'd be just one more tragedy in his life. And he's already had his share."

I twist the hem of my shirt until my knuckles go white. Her eyes bore into me—those pity eyes that make my skin crawl. I can practically hear her thoughts screaming: How the hell did this broken girl survive? The truth hammers in my chest: Did I survive? Or am I just a walking corpse of the girl who got buried alive in her own trauma?

"What exactly did your therapist say?" Her voice cuts through my spiral. "You mentioned something triggered you."

My throat constricts. "She asked if I deserved to be happy." The words burn coming out. "And I just... froze. Completely fucking froze."

"Sit down," she commands, leaning forward with an intensity that matches the storm in my head. "I'm going to tell you everything I know."

I drop into the chair, hands trembling.

She takes a deep breath. "How much do you remember about those years?" she asks.

My throat tightens. "Too much." I shake my head. Remembering isn't the problem. I can still smell vomit on carpet. Can still see pills scattered across bathroom tiles. Can still remember having to drag Mom's unconscious body into recovery position at thirteen. I can vividly remember every time the social worker came over to take me out of the home. Can remember every home I was in during those years. So, yeah, it's all there in vivid detail. But, at the same time, I'm so emotionally stunted about that time that it all seems like a dream.

She nods. "Too much. How is your relationship with your mother now?"

I dig my fingernails into my palm. "She lives with me now. Bipolar disorder. The whole time she was just—" My voice cracks. "She takes lithium and Abilify now, and it's like living with a different person. A stranger wearing my mother's face." I laugh, but it sounds more like choking. "Some nights I stand in her doorway watching her sleep, and I want to scream until my lungs bleed. So my brain just... erases it all. Survival, right?"

"The mind builds walls around trauma," she says softly. "Like scar tissue forming over a wound that would otherwise never stop bleeding." Her eyes darken. "It's like the pandemic. We all act like it never happened, but two years of our lives were stolen. Two years of isolation, fear, death. Nobody's forgotten—how could we? The nightmares, the empty streets, the sirens all night, over a million dead. We just buried it alive, pushed it down deep where all the other horrors go, because that's what humans do when reality becomes unbearable."

The pandemic feels like a fever dream now—something we all lived through but can barely remember. Back then, it consumed every conversation, every thought. Maybe she's right about trauma. Once it's behind you, what good does it do to keep looking back? Except I know the years bouncing between foster homes left their mark on me. If they hadn't, I'd be wearing Cameron's ring right now, planning my future with him instead of his planning a possible future with somebody else.

And I know that Cameron would fucking marry me tomorrow because he's made that crystal clear. Not just when he whispered it against my neck that night in bed at the chalet, but every goddamn time we're doing something mundane—his hands freezing mid-air while folding Brinley's onesies, his eyes burning into mine over steaming pots in the kitchen. He's told me he loves me and wants to marry me so many times I could choke on the words, but I always act deaf and change the subject so fast it gives me whiplash. Can't deal with that shit. Won't. If I pretend hard enough, maybe those words will evaporate into nothing.

"So, yeah," I say. "My brain doesn't seem to process what I went through. But it's there, always. It's buried deep but it seems to really be the one thing that's standing in the way of my being happy. Truly happy with my little girl and this amazing man."

"So," she says. "I guess you need my feedback on what you went through and you might even want my opinion on why you're standing in the way of your own happiness, then?"

I inhale a breath. "No. I remember what I went through. Intellectually, anyhow. I remember it all. In vivid detail. So, that's not the problem. The problem is - how did my brain process everything that happened? Did I give you any clues on how I handled things back then?"

"What kind of clues?"

"Oh, I don't know. You oversaw the caseworkers that

would come to the house. Did they tell you anything about me and how I handled the chaos?"

She nods, manila folder open on her lap. "I reviewed your file before our session. Your previous caseworkers were quite thorough in their documentation. One pattern stood out—you consistently assumed responsibility for your mother's issues."

"That can't be right," I say, but my protest sounds hollow even to me. Here I am, after all, giving my mother my spare bedroom, counting her medications, making sure she eats three meals a day. I never once demanded an apology for the nights I went hungry, or the school events she missed, or the times I had to hide her empties before CPS visits. I should hate her. Why don't I?

Maybe it started with those missed parent-teacher conferences, when I'd sit alone in plastic chairs meant for adults, my legs dangling, watching other kids' moms show up. I'd stare at my B+ and think: if this was an A, she'd be here. Or those mornings I'd find her sprawled across our bathroom floor, vomit crusting the corners of her mouth, pill bottles scattered like landmines around her limp body. I'd check her pulse with trembling fingers, praying to a God I didn't believe in, and feeling fucking horrible that I didn't hide the pills better. Every time she'd clutch my hand and rasp, "You're the only good thing in my life, Tally," my chest would cave in, and I'd want to scream: THEN WHY AM I NOT ENOUGH?

I became a fucking contortionist, twisting myself into whatever shape might keep her sober. If I was quieter. If I was smarter. If I hadn't gotten drunk that one time at twelve—TWELVE—stumbling home at dawn to find her wild-eyed and sober for once, clutching the phone to call the police. I freaked her out so much that of course she went back to using, even though at that time she'd been sober for six months. By that afternoon, she was high again. My fault. My fault. MY FAULT.

It was always like that. Now that Sibley's telling me I always assumed her problems were my fault, I'm drowning in the memories of exactly why I believed it.

Sibley glances at her notes. "You repeatedly told caseworkers you blamed yourself for your mother's addiction and for her getting caught, which led to you being removed from the home."

I stare at my hands. "Yeah, that tracks. Like when she was high at Ralph's grocery and my friend's mother spotted her? That was on me. She'd asked me to go shopping because she needed one thing, but I was being selfish. Just wanted to play Minecraft with my friends." My throat tightened. "If I'd just gone instead, no one would've called CPS that day."

"Tally, you were being a teenager. Teenagers want to play Minecraft with their friends."

My voice cracks. "I was awful that day. Mom just needed cream for her coffee. One simple errand. She never asked me for anything—always did the shopping herself, kept our fridge stocked no matter how tight money got. But I was too busy playing Minecraft." I press my fingertips against my temples. "Every damn day I replayed it. If I'd just gotten off my ass for an hour and walked to the store for her fucking cream, she wouldn't have been tweaking in the cereal aisle while one of my friends' moms saw her and then hotlined her."

Sibley continues to look at her file on me. "And then there was the time your mom was hotlined because of a parent-teacher meeting. You blamed yourself for that, too."

I pick at a loose thread on my jeans. "Yeah. When Ms.

Davos asked where my mom was after she missed that meeting, I just... told the truth. Said she was in bed and didn't want to come. With her history, the teacher immediately suspected pills." I swallow hard. "Which was true—she was passed out on Oxy—but I should've lied. Could've said she had the flu or had to work or something, anything but just saying that she couldn't get out of bed. Instead, I basically handed them the reason to take me away."

"And you blamed yourself for her getting busted for a DUI, which led to yet another hotline and you being taken from the home again. How was that your fault?"

I slam my palm against the table. "That one was a hundred percent on me." I shake my head, remembering that day. "I was at Tara's house after school, ignoring Mom. Every text. Every call. My phone buzzing in my pocket like a fucking time bomb." My throat tightens. "I was pissed at her—can't even remember why now—but I knew exactly what I was doing." I dig my nails into my palm. "So when I didn't come home after school and she couldn't get ahold of me, she tore out of the house, convinced I was being dismembered in some psycho's basement. I knew what the drugs did to her brain, how paranoid she sometimes got. I knew she'd imagine my blood pooling on concrete somewhere. And I let her spiral anyway." I shake my head, blinking rapidly. "So yeah. When she couldn't find me, she jumped in the car after downing half a bottle of pills. Got pulled over three blocks away. Child services showed up the next morning, and I spent the next eight months with the Petersons while she spent 6 months in jail - it wasn't her first offense - and did mandatory rehab."

Sibley slams her file shut. "We've found it, Tally. The poison at your core. This conviction that you don't deserve happiness—it's rooted in carrying blame that was never,

ever yours. Your mother's incarcerations, those humiliating court appearances, every time they ripped you from her arms... you've branded yourself guilty for all of it. And her addiction?" Her eyes bore into mine. "You've crucified yourself for that too, haven't you?"

My throat closes like someone's strangling me. I can barely nod. "Yes." The word scrapes out, barely audible. "God, yes. I believed—I still believe—if I hadn't gotten her caught so many times, if I hadn't been this... this burden... she wouldn't have needed to escape reality. It was this vicious cycle crushing us both—drugs created chaos, chaos demanded more drugs. And I was just this stupid kid who couldn't keep secrets, who kept accidentally betraying her to neighbors or teachers. Who caused her stress because of all the times I vanished without calling her, knowing that would cause her to spiral. I convinced myself if I could just disappear completely, become nothing... she might finally break free."

Sibley smiles and extends her hands across the desk. I hesitate before placing mine in hers. " Tally," she says, her voice gentle but probing, "you've identified that you believe you don't deserve happiness because you feel you betrayed your mother throughout your childhood. You've been carrying the weight of your mother's dysfunction as if it were your responsibility. How do you plan to move forward from this realization?"

I sigh. Fucking fantastic. The million dollar question.

Sure, identifying the problem is one thing. And yeah, it's a huge thing. I never connected those dots before—that I felt responsible for all the shit that went down when I was a kid. But now what? Am I supposed to just snap my fingers and suddenly believe I deserve to be happy? That I deserve Cameron? And if my brain convinced myself that I caused my mother's problems, how can I make it not believe that I won't be poison to Cam just like I was poison to Mom?

If I could figure that out, maybe I'd stop being such a self-sabotaging disaster long enough to let him in.

But I won't hold my fucking breath.

Chapter Thirty-Nine

CAMERON

Willow and Brinley are at the house with me while Marisa tutors across town. I glance at Willow as she moves around my kitchen, a space that feels somehow violated by her presence, even though Tally gave her blessing. "It's fine," Tally had said this morning, not meeting my eyes, "but I'll be back for dinner." Then she'd slipped out the door without telling me where she was going.

Now Willow stands at the cutting board, knife flashing through garlic and onions with practiced efficiency. The sharp scent fills the kitchen as she preps ingredients for Arrabiata sauce—the spicy base for Tally's favorite penne with vodka cream. I watch Willow's hands, competent and sure, just like Tally's have become since I taught her to cook. The grocery trips, the recipe planning, the careful filleting of meat—these are our rituals, mine and Tally's. Seeing Willow in her place makes my stomach twist, though I force a smile when she looks up. She's good, maybe even as good as Tally in the kitchen. But it's not the same.

Damn. I'm doing to Willow exactly what Tally does to

me. Keeping her at a safe distance, never letting her past the outer walls. Sure, we laugh together, talk for hours, and I genuinely enjoy her company—even look forward to seeing her. But that's where it ends. My heart remains stubbornly elsewhere, locked in Tally's possession despite her refusal to claim it fully. I should be asking myself when I'll finally reclaim it, not when she'll release it. If I can't reclaim it, I'll eventually have to tell Willow the painful truth: there's only one woman I want, and it isn't her. For now, though, I'll keep seeing Willow, waiting for that same electric shock that jolted through me the moment I first saw Tally at Max and Celeste's wedding.

But I'll give it some time. Willow is so perfect on paper, she has to eventually become right for me.

Right?

Chapter Forty

TALLY

The scent hits me first when I open my door—penne with spicy vodka creme sauce wafting through my apartment. Then I see her. Willow. Standing in my kitchen wearing an apron. Thank god it's not one of mine, or I'd have to cut a bitch right here and now.

After spending the day at Sibley's office dredging up every painful memory about Mom, I'm already on edge. And there they are—this perfect little domestic scene. Willow stirring the sauce, Cameron chopping vegetables beside her, both with glasses of wine in front of them. My mouth waters, not for the pasta, but for that cabernet. Five more weeks. Five more weeks until Brinley hits six months and my pediatrician gives me the all-clear to stop breast-feeding. Five more weeks of watching everyone else drink while I'm stuck sober. The wine glasses gleam under my kitchen lights, mocking me.

Cameron looks at me and smiles. "Tal," he says. "You're home."

"So observant," I say, narrowing my eyes. Then I shake

my head. Dammit. I suddenly have the urge to throw his ass out of the house and set his clothes on fire like in that scene from *Waiting to Exhale*. I close my eyes, seeing the fantasy of me pouring gasoline over his clothes, then lighting the match and walking casually away.

I lift Brinley from her walker. Her face lights up as she reaches for my nose, tiny fingers grasping. I retreat to the bedroom, settling into the rocking chair with her warm weight against me. I can't bear to watch Cameron and Willow playing house in my kitchen—a situation I created myself. I have no grounds for this anger. Cameron was thoughtful, asking permission for Willow to meet Brinley here rather than somewhere impersonal. I agreed readily, even enthusiastically. But that was before I dug up all those buried feelings. Now that I've unearthed them, every nerve ending seems exposed.

Cameron eases into the bedroom and perches on the edge of the bed. "Tally," he says softly. "Talk to me."

My vision blurs as tears well up. "I thought I could handle this, Cam, but I was wrong." My voice catches. "Your happiness matters to me—no, it's more than that. I need you to be happy. But seeing you with Willow..." I inhale shakily. "You should move back to your home. Except that makes no sense, right? You're all the way in Brentwood, I'm here, and shuttling Brinley between us would be a nightmare." Running my fingers through my hair, I whisper, "God, I'm such a mess right now. I'm sorry."

Brinley's wail pierces the silence. I yank up my shirt and she latches on with desperate hunger, her tiny fingers digging into my skin. Her eyes flutter shut, milk-drunk, as I rake my fingers through her downy hair. Thank God for those baby blues pills. Before them, I'd stare at her perfect face and feel...nothing. A void where maternal love should have been. The pills Cam prescribed saved me—saved us both.

"Tally," he whispers, his voice raw. "I'll end it with Willow tonight. Just say the word."

I jerk my head. "No." My chest tightens. "I refuse to be the reason you lose someone who might actually make you happy. I'm drowning in enough guilt already." My hair falls into my eyes and I blow it away violently. Brinley suckles harder, sensing my tension. Cameron's eyes bore into mine—confusion, concern, something else I can't name.

The truth sits like acid in my throat. Today, Sibley held up a mirror to what I've been carrying since childhood—this twisted belief that somehow I caused my mother's spiral into addiction, that I'm the reason she was taken away again and again. This poison has seeped into every relationship I've touched. I can't ask him to leave Willow, not when I'm still wrestling my own demons. If he chose me now, he'd just become another thing I ruined before I was ready to be what he deserves.

Brinley stop suckling and starts crying, her diaper needing changing. Cameron takes Brinley from me, his fingers brushing mine for a heartbeat too long. "I'll handle this," he gently says, laying her on the changing table. The muscles in his forearms flex as he works. I collapse against the headboard, throat burning with unspoken words.

"Tally," he says, eyes locked on mine even as he expertly secures the fresh diaper. "What is really going on?"

"Nothing," I whisper, then louder: "Everything. I'm ripping myself apart trying to understand why I can't—" My voice breaks. "God, Cam, I told you to leave, but the truth is I'm terrified you might actually go. I need you here. Not just for her. For me." My hands tremble. "I can't do this alone."

Cam freezes, diaper wipes forgotten in his hand. "Christ, Tally. You're actually asking for help."

"Yeah." My laugh sounds like shattered glass. "Miracle of miracles."

I've cracked myself open for him to see the mess inside.

Maybe I'm not beyond saving after all.

Chapter Forty-One

TALLY

Christmas is coming, and Willow is still around - so Cam and Willow have been hanging out for the past three months or so. I've been watching her with Cam—the way she touches his arm when she laughs, how she remembers exactly how he takes his coffee. I still hate that someone else occupies the space beside him, but I can't deny she's good to Brinley.

Tonight she's bringing over her box of heirloom ornaments for our tree. I want Brinley to have these moments—the pine needle smell, the tangle of lights, the careful unwrapping of decorations. My foster families gave me Christmases: the Johnson's neighborhood light tours, the Martinez's matching pajamas, the Petersons' midnight mass where I dozed against Mrs. Peterson's wool coat. But watching other families' traditions always felt like pressing my nose against a window, looking in. Those Christmases were borrowed, like everything else.

I mean, yeah, we did the whole Christmas thing with Mom too, back before Dad bit it and Mom went off the deep end. Can't say I remember much—I was just a tiny kid—but there's photographic evidence somewhere: little me sandwiched between Mom and Dad, who apparently always dragged his ass home for December 25th. Sometimes I stare at those pictures like they might suddenly start moving, you know? Like maybe I could catch some detail I missed, some memory that isn't just a blur of lights and noise.

Brinley army-crawls across the living room floor, her tiny hands slapping against the hardwood as she makes a beeline for the remote control. When I move it, she points and lets out a string of "ba-ba-da" sounds that somehow manage to convey complete outrage. Christ. Between her father's money, my attitude, that face and those dimples, this kid's going to own the world if I don't watch it. I can already picture the kindergarten playground, some poor five-year-old boy offering her his juice box while she bats those eyelashes. God help us all.

I scoop up Brinley mid-lunge toward Kitty's swishing tail. "So," I say to Cameron, balancing my squirming daughter on my hip. "Think we should take the munchkin to see Santa? You, me, and Willow?"

The cat—named Kitty because creativity isn't my strong suit—darts under the couch, probably convinced my daughter is some kind of pint-sized predator. Can't blame her. Brinley's obsessed with that poor animal, always crawling at top speed after her, and when she catches up? Full-body tackle accompanied by high-pitched babbling that I'm pretty sure translates to "I LOVE YOU SO MUCH I MUST SQUISH YOU."

I'm weirdly excited about the Santa photo. There's something hilarious about those first-visit meltdowns—the red-faced screaming, the terror in their eyes. My own baby picture with Santa is framed evidence: six-month-old me howling like I'm being murdered, clutching a torn chunk of synthetic beard in my tiny fist. Apparently, I've always had trust issues with men in disguise.

"Sure," Cameron says. "Next Saturday afternoon would be good."

So, we're all set to ask Willow about the Santa visit when she arrives to help decorate.

She shows up in one of those "ugly" Christmas sweaters that's actually cute as hell—Jack and Sally from *Nightmare Before Christmas* dancing under a moon surrounded by tiny skulls and pumpkins. Of course she'd wear my favorite Christmas movie. Damn her.

She's brought Brinley a silver bell ornament, engraved with "Brinley's First Christmas." When she hugs me and then Cameron, my stomach twists the same way it always does. I've just gotten Brinley weaned, which means I can finally drink again—and watching them together makes me want to. If Cameron pulls out a diamond ring tonight, I'll need a whole bottle.

I tell myself I'm fine with their relationship. I'm not. But whenever I imagine confessing to Cameron—telling him I love him—I panic. Because I know exactly what would happen: he'd drop Willow in a heartbeat and that ring would end up on my finger instead. And then what? The walls would close in, and I'd be trapped. How could I ask him to dump her, only to realize I'm too scared to follow through? That would be beyond cruel. So I'll paste on my smile and deal with whatever happens, even if it kills me inside.

"Oh, I'd love to take Brinley to see Santa!" Willow says, clapping her hands with such enthusiasm her silver bangles jingle against her wrists. Brinley, with her wispy dark curls bouncing, immediately mimics the motion, clapping her chubby little hands, her rosebud mouth stretching into a gummy smile that reveals her two tiny bottom teeth. She lets out a string of delighted babbles that sound almost musical.

So we make plans to take Brinley to the Westfield mall in Century City, with its gleaming marble floors and soaring glass ceilings that capture the California sunshine. The place drips money—Gucci handbags displayed like museum pieces, the unmistakable orange of Hermès boxes, Rolex watches glinting under spotlights, and mannequins draped in Prada that cost more than my monthly rent. It's not one of those dingy strip malls with flickering fluorescents and discount stores; this place is all polished brass, designer perfume wafting through the air, and shoppers carrying those stiff paper bags with fancy rope handles.

We have a blast trimming the tree while Mariah Carey belts out Christmas tunes from my Amazon Music playlist. Willow's Christmas cookies—the bitch can bake, I'll give her that—disappear almost as fast as we can frost them with red and green buttercream.

Brinley's chubby little fist mashes the cookie into her cherub cheek, leaving a trail of sticky brown crumbs down Rudolph's shiny red nose on her crimson holiday onesie. When I reach for her with the damp washcloth, her rosebud mouth twists, her face scrunches up like a wadded paper bag, turns the color of an overripe tomato, and she lets out a glass-shattering shriek that makes my eardrums throb. Mrs. Henderson next door, with her collection of ceramic cats and paper-thin walls, probably thinks I'm performing some sort of ritualistic sacrifice instead of just wiping cookie goop off my daughter's dimpled face. No matter. I scoop her up, feeling her warm, squirming weight against my chest, and take her upstairs to change her, her howls of indignant protest—worthy of an opera diva—echoing down the hardwood stairs the entire time.

Crisis averted and Brinley in a new onesie with a new cookie - apparently I'm a glutton for punishment - we all decorate the tree. The seven-foot Douglas fir transforms under our hands, first with classic white lights, then my signature touch—a strand of pale pink ones. Cameron's life story dangles from the branches: the family photo with Stephanie and Alecia; the miniature hockey skates from his Harvard Westlake days; that handblown glass football helmet; even his crew team ornament. Father Christmas watches it all from his perch at the top.

His face crumples when he pulls out the Clara ornament from The Nutcracker, followed by the Sugar Plum Fairy, the delicate figurines dangling from his trembling fingers.

"Alecia and I took Stephanie to see *The Nutcracker*," he chokes out. "She screamed with joy when Clara appeared. We'd already signed her up for ballet lessons the next morning. And maybe she would've been a star if—" His voice shatters.

My chest feels like it's being crushed in a vise. Jesus Christ. A child ripped away forever. All those firsts stolen—first heartbreak, first rebellious tattoo, first time telling her parents to fuck off. I can't tear my eyes from Cameron as he white-knuckles that tiny Clara ornament like it's the only thing keeping him tethered to earth. My arms ache to hold him, to absorb some of that grief, but Willow beats me to it, wrapping herself around him while he pinches the bridge of his nose so hard I can see the skin blanch, fighting a tsunami of tears.

He nods. "Don't worry about it. These ornaments just... they get to me every time." His voice catches slightly as he exhales, blinking away the moisture gathering at his lashes. "I was thinking—maybe I could get that photo of Brinley with Santa framed. Turn it into one of these." He taps a glass ball gently with his fingertip. "Or if it turns out really well, we could use it for Christmas cards this year."

I plaster on a smile, frozen in place. My fingers twitch at my sides, wanting to reach for him, to offer comfort the way I always have. But Willow's already there, her arm sliding around his shoulders as they settle onto the couch. Cameron pulls out a worn photo album, their heads tilting together over the pages. No glance my way, no patting the empty cushion beside him. Just the two of them in their bubble while I hover on the outskirts. My stomach knots as I watch them. Shit. I always thought he'd be waiting in the wings for me, ready whenever I finally made up my mind. The realization hits like a slap—he might actually choose her, even if I confess to him how I really feel. My chest tightens, panic rising in my throat.

I wish Mom was home instead of playing piano at that fancy-ass club. I'm just a third wheel here, and I can't take another second of it.

"I'm out," I announce to the lovebirds on the couch with their precious photo albums.

Cameron barely looks up, just nods. Willow, though—she bounces to her feet and wraps her arms around me. Always with the hugging, this one. Used to make my skin crawl, but whatever. She's genuine, I'll give her that. Plus she smells expensive, like some boutique perfume that's all sandalwood and jasmine.

"Bye, Tally!" Her voice is sunshine and puppies. "'Next Saturday's Santa day with Brinley—it'll be magical!"

I end up at Celeste's without even meaning to, like my Jeep has a mind of its own. One minute I'm aimlessly cruising, the next I'm pulling into her fancy-ass circular driveway. When I hit the doorbell, Celeste appears with little Violet practically doing backflips on her hip, red-faced and howling like she's being murdered.

"Tally!" Celeste's face lights up despite the chaos. She yanks me into a one-armed hug. "Get in here!" She whispers something into Violet's ear, and the kid's tantrum magically downshifts. Within seconds, the two-year-old terror is thumb-in-mouth, head heavy against her mom's shoulder, eyelids drooping like she wasn't just raising hell.

Celeste adjusts the sleeping baby on her shoulder. "Let me put Violet down to sleep. Wait by the pool and we'll talk after."

I wander through rooms that could swallow my entire house whole. Marble floors that echo with every step. Ceilings so high they might have clouds. I remember the first time I visited—how I'd gawked like a tourist, thinking my best friend had hit the jackpot. Now all I see is three people rattling around in twenty thousand square feet while Rosa, their housekeeper-slash-therapist, lives in the guest cottage out back. Like buying a cruise ship to paddle around your bathtub.

Celeste emerges with a bottle of wine and two glasses. God, it feels fucking amazing to drink again after all those months of pregnancy sobriety. "Max not around tonight?" I ask, taking a greedy sip.

"Paris," Celeste says, pouring herself a generous glass. "Some French film company Kensington Films wants to swallow whole."

"What about Esme? She watching Violet?"

Celeste's smile falters. "Let her go last week. Told Max it was ridiculous paying someone to do what I'm perfectly capable of handling myself." She swirls her wine, not meeting my eyes. "I'm home all day anyway. Besides, at Violet's age, having two mother figures around just creates attachment confusion. Better if I'm the only woman in her daily life."

Makes sense. Poor Brinley, though—shuttled between three different women. Me, my mom when neither Cam nor I can be there, and Willow. Fucking Willow. Last night I caught myself staring at Brinley while she slept, wondering if someday she'd look at me and just see the screw-up who gave birth to her, while perfect Willow became her real mom. The thought made my stomach drop like I was falling off a cliff. I'd lose everything—Cam to Willow, and my baby girl right along with him. Who could blame her? Willow's got her shit together. I'm the one with bright red nail polish and baby food in my rainbow-streaked hair. Game over. If I were tiny enough to fit in Brinley's shoes, I'd probably toddle right over to Willow's perfect arms too.

“So you're flying solo with Violet now, huh?” I sigh. And then, just out of the blue, I start crying.

Celeste narrows her eyes. "You look like hell. What's wrong?"

I sink into her patio chair, staring at the ripples in her saltwater pool. She knows I traveled thirty miles in LA traffic to get to her house. I wouldn't be here if I wasn't desperate.

"It's Cameron," I finally say, my voice catching. "I always thought he was just killing time with Willow. That I could snap my fingers whenever I wanted him back. But tonight..."

"What happened tonight?" she asks, settling beside me.

"We were decorating the tree and he pulled out these Nutcracker ornaments. Apparently Stephanie loved the ballet, and he and Alecia had this whole fantasy about her becoming a dancer." I take another gulp of wine. "He got all teary, and Willow—fucking Willow—was right there holding his hand. They curled up with his photo albums and when I left, he barely noticed." I stare into my glass. "What if he proposes to her at Christmas? What if Brinley ends up carrying their goddamn wedding rings down the aisle? What if my own daughter starts calling her 'Mommy'?"

Celeste's eyes find mine. "Tally. You had to know Cameron would eventually stop waiting for you and commit to someone else."

I look at my blood-red nail polish. "Yeah. I knew." My throat tightens. "And sometimes I almost cave—almost tell him everything about how I love him so desperately I can't breathe sometimes. But then what? That's me making promises I'm not sure I can keep." I look up at Celeste. "I can't ask him to dump Willow when I don't even know if I can give him what he wants. That wouldn't be fair to anyone."

Celeste takes a deep breath. "Oh, Tally."

Something in her voice makes my stomach clench. "What? You're holding out on me, aren't you?"

She shakes her head. "No. I mean. Oh God."

The floor seems to tilt beneath me. Cameron must've told Max something—something Celeste is keeping locked up tight. Whatever vault Max asked her to stash it in, I'm about to crack the combination.

"Tally. I promised not to tell."

"Tell me what, exactly?"

"Cameron bought a ring for her."

The air leaves my lungs like I've been punched. My ears ring. Fuck. FUCK. FUCK!!!!! I did this to myself, didn't I? I torpedoed everything. That diamond Willow's getting for

Christmas had my name on it once—would've been mine the moment Cameron learned Brinley was his. I see his face at the chalet, feel his hands on my skin, hear him whispering he'd marry me tomorrow if I'd just say yes. If I'd just opened my damn mouth and told him how I felt, that ring would be mine.

Now it's too late. He's slipping that ring onto Willow's finger, and my worst fear is coming true right before my eyes.

I nod. "So my gut was right. Cameron's really gonna put a ring on it." My hands won't stop trembling, and my stomach lurches like I might hurl right here. Hot tears spill down my cheeks before I can stop them. That sick feeling I've been pushing away for months crashes over me like a wave. Cameron and Willow. Together. Forever. Moving forward while I stand frozen in place. I've been lying to myself this whole time, repeating that bullshit mantra: I'm fine with whatever happens. I can handle it.

But watching my words crumble against reality, I finally admit the truth.

I can't handle this.

Not even a little bit.

Chapter Forty-Two

CAMERON

The ring box digs into my thigh through my pocket. I shift in my seat, trying to quiet the voice in my gut screaming that this is wrong for both me and Brinley. On paper, Willow is perfect. Smart as hell, genuinely kind, and Brinley lights up around her.

Yesterday at the hospital, I hung back by the nurses' station, watching Willow sit with a bald little boy. She held his tiny hand in hers, nodding seriously as he asked her about angels and what happens after you close your eyes for the last time. And she was giving him comfort, telling him that there would be no more pain and he would feel only love, peace and joy. Then he asked, very seriously, about his mother and father. Would they be okay? And Willow assured him they would. That they would never forget him, that he would always be in their hearts with love.

My vision blurred, thinking about that brave kid facing the end, and Willow giving him exactly what he needed in that moment. I bought the damn ring that afternoon. What father wouldn't want someone that compassionate raising his daughter? What man wouldn't want that kind of heart mothering his future children?

Willow checks every box. She's smart, beautiful, kind—the complete package. Anyone would be lucky to call her their wife. So why am I hesitating?

Every night I lie awake in the attic bedroom Tally's loaned me, staring at the ceiling, listening to the sounds of her moving around downstairs and wanting desperately to join her in her bedroom. Even if it's just to hold her, to sleep in the same bed like we used to, to feel her warmth against my skin. But I don't dare. That would be breaking the rules. I hate her rules, but I have to respect them because I know why she made them. I break the rules and then she feels suffocated and, before you know it, we're fighting and I'm back in Brentwood.

Four months of dating Willow, and we haven't gone beyond goodnight kisses at her door. It's not for lack of attraction—God knows I've imagined what it would be like. But something stops me every time. Like crossing that line with Willow would be some final betrayal of Tally. Which makes no sense when Tally herself keeps nudging us together. Yet I can't shake the feeling that having sex with Willow means saying a permanent goodbye to Tally, and I'm not ready for that. Not even close.

Once my sports medicine fellowship starts in January, I'll be pulling seventy-hour weeks at UCLA. My place in Brentwood is right there, so moving back makes sense logistically. But what about Brinley? These past six months, I've been home every night by ten—even with dating Willow since August—and I'm the one who gets up when the baby cries at 2 AM. Tally needs her sleep for work, and I've been happy to handle those nighttime wake-ups. But now? We'll need a whole new parenting schedule, coordinated around both our jobs. I keep picturing Tally exhausted, dark circles under her eyes, trying to tattoo someone with Brinley screaming through the baby monitor. What happens when I'm not there anymore?

Tonight's the monthly Kensington brothers dinner—just me, Silas, and Roman this time. Next month it'll be Max and Asher, then Ansel and Connor after that. We rotate.

I check my watch and sigh. Silas. The one who dragged Willow to that damn retreat and started this whole mess. And Roman... At least he's mellowed out. The old Roman would've had three arguments with us both before the appetizers arrived. We always got along though—I understood his rage at Dad for vanishing without a word, and his frustration when none of us joined his crusade against forgiving the old man.

Something changed in him when he met Lilith. That tarot reader turned his life inside out, and now they're married and disgustingly happy. She's all honey sweetness and saint-like patience while he's still vinegar and hot pepper. Somehow, it works perfectly.

I spot Silas and Roman at our usual corner booth at Nobu, a bottle of sake and rainbow roll already waiting. I slide into the seat with a nod.

Roman fills a small ceramic cup and slides it toward me. "So Silas played matchmaker with you and Willow. And now there's a ring?"

Silas beams with self-satisfaction, looking so pleased with himself I have to resist the urge to jab my chopsticks somewhere painful. His intentions might be good, but I'm still irritated by his interference.

"I bought one," I admit. "But I've got reservations."

"About what?" Silas scoffs. "Or is this still about Tally?"

Instead of answering, I turn to Roman. "What's that thing Lilith always says about intuition?"

Roman swirls his sake thoughtfully. "That gut feelings aren't mystical—they're your subconscious processing millions of details your conscious mind misses. Lilith says your subconscious is like quantum computing while your conscious thoughts are running on dial-up."

I nod. Damn, this sounds so familiar.

I clear my throat. "So what's the verdict when your gut says one thing but your brain's screaming another?"

"Trust the gut," Roman says without hesitation. "Always."

Silas leans forward, eyes narrowing. "Why? You're not thinking about bailing on Willow, are you?" He jabs a finger in my direction. "I swear, Cameron, if you pull some dumbass move—"

To my surprise, Roman doesn't back Silas up. Instead, he rubs his jaw thoughtfully. "I used to be Team Brain all the way. Logic over feelings, every time. Then Lilith happened." A small smile plays at his lips. "Suddenly I'm believing in intuition, energy fields, the whole nine."

"Right," Silas snorts, elbowing Roman. "You're also reading tarot cards now, so maybe Cameron shouldn't be taking your spiritual awakening too seriously."

"Hey, dickhead," Roman snaps, "mock all you want, but Lilith read me like an open book with those cards. My wife sees things others don't."

When Silas opens his mouth to protest, Roman's expression shifts. One moment he's our brother—the next, he's that *other* Roman, the one who once broke a guy's wrist for keying his car. His face hardens like concrete setting, and the temperature around him seems to drop ten degrees. The wedding band on his finger catches the light as his hand tightens into a fist on the table. We all know the unspoken rule: Lilith is sacred ground. Question her beliefs, her choices, her anything—and you'll face that arctic stare that makes even Silas, six-foot-three and built like a linebacker, suddenly find something fascinating to study in his beer glass.

Silas retreats. No surprise there. Nobody wants to tangle with Roman, who's carried the family reputation for throwing fists since we were kids. Even now, with medical degrees and designer suits between us, if you asked any Kensington which brother you least wanted to piss off, Roman's name would come out first every time.

Silas shoots Roman a look. "Tell me you're not about to torpedo things with Willow over Tally."

I clear my throat, fingers tightening around the sake bottle. The bottle feels warm against my palm. If Tally walked through that door right now and said she wanted me—really wanted me—I'd probably trip over myself getting to her. But every time I think I see a crack in her armor, she seals it back up twice as thick. Sure, she's made comments about Willow, little digs that betray something beneath the surface. But that's not the same as being ready for us. For this.

The tattoos on Tally's skin tell stories, but the ones beneath run deeper. I understand why she guards herself—why wouldn't she, with her past? Yet understanding doesn't bridge the gap between us. Her walls make sense, but they still stand between what we could be. But I've spent enough time waiting. When I met her, something shifted in me—like I could finally breathe after drowning in what happened with Alecia and Stephanie.

I want Sunday mornings with pancakes and bedtime stories. Brinley needs that too—a home where the foundation doesn't shift. And Willow... she'll give my daughter something steady to hold onto, someone whose kindness won't disappear overnight.

I shake my head. "No way. Willow's the one." The words come out hollow, like I'm trying to convince myself more than them.

Roman narrows his eyes. "Cam, I'm getting weird vibes here." He leans forward, elbows on knees. "Call it intuition or whatever, but you don't sound like a guy who believes what he's saying."

Silas scoffs, shooting Roman a look. "Oh, for fuck's sake. Ever since you married that crystal ball lady, everything's 'cosmic vibrations' and 'aura readings.' Try using logic for once." He shifts toward me, one eyebrow cocked. "What's your take on this, Cameron? Your actual take?"

Roman's jaw tightens. "Lilith's not a crystal ball lady. She's trained in tarot interpretation and energy work. Show some fucking respect."

Silas knocks back more sake, then sets down his cup with a sigh. "My bad. Tarot interpreter." His attention swings back to me. "But seriously, Cam. What's your brain telling you?"

I exhale slowly. "The logical choice is Willow. She's perfect on paper—we speak the same medical language, she's got a heart of gold, Brinley adores her, and she's gorgeous. We've walked the same paths, held the same dying hands. And both of us know what it's like to lose the center of our world - she lost her husband, I lost my wife and daughter. So, we know each other's pain."

I don't mention that despite the attraction—which is definitely there—we haven't slept together. They'd never understand why: every time I get close, Tally's face flashes in my mind like I'm betraying her somehow. It's absurd, I know. But when Willow kisses me, I respond. The chemistry isn't our problem.

"So, there you go," Silas says. "You try to make a list of pros and cons, and if you make a list of the pros with Willow, you'll have a shit ton. Do the same list for Tally, and it's all cons, man. All cons."

I nod, but something twists in my gut. If Tally's so wrong for me, why does everything about her feel so right?

But I know one thing - I need something solid to believe in. Tally's given me nothing—not a single foothold to climb toward her. She won't even step out of her own way long enough to let me in. Meanwhile, Willow keeps painting this future for us. "I'm falling for you," she says. "I can see forever with you." Those words, right out in the open.

Does Tally love me? Hell if I know. She's never said it, never shown it. That night at the chalet, when everything between us felt so real, so raw—I let those three words slip out. Couldn't hold them back. And what did she do? Pretended not to hear me. Just kept moving like I hadn't laid my heart bare between us. And I've told her I love her several more times since then, and she's always played deaf when I say those words. If that's not my answer right there, what is? When someone can't even acknowledge your love, they've already given you their response.

Roman leans in, lowering his voice. "Look, Cam. You need to understand something about Silas. He's got skin in this game with you and Willow. He played matchmaker, and Willow's in his inner circle. If things crash and burn, he's the one who'll catch hell from her, not to mention looking like a complete idiot. And you know how Silas hates being wrong about anything." He taps his finger on the table. "Just... filter whatever advice he gives you, alright?"

Silas narrows his eyes at Roman. "Shut the fuck up,

bro." He rolls his eyes. "You think I'd steer Cameron toward a lifetime of misery just to avoid admitting I'm wrong? Listen, logic beats instinct every time. Period. Your brain's the reliable one here." He makes a dismissive gesture. "Look at the facts—one woman keeps pushing Cameron away while the other is all in. And bonus, she actually shares his interests." He jabs his chopsticks in my direction. "Trust me on this—being able to talk until sunrise about shit you both care about? That's the foundation. Not whatever primal thing you had going with Tally."

Guy's got a point. I give in with a smile and pull out the ring for my brothers to inspect. The princess cut diamond catches the light, its platinum setting gleaming. Nothing like Max's extravagant pink diamond that cost him millions, or Roman's rare blue stone he hunted down for Lilith. My brothers and their damn colored diamonds. Me? I went classic. Simple. And yeah, I didn't agonize over catalogs for months or whatever, but that doesn't mean I don't care. I just... didn't want to make it complicated. That's all.

I sigh. Who am I fooling? For Tally, I wouldn't just walk into a jewelry store and point at something behind glass. I'd lose sleep sketching designs. I'd corner Celeste and Olivia for intel on what would make her eyes light up. Not just any stone would do—I'd need something as complex as she is. I've actually pictured it: a natural black diamond with hidden fire inside, revealing different colors every time she moves her hand. Pure Tally—darkness with unexpected brilliance underneath. God help me, I've already researched suppliers and bookmarked designs that might be worthy of her finger. That's how far gone I am.

Roman and Silas look at the ring, and Roman looks back at me. "Pretty," he says and then raises an eyebrow. He knows that this generic ring means I'm just not really feeling this. Silas is right about one thing - Lilith has changed him. He's much more sensitive now, much more likely to see what's under the hood.

Silas, on the other hand, beams at the ring and nods.

"Now that's what I call an engagement ring. Flawless clarity, platinum setting, princess cut." He nods approvingly. "Knocked it out of the park, Cam." Leave it to our resident gemologist to recognize a six-figure stone when he sees one. In his mind, that price tag equals commitment.

Roman's eyes narrow, reading me like a book he'd rather not finish. "Cam," he says, shaking his head slightly, "just be true to yourself, alright? Whatever you decide, we've got your back. I just want to make sure it's what you actually want."

I swallow hard and take a sip of sake. "It's what I really want."

Roman shakes his head, but Silas claps a hand on my shoulder. "Time to make it official and bring Willow into the fold! Let's have Asher handle the engagement bash—you know what he's like when he gets his hands on party planning."

I nod. "Asher's the man for the job. Once I get that 'yes,' I'm handing him the reins. Between my sports medicine fellowship kicking off and everything else, wedding planning's the last thing I've got bandwidth for. Engagement party, venue hunting—all that stuff. Asher can work his magic."

After dinner, Silas heads out while Roman and I hang back in front of the restaurant. "I can tell something's up," he says, crossing his arms. "Either you tell me what's going on, or I'm asking Lilith. And we both know once she gets her cards involved, there's nowhere to hide. Your choice—talk to me now or face the tarot inquisition."

I sigh. "I just can't shake Tally. There's just a big part of me that still thinks she's end game. But Silas is right. That's just my heart talking. My brain is screaming at me to put a ring on it for Willow. I know you're worried about me, and I love you for it, but here's the thing. I'm not settling. It's not like forcing myself to marry somebody completely wrong for me. On the contrary, Tally is completely right for me."

"You mean, Willow is right for you, don't you?"

I nod. "Yes, yes. Right. Willow is completely right for me. So I'll be happy with her. Everything about her is right for me."

Roman grabs my shoulder, fingers digging in. "Listen to yourself, man. We both know Tally owns you. But if she won't have you—" he shrugs, his expression darkening. "Life's brutal that way. You can't always get what you want, but sometimes you get what you need. The Stones knew that shit."

I nod.

Yes, you can't always get what you want. But sometimes you can get what you need.

And, on paper, Willow is everything I need.

Chapter Forty-Three

TALLY

The front door clicks open and Cameron comes in. No idea where the fuck he's been, but I can imagine. No. I actually only have one guess - fucking Willow.

I'm sprawled on the couch, empty tequila bottle on the coffee table. Last night's bombshell about him buying Willow a ring still burns in my gut. This morning I couldn't even look at him. He knew something was up but didn't have the balls to ask, so I escaped to my studio. Bad idea. I snarled at everyone who walked through the door, but hey—the clients ate it up. Nothing sells tattoos like an artist with a chip on her shoulder and a middle finger ready to fly.

Now I'm three sheets to the wind with Brinley asleep upstairs. Mother of the Year, right? If she needed the ER tonight, I'd be screwed. But fuck it. I've been dry for months, and tonight I earned this bottle. Problem is, tequila's just making everything worse—like pouring gasoline on my already raging dumpster fire of anger. Each shot just cranks the dial from pissed to nuclear.

So when Cameron comes home, and I just assume he had been out with Willow, I let him have it.

“Cam,” I slur. "You need to get your shit and get out. Tonight.”

He looks at me with an expression of bafflement and concern. “Why?”

“Because I don't want you here anymore. You obviously don't wanna be with me, you wanna be with Willow, so be with her already! Just be with her! Just put a ring on her, I know you're going to.”

His face drops like a fucking stone, and I spot the bulge in his coat. Before he can say a goddamn word, I lunge across the space between us, ripping into his pocket like a woman possessed. My fingers are trembling so hard I nearly drop the tiny velvet box. Holy shit. Holy SHIT. Inside sits a ring that catches the light like a supernova—platinum band, diamond the size of my knuckle. Not what I'd have picked in a million years—my dream ring would have rose engravings or black diamonds or something that screams ME—but Jesus Christ, it's stunning enough to knock the breath clean out of my lungs.

I see it and my stomach turns inside out. Fuck. FUCK! FUCK!!!!! That diamond could pay off my student loans twice over. I can already picture it sparkling on Willow's perfect little hand with the perfect manicure that she obviously takes the time to get every week. Of course he'd end up with someone like her. Little Miss Perfect was written in his stars from day one. So much for the guy who played Chopin at 2 AM and looked at my mom like she hung the moon. Looked at me like I mattered. What a joke. He's running right back to his comfort zone—a shiny-haired brunette who probably has a designer reusable coffee cup for her oat milk lattes and a closet full of beige everything.

Someone he can parade around his fancy doctor cocktail parties without having to explain away her tattoos or her language.

Cameron's face transforms before my eyes as he snatches the ring with shaking hands. His usually placid features harden, jaw clenching tight enough to make the muscle twitch beneath his stubbled cheek. His eyes narrow to slits, pupils dilating until they nearly swallow the sapphire irises. The vein at his temple pulses visibly.

His face shows rage. Pure, undiluted rage. His nostrils flare as he takes a sharp breath, shoulders squaring as if preparing to lunge. He looks like he's finally gonna fight back instead of taking my shit like he always does. And I say, bring it fucking on.

Cameron drags both hands through his hair, yanking at the roots. "What the *fuck* did you think would happen, Tally? You practically gift-wrapped me for her." He stalks across the floor, each footfall like a thunderclap. "Every goddamn time I said 'I love you,' you froze like a corpse. Every single time I mentioned marriage, you looked at me like I was speaking fucking Mandarin." His jaw clenches so tight a muscle jumps beneath his skin. "So yeah, I'm asking Willow to marry me. But don't you dare think I didn't have it all planned for you. But not this ring—Christ, this ring isn't even in your universe. I would've gotten you something that would've made people's eyes bleed. Platinum with those twisted roses you worship, like some gorgeous Ed Hardy dream. A natural black diamond that burns between blood-red, midnight-blue, and poison-green when it catches even a whisper of light." His eyes bore into mine like drills. "Silas would've moved heaven and earth to help me get it too, if he didn't think you were absolute fucking venom. Which he does. And right now?" He leans in, voice dropping to a lethal whisper. "I'm starting to think he was too damn kind."

That bastard. The ring he described—black diamond, colors that catch the light, tiny roses wrapped around the platinum band—it's like he reached into my dreams and stole the image right out of my head. He's doing this on purpose, showing me what I could've had if I hadn't been such a coward.

"Get out! Get out! Get the fuck out!" My finger jabs toward the ceiling, toward the attic room where he's kept his duffel bag half-packed for six months. "Go upstairs, get your shit, and get the fuck out now!"

His whole body trembles, face flushed with anger I've never seen before. "Go to hell, Tally. Just go to hell." He storms out the door without another word.

"What about your shit?" I shout after him. "You're just leaving everything?"

"Mail it. I couldn't care less right now."

I slam the door so hard the windows rattle. Upstairs, Brinley wails—probably terrified by the shouting match and the thunder of doors. Some mother I am, screaming like a lunatic while her father peels out of our lives.

Yet somewhere beneath my anger, I feel a twinge of respect. Sweet, gentle Cameron finally showed some backbone. Found his limit.

And damn me for admitting it, but seeing that fire in him just makes his absence sting even worse.

Chapter Forty-Four

CAMERON

After Tally slammed the door in my face, I drove straight back to Brentwood, white-knuckling the steering wheel the whole way. My blood's still boiling—I can't remember the last time I felt this level of rage. The absolute nerve of her. She practically shoved me at Willow, and now she's acting betrayed? I've laid my heart bare for her. Told her I love her. Told her she's it for me—the one I want to build a life with. And not because of Brinley. Christ, I'd have put a ring on her finger even if there wasn't a baby in the picture. If she doesn't see that by now, it's because she's deliberately looking the other way.

So this is how it goes? She gives me nothing, I try to move forward, and suddenly I'm the villain? She's kicking me out? That's a joke. A goddamn joke. Fuck this bullshit.

I pick up my phone and dial Willow's number. Not because I'm looking for company in bed tonight, but because I can't stand another minute without making her my fiancée. The ring box sits heavy in my pocket, practically burning a hole through the fabric. When she arrives,

I'll keep my distance—tell her I want to save ourselves for our wedding night. The real reason gnaws at me: some foolish part of my heart is still holding out for Tally, and I can't bring myself to have sex with Willow while that door remains even slightly open. God, listen to me. What kind of man proposes to one woman while pining for another? But I know Willow will say yes when I drop to one knee. Her emotions are transparent, honest—everything Tally's aren't. Willow's never been shy about wanting a future with me.

It's late, midnight, but I know that Willow does not work tomorrow. So, even though I apparently woke her up when I called her, she agrees to come over. "I've never been to your house, "she says. "I'm excited to see it."

Yeah, this house is going to shock her after seeing the place I shared with Tally. Tally's bungalow has its charms—weathered oak floors that creaked with every step, those hand-painted Mexican tiles in the kitchen, and that wrap-around porch where we'd watch fireflies dance around the century-old magnolias in the front yard.

But my Brentwood estate? It's another world. Marble floors cool against bare feet, vaulted ceilings that make even whispers echo, floor-to-ceiling windows that frame the Hollywood Hills like living artwork. The infinity pool seems to spill into the canyon below, and sometimes I'll spot Harrison Ford walking his dog or Clooney waving from his balcony. I bought this 5,000-square-foot monument to success when I finished my residency for one reason - Alecia fell in love with it and really wanted to live here. She gasped when she first saw the spiral staircase, trailing her fingers along the wrought iron railing. After the accident, I couldn't bear to erase that memory, which is the only reason I haven't sold it and bought something smaller.

Willow comes over, and I suggest we sit by the pool.

Despite the winter chill, I switch on the heat lamps and we settle in. Then I pull out the small velvet box.

"Willow," I say, my voice oddly flat even to my own ears, "these past few months have been great. Will you marry me?"

The words hang in the air like unwelcome guests. I've said nothing about love or forever or any of that stuff people usually say. Probably the worst proposal in history, yet I feel strangely detached about it.

With Tally, it would've been different. For her, I'd have created something unforgettable. Maybe composed a song, or enlisted Asher to help design something that spoke to her artistic soul. I'd imagined a scavenger hunt across the city—each stop a gallery or mural or sculpture she loves—culminating in that perfect moment when I'd kneel and offer her the ring I've pictured a thousand times in my dreams.

Willow doesn't seem to notice how hastily I've cobbled this proposal together. She flings her arms around me, tears streaming down her face. "Yes, yes, oh, God, a thousand times yes!!!!"

That's that, then. I'm going to marry Willow, and I swear to God I'll make it work. Why shouldn't I? On paper, she's perfect—brilliant doctor, kind heart, gorgeous smile. We click. We talk for hours. The chemistry's there. She ticks every box. She'll be good for me, good for Brinley. She has to be.

I clear my throat. "I should call Asher about throwing us an engagement party. We could do it here, or maybe at the Centurion—you know, that restaurant at The Patrician? My family's belonged to that country club since practically the Stone Age." I tap my chin. "Fun fact: archaeologists found cave paintings of the first Kensingtons filling out their membership applications." She giggles at my lame attempt at humor, and I feel a twinge of something I can't quite name.

Willow's eyes light up like a kid on Christmas morning. "Oh my god, I was hoping for this!" She bounces on her toes, her voice rising with each word. "We fit so perfectly together, don't we? I knew we were endgame." Her fingers lace through mine as she gazes around, already claiming the space. "Just imagine—you, me, Brinley. Our little family." She gives a dreamy sigh. "And maybe two more little ones running around someday." Not once does she ask why I'm here instead of at Tally's. Either it hasn't crossed her mind or she's deliberately avoiding the question. She squeezes my arm, her smile dazzling. "So, Cam. Show me our new kingdom."

I take her hand and we go into the house. I show her everything—the state-of-the-art kitchen with its gleaming Wolf range and Sub-Zero refrigerator that cost more than my first car, the living room with its soaring twenty-foot ceilings and floor-to-ceiling windows that frame the ocean like a living painting, the glass-walled atrium where morning light dapples through tropical plants, the temperature-controlled wine cellar stocked with vintages that would make a sommelier weep. The master bedroom features a California king on a raised platform, and the bathroom which has a rainfall shower big enough for six people and a Japanese soaking tub carved from a single block of marble.

This house is an architect's dream, which is why I love it —and it's Asher-approved. Ash is our resident art critic and architectural buff, the one who can spot a fake Eames chair from fifty paces, which is what he's chosen to focus his genius IQ on as opposed to science and physics, although if he did choose to focus on physics and chemistry, I have no doubt he'd have a Nobel Prize by now.

Willow's eyes widen as we finish the tour. "This place is incredible. And you traded all this for an attic bedroom just to be near your daughter?"

I rub the back of my neck, looking away from her searching gaze. The mansion suddenly feels hollow around me, each echo bouncing off marble and hardwood a reminder of what's missing. My throat tightens as I think about mornings with Tally's off-key humming drifting up through the floorboards, nights when I'd pass her door and pause, just to hear her breathing. How Brinley's tiny fingers would curl around mine while Tally pretended not to watch us from the doorway. This mansion with its perfect staging feels like a museum compared to the cramped, chaotic warmth of that little house.

"It wasn't really a sacrifice," I finally say, turning back to Willow with what I hope passes for a smile.

She clears her throat. "I mean, you were living with your daughter in Echo Park." She hesitates. "How will you manage visits now that you're back here?"

Brinley's face flashes in my mind. I stormed out so fast I didn't even think about visitation arrangements. Tally might be furious about my engagement, but she'd never use our daughter as a weapon. Even so, my fellowship barely leaves me time to breathe—twelve-hour days, six days a week. Now I'll waste precious hours crawling through gridlock between here and Echo Park just to see my own child. The thought makes my jaw clench. This whole situation is a disaster, but I didn't create it. She did. I should probably be more understanding, but Christ. After everything I've done, I don't deserve to be jerked around like this.

I exhale slowly. "It's complicated. Tally and I aren't exactly on speaking terms right now. We need to sort things out."

Willow nods, her expression careful. I can tell she's curious but trying not to push. "I was afraid of this. I never wanted to come between you and your daughter." She squeezes my hand. "I hope you two can work through it."

"We will," I say, not entirely convinced.

Her fingers slide over mine. "What do you say we head upstairs and celebrate our engagement properly?" The suggestion in her voice is unmistakable.

Throughout our relationship, I've kept a careful distance—always a goodnight kiss at her door, never accepting her invitations for "nightcaps" that would inevitably lead to her bedroom. At Tally's house, intimacy was never an option, which made visits there safe. Now we're alone in my home with nothing stopping us except the image of Tally's face that appears whenever I close my eyes. Something tells me crossing this line with Willow would permanently sever whatever remains between Tally and me. Some bridges, once burned, stay ashes forever.

What kind of man was I becoming, obsessing over whether Tally and I could ever find our way back to each other? I pushed the thought away. Marriage to Willow would close that door forever anyway. Better to stick with my original plan.

"Uh, let's wait until after we're married, okay?" I say, then inspiration strikes. "After what happened with Tally—you know, the pregnancy—I'd rather not risk repeating history. It just seems smarter to wait."

The words hang between us, concealing my deeper fear: if Willow gets pregnant and our engagement falls apart, I'd be drowning in complications. One child with a woman I'm not married to is difficult enough. Two children with two different women? The thought of juggling these relationships makes my stomach turn. But I couldn't tell Willow that —she'd think I was already planning our failure.

She nods, her lips pressed together in that way people do when they're pretending to understand but don't. I can see the questions flickering behind her eyes. Chemistry isn't our problem—my body responds to her like a tuning fork struck against stone. But every time I lean in, Tally's face appears in my mind. My rational side argues this is ridiculous; Tally and I aren't together, probably never will be. Yet something in my chest tightens, refuses to budge. Like trying to force a key into the wrong lock—it simply won't turn.

Willow's brows knit together. "Okay," she says, hesitating. "I just figured that you calling me this late at night... well, maybe I was reading too much into it."

I run my hand through my hair. She's right—who calls someone at midnight unless they want something? This whole thing was impulsive. The second Tally shut me down, I called Willow, desperate to put a ring on her finger before I could think twice. That's not me. I don't make life-altering decisions on a whim. I should have waited, done this properly.

What if this proposal is just a reaction to Tally's rejection? If that's true, we're screwed from the start.

Hell, we probably are anyway.

No. I shake my head. I can't go into marriage already assuming failure. Think positive. Willow is perfect for me. She is.

She's perfect for me.

But she's not Tally.

Chapter Forty-Five

TALLY

Mom finds me on the couch at 3 a.m., tequila bottle on the coffee table, while Brinley screams bloody murder upstairs. The kid who's been sleeping through the night for weeks is suddenly channeling a banshee, like she knows everything's gone to shit.

"Tally, what happened?" Mom's eyes dart from me to the empty driveway where Cameron's car should be.

The evidence is all there—drunk daughter, crying baby, missing baby daddy. Mom doesn't need a geology degree to see the seismic event that just leveled our lives.

"Cam's gone," I say, my voice cracking. "I kicked him out. He left furious." My stomach churns with alcohol and rage while my hands shake. "We'll need some custody arrangement, but how the fuck am I supposed to look at him now?"

I pace the living room floor, yanking at my hair while Brinley's wails echo through the ceiling.

"Everyone does this shit—exes passing kids back and forth like fucking parcels. But how?" The words tumble out.

"How do you stand there making small talk with someone who used to be your everything without breaking apart every single time?"

Mom slams her mug down. "Tally, why the hell did you kick him out?"

"Because, Mom," I spit the word like venom, "he was going to leave anyway. He's putting a goddamn ring on Willow's perfect little finger for Christmas. I just accelerated the inevitable before he could rip my heart out."

Mom's eyes narrow to slits. "What did you expect? Jesus Christ, Tally! You've been playing with fire this entire time." She jabs her finger at me. "You practically shoved Cameron at that gorgeous doctor with her perfect hair and perfect teeth. Everyone could see he was miserable—that he's desperate for you. But you pushed and pushed until he broke, and now he's gone. Are you fucking satisfied now?"

I slam my glass down, tequila sloshing over my fingers. "That's rich coming from you. I'm supposed to take relationship advice from the queen of bad decisions?"

"What's that supposed to mean?" Her voice drops dangerously low.

"I mean your revolving door of men, Mom! You couldn't keep a man if you handcuffed him to the bed! You wouldn't recognize a healthy relationship if it slapped you across the face!"

"Well, neither do you, obviously!" She's shouting now, face flushed.

"AND WHOSE FAULT IS THAT?" I scream, hurling my glass against the wall where it shatters, Patrón streaking down the paint. "Who showed me exactly what love looks like? You were my fucking blueprint!"

Something inside me knows I should stop, but the alcohol has unleashed the beast I keep chained. It claws its way up my throat, shredding every careful boundary I've built. The rage I've buried under smiles and tattoo ink is breaking free, and I can feel myself burning bridges I might never rebuild.

Mom bolts up the stairs.

"Where are you going?"

"Your daughter's been wailing since I pulled in the driveway. God knows how long before that."

Shit. Brinley. I'm down here getting hammered while my baby screams her lungs out upstairs. Some mother of the year I turned out to be—kicking out her dad, then drowning my guilt in top shelf tequila. With Cameron around, I could fake the whole responsible parent thing. Now? My hands shake as I imagine Brinley at sixteen, with my tattoos and my mouth and my taste in losers. The cycle continues, courtesy of yours truly.

Mom descends with my red-faced daughter clutched against her chest. Brinley's cheeks glisten with tears, her tiny mouth working: "Ba-da-ba-ba-ba." Not actual words—she's only six months old—but the desperate babble cuts straight through me. Her eyes dart around the room like she's searching for something. For Cameron? For the mom who had her shit together a day ago? Babies pick up on everything. The tension in this house must feel like static electricity against her skin.

I sink into the rocking chair and hold my arms out for my daughter. Mom hesitates—she can smell the tequila from where she stands—but hands her over anyway. The room tilts slightly as I cradle my baby against my chest, her tiny fingers clutching at my shirt. I hum something soft and tuneless, swaying in time with the chair's gentle motion. Her eyes, so much like his, stare up at me, wide and questioning. My voice cracks on the third verse of whatever lullaby I'm attempting. She shouldn't have to feel the tremor in my hands or see the mess I've become, but tonight, she just needs her mother—drunk, broken, or otherwise.

"Mom," I say. "I need to take her to see Santa. I was supposed to go with Cameron and Willow, but, that's not gonna happen now. But I need to give her as normal of a Christmas as I can. I know she's too little to really appreciate any of it, but, one of these days, she's gonna be looking for pictures of her first Christmas and I want her to have them. So I'm hoping you can go with me to see Santa with her."

"Of course," Mom says. "when do you want to go?"

"I was supposed to go with Cameron and Willow next Saturday. But I think I can say that I'm not going to go to work tomorrow. I mean today, considering it is tomorrow right now. It's OK, Blade's been amazing, and he can hold down the fort. I thought I'd like to do that later on today."

Mom sinks into the couch beside me. "Tally, are the therapy sessions helping at all?"

I shrug. "They're fine. Just—you can't exactly erase decades of bullshit with a few months of talking, you know? But I'm trying."

Mom's eyes soften. "And what about Cameron? Is that door completely closed?"

"He bought Willow a ring, Mom." My throat tightens. I stare at the ceiling, blinking hard. "Look, I don't blame him. I blame me. He's a good man who deserves someone whole, and that's what she is. That's the reality I'm facing." I stroke Brinley's tiny hand. "Some days I feel like I'll never put myself back together. But if he's happy... I'll learn to be happy for him. And maybe someday I'll figure out that me and this little nugget—that we're enough."

Brinley's eyes flutter closed, thumb sliding into her

mouth. I trace the curve of her cheek with my fingertip, memorizing her face like it might disappear. Her baby smell hits me—milk and powder and something uniquely her—and my eyes burn.

"This is it for me," I whisper, the truth of it like swallowing glass. "Just her and me against the fucking world. And you." I look at Mom. "Cameron's gone. Forever gone. And I need to tattoo that reality onto my heart before it kills me."

Chapter Forty-Six

TALLY

I dial Celeste's number. Since she writes screenplays from her home office, her schedule's usually pretty flexible. Sure, she's got deadlines hanging over her head, but I'm betting she can spare a day to join Brinley and me for our Santa visit. At least it's Friday—weekdays mean fewer screaming kids and mile-long lines.

The Westfield mall's something of a unicorn. While shopping centers across America are turning into ghost towns, ours is packed year-round. It's got that outdoor layout with actual walkways and fountains, not just some fancy street of disconnected boutiques like Rodeo Drive. A real mall, and easily the hottest shopping spot for fifty miles.

Celeste balks at first—Century City means a twenty-mile drive for her, fifteen for me—and I know interrupting her workday is asking a lot. Writers don't exactly appreciate being yanked out of their fictional worlds mid-sentence.

"Fine. But Cameron's gone. I kicked him out last night."

The line goes silent. Then I hear rustling, like she's already changing clothes.

"Shit, Tally. I shouldn't have told you about the ring. Max is going to murder me when he finds out."

I roll my eyes. "Please. It's not like I wouldn't find out eventually. What was your plan—wait until I got a wedding invitation? You just ripped the Band-Aid off early. I'm not mad, and Max won't be either."

“Max wanted you and Cameron to have a good Christmas with little Brinley together."

"Right, and drop the bomb after we've taken those perfect family Santa photos for Instagram." I snort, looking at my blood red nail polish. "Whatever. Perfect Willow gets perfect Cameron in his perfect Brentwood mansion. Timing's irrelevant." My voice cracks despite my best efforts. "At least I won't be standing there like a dumbass in line at the mall while they hold hands behind my back."

I squeeze my eyes shut, but the images flood in anyway. Cameron helping Willow unpack her designer suitcases. Her manicured hand on his kitchen counter. The two of them curled up on his couch, planning their future—her voice syrupy sweet as she talks about "our daughter" and the siblings she wants to give her.

My stomach knots. That bastard better make one thing crystal fucking clear to her—Brinley is MY daughter. Mine. The only good thing I've got left in this dumpster fire of a life. And nobody—especially not some country-club Barbie —is taking that from me.

We converge at the mall—me, my mother, Celeste with little Violet in tow, and Brinley strapped to my chest. Violet, all of two years old, bounces with excitement about seeing Santa, while Brinley just drools on my shirt, completely oblivious to the holiday chaos we're about to subject her to.

Celeste adjusts the sunshade on Violet's stroller. "So. Cameron's gone?"

"Kicked his ass straight to the curb," I say, watching Violet babble something that sounds suspiciously like "molecular structure" to her stuffed bunny. Kid's vocabulary is freaky for twenty-six months. "And before you ask—I'm done talking about him and Willow. Filed that shit away like the Ark at the end of *Raiders*. You know that scene? Giant warehouse, endless boxes? I'm storing this whole clusterfuck in the mental equivalent of that giant warehouse, because otherwise I might actually murder someone."

Violet looks up at me and smiles, all baby teeth. "Aunt Tally. Bunny for you." She pushes her small stuffed bunny into my hands, its fur matted from being dragged around all day.

"Thanks, Vi," I say, trying to hand it back, but she shoves it at me again. Her blue eyes lock onto mine with that weird intensity only toddlers have, like she can see straight through my bullshit.

Fine. I clutch the rabbit against my chest, and something in me cracks a little. This tiny human offering me her most prized possession because she somehow knows I'm falling apart? Fuck. I swallow hard and pat her head. Kids, man. They see everything.

"That one's got a good heart," I tell Celeste.

"I know," Celeste says, beaming. "Last week at Gymboree, she spotted this boy hiding behind his mom's legs. Wouldn't talk to anyone. By the end of class, she had him building a block tower with her." Celeste tucks a strand of hair behind her ear, her eyes never leaving her daughter. "And there was this other little girl whose parents were screaming at each other during pickup. My Violet just walked over and held her hand until they were done."

I nod, feeling something warm in my chest despite

myself. All the degrees and achievements in the world don't mean shit without a heart.

Shit. Seeing that look on Violet's face—that pure-hearted concern for others—it's like a knife to the gut. Cameron has that same look. The one I pushed away. The one who's probably making breakfast for little Miss Perfect right now, his shirt unbuttoned to show just a bit of his gorgeous and perfect chest. Cameron, who looked at me like I was his forever person. Who showed up when he said he would. Who called when he was running late. Who wouldn't have just disappeared one day like my mom's loser guys. I run my tongue over the sharp edge of my incisor and taste blood as we get closer to Santa.

We reach the front of the line and place both girls on Santa's lap. Violet's an old pro at this—she sits there grinning like she's reuniting with a beloved uncle. Brinley, though? Her little face crumples, then she lets out a wail that probably has elves covering their ears at the North Pole. Click. Annddddd there's our Christmas memory preserved forever.

I can already picture teenage Brinley rolling her eyes when this photo makes its annual appearance. Maybe she'll laugh about it someday. Or maybe she'll add it to her list of childhood traumas to discuss in therapy, right after "Mom forced me to wear matching Christmas sweaters" and before "Mom wouldn't let me get a belly button ring at twelve." Whatever. As long as she doesn't end up preferring Willow over me—though honestly, I just want her to be happy. Santa's lap trauma and all.

Brinley's still screaming bloody murder as I pry her off Santa's lap. So much for holiday magic. We head to Javier's for overpriced tacos while Mom keeps staring at the photo, beaming like Brinley isn't having a complete meltdown.

"This would make the perfect Christmas card," Mom says, pointing to the picture.

"Right. And who exactly would I send it to? Everyone I care about is sitting at this table." I pause. "Well, maybe Olivia."

Mom gives me *that* look. "What about Cameron? Don't you think he'd want—"

"Not. Another. Word." I stab my fork into a chunk of avocado. "And hell no."

The truth hits me like a hangover. Part of me knew Cameron was dying to take Brinley to see Santa himself. And maybe—okay, definitely—I rushed to do it first so he couldn't have that moment with her. I don't know why I'm being such a bitch about it, but the thought of him and Willow creating Christmas memories with my daughter makes something twist inside me that I'm not ready to examine.

Celeste methodically hands animal crackers to Violet, who's washing them down with apple juice. Brinley's passed out in her carrier after her Santa meltdown, having gone from 60 to 0 like she does. I catch Celeste's eyes darting to me, then away. Shit. That look means trouble.

"Tally," she finally says, voice too careful. "You know Cameron's not just Max's brother—they're practically joined at the hip."

My stomach drops. "Yeah?"

"The wedding stuff will be starting. Engagement dinner at the Patrician next month, then the shower, bachelorette party, rehearsal dinner…" She trails off, twisting her wedding ring.

My hands go cold. Here it comes—my best friend asking permission to celebrate the marriage of the man I'm desperately in love with to someone else. And what can I say? Of course she has to go to all these things. Willow will be her sister-in-law or something like that - I'm never good at who's a sister or brother-in-law, let alone who's a second cousin twice removed. But Max and Cameron are brothers. All the Kensington men stick together like glue. It's just how it is.

I shrug. "Whatever. Just don't expect me to follow your socials for a while. That shit's gonna be all over my feed—tagged photos, group selfies, the works. I don't need to see it."

Celeste's shoulders drop. "God, Tally. This sucks. I feel like I'm betraying you just by going to these things. You know you come first with me, right? But it's happening whether we like it or not."

I force a smile and jingle my car keys. "Yeah, yeah. Anyway... you up for a good Marvel flick at the Cineplex?"

"You good?"

I nod. "Fine."

Fine? I'm about as fine as a fresh tattoo in salt water. Every time I picture Celeste getting dragged to all these wedding events, it's like someone's twisting a knife right in my gut. God knows how many parties these people have planned. The Kensingtons don't do anything small—they're throwing the engagement party at some fancy-ass country club, for Christ's sake. And the bachelorette party? Probably jetting off to some exotic locale. I don't know if Willow's family has a mansion in Italy or whatever, but the Kensingtons sure as hell do—some sprawling villa on Lake Como.

If they end up having the bachelorette party there, I'm literally going to vomit.

Chapter Forty-Seven

CAMERON

Events are moving too fast, and I can't seem to hit the brakes. My sports medicine fellowship consumes nearly every waking hour—I haven't seen Brinley in months, which gnaws at me constantly, though Tally hasn't exactly been pushing for father-daughter time. Despite my insane schedule, Asher managed to throw us an engagement party at the Patrician that would make Hollywood jealous. My colleagues from the hospital showed up in force, but I was blindsided by Willow's guest list. All this time together, and she never mentioned her father's photography career puts her on a first-name basis with supermodels, actresses, and other camera royalty.

Not that I was taken aback by this, mind you. I've grown numb to the spectacle of wealth. When your brothers include Max and Roman, who make billion-dollar deals before breakfast; Connor and Kalen, whose faces appear on magazine covers monthly; Silas, who designs jewelry for actual princesses; and Ansel, whose Grammy shelf requires its own wall—well, you develop a certain tolerance. Even

Asher, who orchestrated our engagement event, counts Hollywood royalty - not to mention actual royalty - as his regular clients. I may have chosen the "humble" path of medicine, but the Kensington name still means I've shaken more famous hands than most people ever will. Yet watching the flash of cameras outside as another celebrity arrived to our party, I can't help wishing we'd eloped.

And that was just the engagement party. The celebrations continued with impressive frequency—Willow's bachelorette weekend was held at her Tahoe estate, where I'm told the ladies demolished several cases of Veuve Clicquot.

The countdown to my wedding day has begun—just one month to go. Everything's happened at warp speed since Willow and I got engaged at Christmas. Now it's May, and June 14th looms on the horizon. I keep repeating that this is what I want, that after all these engagement parties and wedding showers and deposits paid, there's no turning back. Yet I catch myself staring out windows, wondering what Tally's doing right now, how Brinley's liking her Gymboree (I only know Brinley's enrolled in Gymboree because Celeste told me) classes and if they ever think of me.

Especially Tally. Dammit, I catch myself staring at Willow's profile, searching for Tally's jawline, her smirk. The engagement photos scattered across our coffee table—posed kisses at sunset on the Santa Monica Pier, champagne toasts at the Griffith Observatory—they all feel like someone else's life. Meanwhile, Brinley's turning one next month, right around the time I'll be married to Willow.

Celeste texts me updates: "Got her first top tooth." "Started walking yesterday, so she's an early walker!" "Said mama and pointed to Tally." "Said 'kitty' today and chased it across the living room." I read these messages in the middle of meetings, in bed at 3 AM, when I'm having dinner with Eli or Willow or one of my brothers or my father, and each one is a knife twist I can't stop reaching for. The video Celeste sent me of Brinley running across the floor after the cat while screaming "kitty here!" brings tears to my eyes, yet I can't stop watching it and demanding more.

My bachelor party will be taking place in Paris this weekend. We'll all be traveling to Max's place in the Grós-Caillou district - a sleek penthouse with floor-to-ceiling windows with a view of the Eiffel Tower, marble counter-tops cold to the touch, and that distinct scent of luxury that only comes with seven-figure real estate. He uses it for his quarterly business trips and took Celeste there during their honeymoon, where they apparently drank champagne on the wrought-iron balcony every sunset.

From there, I'm told we'll sample rare vintages in dimly lit cellars with centuries of dust on the bottles, pedal through the manicured gardens of Versailles with their geometric precision, and engage in other sophisticated pursuits befitting a guy who'd rather sip aged Bordeaux than wake up with a misspelled Chinese character tattooed on his ass and a Bengal tiger prowling the bath-room tiles.

Roman pulls up in his Aston to drive me to the airport. He's been able to read me like a book about this whole wedding—probably because Lilith keeps feeding him intel. His wife may not be psychic in the traditional sense, but she reads tarot and claims she can see auras around emotionally charged people. My aura, according to her, might as well be flashing warning signs.

I see Roman, who's looking like he wants to be anywhere else and I wonder what Lilith has told him about me. I shake my head. "I've told her to keep her cards in their box," I say as I toss my bag in the trunk.

Roman shrugs. "Doesn't need them to see you're having doubts." He gets into the driver's seat and I get in the passenger seat and look out the window. We're silent for a few minutes. "Listen, bro," he finally says, eyes on the road. "You can bail anytime. Nobody's gonna hold it against you —well, except maybe Silas, since he orchestrated this whole setup."

I've heard this speech before. Each time, I insist everything's fine, this is exactly what I want. But the truth? If Tally showed up right now, I'd cancel everything and marry her by sunset. No elaborate reception, no three hundred guests. She'd hate all that anyway. Tally would probably want something simple—maybe at that gallery she loves, with just a few people - Brinley, her mother, Celeste, Olivia - and the artwork as witnesses.

"Nope," I say, gut-punched by the thought of hurting Willow. She's decent through and through. I like her, no question. Can't find a damn thing wrong with her, which is weird. Everyone's got their shit. Most people, anyway. Maybe Willow really is perfect.

So why the hell am I still so drawn to Tally's mess?

And Christ, Willow's family—her dad shoots for National Geographic, her mom saves kids' lives as a pediatric surgeon, and they welcomed me like I'm already wearing their family crest. Night and day compared to the chaos Tally grew up in.

But Tally's moved past it all, and she's solid with her mom now. And Marisa—she's not just her diagnosis or the pills that made Tally's childhood a minefield. The woman's brilliant. Destroys me at chess half the time. Fuck, I miss those games—Marisa across the board, that little smirk when she's about to corner my king eight moves out. I'd see that look and know I was screwed, but whatever. Never cared much about winning anyway. Just liked watching her work.

I stare out the window, letting out a heavy breath. Roman tilts his head, those designer sunglasses hiding his eyes but not his disapproval.

"Dude, just cancel already. We're supposed to be hitting Paris this weekend, and you look like you're walking to your own execution."

"I said I'm fine," I snap, my tone sharper than intended.

"Bullshit. When I was marrying Lilith, I was counting down the hours. Couldn't sleep, couldn't eat—just wanted her to be my wife already. You? You've got that same look you had when we took old Bear to the vet that last time."

My stomach twists at the memory. "Don't bring the dogs into this."

"Cameron." Roman's voice softens, using my full name like he means business. "You've always been the one who faces problems head-on. When Dad walked out, you stepped up—fourteen years old and already the family backbone. Every scraped knee, every broken heart—we all came to you. So why are you running from this?"

What am I supposed to say? That for once in my life, I acted without thinking it through? I was just... responding. To Tally and her damn walls. To her practically gift-wrapping me for Willow. To facing the fact that Tally might never want what I want—a real future—while Willow's been ready for that all along. And Silas got in my head with all that talk about how sometimes you need to override your heart with your brain. Because hearts can be idiots, right? Hearts lead people into train-wreck relationships every day. We've all seen it—couples who are clearly poison for each other, but they "followed their hearts" straight into misery. That's the road Tally and I would be heading down if she can't get past her commitment issues. Just another relationship dumpster fire. So maybe Silas is right. Maybe the smart move is to ignore your heart when it's clearly steering you toward a cliff.

I shake my head. "I'm not running away from anything." Roman arches one eyebrow, his expression calling bullshit without saying a word. "Look, can we just—" I sigh. "Fine. Yes. I'm in love with Tally. Happy now?" I drag my palm down my face. "But I like Willow and she would be perfect for Brinley. I know that. She'll be a great mother, a fantastic role model." What I don't say is that I've been holding back with Willow, physically and emotionally, because some part of me is still waiting for Tally. "But Tally and me together? We're like those tragic couples in literature—doomed from the start. You know those stories, Roman. Tristan and Isolde. Romeo and Juliet. Paris and Helen. Heathcliffe and Catherine. When passion burns that hot, it doesn't keep you warm—it incinerates everything in its path."

Roman leans back in his seat, his eyes still carefully watching the road. "Look, bro. You're acting like it's either safe-but-boring or passionate-but-destructive. Why not hold out for both passion and stability? You say Willow's great, but where's the fire? Why not wait for someone who gives you butterflies without all of Tally's drama? What's your hurry anyway?"

I rub my temples. What *is* my hurry? The question hits harder than it should. Am I just trying to hurt Tally the way she hurt me? To show her I can move on too? Christ, I hope that's not it. There's got to be more to this than petty revenge. This isn't me—rushing into forever because my pride took a hit. Roman sees right through me. I've always been the rock, the one my brothers call at 3 AM when their lives are imploding. The Cameron I've built myself to be wouldn't make a decision this big for such small and petty reasons.

I clear my throat. "I just need to lock it down. So I can provide a stable home for Brinley."

The words hang in the air like a bad joke. What stability am I offering my daughter? A father who's about to marry a woman he doesn't love, and a mother, who he does love, living across town with her tattoo needles and that goddamn smile that still keeps him up at night. Soon I'll be signing custody papers, watching the clock during weekend visits, and passing Brinley back and forth in some parking lot. And every time I see Tally—those eyes, those lips, that attitude—I'll have to pretend my chest isn't caving in, that I'm not still completely fucking wrecked by her.

We get to Max's plane and I paste on a smile. Roman's the only one who really gets me. It's like he once said—the other guys all paired up naturally. Silas and Asher share a face, same as Connor and Kalen. Max and Ansel, barely a year apart, might as well be twins too. That left Roman standing alone, same as me. We gravitated toward each other like the last two kids picked for dodgeball. Not that I don't love all my brothers—I do. But when shit hits the fan, it's Roman I call first. Or it was, anyway. Now he's running triathlons with Max, and I'm wondering if Ansel might need a new buddy. The thought makes my smile feel even more plastic.

Fine. I'll just put on my big boy pants and enjoy Paris, damn it.

But when you have to give yourself a pep talk about a vacation in the City of Light, you're already screwed.

Chapter Forty-Eight

TALLY

I need to get the hell out of town. Cameron's tying the knot with Willow this weekend, and I can't stomach being anywhere near it. Celeste has been my reluctant informant—I practically have to waterboard her for details, and then she watches me melt down over each update. Tahoe bachelorette extravaganza. Peninsula Hotel shower number one. Spago for shower number two. Claire-fucking-Pettibone sewing the dress by hand. Paris bachelor party. 71Above for the rehearsal dinner.

"So the Peninsula penthouse suite shower wasn't enough?" I'd snapped at Celeste when I saw the pictures from Spago. "She needed TWO fucking showers?"

"You asked," Celeste had sighed, showing me photos of Willow unwrapping Hermès boxes at Spago while wearing a white sundress that probably cost more than my monthly mortgage.

Jesus Christ. Could it all be any more pretentious? I always knew he'd end up with someone like her—little Miss Connections, whose mommy and daddy have famous designer friends on speed dial because heaven forbid she shop retail like a peasant. The kind who casually drops "Let's just book out Spago" like she's ordering pizza. Meanwhile, Cameron jets off to Paris with the boys. What a predictable asshole he turned into.

I slam my phone down after seeing Celeste's latest Instagram post: Cameron and Willow toasting with champagne flutes at 71Above, the L.A. skyline twinkling behind them. Their rehearsal dinner. My stomach knots. Five days until their wedding. I need to be anywhere but here.

I glance at Mom. "You're still okay watching Brinley for the week, right?"

"Absolutely," she says, waving her hand dismissively. "The band can survive without me for a few days."

"Just remember I'll be calling every night from the campsite. Gotta make sure you're taking your pills and handling the baby okay. If it gets to be too much, I've got cash set aside for one of those Nanny Pod sitters." I've got it all planned out—days hiking through the Sierra Nevadas near Mammoth Lake, nights at the RV park where I can get decent reception. No way I'm going completely off-grid while leaving my kid and my recovering mom behind.

Mom's face softens. "Tally, honey, we'll be fine. After everything you've done for me..." She reaches for my hand. "Six days with my grandbaby is nothing. You deserve a break."

Later, I watch Brinley toddle across my living room, her chubby legs moving with surprising confidence for someone who's only been walking a few weeks. "Mama up!" she demands, raising her arms, marinara sauce still smeared across one cheek. I scoop her up, breathing in her baby-shampoo smell, and think about how Cameron has never heard her laugh—that full-body giggle that starts in her belly and explodes out like she's discovered the funniest thing in the universe.

The next early morning, I get up at 4 and take the Jeep - I finally came up with a name for her, and it's Sophie, don't ask me why, it just seems to fit her - and head up to the Sierra Mountains, right back to Mammoth—yeah, that Mammoth. Ground zero for this whole mess. Where Cameron and I started circling the drain that ended with him putting a ring on someone else's finger.

If I could hijack a DeLorean and blast back to that weekend, would I play it different? Now that I know he's marrying the chick I practically shoved into his arms, even though his eyes were on me the whole damn time? Shit. Million-dollar question right there. Part of me wants to curl up and die knowing he's with her. But I genuinely want the guy happy, you know? I just wish to hell I could be the one to do it. Maybe I could be, eventually. Or maybe that's the real problem—I don't know if I've got what it takes to make anyone happy, and that's the black hole I can't escape.

I pull into a gas station halfway up the mountain to fill my tank and grab some road snacks. When I come back out, there it is—another rubber duck perched on my bumper. Number twenty for my collection. They're all lined up across my dash now like some kind of weird rubber army.

This Jeep duck thing, whoever started it deserves a kiss. Nothing like finding a tiny surprise that doesn't cost anything but makes your whole day better. I've got the whole celebrity squad—an Elvis duck with his slick hair and rhinestone vest, a Marilyn duck in that white dress, an R2D2 duck, a Dolly duck with her big blonde hair, even a pirate duck with an eye patch. Each one makes me snort-laugh when I find it, which, considering the weekend I'm facing, is exactly the kind of stupid little joy I need right now.

The new duck bobbing on my dashboard makes me smile, and I crank the volume on Lithium—my go-to Sirius station for 90s grunge. The Red Hot Chili Peppers blast through the speakers with "Give It Away," not exactly matching my dark mood (that would be Pearl Jam territory), but maybe the upbeat rhythm will lift my spirits. I gnaw on a Twizzler, feeling the wind whip through my hair with the Jeep's top down. Goddamn it, it is a beautiful day. Mammoth Mountain awaits—cooler temps, 60s during the day, 30s at night. My backpack's stuffed with layers and a tent for the nightly campground stay.

I need this time to myself. I need anything to keep my mind off what's happening back in LA: that fancy-ass wedding at Greystone Mansion, the historic Beverly Hills Tudor estate. Garden ceremony, courtyard reception, and an open bar I won't be drinking from.

The scent of pine and mountain air hits me as I reach the trailhead. Not like that disaster weekend in Mammoth —today I've got real hiking boots and a pack that doesn't dig into my shoulders. Convict Canyon Trail is 14 miles round trip of rocky terrain with steep drop offs to the river below, with those killer switchbacks that make your calves scream. The trail guide calls it "difficult" with that cute little black diamond next to it. Four alpine lakes. Thin air that'll make my lungs burn. Perfect. After everything with Cameron, I need something that hurts in a way I can actually handle.

Three hours later, I'm sitting by one of the lakes, gnawing on beef jerky and washing it down with lukewarm coffee from my thermos. The mountain air fills my lungs, and for a moment, everything feels... okay. That'll change when I get back to LA and open that email from Celeste—the one with Cameron's wedding photos that I practically begged her to send, despite her protests. I need to see them like I need oxygen. Without photographic evidence, I can pretend it never happened. With them? Maybe I'll finally stop checking his Instagram at 2 AM. Maybe I can finally move on with my life.

Still, every time I picture his hand without that gold band, this stupid hope flares up. What if he bailed? What if he's waiting for me to unfuck my life? God, that would be perfect—him making the choice without me wrecking anything. Then someday—after enough therapy sessions to build a fortress and then demolish it—if he's still out there... maybe we'd get our shot.

Yeah, right. And maybe I'll wake up tomorrow with a unicorn in my backyard.

Chapter Forty-Nine

CAMERON

My wedding's in five days and everything is in place, though my stomach's still doing backflips. But everything's on track. My bespoke Armani tux hangs in my closet, black as motor oil with these satin lapels that catch the light.

The wedding cakes—his and hers—are sitting at Magnolia Bakery downtown. Willow and I both want the same thing: dark chocolate that hits you in the back of the jaw, with these orange peel bits that explode with flavor, topped with raspberry buttercream frosting the color of a setting sun. At least her cake has frosting the color of a setting sun. My cake, same flavors of chocolate, orange, and raspberry is a doctor cake—a light blue fondant base sculpted to look like scrubs, topped with a realistic torso in a pristine white coat, complete with a tiny silver stethoscope draped around the neck and even miniature pockets filled with icing pens and a name badge that reads "Dr. Kensington" in perfect cursive.

The reception menu is insane: Wagyu steak so tender you barely need to chew it, salmon with skin that crunches between your teeth, and for the vegans, these mushroom pastry things that are actually pretty damn good - mushrooms and toasted walnuts in a puff pastry. Probably will try one of those myself. Every plate comes with grilled asparagus and cheesy potatoes or vegan mashed potatoes.

Asher's handling all the shit I'm too exhausted to deal with—thank God I dumped it on him. The guy's got an eye for detail. He keeps texting me pictures of orchids cascading throughout the reception courtyard and drawings of the gazebo with lights and fabric. Willow's obsessed with flowers so we'll have them everywhere—peonies the size of baseballs, roses in various unique colors of orange, pink and coral. Asher will turn that mansion into something straight out of a magazine, with those old chandeliers and hand-painted plates.

This whole situation has me in a funk. I keep asking myself if you really need love for a marriage to work. Plenty of couples stay together for decades based on friendship and shared goals, right? I genuinely like Willow—shouldn't that be enough?

Roman sees right through me. He keeps giving me these looks, like he knows I'm settling for less than I deserve. And once those wedding bells ring, that's it for me. No divorce. I've never believed in escape hatches.

Then today, Roman ambushes me with Lilith, of all people. She shows up with their new daughter, Aria, on her chest, takes one look at me and declares I shouldn't marry Willow because apparently I'm surrounded by some "black aura" indicating unresolved trauma or deep depression.

She's not wrong. Losing Tally broke something in me that I haven't fixed. Of course, losing Stephanie and Alecia are wounds that'll never fully heal, but Tally... she was the one who made me feel alive again after all that. With her gone, I'm just going through the motions, pretending I've moved on when I clearly haven't.

Lilith's brow furrows. "Roman, at least take this." She presses a light pink stone into my palm before I can object. "Rose quartz. Opens the heart chakra. Might help."

"Don't suppose you've got something stronger? Like a spell to make me fall for my fiancée instead of pining over someone else?" I try to laugh, but it comes out hollow.

"That's not how it works," Lilith says with a gentle smile. "No spell can override free will. I could do a red candle ritual for passion, though that's not really my specialty. I have friends who are better at those, if you want."

I pocket the rose quartz with a sigh. What I need is something to scrub Tally from my memory so I can give my heart to the woman I'm actually marrying.

But even in Lilith's world of crystals and candles, some magic just doesn't exist.

Chapter Fifty

TALLY

Convict Canyon Trail is famous for its steep climb, and that's exactly where shit goes sideways. I'm hauling myself up with hiking poles around the 4 mile mark, so I didn't get too far on the trail, when this massive mountain lion comes bounding down the trail like he owns the place. I freeze, thinking, "Don't run, don't run," but the shock sends me stumbling backward. Next thing I know, I'm tumbling ass-over-teakettle down this ravine, watching my phone fly out of my pocket somewhere along the way. By the time I stop rolling, the mountain lion's already forgotten about me—he's up there munching on some poor rabbit while I'm sprawled at the bottom realizing something in my body is definitely not right.

I squint at the Convict Creek basin about a hundred yards away. Most hikers avoid it—the terrain's a bitch to navigate, all loose scree and hidden drop-offs. I might get lucky and spot someone headed that direction, but fat chance. And here I am, ass-deep in wilderness with the actual trail far, far away.

Stay calm, Tally. Hikers come through the trail all the time, but am I too far away? *They'll hear you if you yell.* Right? Fuck. I try to move and nearly black out from the pain shooting through my leg. Broken. Definitely broken. Though weirdly, it doesn't hurt as much as it should—my body's pumping me full of whatever chemicals keep you from losing your shit in emergencies. And my goddamn phone is MIA, probably smashed against a rock somewhere between here and the trail. Even if I had it, what are the chances of getting a signal in this wilderness anyway?

The sun's dipping below the ridge now. Fuck. Soon it'll be thirty-something degrees out here with God knows what prowling around—like that mountain lion that sent me scrambling earlier. I know the statistics. Attacks are rare. Doesn't stop my heart from jackhammering every time a twig snaps.

I strain my ears for hikers on the trail above, saving my voice. No point screaming into empty wilderness and draining what little energy I have left.

Night creeps in. Nobody's coming. I yank the emergency blanket from my pack, wrap it around my shoulders. Still shivering. This wasn't the plan—I was supposed to loop Convict Canyon Trail and be back at the trailhead by sunset, driving to Mammoth Mountain RV Park with actual Wi-Fi to text Mom that I'm alive. Tomorrow was meant for Devil's Postpile, a six-mile hike that leads to Rainbow Falls, that hundred-foot waterfall everyone raves about.

Instead, I'm trapped in this ravine with one water bottle and a granola bar. Day hiker's rations. Stupid, stupid, stupid.

I don't sleep a wink. When the sun finally peeks over the mountain, I hear voices on the trail and my heart leaps. Thank God! Someone's bound to hear me screaming and haul my sorry ass out of here. People get emergency-evac'd all the time—and yeah, I used to roll my eyes at those dumbasses wasting rescue resources. Used to think Darwin should just do its work and take those idiots out of the gene pool instead of their asses getting rescued on the taxpayers' dime.

Funny how being the dumbass changes your perspective.

"HELP!" My throat burns raw as hikers pass by. Not a single one stops. "HELP!" I scream it six times, like that'll make a difference. Am I too far off-trail to be heard? The thought slithers in: I could actually die here. No. I refuse to think like that. But as the tenth group of hikers strolls past—close enough I can see their goddamn water bottles glinting in the sun—reality sinks in. They can't see me. They can't hear me. And I'm screaming myself hoarse for nothing.

Hikers tromp past overhead all day, their voices fading in and out like bad radio reception. None of them hear me screaming.

Night blankets the ravine again. My tongue feels like sandpaper against the roof of my mouth. My water bottle's been empty for hours. My stomach's given up growling. The thought hits me like a rock slide: people vanish on these trails every year. They slip down some forgotten crevice and waste away while search parties walk right past them. Their bodies don't turn up until some random hiker stumbles across bleached bones months later.

That could be me.

Fuck.

That's probably going to be me.

Chapter Fifty-One

TALLY

Three days now. No water left. No hope either. I'm hallucinating—Cameron stands right in front of me, clear as day. I reach for him, but my fingers pass through empty air. Then I see little Brinley wobbling toward me on unsteady legs. Yeah right. Like a toddler would be out here alone on this godforsaken trail.

Nothing to do but replay my life's greatest hits and, believe it or not, pray. Something inside me knows there's gotta be more than this. Maybe it's some glowing Jesus-looking dude with his arms wide open, or maybe it's one of those goddesses Lilith's always going on about—Brigid or whatever. Something's out there. Has to be. Otherwise, how do you explain the cosmic joke where some people get dealt royal flushes while others get nothing but garbage hands? Rich kids born with silver spoons, while others dodge bullets in war zones or starve in the same damn country where people throw away enough food to feed them ten times over. If this is all there is, the universe has one sick sense of humor.

I stare at the top of a pine tree until it blurs, then squeeze my eyes shut. "Hey, dude in the sky. We haven't exactly been on speaking terms since the Wilsons hauled my ass to church every damn Sunday when I was twelve. Even then I was mostly checking out that hot skater boy in the front pew instead of giving you thanks or whatever. Sorry about that." My broken leg throbs like a bastard now that the adrenaline's wearing off. No hikers. No rescue. Just me at the bottom of this ravine. "Listen, God, Universe, whoever's tuned to this channel—I make it out alive, I'll get my shit together. No more running when things get real. I swear it."

Jesus Christ, I'm such an idiot! Is this really how it ends for me? Shit, I thought I had decades left to get my act together. To find that perfect guy who'd step up for Brinley. Someone I could actually build something real with, who'd make me want to be better.

Cameron would've been perfect, damn it, but that ship has sailed. Still, I'd love to find someone like him—a guy who'd croon lullabies in that deep, slightly raspy voice, who'd make pancakes shaped like dinosaurs, who'd remember exactly how much cream I take in my coffee without asking. Someone who'd fight for me if it came to that. Who'd teach Brinley to ride a bike without training wheels, who'd sit on her bed at midnight when some teenage asshole breaks her heart, who'd say, "Listen, kiddo, about those raves your mom's warning you about? Trust me, I've patched up enough ODs to know she's right for once."

Someone to balance me out—steady when I'm a hurricane, gentle when I'm all sharp edges. Brinley deserves that good cop/bad cop tag team. Every kid does. Christ, if I don't find her someone like Cameron, she's stuck with just me, the bad cop, and my chaos, and I'll screw her up beyond repair.

Dammit. Now it's too late.

It's all too late…

If I die here, at least Brinley will have Cameron and Willow. A real family. Maybe she'll forget me completely—hell, maybe that's better. No confusing "this is Willow, your new mom, but remember your real mom?" bullshit.

I squeeze my eyes shut and picture my baby girl running through Cam's Brentwood mansion—the one Celeste won't shut up about. All those uncles doting on her. Celeste not just playing auntie, but actually being Aunt Celeste by marriage. No more cramped house with me. No more mac and cheese three nights a week when money gets tight. No fucking chaos.

Who am I kidding? Somebody else might've wanted to pretend I never existed. Start fresh with Willow. Happens all the time.

But not Cam. He' s not that guy.

Never that guy...

Chapter Fifty-Two

CAMERON

I'm getting married at 7 PM tonight, but it's only 3 and I'm already noticing weird shit. Celeste keeps glancing at her phone like it might explode, her fingers twitching every time it buzzes. She's practically vibrating with tension. And what the hell is up with Max? He's doing the exact same thing—staring at his screen, shaking his head, then checking it again thirty seconds later like some kind of compulsive tic. Something's definitely up with those two.

My place has become wedding central. Limos idling out front soon, tuxedos hanging on every doorknob. Earlier, Celeste was in my guest bathroom with some lady wielding hot tools and another dabbing her face with brushes. Willow asked her to be a bridesmaid, but Celeste refused—Team Tally all the way—though she still agreed to get dolled up for photos. That was the plan, anyway. Now I watch her pacing my living room floor, obsessively checking her phone with shaking hands, half her hair curled and pinned up, half not, as if she'd abruptly made the stylist quit mid-session.

"Sharp, bro!" Silas says, elbowing my ribs as he passes. My bow tie's already knotted, cufflinks secured. The reception should be decent enough—some cover band cranking out The Cure, Depeche Mode, English Beat and Echo and the Bunnyman type music, premium open bar, fancy catering. I'm not dreading the ceremony itself, just everything after. Though maybe that's the answer—maybe once Willow and I say our vows and finally sleep together, something will click. Some magical connection will spark and I'll suddenly feel what I'm supposed to feel for the woman I'm marrying.

Stranger things have happened.

Celeste's face crumples like she's been slapped. She bolts through the French doors, her heels clicking sharply across the pool deck. Max charges after her, his jaw tight. Through the open window, I catch the scent of chlorine mixing with the late afternoon air as Celeste collapses onto a lounger, shoulders heaving as she sobs. Max crouches beside her, his hands steadying her trembling frame.

Celeste's mascara runs black down her cheeks. "I can't go to this wedding," she says, her voice catching on the last word. "Not if she's missing." She can't finish the sentence. Her fingers twist her wedding ring over and over again. "Max, you don't understand. Tally's like my sister. Yeah, she's got that mouth on her, but when I needed someone? There she was. Every time." She looks up, eyes red-rimmed. "I refuse to believe she's gone. I can't."

My stomach drops to my toes. Something terrible has happened.

I catch Max's eye. "Spill it. Now."

He avoids my gaze. "It's nothing, really."

"Cut the crap! Something's happening, and I want answers!"

"Cameron, you're about to walk down the aisle. Whatever it is can wait until after the ceremony."

My hands clench at my sides. "Max, I'm not asking. I'm telling you to come clean." I step closer, my voice dropping. "If you're hiding something that I could fix, and I don't get the chance because you kept quiet? I'll never forgive you. Never."

Celeste stands up, mascara streaming down her face. "I just got a call from Marisa. Tally is MISSING!" she screams, her voice cracking. "Three days. THREE FUCKING DAYS! She was supposed to call her mom Wednesday night and every night thereafter. Nothing. NOTHING! Since I found out, I've called her phone fifty times. Her mother's called hundreds since Thursday morning. Voicemail. Always voicemail." She grabs my arm, fingernails digging into my skin. "She SWORE she'd check in every night from that campground."

Celeste's sob rips through the air like a wounded animal.

My blood turns to ice. Tally. Missing. The words hammer in my skull. Celeste said she went hiking alone in the Sierra Nevadas. Convict Canyon Trail. That death trap with thousand-foot drops that even experienced hikers avoid. And Tally—stubborn, fearless Tally—would've taken it as a challenge.

Reckless. Foolish.

MINE. Dear God, she's MINE.

Wednesday to Saturday. Seventy-two hours. My heart threatens to explode. My mind floods with images: her body broken at the bottom of a ravine, attacked by a mountain lion, kidnapped by some backwoods psychopath. NO. She has to be alive. She HAS to. She wouldn't leave her daughter motherless. She wouldn't do that to her mother.

She wouldn't do that to me.

Before I know it, I'm sprinting to my bedroom, my heart hammering against my ribs. I tear at my bow tie, fingers trembling so badly I can barely work the buttons of my crisp white shirt. Sweat beads on my forehead as I wrestle out of the $10,000 bespoke Armani tux. Five frantic minutes later, I've traded wedding finery for worn jeans, scuffed hiking boots, and a thick cable-knit sweater the color of storm clouds.

Max appears in the doorway, his own tux still immaculate, face flushed with concern. "Cam, what are you doing?"

"What does it look like I'm doing?" I snap, grabbing my keys from the nightstand. "I'm getting ready to drive up to Convict Canyon Trail and search every goddamn inch of it myself."

"Cam, you have 300 guests who are already filing into the Greystone Mansion as we speak," Max says, his voice rising. "The champagne is chilling, the five-tier cake is set up, the twelve-piece band is tuning their instruments, and Judge Reynolds is waiting. People have flown in from across three continents for this. You can't back out now! Anyhow, Tally's mom called Search and Rescue—professionals have spent the last 48 hours looking for her."

I fix Max with a glare that could freeze hell. "I'm not saying 'I do' while Tally is out there missing. Do you think I could live with myself if something happens to her? Especially knowing I was sipping champagne instead of helping?"

Max shakes his head, his green eyes clouding with resignation. He knows what's coming—I'm bolting, leaving skid marks on this marble floor. My phone feels heavy in my pocket; I'll call Willow from the car, stammering through explanations she won't accept.

Max is right about the consequences—this lavish affair

cost half a million, crystal champagne flutes and peonies and roses everywhere, guests who crossed oceans to be here. But the weight of the platinum ring in my pocket means nothing compared to the image burning in my mind: Tally out there somewhere in the wilderness, her lips cracked from thirst, maybe curled under a tree for shelter.

Three days without proper water in that merciless sun would leave anyone delirious. Three nights in the 30 degree weather would induce hypothermia. And Tally would have packed light—just enough for day hikes before returning to a proper campsite with facilities, not for surviving alone in the backcountry where cell signals die and trails disappear into nothing.

I'm already on the highway when I call Willow.

"Cameron!" Her voice crackles through the speaker. "The ceremony starts in a few hours!"

"Something's happened, Willow."

The silence stretches between us. My knuckles whiten around the steering wheel as I count one, two, three heartbeats.

"What is it?" Her voice shrinks to a whisper.

"Tally's missing." My throat tightens. "She's my daughter's mother. I have to find her. That comes before any wedding."

"You want to postpone?" Disbelief edges into her tone. "People flew in from three continents for this. The costs alone—"

"I know about the band," I cut in. "The cake, the catering, the guests being seated right now. But Tally's out there somewhere. Search and rescue is looking, but I need to be out there too. I just—I have to do this, Willow. I have to."

"Cameron, for God's sake—there are professionals

looking for her. What do you think you can do out there?" Her voice cracks with desperation.

I grip the steering wheel as I hop on the 395, my jaw clenched so tight a muscle jumps in my cheek. "I'm going to find her. I don't give a damn about search and rescue protocols. Every second counts." I merge into another lane, almost cutting off a car, so I wave an apology out the window. "You think I could stand around tonight in a tuxedo, drinking champagne, nodding at Silas's toast while Tally is out there? Freezing? Hurt? Dying?" My voice drops to a dangerous whisper. "That's. Not. Happening. And if you think I'm the kind of man who could smile and make small talk while the woman I—" I stop, breath ragged. "Then you don't know me at all."

Willow's voice rises with each word. "Cameron. Please. You can't be serious. It's our wedding day."

I grip the wheel tighter, still seeing that sedan I nearly sideswiped. My knuckles go white. Arguing with Willow while I'm already this emotional and flying down the highway at eighty? Recipe for disaster.

"I have to go." I end the call and press my foot harder on the gas, watching the needle climb.

Five hours. Five goddamn hours by car. My hands grip the steering wheel so hard my knuckles turn white. I need to get to her faster. Roman. Roman could fly me.

I talk into my infotainment panel, "Call Roman." He answers on the second ring.

"Rome, I need you," I say, my voice tight.

"Name it, bro."

"Tally's gone missing up at Convict Canyon Trail—Mammoth Lakes area. I'm looking at a five-hour drive to the Sierras, and I—"

"Chopper's fueled and ready," he cuts in. "Meet me at Hawthorne. I'll have her warmed up."

I race back to Hawthorne municipal airport and sprint toward Roman's private hangar. He's waiting by his helicopter, bow tie undone against his white collar, tux jacket slung over one shoulder. Lilith stands beside him in her evening gown, checking her phone.

"Where's the baby?" I blurt, noticing Aria's absence.

Roman runs a hand through his wind-tousled hair. "Celeste insisted on babysitting. She wanted to join the rescue mission, but when we explained she'd be more hindrance than help, she volunteered to watch Aria instead."

I rake my fingers through my hair, trying to keep it together. "Okay, so once we reach Convict Canyon Trail, then what?"

“We fly to Mammoth Yosemite Airport then rent an SUV. Then we go on the trail with my equipment and yours.” I have several things that will be needed to search for her, including Personal Locator Beacon and GPS Satellite that can transmit our signal to rescuers and a bright light that goes on my forehead. I also have a 1,000 Lumen lamp that’ll illuminate miles of forest, and a whistle.

Roman slides his headset on as we board—me riding shotgun, Lilith taking the back.

I feel Lilith's hand on my shoulder, surprisingly steady. "She's out there. I know it." When I glance back, she's already laid out her tarot deck across the seat. Normally I'd roll my eyes, but right now, I'll take whatever hope I can get.

"The Sun card," she says, her face brightening. "Thank God. She'll make it through this." Her finger traces another card, upside down. "Though this Reversed Star means the path won't be easy."

I nod, not hearing her. I mean, she's giving me comforting words, but what does she really know?

The helicopter cuts through the air towards Mammoth Lakes, the journey taking less than an hour. Roman keeps his headset on, maintaining contact with the other search teams scanning the wilderness for any sign of Tally. When I catch his eye, he just shakes his head grimly. "Nothing yet."

After touching down at Mammoth Yosemite Airport, we waste no time securing an SUV and speeding toward the Convict Canyon trailhead, where the search continues on foot.

My heart hammers against my ribs as we trudge along the trail. The beam from my high-powered lamp sweeps across the path and into the darkness beyond, revealing only glimpses of the wilderness. Dammit, this trail stretches for ten miles round trip and takes six hours to complete. Tally could be anywhere out here. I find myself oddly reassured that Lilith came with us. She's no psychic, but her intuition runs deep—she might sense Tally's presence in ways Roman or I never could. I don't understand the concept of a psychic connection, but I'm praying Lillith can somehow tune into Tally's frequency tonight.

Roman ditched his tuxedo at the airport for more practical gear—heavy coat, hat, the works. Lilith changed in the helicopter and now sports jeans and hiking boots with her own winter layers. I'm bundled up too, but it's still brutal out here. The cold bites through everything. My mind keeps circling back to Tally. She was only planning a day hike—would she have brought proper winter gear? Who packs a heavy coat for a quick afternoon trek? The image of her shivering somewhere in these mountains makes my stomach knot. Hypothermia sets in fast. And while I know wild animal attacks are rare, they happen. But it's the cold and dehydration that terrify me most. I force the thoughts away, but they keep creeping back.

She has to be alive. There's no other possibility I can accept. When I find her—and I will find her—I'm never letting go again. Even if she doesn't want the same things I do. Even if she pushes me away. I'll wait as long as it takes for her to realize what we could have together.

God, I was such an idiot bringing Willow into this mess. I shouldn't be thinking about her right now, but I can't ignore that I've hurt someone innocent who didn't deserve it.

Roman was right all along. "Follow your heart, not your head," he always said. Should've followed his advice. If I had, Tally would be safe with me now. Not married, maybe, but protected. She'd hate that word—"protected." She'd roll those fierce eyes and tell me exactly where I could shove my protection. But she could be as angry as she wanted, call me every name in her colorful vocabulary, as long as she was here. As long as she was mine.

Roman is right behind me.

Goddammit. The forest stretches for miles in every direction. We're talking worse than a needle in a haystack—more like one particular raindrop in a monsoon. But we can't stop. Every minute matters now. I keep picturing her huddled against a tree trunk, shivering in that thin jacket she always wears. Did she have the foresight to stuff a blanket in her pack? The temperature's dropping fast. No. Can't go there. Can't imagine her lips turning blue, her body growing still. She's alive. She has to be.

Lilith's hand lands on my shoulder, warm and steady. "Cameron," she says, her voice soft. "The search team has equipment, but you have something better."

"Like what?"

"A connection to Tally that runs deeper than logic. I've seen how you two are together. Close your eyes. Picture her. Send your thoughts to her. She might just answer back."

A spiritual bond? Maybe that explains the pull I've felt since day one. I don't buy into that mystical stuff, but with Tally missing and the sun setting—I'll try anything Lilith suggests.

I lower myself to the ground, crossing my legs and shutting my eyes. The forest goes quiet around me as I focus on Tally's face—those green-blue eyes, that crooked smile with the tiny scar at the corner.

Where are you? The question pulses through me with each heartbeat. Where are you? Nothing comes back. After five minutes of silence, I slam my palm against the dirt.

"This is bullshit, Lilith. We're wasting time. We need to keep searching, use the flashlights—"

"Cameron." Her voice is soft but firm. "Professional teams have combed these woods for two days straight. If conventional methods worked, she'd be home by now."

Roman's hand lands heavy on my shoulder. "My wife sees things differently than most people. If she thinks you can reach Tally somehow, you should trust that."

"She's not actually psychic," I argue.

Lilith tucks her hair behind her ear. "I don't see the future, no. But I've spent my life listening to what others ignore—the patterns, the connections. And everything in me says you're her beacon home. Not by shouting into ravines, but by becoming still enough that she can find you. Out here, you're searching for one pebble on miles of shoreline. But if you center yourself, you become the lighthouse."

I shake my head. "How do I do this?"

"You need to completely relax. Take deep breaths through your diaphragm and visualize a word. Say it over and over and over in your head. It can be any word. If your mind wanders, then come back to that chosen word."

Ah. Transcendental Meditation. I recognize this. Before heading to my first Doctors Without Borders assignment, a group of us took a class on TM. The stress in those crisis zones hits like a freight train, and drinking wasn't an option —one beer too many could mean a shaky hand when someone's life depended on steady fingers. We needed something portable, something that worked anywhere, even in a tent with gunfire in the distance. TM fit the bill.

I've seen it work. Hell, I've felt it work, those nights in Sicily when the faces of the day's patients wouldn't leave me alone.

I lower myself onto a flat rock beside the trail. The forest breathes around me—owl calls punctuate the darkness, tree branches sway in the wind, crickets chirp a steady rhythm. Something small scurries through dead leaves nearby. Water tumbles over stones in the creek just beyond the next ridge. I close my eyes and let one word fill the space between my thoughts: love. Whenever my mind tries to wander toward tomorrow's problems or yesterday's mistakes, I gently pull it back. Love. Love. Love. With each deep belly breath, tension melts from my shoulders, my jaw, my hands. A warm current of calm washes through me, leaving nothing but stillness in its wake.

“Okay,” Lilith says, somewhere outside my mind. “Now, try to communicate with her. She’ll tell you where she is.”

I open my eyes and point to the map. "She's in the ravine. See the four-mile marker? We need to follow it down to where it meets the basin."

Roman nods. "Got it." He pulls out his satellite radio, speaks into it for a minute, then slams it down with a curse.

"They're calling off the search until morning. Budget constraints, apparently."

I blow out a breath. "Okay. Looks like I'm hiking it." My hiking boots have only ever met well-maintained trails, not the jagged descent of a ravine. But tonight, that doesn't matter. She's down there, alone. I can't bring her back up without proper equipment and the rescue team, but I can reach her. I can share my water, wrap my arms around her, whisper that everything will be okay. That I'm here. My gut screams that she needs this tonight—that she's slipping away.

Roman doesn't try to talk me out of it. It's dangerous as hell, trying to traverse a steep ravine in the dark. I have this powerful lumen light which will illuminate the way, which will be helpful, but still…hiking down a ravine is tricky in the best of circumstances. But Roman knows I have to do this. It's literally a matter of life or death for her.

Roman keeps pace beside me on the trail, his voice low and steady. "When we hit the four-mile marker, you'll need to navigate that ravine carefully. Keep your stance wide—shoulder-width at least." He demonstrates with his hands. "The steeper it gets, switch to side-stepping. Turn your body like this." He pivots sideways. "Small, deliberate steps. Never rush it." His expression turns serious. "One rescue is enough for today. We don't need you tumbling down after her." Then that familiar grin breaks through. "The mountain rescue team doesn't offer two-for-one specials, bro."

I laugh a little, but my stomach's doing backflips. Once I reach the four-mile marker—just a weathered wooden post with peeling red paint—I stare down into the ravine. The beam from my headlamp disappears into blackness. Fuck it. I start down just as Roman instructed, legs spread wide like I'm straddling a horse. The loose dirt and pebbles shift under my boots, sending miniature avalanches tumbling ahead of me. The grade steepens until I'm practically skiing on my heels, grabbing at saplings to slow my descent. My thighs burn. Seventy percent grade is basically a cliff with trees. Jagged rocks jut out like teeth, waiting to shred me if I slip. Even with years of hiking under my belt, this descent makes my heart hammer against my ribs.

It takes me about an hour of a careful and slow descent, my headlamp cutting a weak yellow cone through the midnight darkness. Loose stones skitter away under my boots, threatening to send me tumbling after them. When I finally reach the bottom of the ravine, my light catches something pale against the black earth. Tally. She's curled on her side beneath a thin emergency blanket that shivers with her trembling. The silver material crinkles as I drop to my knees beside her. My heart slams against my ribs like it's trying to escape. She's alive. Her skin is waxy, lips cracked and bloodless, but she's breathing. I slide my arms under her, cradling her against my chest. Her head lolls against my shoulder, dark hair matted with sweat and dirt. Her eyelids flutter but don't open.

"Cameron," she rasps, voice like sandpaper. "Cameron. Cameron."

My name on her lips is a knife twisting in my gut. Her breath comes in shallow puffs against my neck. When I peel back the blanket, her right leg lies at a sickening angle, the denim of her jeans torn and stained dark.

"Tally," I whisper, my lips brushing her temple. "I'm here."

She doesn't wake, just keeps shaking her head against my chest, my name a broken record on her tongue. I press my forehead to hers, breathing in the scent of her—earth and sweat and something uniquely Tally beneath it all.

"Oh, Tally, I wonder if you can hear me. If you can, know this. I won't leave you again. Never again. Maybe we'll be together for the rest of our lives, or maybe you'll only ever have me as a friend. I don't care. We will be together one way or another. I love you, Tally. You're the only one for me."

Thank God, her breathing's steady. I press my fingers to her wrist—pulse is there, but faint. Her skin chills my fingertips. Hypothermia. She'll likely remain unconscious until we get her to the medevac and the team can slowly warm her core temperature.

I kiss her forehead and radio Roman. "Rome," I say. "I found her. Send search and rescue at first dawn. She needs a medevac and a spinal board. Spine appears intact, thank God, but I won't risk movement. And have her flown to UCLA."

My pulse quickens as I imagine her recovery. UCLA is where my fellowship is—where I practically live. If she's there, I can check on her between rounds, bring her decent coffee instead of the hospital sludge. I could even stay overnight in her room; staff privileges have to be good for something. The rescue team will push for the closest ER, but UCLA's only an hour by chopper. I'll make my case. I need to be there for her, and I can't do that if she's across the city or in the Mammoth hospital while I'm pulling 70-hour weeks.

It's so cold my breath crystallizes in front of me like tiny diamonds. I shrug out of my down coat, the nylon shell crackling in the silence, and drape it over her pale form. My cable-knit sweater is thick but useless against the biting wind that cuts through the wool like knives. My fingers have gone numb, and my ears burn. But she needs this coat—her lips had turned the color of plums, her skin like porcelain against the dark earth of the ravine floor. I'd considered bringing her another coat when I spotted her from above, but the treacherous descent down loose shale and gnarled roots was challenging enough without extra baggage.

I pull her against my chest and close my eyes, trying to ignore how violently my body trembles in the cold. Her weight in my arms is both burden and comfort. The shivering that wracked her frame earlier has subsided—a good sign that the down insulation is working. Sleep tugs at me, but I jerk awake repeatedly, pressing two fingers to the delicate skin of her neck, counting the slow, steady beats. Her breaths come shallow but regular against my collarbone. Not once do her eyelids flutter—her stillness confirming what my medical training already knows: moderate hypothermia still has her in its dangerous embrace.

I stay awake all night, monitoring her vitals with bloodshot eyes, counting each shallow breath, waiting for dawn so I could hear that Medevac helicopter slicing through the towering pines.

It finally arrives with a thunderous whump-whump-whump that shakes the ground beneath us, thanks to Roman radioing the guy. Thank God. The medic—a burly man with calloused hands and kind eyes—immediately wraps her in a silver heated blanket that crinkles like Christmas paper. Her head, framed by tangled raven hair, bobs from side to side as if she's trying to wake up, but her eyes, bruised with purple shadows underneath, don't open. But she does make a face—her full lips curving slightly upward, her forehead smoothing out—as if she can feel the blessed warmth of the Ready Heat blanket seeping into her ice-cold skin.

"Take her to UCLA," I say, my voice hoarse from the night's worry. "I'm a doctor there, and I can ensure she gets the best care possible from our trauma team and I can also facilitate her immediate admission."

The medic nods, sweat beading on his temple despite the morning chill. "That can be arranged."

"I'll meet you there." My fingers tremble as I brush a strand of hair from her pale face.

Then Tally's loaded onto a bright orange backboard and she's hoisted into the chopper, which hovers twenty feet above us, blades churning the air into a deafening cyclone that whips my hair across my face and flattens the surrounding grass. My heart pounds against my ribs like it's trying to escape as I watch her in the rescue basket being lifted into the Medevac, her body looking impossibly small and fragile against the vast morning sky. She'll be okay. She has to be. I give a little wave to the medic guy who returns it with a thumbs-up as the two of them disappear into the belly of the helicopter, its red-and-white hull gleaming in the first rays of sunlight.

I watch the helicopter lift off with Tally inside, wrapped in a thermal blanket with an IV drip in her arm and medics monitoring her every breath. Only then does the reality of my situation hit me. I'm at the bottom of this godforsaken ravine with no climbing gear and no poles. Getting down here was pure adrenaline and luck. Going back up? That's another story.

No way am I calling for a second rescue. I eye the steep slope, searching for a path. Each handhold becomes a victory—fingers gripping exposed roots, boots finding purchase on jutting rocks. My muscles scream as I haul myself upward, inch by excruciating inch, until I finally drag my body over the edge onto the trail.

Roman and Lilith rush toward me, Roman's arm coming around my shoulders. "You did good, Cam," he says. "If you hadn't bailed on your wedding to come looking, she wouldn't have made it."

He's right. Another night out here with dehydration and hypothermia setting in—she was already unconscious when I found her. I saved her life today.

Fair exchange, I suppose.

After all, she saved mine first.

Chapter Fifty-Three

CAMERON

Roman touches down at UCLA after getting clearance to land. I hop out and embrace both him and Lilith before heading inside. For the foreseeable future, this hospital will be my second home while Tally recovers. It's familiar territory—I practically live here anyway, working twelve-hour shifts six days a week. I'll steal moments with her between patients and spend my nights beside her, even if it means cramming my six-foot-two frame into that unforgiving chair. Being near her is all that matters.

After confirming she's been admitted, I make my way to her room. The steady beep of monitors greets me as I check her vitals: temperature normal - 98.2, blood pressure 118/70, pulse a slightly low but acceptable 65—normal for someone unconscious. Her right leg rests in a temporary splint; they'll wait for the swelling to subside before casting it next week.

I can't avoid Willow forever. She deserves a face-to-face apology for being caught in the crossfire of my mess. God, I can still picture her standing there in that white dress, probably having to explain to three hundred guests why I wasn't showing up. Maybe they made the best of it—drank the champagne, ate the seven-tier cake, danced to that band that cost a fortune. But what haunts me is how she kept asking if the wedding was "postponed" when I called from the hospital. Not once did she say "canceled." The distinction tears at me. She's waiting for a rain check on a wedding that's never going to happen, and I need to make that crystal clear to her.

Lilith, with all her talk about cosmic signs, would say Tally's accident was the universe's intervention—stopping me from marrying the wrong woman. Because Tally—fierce, complicated Tally—is where I belong. She's my daughter's mother. And damn it, she's the one I love with everything I am.

Lilith would be right. Her accident has to be a sign. The universe doesn't make mistakes. Tally and I were meant to find our way back to each other.

I linger at her bedside until her breathing deepens into sleep, then step into the hallway and pull out my phone.

Willow answers on the second ring.

"We need to talk," I say quietly.

Chapter Fifty-Four

CAMERON

Willow arrives at Plateia, the Mediterranean place just blocks from the hospital where Tally's recovering. I chose it deliberately—can't bear being far from Tally right now.

When Willow walks in, she's still gorgeous, but her smile doesn't reach her eyes. No surprise there. Two days ago, I called her from my car and blurted out that our wedding was canceled because I needed to find my ex. The woman I truly love. The woman Willow probably knew I loved all along, though she never mentioned it. Some things don't need saying.

When I called her about canceling the wedding, I hung up on her mid-conversation, too frantic to even explain properly. Haven't spoken to her—or any wedding guest—since. Now I need to hear how she's doing, what happened after I bolted. Part of me hopes everyone just enjoyed the reception anyway. At least then the champagne and flights wouldn't have been a complete waste.

She slides into the chair across from me, setting her Hermès Birkin on the table—a bag worth more than Tally's beloved new Jeep "Sophie." Her blue eyes meet mine, sad but flickering with hope. I can tell she thinks I've asked her here to reschedule our wedding. She won't speak first though; pride keeps her silent.

"How are you?" I ask.

She shrugs. "Been better."

I clear my throat. "I'm really sorry about everything."

Her hand covers mine. "I understand. Roman explained that Tally would have died if you hadn't gone to Mammoth when you did. The search teams couldn't locate her—only you could, because of some kind of psychic connection? I never believed in that sort of thing, but somehow she reached out to you. She was so well-hidden they might never have found her otherwise."

"The rescue teams had thousands of square miles to cover," I say. "I found her quickly because Roman's right—we did communicate somehow."

It still sounds strange, though Lilith insists there's nothing unusual about it. She believes some things defy rational explanation, and my telepathic connection with Tally falls into that category. What it proves is that Tally and I share something profound. If Willow had been lost instead, I couldn't have found her the same way. I don't have that soul-deep bond with her. That's what matters in the end.

She nods, inhales deeply, then offers a smile. "So. Now that we've moved past all this, and Brinley's mother is safe and recovering with proper care, what do you think about us starting fresh and planning another wedding? I realize we invested quite a bit in the ceremony that never happened, but we could arrange something else. Perhaps something more intimate this time. We don't need the extravagant celebration we originally planned."

My stomach tightens into a knot. I've dreaded this conversation. Somewhere in my mind, I'd hoped Willow understood why finding Tally was so urgent—not just because she's Brinley's mother and deserves to watch her daughter grow up. What Willow can't see is the real truth: Tally owns every piece of me. If she had died alone in those woods, a part of me would have died with her. The loss would have hollowed me out like that night I lost Alecia and Stephanie. I would have walked through the rest of my life as a ghost. I understand now with absolute clarity that my place is beside Tally, however she'll have me. I'll wait as long as it takes for her to dismantle the fortress around her heart, brick by brick. My place is with her—through anything, everything.

I take Willow's hands, my voice gentle but firm. "Willow, listen. I care about you deeply, but what Tally and I have... it's something I can't explain. When she was in trouble, I just knew where to find her. That kind of connection—it's rare. I should never have started this with you when my heart was elsewhere. I'm so sorry."

Willow's shoulders drop as she exhales. "Deep down, I always sensed it. The way you looked at her..." She shakes her head. "I kept telling myself I was imagining things. That we'd end up married, growing old together." Her voice catches. "Like Theodore and I would have. Or you and Alecia."

I say the only words I can manage: "I'm sorry." Offering friendship would be an insult after what we've shared. She's losing not just me, but little Brinley too—I've seen how her face lights up around my daughter. Part of me wants to blame Silas for his meddling, for putting her in my path when I was vulnerable. But the truth is, I knew better. I knew from the start this was wrong, yet I charged ahead anyway. Why? Because I convinced myself that if I couldn't have Tally, I should settle for someone who wanted me. What nonsense. Real love doesn't work that way. Real love waits. Real love endures while the other person figures their life out. Patient and kind—just like that old poem says.

She gives a tight nod. "I see. Well, your mind's clearly made up, so I'll just..." She reaches for her purse, her knuckles white around the handle.

When she walks out, her heels click a steady rhythm against the tile. Not a stumble. Not a backward glance.

My shoulders drop as the door swings shut behind her. Relief mingles with the acid burn of guilt in my stomach. I press my fingertips against my temples. Christ. I had no business dragging her into my mess. But watching her walk away only confirms what I've known since I met that tattooed hellion who crashed into my life—there's only one woman I want. Tally.

Maybe she'll open her heart to me again. Maybe she'll choose me, build a life with me.

Or maybe she won't.

Either way, I belong beside her.

Chapter Fifty-Five

CAMERON

Later, I pull Max aside to get the full story on what happened after I called off the wedding. I half expect him to report guests flipping tables or my almost–mother-in-law having a public breakdown. Really, though, I just need to know whether those six months I spent agonizing over centerpieces and cake tastings were completely wasted.

Max shakes his head. "No, everyone was fine. Word got around that you had an emergency, though nobody knew exactly what it was. But I promise you, nothing went to waste—the food, the cake, even the band showed up. People drank at the open bar, they loved the spread, and both cakes were a hit. You did great, Cameron. Well, actually Asher did great—he planned the entire thing."

I nod. "Asher does have good taste."

"Yeah, so everyone partied."

I ask, "How did Willow's parents take it?"

Max shrugs again. "They figured that if you had an emergency, you had to deal with it. They thought the event would be postponed, not canceled outright."

My chest tightens. Now that they know what really happened, I'm sure they hate me. I don't like making anyone hate me—especially when I deserve it. And in this case, I truly deserve their anger. Not for ditching the wedding to look for Tally—I could never regret that. That rash decision is the only reason Tally's alive. But I deserve their hate for dragging Willow into my disaster in the first place.

I clear my throat. "How's Silas handling it all?"

Max takes a deep breath. "He's upset. To be honest, most of us are. We thought Willow was perfect for you. We know Tally has her issues and might never give you what you need. But the heart wants what it wants. So we all wish you'd fallen for someone more stable. If you're happy with Tally, though, that's what matters. We just hope you're happy."

I grimace. Tally and I still have a lot to figure out. I don't know exactly what we are to each other, or where this road leads. Being beside her feels right, but whether we're building something permanent remains unclear.

Still, I know staying was the right choice.

For now, that's all I need to know.

Chapter Fifty-Six

TALLY

I open my eyes and holy shit, it feels like I got hit by a semi. My leg's wrapped in this bulky splint, and I'm somehow in a private hospital room—just me. No roommate. No idea who pulled those strings, but my bank account's already screaming. Sure, I've got insurance, but it's nothing fancy. That $15,000 deductible plus 20% coinsurance? I'm screwed.

Then it all floods back. The fall. The ravine. My leg snapping like a twig. Screaming until my throat was raw, but nobody came. No water. Just that pathetic excuse for a blanket while the wind cut through me at thirty degrees. I remember thinking: this is it. This is how I die. Even heard search helicopters at one point, their spotlights sweeping the darkness, voices booming over loudspeakers asking hikers to keep an eye out for me. They were looking in all the wrong places.

So who the hell found me?

Then Cameron walks in and my pulse stutters to a halt. My eyes dart straight to his left hand—bare. No ring. Shit.

That doesn't necessarily mean anything though. Could be at the jeweler's getting sized. Maybe the platinum gave him a rash. Whatever. I'm not about to assume he ditched Willow at the altar.

But wait...I rub my temple, trying to sort through the fog. During that nightmare in the ravine, didn't he call out asking for my location? And didn't I mumble something about mile four? Christ, I was so out of it. I also thought I saw my toddler scrambling down that same rocky slope—which is obviously batshit impossible. So yeah, probably just another fever dream from my screwed-up brain.

"Cam," I say, my voice catching in my throat. "What' s going on?" Dammit, it's been, what, six months since I've seen him? Six months since I've seen those ocean-blue eyes, that perfect jawline with just enough stubble to make my fingertips tingle. My heart hammers against my ribs like it' s trying to escape. I don't want this reaction. I don't want to feel like I'm seventeen again, breathless and stupid.

I have to remember, he's a married man. Presumably anyway. I mean, of course he is. That entire wedding was locked and loaded, and from what Celeste told me, it was going to drain a small fortune. Grass-fed Wagyu beef with caramelized edges, wild-caught Alaskan salmon drizzled with some fancy French sauce I can't pronounce, all prepared by some hotshot five-star Michelin chef with a name like a sneeze.

Celeste bombarded me with pictures of the cakes—her bridal cake towering six tiers high, pristine white frosting with delicate swirls the color of a Hawaiian sunset, and sugar pearls that glistened like morning dew draped all around each layer. His groom's cake was this clever little masterpiece with a baby blue fondant base topped with the sculpted torso of a doctor, complete with a real stethoscope wrapped around it and tiny edible surgical instruments scattered across the top.

They had that sprawling Victorian mansion with the manicured gardens and amazing courtyard all booked, with guests flying in from as far as Sydney and London. And her dress—God, her dress was hand-stitched by that famous designer, Claire Pettibone, whose gowns have graced everyone from Silicon Valley royalty to Hollywood A-listers, all those intricate lace patterns and beadwork that probably cost more than my Jeep. So yeah, there wasn't a penny pinched for this whole extravaganza, which means the chances he actually left her at the altar are about as likely as me winning the lottery while being struck by lightning.

He slides onto the bed beside me, taking my left hand in his. I can't help but stare at his fingers, searching for that telltale indentation—the ghost of a wedding band hastily removed before walking through my door. Maybe that's it. Maybe he's just trying to spare the almost-roadkill girl any additional trauma. But something in those eyes of his tells a different story.

When he brushes my hair back from my face, his gaze lingering on mine, my chest tightens. Fuck. That's the same look he used to give me. If he's somebody's husband now but still looking at me like that? Hard pass. I've got enough shit to process—like how I nearly became a skid mark on the highway of life, how I almost left Brinley without a mother. Out there in that ravine, I'd made my peace with Cameron and Willow raising her. Christ, they might've erased me completely from her life. Mom wouldn't stand for that—her precious grandbaby and all—but still.

So, here we are, the two of us laying in this hospital bed together, my body curled against his like a question mark. His fingers trace slow circles through my hair, each movement sending tiny electric currents down my spine. That cologne of his—Dior's Sauvage Elixir—wraps around us like a velvet shadow. It's all dark notes of truffle and night-blooming flowers, so at odds with the sunshine of his personality, like he's carrying midnight with him in broad daylight.

His chest rises and falls beneath my cheek in a rhythm steady as a metronome, and the thump-thump of his heart pulses against my ear. I just want to freeze this moment, pretend he's not married, that the antiseptic hospital smell isn't reminding me this isn't real. I nestle deeper into the hollow of his shoulder, and the sigh that escapes him ripples through us both.

"So," I finally say. "How was the wedding?"

He lets out a soft laugh. "The wedding never happened. A certain someone decided to play hide and seek in the forest, and I had to join the search party."

Me. He means me. Wait—what? I remember the helicopter blades chopping through air above me, remember being half-delirious when they finally found me. But did he seriously put his wedding on hold to come looking for me?

"You canceled your wedding day because I got lost? God, I'm sorry. That mountain lion came out of nowhere and I just... fell. Kept falling until I couldn't hear anyone from the trail anymore. Not my finest moment."

"It's poetic, in a way," he says, eyes crinkling at the corners. "First time we met, it was because a deer sent your Jeep rolling. Now a mountain lion sends you tumbling down a mountainside and back to me. The universe has a strange sense of humor."

His words bounce around my skull like a pinball. Me tumbling down a mountainside and back to him. Back. To.

Him. Nope. Not getting my hopes up. Not happening. But damn if it doesn't sound like he might've called off his wedding for me. For real. If that's true, I've gotta come clean about everything. When I was out there thinking I was toast, I had this moment of clarity—I'm a complete moron. Staring death in the face makes you realize how much it'll suck to die without ever really living. That's what hit me. I was about to check out without ever telling Cameron how I felt. I made this bargain with the universe: get me out alive, and I'll stop half-assing life. I'll ditch all the commitment-phobic garbage that's been keeping me from Cameron. I'll just be with him. All in. Wife, whatever. If I could just get one more shot.

I squint up at him. "Cam, what exactly did you mean about the mountain lion bringing me back to you? Aren't you still marrying Willow?"

"No." His fingers continue their gentle path through my hair as he exhales deeply. "I couldn't go through with it. Not when it's you I'm in love with. It's always been you, Tally." His voice drops lower. "Maybe you don't want to hear this. Maybe I'm scaring you right now, but I stopped caring about that." He pauses, shaking his head. "That came out wrong. Your feelings matter more than anything. What I mean is—I'll take whatever part of your life you're willing to share. Because I finally understand something." His eyes lock with mine. "You own my heart completely, and I refuse to settle for anyone else. Not anymore."

I blink hard, wondering if I'm still lying in that ravine, my mind spinning fever dreams. Is this real? Cameron's words echo in my ears—he wants me, baggage and all. No ultimatums. No pressure. He'll take whatever scraps of myself I'm willing to share.

My chest tightens. It's like some twisted version of that

old Christmas story—he's offering patience when I'm finally ready to leap.

I look at him—really look at him. Those steady hands that have never struck out in anger. Those eyes that have never gone cold with disappointment. He's nothing like the parade of losers my mom dragged home, nothing like the ghosts I've been running from.

That social worker was right. I've spent my whole life believing I broke my mother, carrying that weight. But with Cameron? For the first time, I'm not afraid of what I might destroy. I'm only afraid of what I'll miss if I don't say yes to everything—the ring, the vows, the whole damn fairy tale. Because I love him. God help me, I love him completely.

I grip the edge of the hospital bed. "Cam, if you're serious about not marrying Willow, if I'm really—" My voice catches. "If this mess of a woman is truly enough for you, there's something you need to know."

His fingers find mine. "Nothing you say will change where I stand. I belong with you, Tally. That's non-negotiable."

I squeeze his hand, feeling the calluses from years of medical work. "Cameron Kensington," I whisper, my throat tight. "When I was stuck in that ravine for those few days, when I thought it was all over—" I swallow hard. "I realized I'd been half-dead anyway. Walking around breathing but never actually living. Never saying the one thing that mattered."

His blue eyes lock onto mine, pupils dilating. I feel his pulse jump beneath my fingertips.

"Cameron fucking Kensington," I say again, savoring each syllable like the whiskey on my tongue. "I love you. God help me, I've loved you since you stitched me up that first night when I rolled my Jeep all those months ago. I've just been too chickenshit to admit it. But nearly dying out in the wilderness, alone, has a way of cutting through the bullshit. I love you. I want you. I'll marry you tomorrow if you'll have me."

His eyes go soft. "Tally," he whispers, like my name is something fragile. "I've been waiting to hear that since the moment I saw you."

His lips find mine, and suddenly words don't matter anymore.

Chapter Fifty-Seven

TALLY

Four Months Later

Everyone who matters is here—Cameron, Olivia, Celeste, my mother, Brinley, Cameron's brothers, father and step-mother and his best friend Eli and his family—all of us gathered in this underground art museum with its soaring ceilings and dramatic lighting. Lilith stands at the altar looking serene in her ministerial role, a role she took on specifically for today. When she pronounces us husband and wife, I'll officially become Mrs. Kensington—a name change I once swore would never happen, not for any man on earth. Yet here I am, practically vibrating with anticipation. That's the thing about Cameron: he makes me want to break all my own rules.

I'm so fucking grateful for this second shot at everything—life, motherhood with Brinley, love with Cameron. The docs at the hospital didn't sugarcoat it: eight more hours and I'd have been a goner. Cameron finding me wasn't just lucky timing; it was the difference between my breathing and…not breathing.

And now? Pure, unbridled fucking joy. You know those people who flatline and come back talking about how everything's more vivid after? They're not bullshitting. That first pancake after nearly dying tastes like heaven drizzled in maple syrup. Flowers smell like they're pumping out pure ecstasy. Makes me think of that scene in *Fight Club* where Tyler Durden puts a gun to some convenience store clerk's head just so the poor bastard would finally wake up and actually live. I get it now.

So, yeah, after that shit went down in the woods, I stopped taking the good stuff for granted. My mom's been sober over a year now—longest stretch since I was ten. My kid's already stacking blocks like she's building a damn skyscraper, and she's not even supposed to do that for another month. Liv and Celeste would hide a body for me, no questions asked—and I'd do the same for those bitches. Got my name on the deed to Manic Muse and a mortgage that's all mine. Fucking miracle, when you think about it.

And, most of all, having Cameron—the kind of man who leaves notes in my coffee mug and brings home takeout from that Thai place across town just because I mentioned craving it once. The kind who, despite working those brutal hospital shifts, still has enough energy to pin me against the kitchen counter the second he walks through the door. Jesus, we've christened every surface in this apartment since I got discharged. Ten hours a day is all we get because he works so much, and we've made damn sure to use them. Not just the sex—though holy hell, the sex—but the way he looks at me after, like I'm some kind of miracle he's afraid might disappear if he blinks.

And, yes, we make love all over our house, up against walls, on countertops, bent over furniture—anywhere but in front of the baby. Thank God Brinley, at just over a year, sleeps like the dead for 14 hours straight. The second that monitor shows she's down, Cameron's hands are already tearing at my clothes, and I'm clawing at his belt. We're insatiable. Mom? She's tucked away in the ADU behind our Hancock Park mansion—far enough that she can't hear me screaming his name. The space fits her grand piano perfectly, which ranks just above oxygen on her priority list, followed by Cam, Brinley, and maybe me. Sometimes I swear she'd trade me for him in a heartbeat—she worships the ground my future husband walks on.

Yes. Our new house is in Hancock Park, where the air smells like jasmine and money. It's almost halfway between Cameron's sterile white halls at the UCLA Hospital and the buzzing needles of my tattoo studio. I expected suburban hell—cookie-cutter houses and pearl-clutching neighbors eyeing my sleeve tattoos—but this place has character. The streets are lined with jacarandas that rain purple blossoms onto pristine sidewalks. Massive 1920s mansions with red-tiled Spanish roofs and imposing Tudor facades hide behind wrought-iron gates and perfectly trimmed hedges. Every Wednesday and Sunday, I can walk three blocks to a farmer's market where hipsters in designer sunglasses sell $15 jars of honey next to old Italian men hawking heirloom tomatoes the size of my fist.

Our new house, which Cameron bought for us, sits like a fairytale castle on an acre of land—all steep gables, decorative half-timbering, and leaded glass windows. The five-thousand-square-foot Tudor Revival sprawls across its lot, an English manor transplanted to Los Angeles, complete with a stone entrance archway and climbing roses that somehow thrive in the Southern California heat. He insists it's a slum compared to his brothers' homes, and I'm sure he's right, but to me, it's a fucking palace. A palace I barely contributed to, as my Echo Park home was barely above water, which means when I sold it, I only cleared about $5,000 after all the fees were factored in.

Cameron unloaded his Brentwood mansion—and I'm talking actual mansion, not just realtor-speak—then dropped straight cash on this gorgeous Hancock Park place. Three million bucks, and he still had enough left over to buy me this insane ring.

Jesus, this ring though. His brother Silas tracked down this natural black diamond that flashes with these secret colors when it hits the light—deep reds, blues, these moody forest greens. The platinum band twists around like some badass roses-and-thorns situation. He says it reminds him of me—which, yeah, the thorns part is pretty damn obvious. But then he goes and says I'm mostly roses to him. Beautiful. Colorful. Sweet, if you can fucking believe that.

Cameron's been a freaking saint about this wedding. When I told him I'd rather get a full-body tattoo of Satan than have some big white circus, the relief on his face was priceless. Probably still traumatized from flushing half a million down the toilet on that Willow disaster. I shut down the Vera Wang nightmare scenario real quick. "One bow tie shows up, and I'm pulling a Julia Roberts in *Runaway Bride*," I warned him, though I've never actually seen that movie—Celeste has, because of course she has.

I shot down the fancy catering (told Olivia to leave her chef hat at home and just bring her dancing shoes), and vetoed any cake that that's taller than my forearm. Cameron gets it. He's done the whole society-page bullshit before—that Italian villa place with Alecia, and the Beverly

Hills mansion he almost used for Willow. Now he just says, "The only thing that matters is you showing up."

Last night in bed, with moonlight slicing through our vaulted ceiling and spilling across that massive fig tree outside our balcony—the one I'm definitely hanging a tire swing on for Brinley—he gripped my waist and breathed against my neck, "Jesus Christ, Tally, I wish we were married already. Right fucking now."

"Well, you better," I said, digging my nails into his shoulder. "Because if you aren't desperate to marry me, we have a serious fucking problem, don't we?"

He crushed his mouth against mine before pulling back. "No. Listen to me. When I was about to marry Willow, my stomach was in knots—the bad kind. Roman saw it. He told me how he couldn't sleep for three days before marrying Lilith, how his heart hammered every time he thought about making her his. With Willow? I would've been counting the hours till it was over." He seized my hand, the one with the blinding 3-carat diamond, and pressed it hard against his thundering heart. "But with you...God, Tally. I can barely breathe when I think about making you mine forever. I'm burning alive waiting to call you my wife."

It's fucking surreal - when we're in bed, his fingers weave through my hair like he's memorizing every strand, his hand grips mine so tight I feel our pulses syncing, and he wraps around me like he's terrified I'll disappear. All the shit I used to run from, I now can't live without. Post-sex, my head against his thundering heart, his fingertips tracing the ink on my skin like sacred text, whispering things that crack me open - that's what destroys me. The sex? Christ, it's nuclear. When he's inside me, I scream until my throat burns. When his tongue claims me, I shatter so completely I forget my own name. But after? When we're sweat-slicked and breathing like we've been drowning? That's when I feel branded by him. Owned. Saved. That intimacy hits harder than any orgasm, and I never saw it coming.

"Ha. Well, I guess that says it all. We were meant to be, as much as I tried to pretend otherwise."

Yeah, Cameron gets it. He knows now I've been in love with him since that first night, even if I couldn't admit it to myself, let alone him. I finally told him everything—how I pushed him away because I was convinced I'd wreck his life like I thought I'd wrecked my mom's. How Sibley helped me see I'd been carrying my mother's addiction like it was my own damn fault. Like if I'd just hidden her pills better or hadn't set her off, she wouldn't have relapsed again and again. Like her getting caught was somehow always on me.

So now he knows. All of it. And when he understood I pushed him away because I loved him too much to drag him down with me, everything shifted. He hauled me to a couples therapist—Dr. Wallace, a thousand bucks an hour—who turned out to be worth every penny. Six sessions, three times a week for two weeks, and suddenly I could see my patterns clear as day. The work I'd been doing with my regular therapist for months had laid the groundwork, but nearly dying was what really woke me up. Dr. Wallace just helped me cross the finish line—to where I'm standing today, about to marry Cameron without a single doubt in my heart.

So, now, here we are, in this sun-drenched art gallery with its gleaming hardwood floors and white walls adorned with vibrant local artwork, surrounded by the people we love in their casual attire and genuine smiles.

No stuffy reception—we're all heading to O'Malley's, that dimly lit dive bar with the cracked leather booths and neon beer signs, to shoot pool on the worn felt tables and throw darts at the cork boards with years of tiny holes. We'll buy everyone pints of frothy local IPAs and greasy loaded nachos, of course, and then we're going to Indigo, with its intimate stage and blue mood lighting, to hear my Mom's fingers dance across the ivory piano keys. To me, that's a perfect reception.

Only problem is that Brinley can't go, with her chubby cheeks and wispy dark curls, but she'll be hanging out with Violet and Esme, Violet's nanny who smells like cinnamon, at Celeste's mansion, so it won't be too terrible. She'll be at the wedding, though, toddling down the aisle in her tiny cream-colored dress with the satin bow. She doesn't understand, although she's 16 months old with those bright, curious eyes that follow everything, so maybe she understands more than I think she does.

And Brinley is hilarious now. In her Gymboree class, she builds wobbly towers of primary-colored blocks, dances with her arms flailing wildly to "The Wheels on the Bus," and creates finger-paintings with bold purple and green swirls that show me she'll have the Steele gene for artwork because it's pretty damned good for a sticky-fingered kid her age.

She's learning all the things I didn't learn until I got into kindergarten—how to share her favorite stuffed giraffe with the drooling boy next to her, how to wait her turn on the mini-slide, how not to scream and throw a tantrum on the polished marble floor of the Westfield Mall, which she actually did one day, becoming dead weight in her little denim overalls and screaming loudly enough to wake the dead. But she's doing well in Gymboree, and her social skills, according to her Gymboree lady with the perpetually cheerful voice and rainbow-colored scrunchie, are exceptional.

I'm hoping that what's showing up in her this young will be what she'll end up being—she's already empathetic when she pats crying kids on the back and creative with her finger paints and I know she's extremely intelligent as she was talking and walking earlier than many of her peers.

Yeah…I'm one lucky bitch, that's for goddamn sure.

Chapter Fifty-Eight

CAMERON

Four Months Later

The difference between marrying Tally and what would have been marrying Willow couldn't be more stark. With Willow, every morning felt like waking up to dread. I'd lie there staring at the ceiling, mentally rehearsing the pep talk I needed just to make it through another day of our engagement. "Just get through the ceremony," I'd tell myself. "The feelings will follow." When Roman confessed how he'd been counting down the days until he could make Lilith his wife, how he couldn't sleep from excitement, I had nothing to say. The truth hung between us—he'd always seen through my relationship with Willow.

My other brothers adored her, naturally. However, Dad, who liked Willow well enough on paper, would get this look sometimes. Nothing you could point to, just a flicker of something uncertain when he watched us together. I think he knew what Roman knew.

I finally understand Roman's impatience before he

married Lilith. Every morning I wake up with this ache in my chest, counting the days until Tally becomes my wife. I want it yesterday. I want it now. That's how it should feel, right? When you've found the one person who completes you. And Tally—tattoos, sharp tongue, trust issues and all—is undeniably mine.

Sometimes I catch myself in cold sweats thinking about the near miss. If Tally hadn't gotten lost in those woods... Christ. I'd have gone through with the wedding to Willow instead. In that shadow life, I'd only see Brinley on weekends and holidays. I'd pass Tally in hallways, at birthday parties, at school events—always keeping a respectful distance while something essential inside me withered.

I've treated patients with phantom limb pain. That's what life without Tally would be—a constant ache for something vital that's missing. I'd be trapped in the worst possible scenario: waking up beside someone I settled for while dreaming of the woman carrying my child across town. Half-alive. Half-dead. Wanting what I couldn't have while having what I didn't want.

And Willow... well, she's doing fine. Last I heard, she found another pediatric oncologist to date—someone who understands her crazy schedule, her dedication. My buddy in radiology says they're practically inseparable. Maybe he's the one she was meant for all along. I genuinely hope she's happy. Surprisingly, she seems to harbor no ill feelings about me walking away the day of our wedding. The proof arrived yesterday: sterling silver champagne flutes with our names and wedding date engraved on them. Classy move, Willow. Always classy.

Of course, Tally has called the shots on the wedding, and what she wants is a cool breeze of relief washing over me. She wants it all low-key, which is sweet, sweet music to my ears, because the thought of planning another wedding like the one I planned with Willow…I'd sooner scoop out my eyeballs with a rusty spoon while sitting in a bathtub full of lemon juice. It was excruciating enough doing that once, even though Asher handled most of the details with his color-coded spreadsheets and minute-by-minute timelines because that's his thing.

But if Tally wanted something elaborate - the five-star catering with those tiny appetizers nobody can identify, the premium open bar with signature cocktails named after us, the six-tier fondant masterpiece, the photographers stalking our every move, the sprawling mansion with crystal chandeliers, the cascading exotic flowers flown in from three continents, the rehearsal dinner that costs more than my first car, endless showers where people play ridiculous games, overseas bachelor parties, and all the other trappings of wedding insanity, then I would've done it all with a smile plastered on my face. Because it's Tally with her wild laugh and constellation of freckles across her nose, and I'd walk barefoot through a mile of burning coals for her.

Still, I'm beyond thrilled to do exactly what she wants, which is to rent out that industrial art gallery downtown with the exposed brick walls, make sure everybody wears whatever the hell they want - including the two of us, although I plan on wearing my favorite light blue button-down that she says brings out my eyes, that herringbone tweed jacket with leather elbow patches, and those black pants she can't keep her hands off me in. And she'll be wearing that black skirt that hugs every curve, that vibrant top with delicate lace sleeves that showcase her tattoos perfectly, and the necklace I bought her so many months ago, giving it to her right before I left for Sicily. It's the necklace she touches absently whenever she's thinking – with its cascade of different jewels catching the light, emerald green as her eyes, amber topaz like whiskey in sunlight, sapphire blue as midnight, ruby red as passion, and pale green beryl like the first leaves of spring.

Tally thinks we're just going to Indigo to watch her mom's piano set. She has no idea I've arranged with the manager to take the stage after her mother finishes. My palms are already sweating at the thought of sitting down at that piano bench, looking out at her, and playing the melody I've been practicing for weeks. The lyrics are raw—everything I've wanted to tell her but couldn't find the right moment for. My brothers will absolutely roast me for it. I'm totally expecting lots of shit being given by them in the months to come. Total cheese-fest. But watching her face when she realizes the song is for her? Worth every second of potential humiliation. This is happening, cringe or not.

The gallery's exposed brick walls frame us perfectly as Lilith prepares for the ceremony. She got ordained online specifically for today, and honestly, I can't imagine anyone better. She's been insisting for months that Tally and I share some cosmic connection—these "tendrils of light" that she claims to see linking souls who've traveled together across lifetimes. Sounds mystical, but I get it. Some people just click like they're picking up a conversation they started centuries ago. That was us from that first night in the ER—I knew she was it for me, and turns out, she felt the same way too.

God, the time we wasted. Her keeping me at arm's length because she was convinced she'd "destroy" anything good that came her way—including me. "I love you too much to ruin you," she said. I understood her fear, but understanding doesn't make the lost time hurt any less.

Even now, part of me worries she might bolt before

saying "I do." But therapy helped, and nearly dying in those woods changed everything for her. "It was like having ice water thrown in my face," she told me afterward. "I've been pushing away everything good because I was afraid I'd break it. What a waste."

But everybody's here, and it's go time. Lilith calls everybody to order, and I take Tally's hands in mine, those skilled artist's fingers that have marked so many bodies but somehow left the deepest marks on my heart. "I promise to be your anchor when the world gets rough," I tell her, holding her hands. "Your partner when you need backup, and your biggest fan when you kick ass—which is pretty much always."

Tally's eyes shine as she squeezes my hands. "Cameron Kensington, I promise to love you fiercely, honestly, and without filter—just like everything else I do. You saw me, really saw me, when I was trying my hardest not to be seen." Her voice breaks when she vows to trust me with her scars, both inked and invisible, and with the greatest gift she's ever given— our child. Her fingers squeeze mine when she says, "I spent my life running, but I'm done. I'm home now."

Home now. Home now.

Damn, those words are music to my ears.

Chapter Fifty-Nine

TALLY

The ceremony is over, and now it's time to party. The dive bar, O'Malley's, is packed with sweaty bodies, neon beer signs casting everyone in a blue-red glow that makes even the Kensington boys look a little rough around the edges. Cameron and I buy everybody drinks—whiskey shots that burn all the way down and leave my throat feeling scorched. We play pool on a table with cigarette burns in the felt, and throw darts at a board so worn you can barely see the numbers. I even get to know his brother Silas, who's been on my shit list since day one. After all, he was the one who started the whole Willow thing in motion by bringing her to that weekend at the cabin, throwing her together with Cameron right in front of my eyes while I sat there like an idiot.

But he breaks the ice by coming up to me, his designer watch glinting under the bar lights as he apologizes. "I'm sorry for pushing Cameron and Willow together," he says, his manicured fingers wrapped around a bottle of Heineken—not a Bud Light like the rest of us peasants. The fact that he's drinking beer from a bottle at all impresses me, because I get the impression that of all the Kensington men, he's the most bougie with his perfectly styled hair and cashmere sweater that probably costs more than my rent. "But you have to understand one thing. I'm very protective of Cameron. We all are. And the thing of it is, Cameron deserves everything in life. And he's been given a really raw deal, losing his wife and daughter in that accident, after suffering from the tragedy of our father leaving for so long and our mother dying so young."

"Don't worry about it. I get it. You were just trying to play matchmaker because you care."

"Yeah, well, I screwed up. Got too caught up in how perfect they looked together on paper."

"Meanwhile, I'm a walking red flag." I snort, tugging at my sleeve to hide the tattoo that crept up my wrist. "My life's a dumpster fire compared to the Kensington dynasty. But hearts don't read résumés, do they? Mine's been stuck on Cameron forever, and turns out, his has been stuck on me too. He was brave enough to admit it. I just kept running."

Silas laughs, not bothering to contradict me. Cameron's taken to calling me his "beautiful disaster" lately. He knows better than to pretend I'm not chaos incarnate—I'd call bullshit faster than he could blink. But the way he says it makes me believe that maybe my mess is exactly what he wants.

That evening at Indigo, the crowd hushes as Mom takes her place at the piano. Then Cameron appears on stage—a surprise I hadn't expected. His calloused fingers stretches across the keys, and when that gravelly voice of his fills the smoky air, my lungs seize up. Each note seems torn from somewhere deep inside him, raw and unfiltered. The lyrics wrap around me like they were written in my skin. His eyes find mine across the room during the chorus, just a flicker, but enough.

When he announces the title—"Beautiful Disaster"—I nearly knock over my drink. If I had any doubt that this gorgeous love song was about me, I don't anymore.

And, as I clap, tears explode from my eyes like I've been gut-punched by happiness. My chest heaves. My mascara's probably running down my face like black lightning bolts. When have I ever lost my shit over being happy? But Christ, I'm not just happy—I'm obliterated by joy. Married to the most phenomenal man who's ever drawn breath, mother to a little girl so perfect it makes my teeth ache, and my mother finally clean after drowning in pills and bastards for decades.

Fuck me. So this is what it feels like when life doesn't suck.

More by Bella Christina as Annie Jocoby

vinci-books.com/beautiful-illusions

Some encounters change everything... forever.

A struggling lawyer's life flips when the irresistible Ryan claims they've already slept together. Wealth, passion, and dark secrets pull her into a world she can't escape—and a man she can't stop falling for.

Turn the page for a free preview...

Beautiful Illusions: Chapter One

IRIS

I woke up in a strange hotel room. Cotton mouth, a strange, sweet taste on my tongue, a feeling that every muscle was bloated and filled with liquid. My head was pounding, my hands shaking. My hair hurt, and the light streaming through the window was just.too.bright. I attempted to run one hand through my hair, but the hand was caught in a massive tangle. I pulled on my hair and then gave up. The tangle wasn't going to come out. I felt nauseated, and the sensation that came over me was that I was about to hurl. I swallowed hard several times until the feeling passed. I had no idea where the bathroom was, and the last thing I wanted to do was throw up in the bed. Where was I? And who was this guy in this bed? A head of dark hair, but the body was covered in a sheet. He was breathing heavily, evidently knocked cold.

I surreptitiously snuck out of bed, hoping my clothes were around somewhere. On tip-toe, I prowled around the room. It was a very nice room. A suite, in fact. I didn't have time to look around. I had to get out of there. I got on my hands and knees, looking under the bed. Nothing was there. I crawled around the room, becoming frantic at the prospect of being unable to find my clothes. I finally got up and tip-toed out of the room and into the next room.

Through bleary eyes, my head pounding like a Stewart Copeland drum solo, I finally saw my clothes in a pile. My precious red Mary Jane Jimmy Choos, which I spent way too much on, were next to the white sofa. My skirt and shirt were next to them.

I breathed a sigh of relief.

I looked at my hand, which was shaking. I didn't know if I was shaking because of the situation or the effects of the hangover.

Probably both.

I got dressed and then realized I had no idea where my purse was. Panic started anew in my throat. By now, I was beginning to understand that this particular suite was gorgeous. Modern art on the walls and the furniture was modern as well. Distinctively modern. Soft white leather, chrome feet. Marble coffee table in front. Enormous flat-screen TV. There were orchids on a glass table by the window.

This guy certainly had taste.

Just then, I heard my ringtone. Radiohead's *Creep.* It was across the room, and I shot over to my purse. My ringtone was so fucking loud! I immediately silenced it. But the phone helped me find my purse, so there was that.

Then I crept out the door, shutting it gently behind me.

In the cab on the way home, I tried to piece it all together.

Where was I? I was doing shots in a bar. Happy Hour. I met a guy last night. Obviously. I couldn't remember much about him. I couldn't pick him out of a lineup at this point.

You're too old for this shit. It had been a good five years since I was in college, and college was the last time I had this kind of slutty one-night stand. I didn't remember why I started drinking so much. My thoughts were hazy, and I felt exhausted like every cell in my body was filled with alcohol.

Let me see...I was going to meet a guy off the internet. That didn't pan out. Of course. The dude didn't show. And I...went up to a guy and started chatting with him. Which was totally like me. When I'm drinking, anyhow. Otherwise, I'm painfully shy and insecure about myself.

I only remembered a few details. Most things were a blur.

I examined my phone, holding my breath. *Please, please, please let there be no dialed calls late last night.* Shaking, I looked through my log of dialed calls. Drunk-dialing would be just like me. There should be an invention where the phone can tell if you've had a few too many and prevent you from calling anybody.

Nothing was on the dialed calls log.

I sighed in relief.

Then I just sighed.

I'm too old for this shit.

I looked again at the call log to see who'd called me this morning. It was my best friend, Debbie. I called a cab, then called her on my drive home.

"Yeah," I said. "What's up?"

"Hey there, girlfriend, how you doing?"

"Great, great." Or, I would be doing great if I didn't have the overwhelming feeling I was about to hurl. The motion of the cab was literally making me gag.

This was going to be a long cab ride home.

"Oh, I did something really stupid," I said.

"What's that?"

"I met somebody and went home with him. I just got done taking the walk of shame, and I'm in the cab right now."

"Awesome," she said. "You need to get laid. How long has it been?"

"Since the early stone age," I said. "At least. One thing, though."

"What's that?"

"I don't remember any of it. I have no idea who was in the bed next to me this morning." *Oh, God, this is so embarrassing.*

"So, what're you doing now?"

"I gotta pit bull rescue to do. I really don't feel like it. I just want to go home and go to bed. And puke. I need to seriously puke. But that dog needs me, so I gotta go."

"That's too bad. I was calling to see if you wanted to have lunch somewhere."

"Maybe tomorrow. Sunday brunch, maybe."

"Sure, let's meet for brunch."

We decided to meet at a restaurant that was central to both of us. It was a place that served a hearty brunch buffet. Right at that moment, though, any kind of food sounded unappetizing, to say the very least.

I went home, made myself throw up, changed, and then went to the abandoned house where a pit bull was left in the basement after the owners were foreclosed. It was scary how many of these calls we got. I went to the house, permit to enter in hand, opened the door and went downstairs. There was a 9-month-old puppy down there, whining and barking. When she saw me, her entire little body squirmed with delight. I kneeled down, and she licked me on the face profusely. I had a bag of food, a jug of water and a bowl, and I fed her and gave her the water. She wolfed down the food, looked to me for more, and gulped the water.

"There, there, my little one," I said. "That's all you can have for now, but you'll get more in the shelter, I promise." She licked me some more as I unchained her, leashed her, put her in my car, and took her to a shelter. I had a large carrier in the car, and I could hear her whining.

I prayed she'd find a forever home quickly.

Pit bulls really are the sweetest dogs.

After my rescue mission, I headed home and passed out on the couch.

Oh, I'm never drinking again.

Beautiful Illusions: Chapter Two

On Monday morning, I arrived at my law office, where my assistant greeted me. Melinda had hair that was variously blue or green in the front, and when I called her, I was subjected to a Ramones song. I didn't generally dig the Ramones. The Sex Pistols, maybe, but not the Ramones. Still, she was fun, cool and efficient. Everybody loved her, including me.

I noticed a guy sitting on the couch in my peripheral vision. I was surprised to find out I had somebody coming in.

I looked quizzically at Melinda.

She motioned me to come a little closer. I bent my head down, then she said in a low voice, "this guy's here to see you."

I looked at the man, and my heart quickened. He was the most beautiful man I had ever seen. In.my.life. Thick dark hair. Eyes greener than I'd ever seen. He looked at me, an impish smile on his chiseled face, and when he smiled, I noticed his teeth were perfect like he spent his entire younger years in braces. He was wearing an expensive-looking tailor-made grey suit with a silk shirt underneath. Italian shoes.

I wondered why he'd be in my office. He definitely didn't look the type who'd be slumming with a bargain-basement divorce lawyer like myself or filing for personal bankruptcy. Those were my two major areas of practice. I also did some criminal law, and he certainly didn't look like the kind of guy who'd need a criminal attorney. Well, maybe a white-collar criminal attorney, but those are the bigwigs in the high rises. I was as far from a bigwig as you could possibly imagine.

At the same time, he looked so familiar....

No. It couldn't be.

Beautiful man stood up and smiled broadly.

Tentatively, I said, "Hello. Can I help you?"

His smile disappeared. He ran one of his hands through his thick mane of dark hair, his head slightly cocked down, his mesmerizing eyes looking at me questioningly.

I drew a breath.

His face turned red. "Uh, I'm here to see you."

"Oh, ok, sure. My office is right there," I said, pointing to the door.

What the hell?

He followed me in. Files were piled on the desk, on the floor, and on top of the computer.

"Sorry about that," I said, frantically taking the piles on the desk and throwing them to the floor behind me. I was suddenly nervous and had no real idea why. This guy was magnetic, so he made me nervous, but it was more than that. I couldn't quite place him, but my subconscious mind knew exactly who he was.

My subconscious just refused to communicate with me at the moment.

"Have a seat."

He sat down on the red tweed chair. My office was small, about 10 x 10, which was all I could afford. Although I was an attorney, I definitely wasn't highly paid. I spent most of my time worrying about people who didn't pay their bills and chasing after them. Plus, my student loans from 7 years of schooling were choking the life out of me.

He still had a quizzical look in those beautiful green eyes.

Then he began. "You don't remember me, do you?"

I bit my lip and raised my eyebrows in an expression that said, "No, sorry."

He looked down. "I'm really embarrassed. I didn't know you were that drunk the other night."

At this point, I could feel my heart in my throat. No. It couldn't be. Never in a million years would I end up with somebody who looked like him. Never.

I must've been on some kind of candid camera show. There was a Canadian show called *Just for Laughs*, where actors played pranks on unsuspecting people and filmed their reactions. This was probably what this was, although I wasn't aware that there was an American version.

I took a deep breath, not wanting to jump to conclusions, and said, "I'm so sorry. I don't know what you mean."

"Harry's Bar. You and I doing shots together. Any of this ringing a bell?"

It was my turn to be embarrassed. Actually, it should've been my turn to be embarrassed when I first saw him. It was now becoming clear, but I didn't think I'd ever catch the eye of a guy like this.

And I didn't think I'd ever see my hotel mystery man again.

"Um, did any of those shots happen to be te-killya?" I asked.

He smiled. "A few."

I felt tears coming to my eyes. I had no idea why. I lowered my head, putting it in my hands, and then peeked through my hands at him.

He was smiling again, and I was completely captivated. God, this guy could completely light up a pitch-black room. Just the same, ending up with him was a lucky shot on my part that no doubt included beer goggles for him. I was halfway decent looking and could lose a few pounds, but this guy belonged with a Giselle Bundchen clone.

"Gosh, I'm so embarrassed. I didn't act a fool, did I?" Of course I did. I usually did act a fool after tequila.

"Not at all. You came up to me, and before I knew it, we were chatting like old friends. We talked for hours about everything from liberal politics to Oscar Wilde. I was quite impressed with your knowledge of *The Importance of Being Earnest.*" He paused. "I think we even talked about the Kardashians."

The Importance of Being Earnest. I read that play after seeing the movie. But I wondered why I'd be talking about that. Still, it was impressive for me to find somebody who even knew who Oscar Wilde was. I couldn't count how many times I'd met a guy who thought Tennessee Williams was a country singer.

He was looking embarrassed again. "I think I owe you an apology."

I raised an eyebrow and cocked my head slightly. "For what?"

"If I would've known you were that, uh..."

"Smashed?" I said helpfully.

"Yeah. Well, I wouldn't have..."

"Taken me to a hotel room and torn my clothes off?" This was like a mad libs game.

"Yeah."

Oh, the irony. I ended up with a jaw-droppingly beautiful man who was literate, and I didn't even have a good memory of it. I hoped I enjoyed it at the time.

Didn't matter. If I didn't remember it, it didn't really happen. In my mind, at least.

Then it struck me. Why was he here? And how did he find me? The only thing I could think of was I left something in the hotel room, and he was enough of a gentleman to return it to me. But I couldn't imagine what I left there.

I realized something else. This guy was intimidatingly beautiful, yet I felt completely comfortable with him. Mesmerized, captivated, excited – but also completely comfortable.

Like he said, I felt I'd known him all my life.

He was still smiling at me impishly, his head slightly downward, his mouth half-cocked.

"So, I was wondering..." he began, his hand running through his thick mane again. "I was wondering if you'd be interested in having drinks with me sometime."

He wasn't looking me in the eye. Almost like he was shy. This guy, shy? He no doubt had women dripping all over him. Which almost made me turn him down. He had to be a womanizer. Anyhow, he was stratospheres out of my league. Light years. He was the Starship Enterprise, and I was Earth.

Or so went my brain. My heart, however, was noticing how comfortable I felt in his presence. Heart overruling brain, I simply said, "Sure."

He smiled. "Friday night at Harry's? We can meet for Happy Hour and go from there."

"Want to return to the scene of the crime, eh?" I asked with a smile.

"Something like that."

At that, we made a date to meet at Harry's at 5:30 on Friday.

After he left, Melinda said, "Oh, sweet Jesus, that guy is beautiful. Where did you find him?" She was mock-fanning herself as she talked.

I smiled. "You wouldn't want to know." *Your boss is a ho.* "Now, shoo, get back to work."

Friday couldn't get here fast enough.

About the Author

Bella Christina lives with her hubby and two fur-babies in Southern California. When she's not binge-watching *Grace and Frankie*, *Succession* and *Downton Abbey*, she's reading historical and women's fiction and scouring the beach for sea glass and sand dollars.

www.ingramcontent.com/pod-product-compliance
Lightning Source LLC
La Vergne TN
LVHW030915080826
845145LV00013B/2903

* 9 7 8 1 0 3 6 7 3 3 9 3 3 *